RECKLESS ABANDON

Dory pushed his coat aside and slipped her arms around his waist. Though she had held her composure before, she kissed Reid with reckless abandon, forgetting about cautiously starting a new relationship. He was here and she was in his arms, and that was all that mattered. "Oh, Reid," she murmured, molding her body to his. She slipped her hands under his sweater, and his muscles rippled through the cloth of his shirt.

Reid shuddered when he felt the warmth of her slender hands on his back. He felt as if he were on fire, and he could feel his need for her, wanting to shout hallelujah or laugh at his getting himself into this predicament. He knew that he had to stop. Performing inadequately with her just couldn't happen! With great effort, he broke their kiss. His temples throbbed at the tiny whimper she made when he released her and stepped back. He looked down at her and had to steel himself to keep from grabbing her again.

JUST ONE KISS

DORIS JOHNSON

BET Publications, LLC
www.bet.com
www.arabesquebooks.com

ARABESQUE BOOKS are published by

BET Publications, LLC
c/o BET BOOKS
One BET Plaza
1900 W Place NE
Washington, D.C. 20018-1211

All Kensington Titles, Imprints, and Distributed Lines are available at special quantity discounts for bulk purchases for sales promotions, premiums, fund raising, educational, or institutional use. Special book excerpts or customized printings can also be created to fit specific needs. For details, write or phone the office of the Kensington special sales manager: Kensington Publishing Corp., 850 Third Avenue, New York, NY 10022, attn: Special Sales Department, Phone: 1-800-221-2647

First Printing: December, 2000

10 9 8 7 6 5 4 3 2 1
Printed in the United States of America

Dedicated to Margo E. Glover
Miss you, girl. . . .

Special Thanks To:

Trauma-ville! That's where I went when my computer crashed during the writing of this story. I am grateful to Marsha Anne Tanksley and her brother, Eugene Tanksley, who led me to the expert computer technician, Tony, who saved the day. To my son, Mark Johnson, for his expert advice, and to my daughter-in-law, Bonnie Johnson, whose help was invaluable. Carla jeanne Bingham for an insightful look at Albuquerque, and to Judy Walker and her friends who were a delight, giving me a peek at Chicago. Linda Bain Green and Arthur Rivers, for the tip about the excellent orchid expert. Thanks, Tom Mirenda. Any inaccuracies are all mine.

As always, love to my husband, who helps to make all of this possible.

PROLOGUE

Dory Morgan woke up, her heart hammering wildly. Scrambling out of bed, clutching her chest, she ran to the wall switch and flooded the room with light. Glancing around at the familiar bedroom, she felt her heart begin to slow. She was in her own room; she wasn't running around in the dead of winter, half-naked. It had been a dream! She began to laugh, shaking with relief. It had all seemed so real. Suddenly, it dawned on her: *It was my story!* "Must get it down," she mumbled. "Must remember." Barefoot and without a robe, she ran to her study and booted up the computer. "Must write it down before I forget," she muttered, rubbing her gooseflesh arms to keep warm. Finally, she was able to type. It was two in the morning. A second later the soft clatter of the keyboard keys was the only sound in the quiet apartment as Dory typed feverishly:

What am I doing here? Nora wondered as she left the strange fourth-floor office and took the elevator back downstairs. She looked around in a panic. People were leaving, going home. She looked wildly about. Where was her office? She'd forgotten! She looked down at herself. A thin cotton dress. No stockings. Plastic thongs on her bare feet. Had she really come to work like this? The building was emptying. She had to find somebody. Didn't anyone know her? "Please," she pleaded, "someone help me." The words stuck in her throat. She was in the lobby of the building. Of course! The directory! If she saw the name of her firm, she'd remember. She would run up to her office to get her bag and coat, and go home. She'd remember. She started down the corridor, and the lights began to flicker. The uniformed guard at the end of the hall was turning out the lights. "No," she yelled running toward him. "Stop! Help me! Don't you see me?" She began to cry. "Please, I can't remember where my office is. Help me." A man jeered at her from behind a closing metal gate. "If you can't remember your office, you don't belong in here." The gate slammed shut in her face. She was near the guard now. "Help me," she tried to cry, but no sound came. She felt herself slumping to the floor, wondering why she was dressed this way. She felt that she was a career woman, that she was improperly attired. She whimpered as she sank to the floor. Darkness surrounded her.

Dory stopped typing and sank back in her chair. She pushed away from the computer and stared at the screen. She was sweating, yet she was cold. What had happened to her? And who was Nora? Her current heroine was named Sara. What was the meaning of her dream? A shiver swept through her body, and Dory turned off her computer and the light to her study and walked back to her bedroom. Still frightened by the intensity of the dream, she left the light on and lay down on the bed. It was a long time before she closed her eyes.

Hours later, on Christmas Eve morning, Dory was awakened by the ringing of the telephone. Startled, she felt her heart begin to pound. Then she realized she wasn't dreaming. She sat up in bed and picked up the receiver.

"Hello?" She was suddenly alert.

"Are you still comin', like you said?"

"What?" Dory shook her head. Only one person in the world spoke in such a direct and toneless fashion. "Miz Alma?"

"It's me," Alma Manning said. "Are you still comin' here to Rockford next week?"

"Ye-yes," Dory stammered. She rubbed her dark brown eyes and peered at the clock. It was six. "Is everything all right?" she asked. She knew that Miz Alma was an early riser from the days and nights when her mother's old friend had watched her, all those years ago. There was a pause at the other end, just the barest catch of a breath, and Dory's skin prickled. She sensed that something was wrong. Knowing that the older woman would speak in her own time, Dory pushed long strands of curly black hair out of her eyes and waited.

"Nothin's wrong with me, Dolores Jones. Just want to know if you changed your plans, seein' as how you're so busy and famous now. And it bein' Christmas, too."

Dory didn't miss the slight strange inflection in Miz Alma's voice. What was it? "I changed my name legally from Jones to Morgan, Miz Alma. I've told you that before." She spoke softly so as not to antagonize her former baby-sitter, who was more than seventy years old.

"You told me. Don't think I can remember? I'm not senile yet, you know. Just wonderin' like I always do. Plenty of time to wonder 'bout things, here by myself all the time. Wasn't Jones good enough for you?"

Dory suppressed a sigh. *So many times.* "My mother, Vera Morgan, was never married to a man named Jones, Miz Alma. She only borrowed his name for my sake. After she died and I discovered that I had relatives, I took my family's name. You know that."

"I told you I remember, Dolores." Alma Manning sniffed. Then, abruptly, she said, "Since you're still comin', no sense in talkin' all this way from Illinois to New York. I'll see you when I see you. Merry Christmas." She hung up.

Dory replaced the receiver. What an unsettling call first thing in the morning, and right on the heels of that weird dream that had awakened her earlier. She pulled the covers over her shoulders, pondering the strange call and Alma Manning. The blunt woman was one of the few people who still called her Dolores. Hardly anyone ever used her given name anymore. She didn't use it much herself, except with her novels and as the byline on her travel articles. Dory was the nickname her mother had given her, and she had always used it at school and at work. After her mother's death, when Vera Morgan's family discovered that a Dolores Jones existed, they'd used her given name briefly in those first few months. Soon after that, she was just Dory to everyone. When she'd legally changed her name, Dory Morgan had sounded strange on her tongue at first. But that had been so long ago. Now, Dolores Jones sounded foreign—except to Miz Alma.

Dory closed her eyes. It was just too early to think about her childhood years in Rockford. Irvington, New York, was her world now. Besides, it was Christmas Eve. Christmas was for kids, but even at thirty-one she was going to have a great time tonight playing Santa for her niece and nephews.

Dory opened her eyes, as if reassuring herself that all was fine. But was it? What did the dream and Miz Alma's unsettling call mean? Dory closed her eyes again, wondering if the joys of Christmas would soon turn to sorrow.

ONE

The snowy Christmas night in Sleepy Hollow, New York, was drawing to a close, and Dory felt as tired as the carolers sounded. Softly, she hummed "Silent Night" to keep pace with the muted strains that drifted upstairs from the singers in the living room. "Shh, little baby boy," she crooned. "Go back to sleep, baby," she whispered to her fretful two-year-old nephew, Ronald Rivers. She drew the blanket close around the sleeping child, then turned to the other crib. Ronald's twin brother, David, was sleeping peacefully, oblivious to the reluctant sounds of a party ending in the Rivers home. Car doors opened and closed amid choruses of "Merry Christmas" and "Good night."

The bedroom door was pushed open, and a shaft of light illuminated the dimly lit room. Dory motioned to the twins' mother, a finger at her lips.

Willow Rivers tiptoed to the cribs and looked down at her sleeping boys. She smiled at her sister and beckoned. Both women quietly left the room, leaving the door ajar. Once in the sitting room across the hall, Willow sighed and sank heavily onto a cushioned loveseat.

"I hear you. Me too," Dory said, joining her on the couch. "But I'd do it all over again in a second." Her normally deep voice turned soft. "Christmas is special to me."

"I know. To me, too," Willow said. "It is to all our family," she added. "Especially for the last few years."

She took her sister's hand and squeezed it. "Ever since we found each other, Dory."

A lump formed in Dory's throat, and tears glistened in her eyes. She returned the squeeze and coughed to cover her emotions. "Don't get me started again," she pleaded. "You know I was filled up tonight."

Willow smiled guiltily. "I saw when you escaped up here." She inclined her head toward the twins' room. "They're going to miss you while you're gone. We all are. Do you really have to stay away for two months? Your new mystery novel must be the size of *War and Peace!* I know all about research, but that's too long for you to be away from us."

Dory laughed at the frown marring her sister's pretty face. It was oval, much like her own, but Willow's skin was light beige, and hers was more of a butternut brown.

"I still have to eat and pay my bills," Dory answered. "I'm making this a working, slash, research trip. I'm committed to three travel articles, and when I return I have to start typing Chapter One on my computer."

Willow groaned. "I hear you. Deadlines. Don't I know about those." Her deep brown eyes twinkled. "But you love those hectic down-to-the-wire weeks just like I do. When I finish my final flower for a calendar, I'm drained, but loving it." She caught her sister's eye. "We're a lot alike aren't we?"

Dory nodded her head in agreement. Like her sister, she had long black curly hair, which she wore shoulder-length. "Yes, we are."

Willow sniffed in an attempt to prevent her sentimental feelings from getting the best of her and causing her to weep. After six years it was still hard to believe that she had a half sister that she'd loved from their first meeting, and to whom she'd grown extremely close. In a bantering tone, she said, "All except for a couple of things that I can name in half a second." Her glance went to the hall again.

It was Dory's turn to groan. "Oh, no, Willow. Not that again."

"And why not?" countered Willow. "I want a brother-in-law, and I want to be called Auntie before I'm forty. I barely have four years to go! What's so wrong with that?"

"Not a thing, except that your husband's niece, Kendra, calls you Auntie, and I haven't a clue as to when or if a brother-in-law for you will ever materialize." Dory grinned wickedly. "Unless you have some more ideas." Several times in the past few years she'd been invited to Jake and Willow's home for dinner, only to find that she was being matched up. All the gents had been turnoffs, and her sister had promised to stop.

"No, fresh out at the moment," Willow answered. But a second later, her eyes glinted with glee. "Unless I see something tomorrow night that interests me. You never can tell what will turn up at these parties."

Dory sniffed. *"What* is right," she said. Alarm settled over her features. "You didn't—"

Willow held up a slender hand. "No, I didn't 'invite' someone especially for you. My husband said enough with the matchmaking."

"Thank God for sensible Jake. That's an understanding man you have."

Willow grew flushed. "Don't I know it," she said in a husky voice.

Dory didn't miss the dreamy look in her sister's eyes. "Now, when you can come up with someone like that for me, call." She laughed at the skeptical look on Willow's face. "I know, I know. Ain't gonna happen, huh?"

"I'm afraid that's a phone call you'll be waiting a long time for, Dory, love."

Both women laughed softly.

Dory stood. "I'd better take myself home before the streets get really messy. Besides, I have to glue a feather back on my mask. Can't attend the masquerade ball of the year unmasked, now can I?" She linked arms with her sister as they walked quietly past the twins' room. She whispered, "However will I hide the fact that I'm checking out the available men?"

Willow chuckled softly. "Don't worry. I'll have my eye out for you."

"I bet you will."

From behind a closed door at the other end of the hall they heard baritone laughter mixed with the giggles of children. Dory and Willow smiled at each other.

Willow whispered, "He's giving them their bath."

Dory nodded, and winked knowingly. From experience she knew that the six-ear-old twins Giselle and Troy would use all the tricks in their very large bag to escape bedtime. And from the sound of Jake Rivers' laughter, the twins had their father hooked. "Then I won't stop and say good night," she said. "I'll see Jake tomorrow at the ball, and I'll be back to see the kids before I catch my train on Tuesday." She and Willow went downstairs.

At the opened front door, Dory shrugged into her coat and looked out at the falling snow. "What a gorgeous night," she said dreamily. "Christmas as it should be."

Willow stepped outside with her sister. "It is beautiful, isn't it?" She smiled at the younger woman, who held her face up to catch drifting snowflakes. "I think you're really a romantic at heart," she accused with affection. Her face took on an impish look. "Hmm. Just think how lovely a snowy Christmas could be when shared by lovers."

Dory's dark curls shook when she laughed. "You're impossible. Get inside before you catch a chill." She hugged the laughing Willow and hurried to her car and got inside.

Willow called, "I'll still have my eye out for you tomorrow night!"

* * *

It had taken only fifteen minutes to drive from the Rivers home to her co-op apartment in Irvington. Before relaxing, Dory had repaired her costume mask. Now it was close to midnight. Dressed in flannel pajamas and robe, Dory was sitting in the living room, sipping tea from a green mug decorated with striped candy canes. Her feet were propped up on a wide tapestry ottoman. The three-way, swing-arm, floor lamp beside the high-back chair was at its lowest setting, cloaking the contemporary room in warm yellow light. Dory looked out at the quiet street. The snow was still falling, and she wondered idly if the streets would be passable tomorrow evening. She wasn't concerned about missing the ball, because after Dory had finally consented to attend this year, Willow had arranged for a limousine to pick her up and return her home. Although the ball was considered a "must attend" event of the holiday season, Dory had begged off going in the past. She'd always been shy about mixing at galas. Having to do it for her daily bread and butter was different. The ball, in Westchester, was always held the day after Christmas. It was given by a well-known, African-American, New York businessman, whose family wealth came from real estate, and it was attended by the social elite from several states.

The day after the ball, Dory planned to finish her packing. She would be gone for close to two months, but she'd learned to pack conservatively, a far cry from when she'd first started traveling around the country. Memories of her first major book tour covering fourteen cities still brought a chuckle. How inexperienced she'd been about everything. How could she have known when she began writing about her complex beginnings that her journal, which she had begun as a form of catharsis, would turn into a best-seller?

Dory refilled her mug of tea and returned to the living room chair. Seeing her novels that were displayed on the coffee table, she picked up the book that had started it all for her and fingered the white raised lettering of the glossy hardcover jacket. *A Family* by Dolores Morgan. Dory opened the semi-autobiographical book to the first page and read the opening sentence: For the first twenty-five years of my life I was called Dolores Jones.

Closing the book, she set it back down on the table. It was hard to believe that in only six short years her life had changed so dramatically. It had been in August, shortly after her mother had died and four months after her twenty-fifth birthday, that she learned she had a family. Until Dorcas Williams had appeared, claiming to be her aunt, Dory had always believed that she had no other relatives. The memory was still vivid, and would remain with her until she died.

Dory remembered the day as being oppressively hot when Dorcas Williams had walked into the offices of *The Black Press,* an influential fifty-year-old newspaper in Jersey City, New Jersey, where Dory worked as a journalist. Dory sensed a familiarity about Dorcas, but she had promptly dismissed her speech and mannerisms as belonging to just another customer seeking service. It was later, in the cool quiet of a nearby restaurant, that Dory had been rendered speechless by a confession. Vera Morgan, Dory's mother, had been the youngest of three sisters. Dorcas Williams was the oldest. Another sister, Beatrice Vaughn, was dead, but had a daughter, Willow Vaughn.

Overjoyed that she had an aunt and a cousin, Dory was flabbergasted to learn that Willow Vaughn was also the famous floral artist, Morgana. Annual Morgana calendars, with her beautiful paintings of flowers in oils, were coveted worldwide.

Dory stirred, frowning at the cold liquid that touched her lips. She set the mug down and rubbed at her eyes. She never ceased to become emotional when remembering. Her Aunt Dorcas had visited her once more that August. That time she'd dropped a bombshell: "Your cousin Willow is also your half sister."

Stunned, Dory had stared at the handsome older woman. "What are you saying?" she whispered.

"Your mother slept with her sister Beatrice's husband, Michael Vaughn."

"Willow's father?"

"Yes."

"Willow is my sister?"

"You were both fathered by the same man."

"My cousin . . . and my . . . half sister?" Bewildered, Dory looked at her aunt. "Which are we to be?"

The sound of skidding tires broke through her memories. Alert, Dory went to the window, and was relieved to see that the car had come out of the skid and the driver was continuing cautiously down the deserted street. Picking up her mug, she went to the kitchen, rinsed it, and turned out the light. She didn't realize that the time had passed so quickly. It was almost one in the morning. She prepared for bed while thinking of the question she had asked her aunt so long ago—sisters? Or cousins?

After their first meeting, there had been no doubt. They were sisters. From the very beginning, they shared everything. Soon after Dory entered their lives, Jake and Willow married. Months later the twins Giselle and Troy were born, and four years later, robust and curious, Ronald and David arrived. Before, Dory had no one. Now, her life was very full. She had a wonderful family and rewarding work. What more could she want? A tiny smile parted her lips when she thought about her sister's not so subtle attempts at matchmaking. Often their long conversations—about everything under the sun—included the subject of men. Willow was certain that there had to have been somebody special in Dory's life in the twenty-five years before they'd met. Finally, Dory had shared her feelings with her sister.

Eight years ago, while she was working at *The Black Press,* she had met a man. She had been twenty-three, and he twenty-eight. She had been attracted to the tall good-looking man, who wore his hair in short dreadlocks. During the three months that he worked at the paper, Dory found that something special was happening between Reid Robinson and her. She'd decided that she wanted to know more about the man, because she'd begun to think about him constantly. His image floated before her at her dinner table.

Dory vividly remembered the day when her budding dreams were shattered. It happened only days after she'd made her monumental decision to invite him into her solitary life, to see if they really could have something special together.

At the Christmas office party, Reid was by her side. He'd needed only to stare at any of the younger men who dared to interrupt them, and they quickly vanished. Dory enjoyed the attention, but questioned his motives. She had never thought of herself as being desirable, and besides, there were more worldly women around the office who were dying to catch the eye of the handsome man. But as she and Reid danced, her doubts had dissipated. As he held her close, she felt cherished for the first time in her life. She closed her eyes and allowed herself to be lost in another world. His chest was hard, and she felt safe enfolded in his arms. She could feel the intake of his breath as her breasts pressed against his chest. As the dance was nearly ending, in the magic of the moment, he whispered in her ear. His warm breath had sent tingles down her spine.

"Just one kiss, Dory."

Dory was helpless to stop his lips from claiming hers, nor did she want to. The kiss was tender, and promised of delicious things. Momentarily forgetting where she was, she moaned a little and sought his tongue. Then, abruptly he'd ended the kiss. The music had stopped. He'd looked at her strangely, almost sadly. Then he whispered, "Thank you," and yielded to another man who wanted a dance. The new feelings that were stirring inside of her had come crashing to a halt. With great fanfare, two men—unmistakably policemen—entered the gaily decorated office and walked straight to Reid, who didn't appear surprised. As he was handcuffed, Reid said nothing, but his eyes sought and found Dory, who was shocked and fearful. He had held her gaze, as if trying to tell her something. Then he was led away. She never saw him again.

Dory shook herself out of her musings. In later years, she had thought of Reid fleetingly, remembering his husky whisper. Bemused, she'd wondered if she was subconsciously comparing the kisses of other men to those of a stranger she'd met years ago. Had that one kiss been her one big romantic moment? When she'd told Willow the story, her practical sister had thought for a moment and then asked, "After all these years why do you think you remember that day so strongly? That man touched your heart." Dory had laughed, calling Willow an incurable romantic.

Now she couldn't help but think about her sister's words. Had Reid Robinson, with just one kiss, shackled her heart?

After several minutes of tossing and turning under her fluffy comforter, Dory turned on the bedside lamp. Sleep was elusive, and she wondered why. As tired as she felt, she should have been in her second sleep by now. Was she afraid of having another weird dream? Had Miz Alma been trying to tell her something? Or was Reid Robinson's handsome face beginning to haunt her again after so many years? With no answers to her questions, filled with frustration, Dory turned out the light.

TWO

"Erectile dysfunction? You?" Leon Robinson's jaw dropped.

Reid Robinson glared at his older brother. He crossed the room and sank down on the wide sofa that faced the astounded man. "Yeah, me: Rochester's most eligible bachelor. Wonder who's the heir apparent?" Reid's expression dared Leon to laugh or make light of what he'd just been told. He laid his head back and closed his eyes. His dark brown rugged features were lined with anguish and disbelief. When he'd left the doctor's office he'd driven straight to his brother's house. Thank God they were alone. He certainly didn't feel willing to unburden himself to Leon's wife, Cerise, or their eleven-year-old son, Matthew.

"But you're only thirty-six," Leon said, still disbelieving. He couldn't look at his virile kid brother and imagine him downing a Viagra tablet.

Reid opened his eyes and sat up, throwing Leon another dark look. "Where've you been? According to the doc, age is nothing but a number these days. Old folks can't lay claim to heart attacks, arthritis, you name it. The club's no longer exclusive." He grunted. "You're thirty-nine—forty, soon—so look out. You might have to come to me for some groovin' pills."

Leon recovered enough from his shock to regard Reid

thoughtfully. He said, "I know what you're feeling, man, but you're not turning cynical on me, are you?"

Reid was silent, staring down at his hands, which he clenched and unclenched. A muscle worked in his jaw.

Leon stood and left the room. He returned with two bottles of Corona beer and handed his brother one. "Drink," he said, and sat down, taking a swallow.

"Little early for this, isn't it?" Reid asked, but he followed suit and took a long swallow. It was only eleven o'clock on a Monday, and his strongest drink of the morning was coffee. He watched his brother watch him.

"Are you going to get a second opinion? And how certain is the doctor about this . . . problem?"

Reid had to grimace. The word stuck in any man's throat. "Impotence."

Leon glared. "All right." He didn't repeat it. "So how real is it?"

Reid shrugged. "As real as I couldn't make it with a woman—more than once," he growled. His eyes darkened again, and he turned the bottle up.

"Can't make it . . ." Leon sputtered. His eyes darkened. "Is *that* the only proof you have? What kind of medical man would give such a diagnosis on that basis? You *are* going nuts if you don't get a second opinion. I thought you'd had the tests, the works."

Reid stared. "Whoa, big brother," he said, "I told you that I was *headed* for erectile dysfunction. I'm close, but I'm not there yet. What will push me to the brink is if I start on high blood pressure medication. I can almost look Mr. Impotence right in the face. That's a given." He gave Leon a thoughtful look.

"You have hypertension?" Leon frowned. "Since when?"

Reid shook his head. "Not yet. Borderline. I can still control it if I follow orders."

"And the . . . ?" Leon asked.

"Works hand in hand. No hypertension medicine, just possibly no erectile dysfunction. It's up to me. I'm told I fall into the ten to fifteen percent of cases that have psychological causes."

"Psychological?"

"Yeah, you know. Anxiety, stress, depression."

"Depression?" Leon frowned again. "Where's that coming from?"

Reid shrugged his broad shoulders. He avoided his brother's eyes.

Leon swore softly. "I thought you put that mess behind you. That was eight years ago, man. Look what the hell you've accomplished since then!"

"Yeah, just look." Reid's face twisted into a grimace that caused his trim mustache and goatee to dance over his rough-hewn features. His round brown eyes became black with anger as his thoughts whirled in the vortex of evil and confusion that had nearly destroyed him.

"Damn right, just look!" Leon said, getting hot about his brother's cavalier attitude. "Eight years ago you came back here from that false arrest, with hurt pride and licking your wounds. But you didn't sit on your butt, crying into your beer, mad at the world. You took our parents' floundering flower shop and made it into the showplace that it is. *I* certainly wasn't doing it. Hell, man, I was going to throw in the towel and sell the place. And I sure didn't have the idea or the know-how to take Ma's orchid-growing hobby and turn it into a million-dollar business! So, yeah, I'm looking. Looking at my kid brother, who after all these years is letting his past jump up in his face and finally knock him out!"

Reid was silent during his brother's vehement outburst. He finished the beer and set the bottle on the floor by his feet, regarding the angry man. All that Leon had said was true. But why get so bent out of shape? Reid was the one with the potential "condition."

Leon wasn't through. His voice was still sharp when he spoke. "What are you going to do about what ails you?" His eyes glinted.

Reid held his threatening smile at Leon's avoidance of the word impotence. Since his first spate of anger and disbelief since spilling his guts to his brother, Reid felt strangely relaxed. He said easily, "Follow the doctor's orders."

Leon snorted. "Without a second opinion? What's his prescription? I'm dying to hear." His heated dark brown skin glistened with perspiration.

"Rest. Disassociate myself from my world as I'm living it now. Reduce the stress in my life. The only way that I can do that is to get away."

Leon muttered, "It's about time." He looked at Reid. "Are you going to do it?"

Reid nodded. "I believe I am. Thought about it on my way over here, but I wanted to sound off to you first." He gave a half smile. "Glad you were here so I could unload." That remark caused both men to smile.

"How long is the recommended rest? Or are you going to dilute the prescription?"

"No. I'm taking the man seriously." He inclined his head toward the portrait on the wall. Leon, Cerise, and Matthew were in a cute family pose: mother sitting, father standing, and child leaning fetchingly on the mother's shoulder. "I want one of those someday. A family. A wife and some kids." He stared steadily at Leon. "Two months."

A low whistle escaped. "You're taking this seriously, then."

"Wouldn't you?"

After the barest hesitation, Leon answered, "I would." Then, "Go for it, man. Things'll be fine here."

"I have no doubt that they'll be, with you and Gil in charge." Reid's voice had changed. Where his business was concerned there were no ifs or maybes, no pussy-footing around. Everyone in his employ was the best of the best, from Leon, who was his top manager, and Gilbert Lane, who was chief botanist, down to the last laboratory bottle washer at the orchid nursery. His decision to take some sorely needed time off was not addressed lightly. On the drive from the doctor's office to his brother's house he had quickly assessed his situation. There were no pending problems, and since he couldn't see into the future there was really no excuse not to heed the doctor's warning. He looked up at his brother, who'd called his name.

"When do you think you'll take off?" Leon asked. He knew that the nursery was in fine shape.

Reid thought. It was the Monday after Thanksgiving, too hectic a time to take off with only a few days' notice. To be away for such an extended time, he needed a plan. "I thought I'd start out after Christmas, bring in the New Year in some strange town. Maybe out west somewhere."

Leon nodded his approval. "Sounds good. I'll miss bringing in the New Year with you, but this is more important." He looked at the portrait. "I want to be an uncle one of these days." After a pause he said, "Will your plans include keeping your promise to attend the masquerade ball in Westchester? Remember, it's good for the business to show yourself. I always go, but the people you do business with all year want to see the CEO in the flesh. They think you're just a voice on the phone."

Reid's dour look said that he thought it was all so much nonsense, but he nodded. "I'm keeping my promise."

"Good."

Reid started to get up, but something bothered him. *Might as well broach it now, rather than later,* he thought.

Leon saw the frown. "What's up?"

Reid's look was steady. "When I first came in here and started spouting off about my problem, I got the feeling that you knew exactly what I was talking about. Then, when you went on about the second opinion stuff . . . well, I was wondering if you'd had some of the same experiences."

The silence was heavy.

Leon sat back and ran his hand through his thinning hair. Unlike his brother, who'd worn his head shaved for the last several years, Leon chose to keep his hair for as long as he could, receding or not.

"A few years ago," Leon finally said. "A year younger than you are now."

"At thirty-five?" Reid fell back in his seat. The doctor was right. The problem was widespread, but men just didn't talk about impotence. He waited for his brother to continue.

"Yeah." Leon nudged his eyeglasses up off the bridge of his nose. "Cerise and I had been having some problems. I was working around the clock at the nursery, and she was busy managing the flower shop. Matthew was seven then, and was practically living with the baby-sitter. There was never any time for us, and we argued a lot." His brows drew together in a deep frown. "Forget about time in the bedroom."

Reid listened. He remembered the rough period the business had been going through around that time. Leon had never let on that his home life was being disrupted.

"One night, all puffed up like a mad demon, I stormed out of here. I needed to get away from Cerise, Matthew, and everything else. I drove until I found myself in a dive twenty miles out of town." He closed his eyes briefly, remembering the anguish of the moment. "I let myself be picked up."

Reid's eyes flickered, but he said nothing.

"We went to her place, and no time passed before I got the hell out of there." He shook his head as if to erase the memory. "I can still hear that chick's caterwauling, and before I hit the door her laughter nearly caved in those paper-thin walls."

"What happened?" Reid asked quietly.

"I couldn't get it on," Leon said in a bleak voice. "Couldn't make it, man."

"You were tanked up."

"Like hell I was," Leon barked. "I'd have been even more of a fool liquored up and driving on these roads up here, man. You know that!"

For a brief moment they both thought of the drunk driver who had plowed into their parents while they were crossing the street to their church. They'd never had a chance.

"What'd you do?"

"Stayed away from my wife for weeks, for fear of not being able to perform." Leon rubbed his hair. "Thank God for intelligent women," he said. "Cerise finally confronted me. Said she couldn't deal living with a stone man. We talked. That's when I got advice from a few different doctors about what had happened." He grinned. "So much for second opinions."

Reid smiled. "What was the diagnosis?"

"Fright. Guilt. Guess you could list me in that fifteen percent of psychological cases," Leon said. "Remember when I suddenly took off a week?"

"Yeah." Reid had reluctantly agreed to let his manager go.

"Well, me and Cerise were having a second honeymoon right here in this house." Leon grinned widely. "Ain't had a problem since."

"I hear that," Reid said, feeling good for his brother.

Both men stood. Reid held out his hand, and Leon clasped it in one of their handshakes.

"Thanks, man. You didn't have to tell me all that." Reid paused. "But I'm glad you did. Sort of makes this a little easier to deal with."

"Sure. Glad you thought enough of your big brother to seek his advice. Coming from the brains in the family, I can't knock that."

Reid snorted. "Don't give me that tired story. After all those years working as a chemist, I'd better have the chemistry know-how, but you've got the boss man skills and the green thumb. *Together* we made this thing work."

Leon knew that his brother was right, but he shrugged and said, "Yeah, yeah. Go on. Get outta here. I have to meet with Matthew's teacher in an hour. See you at the nursery in the morning."

Out in the cold November air, Reid drew in a deep breath. Was it his imagination that he was feeling twenty pounds lighter? Instead of heading home, Reid drove back downtown. A half hour later he entered the office of Rochester Travel Services.

Later that evening, Reid was at home studying the literature he'd been given by a travel agent, going over his schedule. He'd spent almost two hours with an efficient Ms. N. Wind. When he finished explaining his needs she'd taken it from there, and he'd sat, answering a question or two, while she made calls, checked schedules, found the best rates in the best hotels, and gave him a travel date.

Reid lay on his comfortable sofa, which easily accommodated his long form. When his doctor had said to take a trip, he hadn't meant that Reid should go flying around the world. He'd meant slow and easy, as in train travel. Reid had never been on a rail journey in his life, and the thought of one intrigued him. He rested the papers on his chest and closed his eyes. Besides stress, the doctor had said, part of his problem was probably due to underlying pressures.

"Underlying pressures," Reid muttered. The doctor

didn't realize how close he had come to the truth. Leon had hit on it, too, though Reid hadn't admitted it to his brother. But Reid knew what seethed deep inside. True, he'd gotten over the embarrassment of being handcuffed and arrested on his job in New Jersey. True, he had rid himself of the stench of that Wisconsin jail cell that he'd been taken to. True, he had left that state and never looked back. He'd made a new life for himself, from research chemist to hard working orchid grower. And what a lucrative life it was.

Reid knew that what had driven him to be a success was the burning need to forget that he'd ever been to Wisconsin, much less worked there, intending to have a career as a chemist in cosmetology research. He knew that what had happened to him there, resulting in his arrest on suspicion of corporate embezzlement and murder, gnawed at his soul. He had been released for lack of evidence, and his name had been cleared, but maybe it was time to rid his system of the old poison. Maybe it was time to find out who had orchestrated his downfall, who had hated him enough to ruin his career and his life. Maybe then the "underlying pressures" would cease and he could begin to think about having a normal sex life.

Reid picked up the papers again and fingered his destination tickets. He closed his eyes and muttered, "Just maybe."

Weeks later, on Christmas day, Reid was at Leon's. It was all he could do to sit through the fantastic meal that Cerise and her sisters had prepared. The house was full, with Leon's in-laws and a relative or two on the Robinson side. Soon after dinner was over, Reid politely said his good nights to everyone and got his hat and coat. His brother stopped him at the door.

"Hey, man," Leon said. "What's up? You hardly said

a word, and when you did, it was in monosyllables." He looked suspiciously at Reid. "You're not chickening out of flying down to the ball tomorrow, are you?"

Reid grunted. "I told you I was going."

"Then what's eatin' at you? Heavy date last night?"

Reid glared and said, "Depends on what you call heavy."

Leon frowned, then adjusted his eyeglasses. "So that's it," he said in a low voice. "What the devil are you beating yourself up about? It didn't happen, so you want to chew on nails?"

"Something like that," Reid answered, his voice filled with disgust.

"Forget about it, man. It wasn't the time. You probably tried too hard. Give yourself a break and stop fighting. It'll happen for you."

"Yeah, I'll be sure to wire you when it does." Reid opened the door. Then, with a wave over his head, he said, "I'll see you at the airport. Don't be late."

Leon watched his brother until the black Lexus disappeared from view. He closed the door, his forehead wrinkled with a frown. "Don't blow it, Reid. Relax, buddy," he muttered. He nudged the copper wire frame glasses up on his nose and went to join his family.

The ballroom in the Westchester Hotel was a decorator's fantasy. Crystal icicles and glistening snowflakes in all shapes and sizes hung from the ceiling. White doves in a giant cage cooed and flew as if anxiously awaiting the festivities. Green garlands and red-and-gold velvet ribbons decorated the walls.

Dory felt an air of excitement. She watched with shining eyes and expelled a breath, dazzled, as each exquisitely dressed character entered the room. One costume was more magnificent than the next, and the glittering masks were stunning.

"Are you happy you decided to come this year, Dory?" The deep mellow voice, sounding much like Dory's, belonged to Dorcas Williams Hammond. Dory turned to her aunt. "You must be kidding! Why didn't you guys tell me it was like this? I would have started coming a long time ago." The man beside her aunt laughed, his black satin mask moving with the motion. Dorcas's husband of three years, Dr. Bill Hammond, was dressed as a colonel in the United States Air Force, and wore the insignia of a Tuskegee Airman.

"You look dashing, Uncle Bill," Dory said. "As a matter of fact, you two could take the prize tonight." Her aunt wore a fabulous Gay Nineties dress complete with a bustle, and a wide hat with a huge feathered plume. The train of the long red gown swept the floor, and the sparkling sequins shimmered with each movement. A matching red satin mask covered half her face. The happy couple moved on.

Dory spotted her brother-in-law's nineteen-year-old niece, Kendra Rivers. They had shared a limousine and hotel room. Dory had helped zip up Kendra's provocative see-through, harem girl outfit. When Kendra walked, the pale green sheer pants swirled sensuously around her slender legs. Dory noticed that male heads in the room turned at her every move. She could hardly believe that the beautiful young woman was the same shy thirteen-year-old that she'd met years before. Kendra's teen years had been troubled, ever since her father, Nat Rivers, had disappeared from her life. But Jake Rivers had stepped in, acting as caring and loving uncle to the troubled teen, and she had eventually turned her life around. Kendra was now a second-year college student at the University of Connecticut. When at home she lived with her mother, Annette, and her stepfather, Barry Baldwin. Dory and the young woman got on well together, and she wished that Kendra hadn't changed her mind about flying to Chicago during her school break. Dory would have welcomed the company of a family member, especially around New Year's.

"Well, she's a gorgeous child, isn't she?" Willow watched her sister watch Kendra.

Dory laughed. "What's wrong with your eyes? That's a woman I'm looking at!"

Willow sighed. "Where did the time go? It was almost yesterday that she was a teenager, baby-sitting with Zelle and Troy."

"My thoughts, exactly." Dory sighed.

Dory and Willow watched a tall African king dressed in a gold-and-white robe and hat, with a mask to match, in conversation with several bejeweled and gorgeously attired women. Even with a mask, there was no mistaking the regal form of Jake Rivers.

"Hmm," Willow murmured. Her dark eyes shone like black jewels behind her mask. Her costume was that of an African queen, and matched her husband's.

Dory couldn't help smiling. "Is that what jealousy sounds like?"

"You might say that," Willow answered, looking at her husband.

"I don't know why," Dory murmured. "I'd say you don't have a thing in the world to worry about as far as where his heart is. Look." Almost as if he could feel his wife, Jake turned his attention from the women and looked up. His eyes roamed the crowded room until he found Willow. A smile touched his lips, and he dipped his head toward her. Obviously satisfied with the smile that he received, he turned his attention once more to the talkative women.

"See?" Dory whispered.

Willow smiled. "I see," she answered. Her heart was

skipping, and she wondered where the green-eyed monster of jealousy had come from. She was happy that they were spending the night in the hotel. She turned her attention to her sister. "I'm glad you came this year, Dory. Are you enjoying yourself? You're not bored, are you?"

"Not at all. There's an article in all of this. I hope to set up an interview with our host before I leave."

Willow groaned. "This wasn't about work. It's all for fun. I bet you haven't mingled all evening." She looked around at the men who appeared to be unattached, and then sighed. "It's no wonder you haven't," she said in a soft voice. "It looks like you have your work cut out for you, don't you think? What do you say I help you look for your Prince Charming? I saw a fabulous looking Buffalo Soldier a minute ago."

Dory smiled. "Well, I'm afraid you're too late." The music had started, and Jake was on his way to claim his wife for a dance. "Catch you later," she said.

"Dory, don't think I won't be back for you," Willow said softly as she walked into her husband's arms.

"I'll be waiting right here." Dory smiled and waved at the two people who were dearest to her heart.

Reid passed by a mirror on the way back into the ballroom and with a grimace studied his handsome costume. He and Leon had just had a private conversation with several of the wealthy men who did business with Robinson Nursery. Reid had obviously made a good impression. He left Leon talking business and excused himself. It had been worth coming to meet Jake Rivers. The owner of J. Rivers Landscaping was still a loyal customer, years after Reid had started the business. Rivers's orchid displays had been the featured subject of many trade magazine articles.

Reid put his mask back on before entering the ballroom. The rule was that no one went unmasked until after the judging of the costumes. He stood by the entrance to the vast room, his gaze roaming over the crowd, looking in amazement at the array of imaginative costumes. There were African kings and queens, Egyptian gods and goddesses, American folk heroes and historic figures. Many people chose to wear jeweled masks that covered half of their faces, leaving only the nostrils and mouth visible. Others wore short conventional eye masks, festively decorated.

Reid slowly made his way around the room, listening to snatches of conversation, amused at the comments some of the women made about the costumes. As he tried to pass a cluster of happy people, something about one voice made him pause. He started to move on. Then he stopped again, and listened.

"Dory, don't think I won't be back for you." The woman who'd spoken, an African queen, drifted away, leaving a smiling young woman behind.

Dory? Reid remembered a long time ago. Could that be Dory? He watched the masked woman, who was dressed as an African princess. Her simple but elegant white flowing gown did nothing to hide her curves. When she moved, Reid drew in a breath. It *was* Dory. How could he forget the quiet sensuous quality she'd had? It oozed from her with every tiny movement, down to her little finger. She had never been aware of her affect on men. How could he ever forget the sweet taste of her lips, and the touch of that soft moist tongue? He shuddered to think what might have happened if he hadn't stopped himself that evening. Would he have gotten her out of that office and loved her madly? He grimaced at the thought. That decision had been taken from him eight years ago.

Reid saw Dolores Jones being jostled by the dancers. He walked up to her and asked her to dance. When she accepted, he held her in his arms as gently as he had all those years ago.

Dory slipped into the arms of the Buffalo Soldier and realized that he must be the one Willow mentioned. What a man! Tall, strong, and a striking figure. If she could see his face, she was certain that he would be that handsome Prince Charming Willow had been going to help her look for. His mask didn't hide his trim mustache or his short goatee. She couldn't see his hair, which was hidden beneath a wide-brimmed black hat. When he pulled her close, she didn't mind. Something in his manner reminded her of a long time ago when she'd danced like this, if only too briefly. She found herself resting her head against the broad chest of the quiet stranger. Oh, well, she thought, sighing, it was only a dance. She'd probably never see this man again.

Déjà vu thought Dory. The music was ending, and she felt what would happen next. The stranger tightened his arms around her waist and then whispered in her ear. And she remembered a time when her spine had tingled from a man's warm breath.

"Just one kiss, Dory." His lips pressed against her mouth in a tender kiss.

"Reid?" Dory managed to say as his lips captured hers. Instinctively, her tongue darted into his mouth, seeking that sweetness she'd experienced so briefly. Her expectations of what it would be like did not fall flat. Her arms went around his neck as she leaned into him. The music ended, and so did the kiss. Through the slits in their masks, they stared at each other. *"It is you,"* she whispered.

Suddenly, Reid lifted his head. Slowly, he pulled her hands from around his neck, whispered, "Thank you," and strode away.

Dory watched in stupefaction as Reid disappeared from the ballroom. She pulled off her mask.

Shaken, Dory was suddenly aware of Willow—also *sans* mask—by her side. The two sisters stared at each other.

Willow, who'd seen the whole encounter, looked from the closed doors back to Dory. "Reid?" she whispered.

Dory could only nod. "Reid," she echoed.

THREE

For the last two nights Dory had slept fitfully, and her body told the tale. She hurried down the platform toward her sleeping car, and she couldn't reach it soon enough. All she wanted was to close her tired eyes. But then, she might begin to dream again.

It was Tuesday and her train to Chicago was scheduled to leave Penn Station in New York at *12:45* P.M. She'd arrived at noon, and had sat in the waiting room eyeing her fellow passengers behind dark glasses, wondering how many of them would be her company for the next twenty-odd hours.

Dory reached the car and was directed to compartment number nine. She tossed her carry-on bag and laptop on one seat and plopped down on the other. No stranger to rail travel, she always marveled at the compact design of train sleeping quarters. It had taken genius engineers to design to the nth degree the amount of space two people needed to travel in comfort in a confined area. One needn't leave the compartment, except for meals and a walk through the train to stretch the legs. Right now, she wanted to catch a few winks before the announcement for lounge car service was made. She pulled off her boots, put her feet up on top of her luggage, and closed her eyes.

Just as she knew she would, Dory thought about Reid Robinson and those six words he had spoken—the same six that had been the last she'd heard him speak years before. *Just one kiss, Dory. Thank you. How uncanny life is,* she thought. He'd been only a fleeting memory, and now his image crowded her mind. She knew now that he was alive and apparently well, well enough to mingle among such wealth. Since Sunday evening she'd tossed in bed at night, wondering what had happened to him. Had he been in jail all these years, just released? Were the rumors true that he had been arrested for a murder somewhere out West? If he had nothing to hide, why had he disappeared from the ball? He'd apparently left the hotel, because she'd never seen him again. Even on Monday morning, when she and Kendra had checked out and gotten into the waiting limousine, she hadn't even caught a glimpse of him. He was as much a mystery to her now as he had been then.

Dory awoke to the conductor's voice over the intercom, startled to find that she'd slept for almost forty-five minutes. The train was pulling into the Thirtieth Street Station stop in Philadelphia. Voices in the corridor meant that people were getting off to stretch their legs. The routine engine switching from electric to diesel usually took a half hour, and browsing upstairs in the huge station was a popular activity for travelers. It was also an opportunity to get a quick meal, which Dory was about to do. She'd missed getting a snack in the lounge car. She pulled on her boots and slipped on her navy nylon ski jacket. Voices in the narrow corridor kept her from opening the door until the passengers passed. The sleeping car attendant, Kevin, was speaking, but the other voice was muffled. The attendant's words made her pause.

"Okay, Mr. Robinson, we've got it straight now. You were correct. Your agent did book you into the deluxe accommodations that you requested. Our printout somehow had you mixed up with another R. Robinson, who should be here in compartment number seven. Follow me, and we'll get you set up in your room at the end of this car. Sorry for the inconvenience."

Dory froze. *R. Robinson? There's no coincidence as strange as that. Reid can't be on this train!* He had been in the next car all the time? But with the strong, "Thank you," that came in another voice, there was no doubt.

Inhaling deeply before opening the door, Dory hurried onto the platform and walked quickly up the stairs. Rushing because she'd already wasted so much time, she had no choice but to bring her food back to the train.

Fifteen minutes later, Dory was at the cashier paying for a container of chicken noodle soup and a meatball hero. She wouldn't need another thing until dinner was served around five o'clock. By then she would have herself under control if she met Reid in the dining car. First-class accommodations included all meals, and she was certain that between now and eight tomorrow morning she was bound to meet most of her traveling companions—including him. She wondered just how far he was going. Passengers who reserved the pricey sleepers usually were traveling for a good fifteen hours or more.

"Hello, Dory. I thought that was you hurrying from the train."

"Wha . . ." Dory turned and saw Reid standing in line behind her.

"I thought I'd do what everyone else is doing. I'm new at this."

"Reid?" She felt so gauche, standing there, gaping at him. Except for his height and voice, this was not the same man she'd known!

Reid grimaced at her shock. "It's me," he said. He paid for his food and nodded toward the stairs. "I think our thirty minutes are just about up. We don't want to get stranded here in Philly, do we?"

Dory found her voice. "No, we don't," she said, and she walked beside him, matching his quick long stride.

When they reached their car she hesitated as Reid stopped, apparently, at his compartment. He looked at her, then held up his bag.

"Care to have lunch together?" Reid asked.

"Sure," Dory answered. "I'd like that."

"Your place or mine?"

"Mine," she said, leading the way. "I'm in number nine."

Reid raised a brow, but followed her down the familiar corridor. She'd only been a breath away since they'd left Penn Station.

When they'd settled themselves and Dory unwrapped her meal, Reid looked amused. He remembered her penchant for heroes, the messier the better. She'd always been embarrassed about eating the drippy sandwiches in front of her coworkers.

She noticed his tiny smile and guessed what he was thinking. Dory made a face. "Promise you won't lick your fingers, and I won't lick mine."

Surprised at how quickly she'd recovered enough to relax with him, Reid felt his own insides settle down. His rugged features wrinkled in a grin. "Promise," he said, and bit into his giant sausage and pepper hero.

"No soup?" Reid finished the last of his sandwich and tossed his wrappings in the trash bin.

Dory did the same. "No. Can't handle it."

Reid picked up the small container and drank the warm broth. When he finished, he replaced the cover and discarded the cup.

Dory slid the folding tray table back into place, then let down the sink. After running two terry cloth hand towels under the hot water, she gave Reid one and used the other. Moments later, she sat back and stared at Reid. They hadn't spoken a word while they ate, each pretending to be engrossed in a movie that they both had probably already seen. The small TV set was off now, and they watched each other.

Finally Dory broke the silence. "What happened to you, Reid?"

Several seconds passed before Reid spoke. After watching the passing terrain, he turned to her and held her gaze. "I could take that to mean my appearance, Sunday night, or eight years ago,"

Unprepared for his bitter response, Dory could only answer, "All three."

Reid held her stare. "Fair. Which do you want first?"

"You . . . you don't look the same." She stared at his bald head. Seeing it without any warning had shocked her. "You wore dreadlocks, and you were clean-shaven. The mustache, the goatee . . . you look like a different person," she ended on a low note. He looked so much older than the thirty-six years she knew him to be.

"You mean, old?" Reid formed a half smile. "Not you, Dory. You haven't changed a bit. No, let me correct that," Reid said. He looked her over slowly.

Dory flushed under his intense appraisal.

He gave a grunt of approval. "You no longer look like your name. Sorrow. Dolores means sorrow." He continued his study of her. "I always thought you had the saddest eyes. The look in them has changed." He grew thoughtful. "You're happy."

His statement caused her to nod. She remembered that about him—he was a sharp observer. "I am."

Reid studied her face. "I know." Somehow that bit of knowledge didn't make him feel good. He wondered if another man was the reason behind her happiness. He looked at her hand. "You're not married?"

"No," Dory answered, "nor engaged. Are you?"

"Neither."

Dory broke the silence that followed. "You owe me two more explanations," she said gently. She was almost hesitant to ask. Would a man be so willing to talk about being locked up? The dark look that came over his face made her shudder inwardly. It was a bad idea. She chewed on her bottom lip. "You don't have to answer that," she said. "Forget I asked."

Reid stared at her, then said, "Forgotten." Abruptly, he rose, his bulk filling the compact space. "See you at dinner?" When Dory nodded, he slid the door open and closed it behind him with a snap.

She felt overwhelmed. What had started out to be a scenic contemplative journey had catapulted all five of her senses into overdrive. Reid couldn't have known what she'd been feeling. His presence had filled the room so that she almost thought he was still sitting across from her. She had to quell the warring that was going on in her belly and her heart. She'd wanted him to take her in his arms and kiss her senseless. The tender kiss of Sunday and the one eight years ago were nothing compared to what she had in mind. It was all she could do to keep her hands to herself and not run them tenderly over the rough terrain of his cheeks. She wanted to smooth his hurt away and, like a curious toddler, run her fingers over the taut shiny skin of his head.

Dory closed her eyes as she waited for her breathing to return to normal. The words of her wise sister taunted her: "That man touched your heart."

Reid wanted to bang his head against the wall of his compartment. What was wrong with him? After fleeing from her Sunday night, he had invited himself to sit within kissing distance of her? After she'd bitten her lower lip, he'd had to get out of there. This was stress-free travel? Damn! His brain had been on fire while his body remained uncooperative. It had stayed lukewarm. He'd felt nothing. *Nothing!*

He was stretched out on the wide seat, which accommodated his long frame, staring at the ceiling and trying to understand what the hell was happening to him. Any other time, if he'd seen a delectable woman, there would be some kind of reaction: heat in his belly and in his loins. It was just like Christmas Eve, when he'd tried to get it on with a woman he dated occasionally and he'd fizzled again. Then, at least, he'd had the feelings. He'd been hot and ready. But, when the moment of truth came, nothing. His brother had said that it'd happen; to give it time. "You're wrong, Leon," he muttered.

"Now what, doc?" Reid said, bitterly cursing his medical man. He sat up and watched as the train crossed over a body of water, and he vaguely wondered where they were. When he'd kissed Dory Sunday night, his brain had told him to do it. He'd wanted to feel her lips, and her curves under his hands. But when she'd responded so warmly, her lips so tender and moist, he'd expected to feel the warm sensation that meant he was turned on. When it hadn't come, he'd been shocked.

Somewhere, deep within his subconscious, he'd thought that if he felt strongly about a woman he would have no problem; that his body would respond to the messages from his brain. When it hadn't happened with her, he knew that he'd been wrong. Dolores Jones had been the one woman who had always made his body hot when she walked into a room. Right after they'd met on the job in New Jersey, he'd desired her. Waiting all those weeks before he'd even touched her had been agony. Then, after the moment he'd finally held her and kissed her, he had been stripped of his dignity and reduced to a lowlife before her eyes. Now she was here, and he didn't know what to do about her, or himself. How was he going to avoid her on this rolling prison? There was no escape.

* * *

Dory was in the lounge car. Surprisingly, it was nearly empty, with the exception of two booths. One held two couples who sat talking quietly. She watched with interest, as she was wont to do, always on the lookout for potential characters for her novels. This group was decidedly not extraordinary. They appeared to be middle-class retirees on vacation, and Dory guessed that they were friends. The other booth held a younger couple who looked to be in their midthirties. The woman shot her companion a nasty look and then turned away in disgust to stare out the window, resting her pointy chin in the palm of her dark tan hand.

Trying hard not to stare, Dory felt a growing interest in the silent couple, already putting her own labels on them. A lovers' quarrel? Or a quarreling married couple? The man sent an angry look his companion's way, then stared down at his bark-brown hands, which were clenched into fists. He was drumming both lightly on the smooth tabletop. The man's back was to Dory, and he must have spoken because the woman turned her head to look at him. After rolling her eyes, she turned to stare out the window again. Dory wished she could see more of the man's face, but all she saw was his profile and a small gold hoop earring. The resolute set of his shoulders under his short black leather jacket indicated his anger. The tapping of his black leather running shoes confirmed Dory's guess. The man was seething.

Making a mental note, Dory turned her attention to her composition notebook. She always used a bound book instead of a notepad when jotting down her ideas. Frayed and lost pages had made her miserable in the past. She just sectioned off the book into categories, such as plot, characters, and commentary. She disliked using a computer notebook in public, feeling more comfortable and private with the old-fashioned pen-to-paper method. Of course, all her work was stored electronically, and it was easy to add, revise, and compose in the quiet and comfort of her hotel room, especially on lengthy trips. Tonight, in her sleeping quarters, when the train was quiet, she would use her computer. Dory bent her head and began to write down an idea about her heroine, Sara, in her new mystery novel. Intent on her work, she didn't hear Reid approach until he spoke.

"Dory?"

She looked up to see him sitting across the aisle from her. He was holding a paper cup that apparently held a hot beverage. Curious about his choice of seats, she answered, "Hi."

Noticing her expression, he acknowledged her silent question and inclined his head toward her work. "You were engrossed when I walked by. I didn't want to disturb you."

"I've a long ride ahead of me," Dory answered with a smile. "I can do this tonight." After a slight hesitation, she closed her book. "Want to join me?"

After moving across the aisle, Reid said, "Your work?"

Dory nodded. "Research and outlining my new book."

"Book?" Reid acted surprised.

It was Dory's turn to look surprised. Then she remembered that she hadn't had a chance to talk about herself to him. "I'm not a reporter now, Reid. I earn my living writing mystery novels and travel pieces." She tapped her notebook. "My characters are wrapped up in a train journey that includes murder and mayhem."

Taken aback, Reid said, "As in *Murder on the Orient Express?*"

Dory laughed. "Not that involved. The train trip is only a small part. A lot of the mystery takes place in Chicago. I'll get off there, stay a couple of weeks, and then take my characters to Albuquerque. Along the way, I'll be interviewing various people for my travel articles."

Chicago? Albuquerque? Was there some strange destiny at work in their lives? Reid studied the young woman, who'd just amazed him. Somehow, he thought she would have never ventured away from the safe world she'd made for herself in Jersey City.

"You've been published?" Curiosity tinged his voice.

Dory nodded. "About six years ago. I've been writing ever since."

"The urge must have been powerful to make you give up your job. You were a great reporter. What was the novel about?"

"Actually, it was a journal," Dory answered.

"Journal?" Reid's interest deepened.

Dory looked out the window for a moment, then turned to Reid and said in a subdued voice, "About two years after you were . . . after you left . . . my mother died, and I discovered I wasn't alone in the world, after all."

She didn't say, *after you were arrested,* Reid thought. Then he murmured, "My sympathy."

"Thanks," Dory said with a sad look. "The discovery overwhelmed me, and as a catharsis I wrote all my experiences down until I felt cleansed. With my sister, Willow's, urging and the blessing of the rest of the family, I submitted it, and it was published." She paused. "It was a best-seller."

Wonderingly, Reid shook his head. "Amazing. What's it called?"

Dory told him, and he looked thoughtful. "Have you heard of it?" she asked.

"Sounds vaguely familiar. I may have seen it at my brother's house. His wife is a voracious reader. Especially by and about our people." Reid lifted a shoulder. "I should have recognized your name in some bookstore."

"No. Instead of Jones, I use my real family name now. So you wouldn't have given the name Dolores Morgan a second look."

"What happened?" Reid asked quietly. "Your discovery must have been traumatic."

Dory nodded. "It was."

A half hour later, Reid was looking at the young woman across from him who had metamorphosed from a demure curious kitten into a strong feline—a sleek fast-moving cheetah, a hunter. He'd always admired her investigative skills, and she'd parlayed that talent and her family tragedy into a money-making career.

"Dory Morgan." Reid rolled the name over his tongue. "Something I'll have to get used to, but I like it, Dory." He shook his head. "Best-sellers? Congratulations. I'm impressed," he said, "but not surprised." But he *had* been astounded to learn of her sister's celebrity as Morganna and that Jake Rivers was her brother-in-law. Destiny again?

"Thanks."

Reid noticed the sad look on her face. He'd caused her to remember a painful part of her life—a past that only time could heal, and then maybe never. But he was curious. "So no one ever heard from Nat Rivers, the man who taunted his brother all those years?" Reid thought about the close relationship he had with his own brother, and wondered about some families and their secrets.

Dory shook her head. "Only his daughter Kendra, soon after her mother remarried. Nat warned her not to take her stepfather's name. She was frightened because he sounded drunk, and he started saying crazy things about killing himself, that he'd really messed up everybody's life."

"Then he never succeeded in kicking the bottle, even after Jake's help?"

"Apparently not."

"Guess it's best he stay away, then."

"Yes, it is. Especially for Kendra." Dory said. She gathered her things and put them in her briefcase. The announcement had been made that the lounge car would close on arrival in Harrisburg.

Reid slid out of the booth and stepped aside to let her go ahead of him to their quarters, which were two cars away. Sitting for so long had made them both unsteady on their feet, and the jerky motion of the train as it pulled into the station caused them to steady each other.

Dory grew flushed as her back pressed against the hardness of Reid's chest. Even through the bulky red pullover sweater that he wore, his muscles were evident. His hand on her shoulder had brushed the side of her neck, and she had no control over the ripple that passed through her. Embarrassed that he surely couldn't have missed the shock wave, she stepped through to the next two cars rapidly.

Reid stopped at her door. "So what happens here?" he asked, looking out the window. "Another thirty-minute wait?"

"I don't know. After Philly, the rest of the route is new to me, too." They soon found out from Kevin that they would be stopping for about ten minutes. Smokers usually got off.

Reid said, "Good. Then I think I'll walk around myself." He turned to leave. "See you later."

In a few minutes Dory saw him walk by her window. He'd put on the same black nylon ski jacket and a black knit skullcap. His jeans were tucked into dark brown, fleece-lined, leather boots. At six feet tall he was an imposing figure, with a purposeful walk and shoulders that said, "Don't mess with me." Dory wouldn't think of it, and wondered if he'd developed that attitude in prison. She could only imagine the hell he'd gone through. No, she corrected herself, she did know the mess he'd had to endure. As a teenager, she had seen and heard the horror stories of her high school classmates and some of the young black men of her neighborhood. So many had given their lives to the lifestyle they'd chosen—the drugs, the alcohol, crime—and some succumbed to AIDS, as her mother had.

Dory shook off the sudden melancholia, wondering why Reid hadn't invited her to get some fresh air with him. Had he tired of her company?

Staring out the window, she became aware that a man was looking up at her. When their gazes met, he held hers for a moment and then dropped his eyes and moved out of her line of vision. Dory frowned at the intense look he'd given her. Had they met before? she wondered. From the brief look she felt that the years hadn't been all that kind to his deeply lined face. He was about seventy, and his manner of dress struck her as being out of place with the casual travelers she'd seen so far.

Although she hadn't seen it fully, she guessed that, like his long, gray, wool, herringbone coat, his navy-blue suit was just as impeccably tailored. Probably had a nearly invisible gray pinstripe, she thought. His pearl-gray hat with wide, black, grosgrain ribbon was sitting at a slightly jaunty angle. Dory smiled. The old man reminded her of pictures she might run across in somebody's old family album—a relative with a shady past who was best left to memory.

An involuntary shudder made Dory get up. Maybe she should hop off, catch the last five minutes of fresh air. She stepped out her door, only to come face-to-face with the stranger who'd stared at her. He appeared to be as startled as she was when he broke eye contact, muttered, "Pardon me," and followed quickly behind Kevin, who was apparently showing him to his compartment in the next sleeping car.

Dory stared after the man, wondering why she'd begun to breathe so rapidly, with almost the same reaction she'd had to her dream on Christmas Eve. Before she could think clearly about it, the train began to move slowly from the station. She wondered if Reid had gotten back on in time. She'd probably missed seeing him walk by when she was in the corridor. At that moment the passenger in number seven opened the door and stepped into the corridor.

R. Robinson? Dory looked at the black woman, who appeared to be in her early forties. She gave Dory a toothy smile. "Hi," she said, stretching her limbs.

"Hi," Dory answered. She wondered what the R stood for, and how *this* woman could have possibly been mistaken for a *Mr.* R. Robinson.

She peered into Dory's room, then said, "Traveling alone? Me too." At Dory's nod, she stuck out her hand. "I'm Robbie Robinson. Call me Robbie. Nice to meet you. Wish I'd known another lone female was right next door. Well, we can get acquainted at dinner. They'll be making the first call any minute now."

Dory couldn't help smiling. Robbie? No wonder. She rescued her hand from the strong grip and refrained from smoothing her fingers where Robbie had squeezed her garnet gemstone ring into her flesh. "Nice to meet you, too," she managed.

"Hey, I guess you heard the commotion when we were in Philly, huh? Mix-up in the accommodations?" Robbie grinned widely at Dory. "A hunk had my room, and I had his. One of those deluxe compartment types. Too bad they hadn't given mine to someone else. I wouldn't have minded a bit if I had to bunk with the other R. Robinson."

Dory felt a sudden possessiveness. "Oh?" she said.

"Uh-huh. Wait until you see what I'm talking about. Maybe we'll see him at dinner." Robbie stopped. "Well, maybe you're not interested," she said, squinting at Dory's fingers. She groaned. "Oh, you probably would be. You're unattached too, huh?"

Before Dory could respond, the train conductor's voice sounded over the address system. "All passengers please return to your assigned accommodations. Those in coach take the seat you were assigned. Do not switch seats. The lounge car will remain closed until further notice. All sleeping car passengers please remain in your compartments. All tickets must be presented on request. Thank you for your cooperation."

Kevin appeared and walked briskly down the aisle. "Excuse me, ladies. Please have your tickets ready for inspection," he said, hurrying to the next car.

Dory and Robbie listened as he repeated his request to several curious passengers who'd stepped into the corridor. Dory recognized four of them as the same gray-haired mixed foursome she'd seen earlier in the lounge car. The couples, their compartments opposite each other, began to talk excitedly.

Robbie raised a beautifully arched brow at Dory. She had a skeptical look on her good-looking earth-brown face. "This doesn't look good," she said in an ominous tone.

"What do you mean?" Dory asked. That announcement didn't seem out of the ordinary to her. Tickets were frequently inspected after a major stop, where many people might have boarded. But she paid attention to Robbie, who looked worried. Dory had thought she was the type to shrug off something that seemed so insignificant.

"That was the chief of Onboard Services. The conductor would normally make that announcement. Don't you remember the chief's introduction of the staff this morning, and who does what?" Robbie frowned. "Besides, the tone of his voice was too stern and rushed. Usually they sound bored with making the same announcement umpteen times on the same run. Something's not right."

The announcement was made again. This time it was the conductor's voice they heard. "Passengers, *please* refrain from walking through the cars at this time. Have all tickets ready. *Thank you* for your cooperation."

"See what I mean?" Robbie said with a shrug.

Dory nodded. She hadn't missed the sarcasm.

Robbie stepped inside her compartment, but left the door open and the shade up. "I'll see you when whatever's happening is over. Let's make the first call for dinner though. Maybe we'll learn what's going on."

"Sure," Dory answered and followed suit. She got her ticket out of her bag and waited, wondering what had happened. Apparently, all occupants of the twelve compartments in her car were curious, because Dory heard snatches of conversation up and down the corridor. Obviously some of the passengers were in their doorways, speculating.

Curious, she looked at the room directly across from her. The door was closed, and the shade was down. For the first time, Dory wondered who was across the aisle. She didn't remember hearing the door open or close, or seeing the shade up since she'd boarded. But with Reid's unexpected appearance, she'd been otherwise pleasantly distracted. Normally the attendant left the door of an unoccupied room open, with pristine pillows fluffed, hangers and train literature placed neatly on the seat. *Someone must be in there,* she thought. Why hadn't he—or she—opened the door, like everyone else?

She heard the conductor enter the car and begin asking for tickets. When he got to her Dory saw that there were two train personnel doing the inspection. *Curious,* she thought. She noticed the careful scrutiny of her ticket against a roster the stern-looking man held. With a brisk, "Thank you, ma'am," he turned and knocked at the door across from Dory. "Tickets, please," the conductor said, knocking loudly.

There was no answer.

"Open it," he said to his female assistant.

The door was unlocked, and slid back. "Sir, wake up. Wake up. Can you hear me?"

Curious, Dory strained to see around the two conductors. The man in room number eight was sitting on the same side that Dory was, so she couldn't see his face. The seat facing him was empty, but the pillow was rumpled. She could see his pants legs and black leather running shoes. She couldn't hear his response, if any, but the conductor looked at his roster.

"Two in here? Where's"—he checked the names again—"Ms. Lawrence? She's traveling with you?"

Dory heard a muffled response and saw the train personnel eye each other.

"Walking?" the male conductor said. "We'll check back later. Thank you." The man was given his ticket back and the second the conductor stepped back the door slid shut with a bang. Dory never saw who was inside. She shivered. Just then, Kevin appeared. Excited passengers—including Robbie, who was standing by Dory's door—bombarded him with questions.

Good-naturedly, Kevin brushed a hand through his light-brown curly hair, but his dark gray eyes looked worried. "Appears someone got on without a ticket in Philly, and is playing tag with the conductor. But they can't play that game forever. Whoever it is will be caught soon enough. Nothing to worry about, everybody." He gave a nervous grin and continued to the end of the car.

"Well," Robbie said. "Ain't that nothin'? Freeloaders everywhere you go. Now it's creeps like that who make *me* got to pay more for everything." She gave Dory a disgusted look and waved her manicured nails. "I'm going to wash up. It's almost time for dinner. See you later." She closed the door.

Dory glanced at the closed door of room number eight. *Not a sound.* She shut her door and pulled down the shade. She wondered about Reid. Reaching his compartment required going around a short corner and walking down another corridor at the end of the car. From that distance there was no way that anyone could possibly hear anything happening in her area except an extremely loud commotion.

Seconds later an announcement was made that the lounge car was now open for light snacks, and that the first seating for dinner was in progress in the dining car. Dory sighed with relief. Suddenly, she was anxious to see Reid. He had to have heard the announcements, and he was probably just as curious as everyone else.

Dory was tempted to wait for him, as he had to pass her door, but a short rap on the door and Robbie calling her name prevented that.

"Ready?" Robbie asked when Dory opened the door.

"Sure. After you." Dory looked expectantly at number eight, guessing that the occupants would certainly join everyone else on the rush to dinner, but the door remained closed. She followed behind the older woman until they were stopped at the door of the dining car and waited to be seated. On full capacity trains, all booths were filled in first come, first serve order.

"There's something about bald men! I want *that* seat," Robbie muttered.

Dory looked to see Reid facing them. He was alone. Her heart tripped when he looked straight past Robbie and stared at her. He nodded, and Dory did the same.

"You've met the hunk, I see," Robbie observed dryly when she saw the exchange between the two. "Well, no sense in trying to get to know *him* any better," she said under her breath. She stopped at a partially occupied table and promptly sat down. "If you don't mind, I'd like to sit here," Robbie said to the attendant.

Caught off guard, Dory was led to Reid's table, where the lead service attendant, who was the mâitre d', said, "Sit here, Miss. Fill all seats, please." She gave Robbie a look, and went on to seat other passengers.

"What was that all about?" Reid said in a low voice.

Dory shrugged. "Who knows? Maybe her agenda was suddenly messed up." She busied herself with studying the short menu. "I believe you two met earlier?"

Reid stared at the back of Robbie's bobbing head, where she was already engaged in an energetic conversation with her two seatmates, and then turned his astute gaze on Dory's face. "I suppose you heard about the mix-up."

"Yes."

"I'm certain that Ms. R. Robinson will have no problem in finding another agenda, whatever that may be," Reid said in a bored tone. He studied the menu. "What do you like?" he asked smoothly.

Dory couldn't hide the smile that made apples of her cheeks.

FOUR

Reid looked around the emptying dining car with interest. Since there had been no request for them to vacate, he and Dory had sat through second cups of coffee. He was enjoying her company, and didn't know how to say good night to her. The more he thought about spending the next few hours alone, the less he liked it.

Reid noticed a sudden look of puzzlement on Dory's face, and followed her stare to a table behind them and across the aisle.

Turning back to her, he said softly, "I remember that look. Something up?"

Dory was flushed, feeling good that he remembered from so long ago the way she got quiet, and then excited, when doing investigative pieces for the newspaper. He had teased her about having a bloodhound's nose. She answered, with a slight frown, "I don't know."

"Something, though," Reid answered. When he'd given that quick glance he'd only seen a young black man staring out the window. During dinner he had hardly paid attention to the voices around him, and didn't know whether the young man had engaged in conversation with his seatmates or not. Reid was curious about Dory's obvious interest in the man.

Dory gathered her purse. "Can we leave now?" She averted her eyes quickly from the man across the aisle when he felt her stare. She shivered at the questioning look he gave her.

"Sure," Reid said, sliding from the booth. He touched her arm to stop her from returning to their car. "Want to stretch?"

Dory hesitated for a fraction of a second. "Good idea." Several minutes later they reached the crowded lounge car and took seats in the last unoccupied booth.

"Drink?" Reid asked.

"Vodka and cranberry juice." When Reid left, Dory looked around. She recognized some of the passengers from the dining car, and others were travelers she'd seen in the sleeping quarters. It was almost seven-thirty, and she realized that people were restless after nearly seven hours of confinement and were seeking companionship and conversation before turning in for the night. She wondered where Robbie was, and how she'd fared with her dinner companions. The talkative woman had left the dining car with her two new friends. One was a man of Asian descent, and the other was a Caucasian woman. Both appearing to be taken with Robbie's friendliness.

Dory was so engrossed in her perusal of the crowd that she was startled when someone slid into her booth, across from her. A ready smile on her face, she froze. It was the old man who'd stared at her from the train platform in Harrisburg.

"G-good evening." Dory stammered. *Why is he looking at me like that? Have we met somewhere?*

"Evenin'," the stranger responded. He took a sip from his highball glass and looked away.

Approaching Dory and their new companion, Reid wondered at the sudden look of relief in her eyes. Curious as to her reaction to the man who'd joined them, he placed Dory's drink in front of her and then sat beside her. Reid nodded to the stranger, who nodded back, but said nothing. Reid frowned. Was the man rude, or just unfriendly?

"Evening," Reid said in a precise tone, staring at the stranger. He realized that this was the same man he'd caught staring at Dory during dinner. The man had been seated with Ms. R. Robinson and her companions, and then left the threesome after hurriedly eating his dinner. But Reid hadn't missed the man's obvious examination of the back of Dory's head. Whenever she had shifted position the man had craned his neck to get a better view of her profile. At the time, Reid had dismissed it as an old man trying to appreciate a pretty young woman undetected. Now his appearance so close to Dory did not seem so innocent. Did he know that she was traveling alone? His antennae up, Reid watched Dory's reaction to the stranger.

Noting the troubled look in her eyes, wary of the stranger, after a glance at his watch Reid said, "Dory?" At her glance, he added, "That movie you wanted to see is about ready to start. Still want to catch it from the beginning?"

Startled, Dory gave him a relieved look. "I'd almost forgotten," she said. "We'd better hurry. I hate missing the first minutes." Reid was standing, and she caught his outstretched hand, steadying herself with his firm grip.

Dory was grateful for the rock-hard hand and the strong arm that grasped her waist. Reid had immediately understood her apprehension and the need to be far away from the stranger. Without a backward look at the old man, she walked with the rhythm of the train, careful not to spill her drink.

They went to her compartment, left the door open, and sipped their drinks quietly.

Reid was the first to speak. "What's going on?"

"You mean him?" Dory answered with a jerk of her head in the direction of the lounge car.

Reid nodded. "The old man who sat with you, and the one from dinner. They both made you uneasy."

Dory smiled. "I remember that about you."

"What?"

"Right from your first day on the paper, your observation skills led you to such interesting interviews. They were always so clever."

Reid acknowledged the compliment. "Thank you." But he was waiting for an answer, and didn't smile.

Dory drank some more of the sweet, yet tart, beverage. An involuntary shudder rippled across her shoulders. "I don't know what it is," she began. "Something about the way the old man stared at me from the platform in Harrisburg." She shivered again. "Almost as if he knew me, but didn't want me to know it." She explained her two encounters with the old man. When finished, she said, "Do you think I'm imagining things?"

"Your imaginings always turned up something. Why question your intuition now?" He shook his head, regarding her. "Don't quash that natural instinct. It's been known to help in a pinch. What about the other one?"

The other one, Dory thought. "He wasn't traveling alone, earlier. Now he is."

"How can you be so sure? We're traveling alone, yet we've taken two meals together," Reid said matter-of-factly.

Dory thought, then spoke calmly. "He was intensely angry. I could almost feel the heat from his anger touch me. I think that he must have felt my curious stare, though he didn't acknowledge me then. But just now, he did, giving me that evil look."

"Are you certain it was meant for you?"

"There was no mistaking it," Dory answered.

Reid believed her. He caught the underlying fear in her voice, though she was trying to mask it. "Can you elaborate?"

Dory complied, relating her observation of the couple when she'd seen them together. While she was remembering every detail, she suddenly stopped. "The shoes," she exclaimed.

"Shoes?"

"The black leather running shoes," Dory said. "I saw them!"

"Where?" Reid followed her gaze across the aisle to room number eight.

"In there," Dory whispered. The room was silent, even devoid of the faint tinny voices made by a small TV. She listened to the chatter that drifted in the corridor. Most passengers were talking from their rooms with one another. She recognized the familiar voices of the retired group and others she'd heard during the day. In room number six, directly across from Robbie, was an older woman, a widow, who was traveling to Akron, Ohio, to spend New Year's with her sister. Dory saw that the door was closed and the shade pulled down, so she assumed that the bed had been let out and the woman was in for the night. There was no noise from number seven, and Dory could not see whether the door was open. She wondered where Robbie was.

Reid realized that Dory was so engrossed with her thoughts that she hadn't heard him. He repeated his question in a low voice. "What about the shoes, Dory?"

She looked at him as if she just realized that he was still there. "They were the same ones I'd seen in the lounge car."

"How can you be sure?"

"I just know," Dory answered. "They were the same." After a moment, Dory said, "Where's his friend? I didn't imagine her. Someone else must have seen them together at some time, besides me." She was tempted to start asking around.

The car door was heard opening and closing, and seconds later the occupant of compartment number eight appeared. He stared in surprise at the two people who were watching him. Then, without a word, he entered the compartment and slid the door shut.

"It's him!" Dory appeared amazed that she'd guessed right.

"The room was empty."

"You saw?" Dory asked catching her breath. "He moved so fast."

Just then they heard the car door opening and closing again, and the excited voice of Robbie as she spoke to the people who were standing in the corridor. She stopped at Dory's door, took in the presence of Reid, and quickly dismissed him as if he belonged there.

"Did you hear?" Robbie asked. "Remember the earlier announcement about the person trying to beat paying the fare? Well, obviously there were two deadbeats on the train, and one is still roaming around. First he was changing from seat to seat in the coaches, and then he was supposed to be staying back here in the sleepers." Rushing on like a kid anxious to be the first to impart the news, she said, "He was making believe he was traveling with a young woman. Supposed to have threatened her into keeping quiet."

Dory stared openmouthed at Robbie, as if she'd suddenly lost her mind. "What did you say?" Her eyes caught Reid's masked gaze. If his thinking matched hers, he didn't let on.

Reid spoke in low tones to the excited woman. As if mesmerized by his calm voice, Robbie stopped talking and listened. "Ms. Robinson, can you tell us exactly what you heard, and did you hear it from one of the staff?"

Robbie's look said that she wasn't one for carrying misinformation. "You got that right," she answered. "Any second the conductor will be making the announcement. His assistant said that she's sure the story will be blown out of context by now." She took a deep breath. "Ain't that nothin'? That young woman, whoever she is, is being held against her will, and right under everybody's eyes." She paused. "Except mine. I haven't even seen the couple they described. Wonder where they could be all this time?" Her black eyes crackled, and she sniffed as if something bad were in the air. "They oughta stop this train and search the damn thing until he's found. How do they expect anybody to get to sleep tonight with something like this going on?"

The intercom sputtered and the chatter stopped as everyone listened to the conductor, who sounded annoyed. "We have a nonpaying guest on the train. All ticket holders please return to your designated seats. I apologize for the inconvenience."

"That's all?" Robbie exclaimed.

Reid looked at her. "Apparently they're concerned about their passengers sleeping well tonight," he said dryly.

Robbie rolled her eyes at Reid. "Well, I'm in for the night behind this locked door, and nobody had better even *think* about trying to get in *here.*" She looked at Reid, then gave Dory a significant look. "Never can be too careful about getting overly friendly with strangers on a train," she said. "A body can wake up murdered." With a warning look at Dory, she said firmly, "Good night. I hope to see you in the morning."

Dory saw the look on Reid's face, and knew that he'd been reminded of his past. Robbie's words and implication had cut him. *Murder.* He'd been a suspect in a murder. Suddenly she realized that she knew nothing about him. He'd never explained what had happened to him all those years ago. She lowered her eyes, and the skin on her arms grew cold under her long-sleeved sweater. She rubbed her arms to keep from shivering.

Reid was immobile as he watched Dory's face. The sudden questions in her eyes had started a fire in his temples that threatened to blow the top off his head. *She's afraid of me,* he thought. His jaws were taut, and when he felt calm enough to speak, he rose.

Dory looked up at Reid's angry face. *Oh no. How stupid of me. What must he be thinking?* "Reid, I'm sorry . . ."

Reid looked down at her. "Don't say anything, Dory," he said in clipped tones. "You can only make things worse by apologizing." He looked at the closed door across the aisle. "I'd get Kevin in here to set up the bed if I were you. Then, like your neighbor, keep your door locked." He stepped outside the compartment. With one long look at her, he said, "Sleep well," turned on his heel, and walked away.

Reid's long stride took him to the other end of the car in seconds. The walkway was strangely deserted. After Ms. R. Robinson's statement it was no wonder, he thought. Breathing hard, stopping within feet of reaching his compartment, he stood in the short corridor looking out of the window. He could see nothing, but he needed a moment to cool off. He held on to the cold metal railing and gripped it as hard as he could. When he felt the heat of his anger dissipate, he turned back in the other direction instead of heading for his compartment. Maybe the lounge car was still open. He could use another drink. When he rounded the corner and entered the car, he stopped, staring at a figure at the other end of the car. Reid's lips tightened as the startled man looked at him and then—with an almost frightened look on his face—left Dory's door and rushed away. Reid swore, and by the time he'd followed the man into the next car, he found the corridor empty except for Kevin, who was still preparing quarters for sleeping.

That old man is stalking Dory. The thought turned Reid cold. *What the hell is going on in this damn train?*

Undecided about what to do next, Reid was torn between standing guard outside Dory's door, forgetting about her and returning to his room, or demanding an apology because of her evil thoughts about him. He ran his hand over his smooth head and, decision made, walked toward the lounge car. He would take that drink, after all. He walked through the cars, rolling easily with the motion of the train. Many passengers in the coach cars were already taking naps, and others talked in low voices. The occasional squall from a baby and a mother shushing it was a common sound, and most travelers, oblivious, continued to nap, read, or talk. As he passed through one car he stopped at a soft cry coming from one of the rest rooms. Thinking it was his imagination, he started forward when he heard it again. It was unmistakably a woman's soft sobbing.

"Oh, God, help me. Please . . ."

Reid looked around to see if anyone else had heard it, and saw a woman passenger looking at him. When she saw Reid hesitate, she joined him.

"You heard it, too?" she asked, her eyes narrowing with suspicion. "I thought I heard some noise earlier, but I was dozing off and thought I was just dreaming." Before Reid could answer her, she knocked on the door.

"Hello? Miss, are you okay in there? You need help?"

"Please . . . help . . ."

Reid pulled open the door, and the woman rushed inside. "Oh, my God," she yelled.

Reid saw a young woman, who looked to be a teenager, sprawled on the floor, trying to cover herself. Her panties and panty hose were pulled down to her ankles. She looked up at Reid and the angry woman passenger out of blackened eyes. Her face was bloody and bruised. Reid went to her, swearing under his breath. She cringed, and he refrained from touching her, but demanded, "Where are you hurt? Are you wounded?"

She shook her head and started to sob heavily. Reid stood and searched until he found the call button. He pushed it and said to the female stranger—who was cursing and praying at the same time—"Stay with her while I clear the door." The woman nodded, and began to talk in a soothing voice to the young woman.

Reid stepped outside the large rest room, which was built for handicap accessibility, and pulled the door closed against the curious onlookers who'd gathered.

"The conductor's been called, and should be here any second. You can all help by staying in your seats." He wasn't smiling, and many people noticed his no-nonsense demeanor and walked away or backed up, muttering their disgust at the scene.

"Crying shame, brother, when our women can't take a damn trip to the bathroom alone." The angry black man glared at Reid and then looked up and down the car as if the attacker might jump up and wave, identifying himself.

Reid raised a brow at the man's choice of words—"Our women." He was black, and the young woman who'd apparently been raped was white. *The beginning of a new millennium must be bringing about a change in the world,* Reid thought. Could this be the meaning of brotherhood? Like his fellow traveler, Reid was seething inside, too.

"Amen to that," Reid answered with tight jaws as the man walked away shaking his head. Reid stepped aside when the conductor and two other men rushed down the aisle of the coach car, and one of them pulled the rest room door open. Two men stepped inside.

One man, not in uniform, said to Reid in a voice filled with authority, "What's going on? You signaled?"

Reid nodded his head toward the conductor and the other man, who were bending over the woman. "It looks like she was attacked."

"Raped?" the man said.

"Appears that might be the case." Reid met the man's unblinking stare.

"You found her?"

"He was walking by and heard her crying. I heard her at the same time, and we opened the door together." The helpful woman passenger spoke the words defiantly. "I was the one who went inside first." The woman's gray eyes flashed angrily at her fellow Caucasian, who looked at her in surprise. "And if you're an officer out of uniform, why don't you identify yourself to this man, who was walking by and only stopped to help somebody in trouble?"

Reid saw the man's light brown eyes darken at the implied racism. But he calmly said, "You're right, ma'am," and pulled out his gold shield. So much for brotherhood, Reid mused. The assistant conductor appeared and rushed into the rest room, followed by Reid's interrogator. The door was closed.

"My name's Jennifer Moser."

Reid looked down at a petite mixed-gray brunette, who appeared to be somebody's gritty grandmother. He smiled and took her outstretched hand. "Reid Robinson," he said. "My pleasure."

"No sir, the pleasure's mine," she answered in a firm voice. She flung an angry hand toward the closed door and grimaced. "But not under these circumstances," she said as she took her seat. "I saw you in the dining car earlier. You'd be hard not to notice." Her glance covered Reid up and down. "Ever done any modeling?" She was looking up at him, her head tilted at an angle, scrutinizing his face and body.

Reid looked amused. "No." He watched her pull a card from her sweater pocket and offer it to him. He took it, read Moser Models, and suppressed a laugh.

"That's me. I'm always looking for talent, and you've got the look. Pity you're not interested." She stifled a yawn. "Don't find too many men who can go bald that attractively. Well, if you change your mind, you have my number." She threw a look at the door. "If you need me for anything, let me know." She laid her head back and closed her eyes.

There was no mistaking Jennifer Moser's meaning, Reid thought as he walked away. "Did I think brotherhood?" he muttered. Trying hard to squelch his anger at the white detective's instant suspicions, Reid had had his first reminder of the day that he was a black man. *Would the day ever come?*

He knew that word about the attack must have traveled through the train like a swarm of bees. People in the coaches were talking excitedly or rushing to the car where the attack occurred, and in the sleepers doors were open, and people were standing in the corridors, faces and voices filled with anxiety.

Reid found his car eerily quiet compared to the rest of the buzzing train. Unwilling to believe that word of the attack hadn't reached that far back yet, he paused in front of Dory's door. The TV was off and the radio was silent, but he could see that the lights were on. He frowned, suddenly feeling that something was wrong. He knocked and waited. There was no answer. Could he have missed her? Had she taken a walk? Reid walked away, headed for his own sleeping quarters. Then he stopped at a sudden thought—could Dory be avoiding him? Had she been afraid to be alone with him since Ms. Robinson had planted the seed in her mind? Angry, he turned back to her door. There was no way that he was going to allow her to have evil thoughts about him. In fact, he realized that he'd never given her answers to her questions when they'd first talked. Reid sucked in a breath. *It's your own fault, man. For all she knows, you could be an escaped criminal. The last time she laid eyes on you eight years ago, you were in handcuffs.* Silently kicking himself, Reid knocked again. There was no answer. Making a decision he tried the door. It wasn't locked, and slid back easily.

The compartment was empty, and surprise filled Reid's eyes.

Where is she? Trying hard to keep his composure, Reid frowned as he saw Kevin enter the car.

"Mr. Robinson," the attendant said, "ready for me to let out your bed?"

"Sure, go ahead," Reid said, still frowning at Dory's absence. "Any chance you passed Ms. Morgan?" he asked casually.

"No, sir. But with all the commotion, no doubt she's up ahead. Just give me a few minutes to do your room." He walked away.

Certain he would have seen her, Reid dismissed Kevin's suggestion. There was a shower room at his end of the car; maybe she was in there. He passed by the closed door and listened. Silence. Becoming impatient, he played down the dark thoughts that were beginning to invade his mind. But he couldn't forget the attack on the teenager, the old man outside of Dory's door, and the silent man who had aroused her suspicions. Reid's frown deepened. He walked to his bedroom and found Kevin closing the door.

"All set, Mr. Robinson," Kevin said. "If you need anything during the night, just give me a ring. Good night."

Reid opened the door to find the sofa converted into a wide lower berth. He sat down in the armchair but couldn't relax, his mind on Dory.

Dory was afraid. Not since before her days as a working journalist had she felt so frightened and nervous around strangers until she got on the train. Was she letting her imagination work overtime, or living the life of her mystery sleuth, Sara, too realistically? She looked around. The dimly lit reserved club car was usually occupied by commuters. It was practically empty, and she welcomed the closed curtains that shielded the passengers from view of patrons at the snack bar.

Earlier, for a long while after an angry Reid had left her, she had wanted to apologize to him. He'd given her no reason to think less of him, and she was wrong to have acted so sanctimoniously. She'd had to let him know.

Dory recalled the last harrowing minutes. When she'd opened her door, she was surprised to look right into the eyes of the man in number eight. Startled, she'd nodded her head in greeting. Instead of responding civilly, he muttered a curse and gave her a sour look.

"What the hell are you looking at?" he'd said, and slammed his door shut.

Dory heard his lock click. Astounded, she slid her own door closed and then fell back in her seat, wondering what the man's problem was. When she had calmed herself down she heard a door opening and closing, and wondered if it was his. She was hesitant to move her shade up an inch to take a peek. She'd hate another encounter with the man. He was obviously mad at the world, and probably angry because his companion had ditched him. Dory gleefully hoped that the woman had gotten her bags and hopped off, leaving him alone with his bad attitude.

Her heart nearly stopped beating when she heard someone try her door. No knock, just a quiet click of the lock mechanism, which held.

"Who's there?" Dory called. There was no answer, and her heart continued to thump. Seconds later, she heard excited voices in the corridor. Listening carefully, she heard people talking about an attack. A teenager was raped? On the train? *Impossible,* she thought. *There're so many people around! How?* Suddenly, she wanted the company of the talkative Robbie, and wondered why she wasn't in the corridor talking about the latest incident on this episodic train journey. The voices drifted away, and all was silent. Dory decided to chance opening her door. With Robbie's company, maybe she would begin to settle down.

Dory frowned. She knocked again, wondering where Robbie had gone after declaring she was locking herself in for the night. Was that her door that had opened and closed? Shrugging and feeling suddenly frightened at being alone in the corridor, Dory looked up and nearly screamed. Standing at the end of the corridor was the old man. He was just watching her. Had he tried her door? Dory shuddered, and instead of slipping back into her room she hurried away toward Reid's bedroom compartment, grateful for the presence of a man and a woman walking through the car.

She knocked, and there was no answer. It was quiet inside. She heard soft footsteps in the corridor. Had the old man followed her? Panicking, she turned and slipped into the nearby shower room. It was a long time before she opened the door and hurried down the deserted corridor. Where was Reid? She rushed through car after car, hoping to find an unoccupied seat in one of the crowded coaches, but every seat was filled. It was only luck that she'd spied the reserved-seating car. When she pushed aside the curtain, she found the car half full. She slipped inside, taking a seat in the rear, not speaking to the people scattered around in the seats in front of her.

Only then beginning to breathe, Dory listened to the chatter in the snack bar. Unseen behind the closed curtain, she shivered, dwelling on the events that brought her to that car. Peering at her watch, she saw that it was after nine o'clock. The speaker hummed, and then the conductor's voice was heard.

"Sorry for any inconvenience, folks, but we're being detained at this stop. We have a sick passenger who is detraining. We request that all passengers remain patient, and we'll be on our way as soon as possible. Thank you."

The rape victim, Dory thought. She huddled against the window and stared out at the deserted platform. Wondering if she would seem a foolish silly female if she called an attendant to accompany her back to her room, she looked up in surprise. Reid's commanding presence filled the entranceway.

"Reid," she whispered. His eyes locked with hers.

Reid stood looking down at her, not knowing whether to show anger or relief at finding her. When he saw her shiver he sat down beside her. "Why are you here? I've been looking for you," he said in a low voice. He couldn't help noticing the slight tremor that shook her. The lighting was too low for him to read her expression, but he could sense her fear. "You heard about the attack?"

Dory nodded. "I heard." Unable to prevent it, she felt another violent shiver go through her as she thought about the strange incidents. She'd never been so relieved in her life as when she saw Reid standing in the doorway.

"Is that why you're so scared?"

"Partly," Dory answered.

"What's the rest?" he asked.

Dory was slowly beginning to relax, and now felt silly about repeating her fears. Her imagination was just working overtime, she assured herself. Telling Reid would make her seem a foolish female. She was hardly a tenderfoot who couldn't cope on her own. Travelling solo was part of her job, and after many years she was a pro. This trip was just something out of the ordinary, and she wasn't going to let it knock the good sense out of her. She looked at Reid, who was waiting patiently for her to answer.

"It's nothing, Reid," she said. "I'm feeling tired. Would you mind walking back with me? Kevin has probably turned my bed down, so I think I'll stretch out for a while, jot down a few notes, before calling it a night."

Reid didn't believe her, but rather than call her on her nervous lie he stood and followed her through the train until they reached her door. They'd been silent all the way. He waited until she opened the door. The bed was prepared.

Dory gave him a curious look. "Why were you looking for me?"

Reid looked down at her. "It's not important," he said finally.

"Oh," Dory said. When he continued to stare at her, she said, "I went looking for you, too."

He looked surprised. "Why?"

"I hoped you would accept my apology." Her look was direct, and her voice steady.

Reid remembered his own reason for seeking her out. "Not necessary," he said. Now wasn't the time for explanations. "Good night, Dory."

"Good night, Reid."

As Reid began to walk away the conductor made another announcement, asking that all passengers return to their proper places, as a security investigation was under way. He ended with the usual apology for the inconvenience.

Reid shook his head in disgust, wondering again at this supposedly stress-free mode of travel, and wondering how many hours the train would be delayed. He reached his compartment without meeting a soul, entered it, and locked the door. Pulling off his boots and bulky knit sweater, he lay down, resting his head on the palms of his hands.

Reid closed his eyes, but he immediately opened them when Dory's face floated before him. He hadn't totally believed her reason for looking for him, and he tried to guess who could have scared her so much; or what?

FIVE

An hour after several police officers had scoured the cars, checking anyone who matched the description the young girl had given them, the train left the station. It was close to eleven o'clock. When Dory pressed the call button, Kevin appeared almost immediately.

"Ma'am? What can I get for you?"

Dory stared at the young man. He looked wide-awake, though she guessed he'd probably been dozing like most of the quiet passengers. "Kevin," she said softly, "there was no official announcement about what took place. Perhaps you'll tell me what's going on? After all, this silence and trying to keep passengers in the dark isn't encouraging, and doesn't say much for patronizing your company in the future."

Kevin studied the woman, who looked to be about his age, and made a wry face. "Guess there's no harm. Everybody'll be talking about it first thing in the morning."

Dory nodded and waited.

"The young girl who was attacked?" Kevin said, as if in confidence. "Well, she finally admitted that it was her boyfriend who did it. They both got on in Philly, but she had a ticket and he didn't. They were running away together."

Dory looked surprised. "He was the one trying to ride free?" Her glance went fleetingly to number eight, and back to Kevin.

"One of 'em," Kevin answered. He shrugged. "Anyway, the deadbeat guy kept picking at her, asking for any cash she had, said he'd take care of the money. She said she got fed up with his lousy attitude and told him she was getting off and going back home. He started slapping her around, and when she tried to get away from him, escaping into the rest room, he followed her."

"Nobody *saw* them?"

"Guess not." He shrugged again. "Even if they did, I doubt if anybody would have said anything. People get killed for buttin' into other people's business. Anyway, she said she couldn't scream because he was all over her in a second."

Dory pursed her lips. "I wish she'd spoken up sooner. It certainly would have saved unnecessary police work, and we'd have been on our way a lot sooner." Dory guessed that with all the delays so far, they were already almost two hours behind schedule.

Kevin made a face. "Guess she was embarrassed. You know, getting taken in by an older guy's fast talk. She said she's eighteen, and he's nearly thirty. Well, glad it's over. Would you like anything to drink? Coffee? Juice?"

"Apple juice, if you have it." He nodded and returned to his station. Minutes later he appeared with the juice and some crackers and cheese.

After thanking Kevin, Dory closed the door. She finished the snack and then closed her computer notebook. She'd added and revised her many notes on Sara's harrowing train journey. It was uncanny how real life was imitating her fiction. Dory suppressed a shudder. In her novel, her amateur mystery sleuth, Sara, encountered many strange people. There was even an attack on a woman, though Sara's victim was middle-aged and married, and the attacker was a stranger. Like Dory, Sara met an older talkative woman like Robbie who obviously had an eye for good-looking men.

Unable to stop the persistent chill that swept through her, Dory thought about the occupant in number eight, and noted that such a stranger was not a part of Sara's mystery. A nervous giggle escaped her. She muttered, "Maybe I should make something out of the surly man and his vanished companion." Shaking off a sudden feeling of apprehension, she opened her computer again. Concentrating on her story would dispel the uneasiness that was beginning to overtake her.

Dory studied her notes. Outlining how she would murder one of the passengers was becoming a little tricky. With the tight security on the train, especially after an unsavory incident, it would be a little difficult to commit a murder and hide the body with so many people coming and going at all times. *Except at night,* Dory thought. She'd made up her mind that it had to be in the late evening hours—less chance of being spotted. Besides, if she had the murder take place in the sleeping quarters, where in the world could a body be hidden in such a compact space? She looked around her compartment. It would be impossible to hide an adult body in the upper berth when not in use. And when it was let down for sleeping, there was no way one could go undetected.

Dory had placed her bags on the adequate shelf space under the TV next to the opposite seat. She hadn't bothered to stash them in the overhead rack, since she was alone in the room.

Suddenly, she had a thought.

Climbing up on the toilet lid and pulling herself up to the luggage rack that reached the ceiling, she stared in amazement. She'd never bothered to utilize that storage area in all her travels. The space was wide, and deeper than she had imagined. Chewing on her bottom lip while she contemplated the logistics of her plan, she thought for a long moment. Finally, making up her mind, she hoisted herself all the way up until she was propped on the ledge above the commode. Grabbing the steel bars used for easy access to the top berth, she reached up and caught hold of the steel guardrail of the luggage rack. With a deep breath she pulled herself up and over the railing, tumbling into the big space.

"Ugh," she muttered, brushing dust off her face. Apparently she wasn't the only traveler who didn't bother to use the space. She curled into a fetal position and calculated how large a body could be hoisted and then hidden up here. There was ample room for pillows and luggage to cover the body. If anyone looked up briefly, all they'd see would be suitcases and nothing else, unless they climbed up and moved things around. Space was left between her head and the wall, and her feet just barely touched the other side. She scrunched back as far as she could, so that she was far away from the edge. She could not see down over the metal guards.

"Hmm," Dory said, "this just might work." Now all she had to do was select the perfect size victim. It had to be a woman, on the petite side and less than five-foot-six. And the villain would have to be strong enough to lift the body without any help.

Her concentration was penetrated by the sound of a door sliding open and then closing. She couldn't be certain whether it was a compartment door or the heavy door that separated the cars. The sound was muted, and she supposed a passenger or a train employee was trying to be considerate of sleepers. She heard a muffled sound and then something that sounded like a thud, as if someone had dropped something on the carpeted floor. Then there was silence. *Probably Kevin,* she thought, *answering a late-night call.* If all the passengers stopped to ask him questions as she had, the poor guy would be dead on his feet.

Unfolding herself before she could become cramped, Dory grabbed the rail, eased her body carefully over it, stepped down on the toilet lid, and then hopped to the floor. Pleased with her experiment, she dusted herself off, then pulled down the sink and washed up, regretting that she didn't have a change of pajamas.

Bent on recording her observations, she typed them while they were still fresh in her mind. After a few minutes, she frowned and turned off the computer. How would she get the murderer and the victim together? Now that she'd found a place to hide the body, she had to get back into the head of the killer. Her rough character profiles had the villain as a slight man, but considering how he was going to commit the murder she had to change his physical appearance. He had to be taller than the five-eight she had in mind, more like five-eleven, maybe even as tall as Reid. As his image flashed before her, Dory felt suddenly ashamed. Why had that thought come to her? Did she really think deep down that he was a murderer? How much time had he served? She closed her mind to all thoughts of him, and once more concentrated on planning her murder.

She knew that the villain had to remain unseen until it was clearly safe for him to strike. But where? The victim was a stranger to him, and wouldn't have willingly let him enter her compartment. Or would she? Dory shuddered again. Hadn't she let Reid into hers? Robbie's ominous words haunted her. "Oh, for God's sake, Dory! What's gotten into you?" she fumed in a hoarse whisper. "Nothing that man did gave any indication he was an escaped murderer!" But he had refused to talk about himself. Annoyed, Dory got off the bed. Now that she'd started, she had to complete the scenarios that were careening around in her head. She listened for sounds in the corridor, and decided now was as good a time as any to work out her plan. At this hour, she reasoned, Kevin would probably be the only one she'd encounter, anyway. She decided that the shower room had to be the place where the killer could hide, waiting for the victim. Earlier, when she'd slipped inside, she'd thought how inconspicuously it was placed. Most people would think it was just storage for the train staff, unless specifically looking for the shower room.

When Dory reached for the lock she was surprised that she'd left the door unsecured all that time. "Careless," she muttered, remembering how someone had tried her door earlier. Refusing to get cold feet, she eased the door open and closed it quietly. The corridor was empty, and still. *Just like it should be when I commit my murder.*

Dory walked stealthily down the aisle, past the silent rooms. When she turned the narrow corner she was engrossed in her character—the villain who was making his way to his hideout. She passed Reid's door without a thought and, reaching the shower door, opened it and stepped inside. Startled by the darkness, she groped for the light switch. Realizing that her murderer would not use a light, she caught her breath and dropped her hand. *Oh, well,* she thought, *so much for getting into someone else's shoes.* Waiting until her eyes became accustomed to the darkness, she felt for the little ledge in the shower stall. She'd sit and wait, as the killer would, listening for sounds in the corridor.

The moment she realized that she was not alone in the room, Dory stiffened. She touched skin. Terrified, she screamed. A string of curses filled the room, and Dory felt a blow to her head. She blacked out, her body falling half outside the shower room. Her attacker stepped over her and vanished down the corridor.

Reid, who had fallen asleep hours ago, woke up. Was that a scream he'd heard, or had he been dreaming? He wouldn't have been surprised if he had been having a nightmare, after the strange events of the day. He looked at the illuminated hands of the miniature travel clock. Nearly midnight. The instant he heard the thud of running footsteps and recognized Kevin's voice, Reid turned on the light.

"Oh, God, not another one. Is she hurt?"

"Don't see any blood. Looks like she's knocked out cold." That was the conductor's voice.

Reid pulled on his robe and opened the door. What he saw made his heart leap into his throat. "Dory?" he whispered. She was lying sprawled on the floor, her head and torso in the corridor and the rest of her inside the shower room. She wasn't moving.

"What the hell happened?" he bellowed to the conductor, who was bending over the still woman. "Did you call a doctor? What kind of train are you people running here?" he shouted angrily.

"Mr. Robinson," Kevin began, but stopped when the Chief of Onboard Services appeared with a security officer.

Reid was on his knees, bending over Dory and feeling for her pulse. Relief flooded through him. "Dory, love," he whispered. "Thank God." He moved aside when the chief took over, taking her pulse and grunting with satisfaction. "Well?" Reid said bluntly. "Are you a medical man?" He stared down at Dory, perplexed. Why had she been wandering about in her nightclothes?

"Enough to know what I'm looking at, sir," the chief answered. "She's been knocked unconscious. How, we don't know yet. But we'll get some answers. You can believe that," he finished angrily. He reached for the emergency medical kit Kevin was holding. After reviving Dory with the smelling salts, he stood and said to Kevin, "Help her to her room."

"She's not going back to her room," Reid said in a tight voice. "At this point, I believe that the female is an endangered species on this train." He put his arms around Dory, who was trying to sit up. "She's staying with me the rest of the night."

"And who are you?" The chief eyed Reid with suspicion. "Do you know each other?"

"We're old friends," Reid answered blandly. "Kevin, would you let down that other berth in my room?"

The chief, whose name badge read A. Brewer, gave Reid the once-over and then looked at Kevin.

"Mr. Robinson and Ms. Morgan were together pretty much all day today," Kevin said.

Dory moaned, "Oh, what happened?" She looked at the men surrounding her, surprised to see that she was in Reid's arms. "Reid!" she cried, remembering what had happened. "Oh, thank God."

Reid helped her to her feet. "Take it easy. You're still wobbly." He looked at the chief, who nodded and stepped aside.

"Ms. Morgan, Mr. Robinson here has offered to let you recover in his room. We have no objection if it's all right with you. Can you remember what happened?"

Dory looked dazed, but she answered firmly, "Someone was hiding in the shower when I went inside. I guess he clobbered me trying to get out of there."

Mr. Brewer said, "Did you get a look at who it was? A man? A woman?"

"It was a man. I felt his neck in the dark. Before I got clobbered he cursed me. Yeah, it was a man's voice. That's all I remember." She stumbled, and Reid held her tightly. "Whew. I need to sit."

Reid glared at Mr. Brewer.

"Okay," Brewer said. "We'll get to the bottom of this. In any case, we're calling ahead to our next stop to have you examined on board. Just a precaution."

"Don't bother. All these delays are getting to me. I'll be *fine,*" Dory muttered. She leaned heavily on Reid's arm as he led her to his room.

The upper berth was made, and after helping Dory to

the lower one, Reid sat down in the armchair. He watched her gather her composure.

"Can I get you anything?" he said finally.

Dory groaned. "Whatever will make me stop seeing two of everything," she answered.

"What?" Reid was on the bed in seconds. "I thought you said you were okay! Why didn't you tell Brewer you needed a doctor?"

Surprised at the intensity of his reaction, Dory moved away from him. His eyes were dark and angry. "It's nothing two aspirin won't cure," she said, looking at him curiously. Why was she here? she wondered. She could have easily been helped to her compartment. She continued to stare at Reid. Why did he want her here?

Reid noticed her sudden apprehension, and could almost hear her thinking. He immediately moved back to the chair, doing an immense job of controlling his anger. *She still doesn't trust me.* He stared at her for a minute, during which she looked increasingly nervous. He stood and opened the door.

"I'll walk with you to your room," he said tersely. "You can call Kevin for some aspirin." He stepped outside.

Dory stood, and after a second of wooziness she walked past Reid. "There's no need. I can find my way," she answered stiffly.

Reid didn't answer, but followed behind her in silence. When they reached her door and she opened it, he said, "Lock it." He turned and strode back to his room.

Dory obeyed the curt command because she had good sense—and because she was scared.

After kicking off her slippers and climbing into bed, Dory turned out all but the small reading lamp above her head. She pushed up the window shade. Although it was pitch black outside, the dark sky was awash with tiny diamonds. The shapes of the looming trees and the faint train whistle were strangely comforting. For the first time in many years, since before she found her family, she felt lonely. She missed Willow and Jake and their kids, and her Aunt Dorcas, with her instant sense of humor and deep laugh.

Dory swallowed the fullness in her throat, amazed at the sudden melancholia that overtook her. Where was it coming from? Then she knew. The Christmas season. Since she was a kid she had looked upon this time of year as magical. It was the time when she had felt closest to her mother, and they had clung to each other, knowing that they were all they had. No aunts, uncles, or distant cousins to visit or come calling. Only their next-door neighbor, Alma Manning.

All during the year, her mother, Vera, lived by her wits, trying to make a living for her and her daughter. There was never an abundance of anything, and Dory had only the essentials. But on every Christmas morning, Dory thought she'd awakened in fairyland. Not only did she get things she needed, but things she'd longed for, too, and couldn't have for lack of money. There was so much of everything! Sometimes, days later, Dory would even uncover a skirt or a sweater that she'd missed. One year, in her happiness, she regretted asking her mother how she'd made it all possible. The hurt and then the anger that appeared in her mother's eyes had made Dory cry. After that she just accepted her mother's bountiful gifts without question.

During each Christmas week, until New Year's Day, Dory had her mother's undivided attention. Vera took the week off from her barmaid's job, and she refused to have company. She stayed home and cooked, talked and played games with her daughter. They went to movies, acted silly at the ice-skating rink, and ate junk food. Then, on the second day of the New Year, the magic went out of Christmas. Her mother went back to work, and soon after that the men returned, accompanying her mother home late at night. Vera called it "entertaining" and warned Dory to never come out of her room when she had company. Later, in her teen years and then college, when her mother became sick, things changed. Instead of happy times, the holidays became days of sadness. Dory and her mother were together, yet Dory felt so alone while watching her mother succumb to her illness. After many years, the drugs and the immoral lifestyle were finally killing her. She could not recover from the AIDS virus. It was a lonely time. On one New Year's Eve when the whole world was celebrating, Dory was fervently saying good-bye to the old year, praying for a new year that held brighter promise. But she knew that she was fooling herself. She and her mother would never recapture that love and closeness they had always shared during that one week out of each year. And when her mother finally died, the loneliness was so acute that Dory had withdrawn into herself.

All that changed when she found Willow. There was laughter and gaiety and love year-round, and the holidays were special again.

Dory pulled the covers around her shoulders as she stared out into the darkness outside her window. In a few days the new year would arrive, and for the first time in six years she would celebrate it alone, without her family. There was no way that she could have avoided being away at this time. She had made a commitment to do a travel piece on gala celebrations. She regretted it now, because celebrating the advent of the millennium with her family would have been special. At the time, she'd had no idea that she'd fall into a sudden funk at being away from home.

Where is all this coming from? she wondered. Had the strange events on the train scared her so much that her imagination was running wild? There had to be a logical explanation for everything, she reasoned. When she thought about the rape, Dory felt anger, but also relief that the attacker was known and would soon be apprehended. She wished that somehow he could be made to suffer the same mental and physical pain he'd inflicted. But a frown marred her face when she thought about the woman who was supposed to be traveling in compartment number eight. Had she really ditched that scowling man? And why had a man been hiding in the shower? Was he waiting for someone, or was he the other person trying to beat the fare, successfully evading the staff? Had he been waiting to slip off the train unnoticed, and she'd ruined his plan?

Dory's mind raced, and when she could find no answers to her questions, her heart began to thump all over again. Suddenly the low whistle of the train as it passed another small town was not so comforting. It was almost like a prelude to something sinister. She wished that she'd stayed with Reid, and wondered why she'd shown such a negative reaction toward him. Deep down she knew there was no way that he had been the stranger in the shower.

Stunned, she suddenly remembered an important fact: That man had hair!

SIX

Reid lay on his bed in the dark, watching the night whiz by. Unable to sleep since he'd returned to his room, he tried to get a handle on his emotions, but hard as he tried, his feelings were a jumble of complexities.

Dory, love. He frowned. Endearments never came easily to his lips, and that one had come as a shock because it was spontaneous. He'd used sweet words appropriately during sexual encounters, and he'd used the obligatory "baby" when he deemed it necessary. His concern *had* to go deeper than his external attitude toward her. Maybe it was time for some heavy introspection.

Since he'd dropped her at her room earlier, he had curbed his thinking about her sexually. He needed no reminder that he couldn't muster up the familiar warmth in his loins which would mean he was sexually aroused—especially where Dory was concerned. Why was that, he wondered? If he wouldn't or couldn't admit it to himself, his subconscious was doing a good job of monitoring his emotions. And his choice of words when he saw her lying unconscious was proof enough that something was going on with him. And that something was connected to a pair of deep brown eyes that had made his stomach do cartwheels years ago. Back then he'd acted casually cool, and when he'd finally made his move on her it had been too late. Now, when it appeared that he was being given another chance, he was a potential candidate for impotency!

Reid turned on the overhead reading lamp. A frown covered his face. His reason for not wanting to be around her was no excuse for letting her walk into danger. He should have hidden his pride and insisted that she stay with him. He knew that she was frightened of at least two men on the train: the silent belligerent young man in room eight, and the suspicious old man. Counting himself, that would make three.

Dory had been knocked cold by Lord knows who, and he was feeling insulted that she didn't trust him. *And there's no reason that she should, you idiot,* he censured himself. *You chose to keep quiet about your past when she asked, so why shouldn't she be leery of you?*

It was one-thirty in the morning, and Reid wondered if Dory had been able to fall asleep after her ordeal. Or was she lying in bed, frightened to death at every sound she heard in the corridor? Earlier, she'd been looking for him, and now he wondered why. Something must have happened for her to seek him out.

It would be next to impossible to lie there until daybreak wondering if the attack on her was intentional or she'd just been a victim of circumstance. Reid got out of bed.

Dory must have dozed, because she woke, startled, blinking to adjust her fuzzy vision. She had heard something. Cocking her ear and holding her breath, she listened.

The compartments were nearly soundproof, but an occasional noise from nearby could be heard, such as a toilet flushing. Earlier, the slightest noise had put her on edge. She wasn't certain of any scheduled train stops, so she reassured herself that any movement or sound was that of passengers preparing to detrain.

When she heard the soft unmistakable thud of footsteps

in the corridor, Dory froze. Expecting them to continue, she waited, unmoving, as if she could be seen. A shadow darkened the dim corridor outside her door. A soft gurgle escaped her, and then her mouth went dry.

Reid stopped at the door, surprised to detect a low light. Was she awake, and working? When he heard the soft sound he frowned and rapped on the door.

"Dory?" he called in a low voice.

"Reid?" Dory nearly cried with relief, but in the next instant, she wondered why he was at her door in the middle of the night.

Impatient, Reid was about to knock again when Kevin appeared and walked briskly toward him.

"Mr. Robinson," Kevin said with a frown on his face. "Anything wrong?" he asked hurriedly, moving past Reid.

"I'm checking on Ms. Morgan," Reid said in answer to Kevin's questioning look. "She decided to sleep in her own room." As he was about to knock on the door to compartment number five, Reid saw the exasperated expression on the man's face. "Is something wrong?" Reid asked.

"Hope not." Kevin knocked on the door.

Dory heard the exchange between the two men and opened the door. "Reid?"

One look at Dory's face made Reid want to kick himself. She hadn't rested since he'd left her. "I owe you an explanation," he said.

Dory looked at him with disbelief. "Now?"

Reid nodded. "If it will change what you're thinking about me, it has to be now."

They both looked down the corridor, distracted by a passenger's excited voice and Kevin's calm voice asking her questions.

"Are you sure, ma'am?" Kevin asked.

"Of course, I'm sure," was the annoyed response. "If

I weren't, I'd be sleeping like the rest of the lucky passengers! I told you, I've been hearing it since I came back from dinner. Now you find where it's coming from, so I can get some sleep like everybody else."

Reid and Dory exchanged perplexed looks.

Kevin knocked on the door of number seven. "Ms. Robinson," he called. There was no answer. "Ms. Robinson," he called again.

Dory caught her breath, and without knowing why she felt a sense of foreboding. She remembered the sinister feeling that had swept through her before, when the plaintive whistle blew. *Stop it,* she scolded herself. *This isn't Sara's mystery playing out here.* Without realizing what she was doing, she caught Reid's hand.

Reid looked down at her. What was she afraid of? Together, they moved behind the attendant.

Kevin tried the door and found it unlocked. He slid the door back.

Reid and Dory peered past Kevin. The bed was made, and the upper berth hadn't been lowered. The room was empty.

Kevin turned to the people in the aisle, looking mystified. "Strange," he murmured, almost to himself. "Wonder if she decided to get off." After a second he said, "I'm sorry you were disturbed, Ms. Gilmore, but there's no one in there to make the noise you've been hearing."

"Young man, if you think you're going to stand there and tell me that I'm hearing things, then we're going to be here all night." Ms. Gilmore, whose head just reached the attendant's chest, glared at him, arms folded against her bosom.

Mr. Brewer, the chief, struggled down the aisle, which was now full of the sleeping car passengers. "What seems to be the problem, Kevin?" he asked in an authoritative voice.

Kevin appeared relieved that his supervisor was on the

scene. "A thumping or scraping sound seems to be coming from this room, and keeping Ms. Gilmore awake. Apparently Ms. Robinson is visiting with another passenger, or she might have gotten off the train," he answered.

The chief stepped inside the room, looking up and down. He felt around the window for loose curtain rods. There was nothing in the room that could possibly move. Everything was tied, bolted, or welded. He looked at everyone and said, "Okay, folks, there's no mystery here. Please return to your quarters. I'm sure Ms. Robinson will be joining us when we reach Chicago in a few hours." To the annoyed Ms. Gilmore, he said, "I'm sorry you were disturbed, ma'am. Whatever you heard is gone now. Enjoy the rest of your sleep."

The corridor had emptied of the grumbling passengers, who were quick to return to bed.

Reid was looking at Dory, who had grown strangely quiet. She still clung to his hand. "I think you could use some company for a while," he said quietly. When she nodded, he looked around her room. "Want anything out of there?"

Dory belted her robe, got her laptop, and slung her shoulder bag over her arm. She pulled the door closed. When she and Reid walked away, she refused to look at room number eight. That door had remained closed the whole time.

Reid pressed the call button. When Kevin appeared, he requested two teas.

Minutes later, Reid handed Dory a container. "Careful, it's hot." He sat down in the chair.

They drank in silence. "Feeling better?"

Dory nodded, relishing the warmth that sped through her and grateful that Reid had allowed her to regain her composure. From his serious expression she knew that he was ready to talk about himself.

"I did not murder anyone, and I never served time," Reid said bluntly. His eyes bored into hers.

Dory blinked, but remained silent.

"I can guess the rumors you probably heard," he said, watching her reaction. "By the time you got the story it had probably mushroomed into a volcano." A disgusted look settled over his rugged face, and he smoothed the skin of his head.

"I never did talk about myself to you, or anyone else at the newspaper." He grimaced. "I should be the last person to be surprised at your thoughts. I was a research chemist in Milwaukee, Wisconsin, in the highly competitive field of cosmetology. I was young, eager, and ready to climb the career ladder. The pay was good, the firm a leader in the field, and my coworkers were great." He shrugged. "What more could there be?"

"What happened, Reid?" Dory felt his controlled anger, and she realized that he was still hurting inside.

"Greed," he spat. "Someone was sabotaging our work. I later found out that the formulas were being stolen, probably sold to the highest taker."

"Later?" Dory didn't understand.

"I'll explain that," Reid answered. "When I discovered some irregularities in the reports and data that had been charted, I knew something was seriously wrong. I investigated, and found that some data had been tampered with. The formulas had been compromised. As leader of a five-man team, I shared my suspicions with my associate, Emily Gibbons, who believed as I did. Someone was cleverly changing the formula." He saw that Dory was still in the dark. Carefully, he explained.

"Competitors will do anything for the marketing rights to highly successful formulas, especially in the perfume business. We agreed that our manager should be informed of our suspicions. Theft of formulas and sale to a competitor could cost the firm millions."

"Did you report it?"

Reid's eyes glinted with the memory. "My manager was skeptical, and he nearly laughed me out of his office with his condescending attitude. He had handpicked his research team, and held us in the highest esteem." Reid laughed bitterly. "My accusations were an affront to his good judgment."

"What did you do?"

"Me? Nothing!" Reid grunted. "It was what *they* did days later. I was fired! I suspected nothing. I went to a meeting, supposedly to address my suspicions with the higher-ups. I was dismissed on the spot. Poor job performance, I was told. My work had deteriorated to such an extent that the other team members had to cover my mistakes. What crap!"

"Couldn't you fight it?" Dory felt angry listening to his story. How many times over the years had she seen or heard about such injustice involving the black male? Vaguely she wondered if the treatment would have been the same if it had been his female associate who'd blown the whistle.

"I tried," Reid answered. "I confronted the manager that I'd gone to first. It escalated into a heated argument. I didn't care who was around. Several people heard me threaten to find out what the hell kind of game he was playing with me. I was escorted off the premises."

"Your firing was related to the data changes."

Reid looked at her with admiration. "I told you about your journalistic instincts," he said.

Good feelings swept over Dory at the look in his eyes. She said. "Was it?"

"I thought so, but apparently I was the only one. Even Emily was surprised at my accusations. She said that I should have shown more restraint, handled it with more intelligence."

"Did you try fighting your dismissal with the proper

agency? Possibly the State Commission on Human Rights?"

"I thought about it," Reid said. "I knew I'd need proof to back up my story, but I didn't have a damn thing for a lawyer to sink his teeth into. Excellent performance ratings would have been something, but that wouldn't have been enough. Besides no substantial defense, there was no money for expensive lawyers. I still had to eat."

"What did you do?"

"It didn't take me long to get the drift that I wasn't wanted in town or the industry. I couldn't find work." He stared at her. "I left the state."

"And wound up in New Jersey." Dory raised a brow. "From chemist to reporter?"

The memory was bitter. "Survival," he answered. "That paper gave me the only positive response I'd had in weeks of waiting for any kind of interview. They were willing to take a chance on me. They could see through the highly slanted resumé." He paused. "Reporting wasn't foreign to me, and I'd liked it. I'd done some in college. Human interest stories can be wake-up calls in many ways. Besides, those three months at the paper helped me to sort things out." *Until I could rid myself of the anger, which I never did,* he thought.

"Why were you arrested so long after you were fired?"

Reid's eyes darkened. "After I left, the CEO suspected something fishy, and began an investigation. During that time, the manager that I'd threatened had a fatal accident. He fell from his twelfth-floor terrace. Supposedly there was reason to believe that he wasn't alone. My name and the argument we'd had came up, and I became a suspect."

Dory snorted. "But you weren't even in the state!"

He eyed her. "Why would that matter?"

Dory thought. "That day"—she hesitated when she saw his eyes flicker—"at the ball, when they came for you, you didn't seem surprised."

"I wasn't," Reid answered. "I knew about the death. Emily had called me. She also said that the wildfire rumor on the job was that I had been the thief, and they were already looking to question me." He watched Dory intently, not realizing that his body was taut. It was important to him that she believe in him. "It was only a matter of time before they came knocking." His voice was bitter.

Dory could hear the anger. "You were taken back to Milwaukee."

Reid nodded. "I was charged with corporate embezzlement and suspicion of murder."

"You said you never served time."

"I didn't." Reid's face was stony. "If it weren't for my family bailing me out . . ." Shrugging off the memory, he said, "That's a long story, Dory." He gave her a pointed look. "I'm not a murderer or a thief. I was cleared of all charges. You have nothing to fear from me."

Dory believed him, and she was angry with herself for not having faith in her own judgment. All those years ago she'd had deep feelings for him, and at that time she'd trusted her instincts. And she trusted them now. Her body fell into a relaxed pose, and she pulled her feet up beneath her on the bed.

Reid could almost see the tension leave her body, and he felt himself relaxing against the chair. After hesitating, he decided that there was something else that had to be resolved.

"I owe you an apology."

"Me? For what?"

"Twice I kissed you and then disappeared without an explanation."

Her voice softened. "The first time you were never given a chance. The second time . . . I was curious about why you vanished from the ballroom so quickly."

"You were?"

"Yes. One minute I was in your arms, and the next I didn't know what to think. I had an awful feeling . . ."

Reid's eyes flickered. "Déjà vu?"

Dory flushed. "Yes," she said, almost embarrassed that he'd guessed her thought. So much had happened since Sunday night.

"I'm glad that it wasn't, Reid," she finally said in answer to his intense look.

He studied her. "Then does that mean I don't have to apologize for stealing your kisses and then disappearing?"

After a moment, Dory answered, "Do you believe that they were stolen?"

Surprised, Reid answered, "Yes."

Dory shook her head. "You're wrong. I was surprised, but . . . I gave them to you. Both times."

"Why?" Reid remembered the feel of her arms around his neck and the slight lean of her body into him as she stood on her toes.

"Because in Jersey I had wrestled with myself for weeks about dating you, and I'd made up my mind when . . . well, it was too late."

"And Sunday night?" Reid could feel his temples pulsing.

"I was shocked." Dory's feelings matched those of that night. "I thought that I was suspended in time. That I was transported back to that moment eight years ago, and we were picking up where we left off. As if the night had never ended." She lifted her eyes to him.

Reid sucked in a breath. "Is that what you were thinking back then? About continuing the evening—before I was arrested?"

"Yes." Dory held his direct stare. "I told you that I'd made up my mind." She tilted her head. "Hadn't you made that decision about me?"

With expelled breath he answered as smoothly as he could. "I had."

Both were silent for several minutes.

Wondering if she'd been too honest with him, Dory was having second thoughts. How did she know what his feelings were toward her now?

Reid was uncomfortable. Should he take her words to mean that she was still interested in something that had been just beginning? *Impossible,* he argued with himself. *After all these years?* He grew angry. Of all moments in time, why had they come together now? Reid was keenly aware that his body was unresponsive to being so close. His thoughts darkened.

Dory saw the change in his posture. He had tensed, and was sitting straight up in the low armchair. Maybe she was being too direct with him. She unfolded her legs and sat straight up. They were probably treading on ground that he was uncomfortable with. She decided to change the subject, but instead stifled a yawn.

"Oh, excuse me," Dory said, yawning again.

"Why?" Reid responded. "You're tired and sleepy." He checked his watch. "It'll be dawn in a few hours. You should get some sleep." He eyed her. "I'll take the top birth." He saw her hesitate. "You're not thinking about returning to your compartment, are you?"

Dory shook her head. "That's just it," she answered. "I was thinking about not going back there, if it's okay with you." She suppressed a shiver, thinking about the day's events and the elusive Robbie. Who had the woman become so friendly with that she would spend the rest of the night with them? And what had Kevin meant when he speculated that she might have gotten off? Had she indicated to him that she might get off before her scheduled stop?

"What's wrong?" Reid noticed the slight tremble.

Dory offered a tiny smile. "Nothing. Just tired. It's been a long day." She settled under the covers.

"And night," Reid agreed. He locked the door, took off his robe, climbed up to the top berth and turned out the lights. "Sleep well, Dory."

"You too, Reid," Dory answered. The room was in total darkness. "Reid?"

"Yes?"

"Would it bother you if I turned on my reading lamp?"

Reid stiffened. "Are you still afraid of me?" he murmured.

Dory thought about what she'd asked, and what he must be thinking. "No, Reid. I'm not." Turning on the room lights, she got out of her berth and stood looking up at his. She couldn't see his face.

"Reid?" When he propped himself up on one elbow to stare down at her, she repeated, "I'm not afraid of you." He continued to look at her with questioning eyes. Dory reached up to the railing and, balancing herself until she was at eye level, held his gaze. She leaned over the railing and kissed him deeply on the mouth. She teetered, and felt Reid grab her arm. When she was steady, she whispered, "Good night." Dory lowered herself to the floor and got back in bed. She turned out all the lights.

Reid was on his back, staring into the dark. His tongue darted out to taste her on his lips. As if to reassure himself that he wasn't hallucinating, he listened to his body. The heat from her warm moist lips had sped through him so fast that his loins were on fire. He'd had an erection! Hands at his sides, he grabbed the blanket and squeezed, anchoring himself to keep from squirming. He could feel a silly grin splitting his face. A yell began to erupt from his throat, and he turned it into a cough.

"Are you okay, Reid?" Dory asked sleepily.

Reid coughed again. "Just fine," he muttered. "See you in the morning."

" 'Night."

Reid heard her moving around and was glad she was finally settling down. He was surprised when she called his name again. "Yes?"

Dory said sleepily, "I never asked. Are you still a research chemist? What do you do?" she mumbled.

Reid smiled. She was beat. "No," he answered. "I'm a farmer. I grow orchids."

Dory's eyes were closing, but they fluttered as she mumbled dreamily, "Orchids? Pretty flowers . . ."

"Dory?" There was no answer, and Reid's eyes glittered in the dark. *Maybe now is the right time, after all,* he thought. He closed his eyes. . . .

Dory and Reid were awakened simultaneously by sounds in the corridor. Voices and the dull thud of hurrying feet caused them to sit up. It was barely dawn.

"What the devil is going on now?" Reid grumbled. He was standing by the door pulling on his robe.

Wide-eyed and fearful, Dory joined him, belting her robe. The train was stopped at a station. Dory didn't recognize the name, but she assumed they had to be in Illinois by then. Her heart pounded as she and Reid waded through the crowded corridor. Deep down, she sensed what was wrong. The train staff, with the help of uniformed police officers, were surrounding Robbie's compartment. Reid's arm went around her waist, and Dory was comforted. Her hip pressed into his.

"Okay, everybody, we need this aisle cleared. Back to your rooms." The voice of authority rumbled like a bass drum. The buzzing crowd, in varying stages of dress, shuffled to their compartments. Dory and Reid pushed their way to hers. Once inside, they sat, leaving the door open, watching and listening. Their suspicion that something was terribly wrong was confirmed with the words, "She's dead." The tone was curiously bored.

Dory's mouth went dry. Her eyes sought Reid's. "Robbie," she whispered in a hoarse voice.

"We don't know that," Reid said, trying to refrain from sounding as baffled as he felt. But he knew that Robbie Robinson was the woman in question. Who else could it be?

"Who else could it be?" Dory said in a whisper. She and Reid listened as the loudspeaker sputtered. "Your attention, passengers. We have an onboard police emergency, and we are being detained until further notice. Those who are scheduled to detrain at this station please return to your accommodations, and you will be given further instructions. Because of this and previous unscheduled holdovers, expect arrival in Chicago to be at least three hours past the scheduled time."

As expected, a collective moan from disgruntled passengers erupted. She raised fearful eyes to Reid, but before she could speak an announcement was made that a continental breakfast would be provided for anyone wishing to eat.

Reid looked at Dory, who appeared to be dazed. He couldn't begin to guess what she was thinking. "We might as well eat," he said. "No telling what time we'll pull out. It's a sure bet that no one will be allowed to leave until every person on this train's been identified and questioned."

Dory heard the bitterness in his voice, and she was certain he was remembering a time when he'd been detained against his will. Would there ever come a time when he could forget? "You're right."

"Wait for me here." Reid stood. Answering her look, he said, "Clothes. For both of us." When she smiled he stepped outside and was confronted by the conductor, who was apparently stopping anyone in the corridor. After identifying himself and being vouched for by Kevin, who was standing guard at the end of the aisle, Reid was allowed to pass. Grim-faced, he strode to his room.

Dory was overwhelmed by the increasing noise the officials made. She overheard their conversation through her closed door. She had pulled down the shades and was washing up when she heard a voice spewing expletives.

"Damn, when will these people learn?" After another string of curses, an angry man said, "What in the world did she wanna go and do that for? Filling her veins with that filth, expecting to feel God knows what. And look what it got her. What'd you say?"

A different man spoke. "How do you know she did it to herself? Could've had a little help, you know."

"Don't be a jerk. Even I can think of a better place than this here train if I wanted to knock somebody off!"

Drug overdose? Robbie? Dory's hand was suspended in midair, and her comb dropped into the sink. She'd never suspected! Stunned, Dory finished combing her hair. Was that where Robbie had disappeared—actually to do drugs with her newfound friends? Disbelieving, Dory pushed up the window shade, then heard the voices on the platform. She swallowed when she saw a stretcher being carried past her window. Minutes later she heard men enter her car, and she opened her door.

"Keep it closed, ma'am," she was told by a uniformed officer. He immediately positioned his back against her door. Pushing the smaller aisle-side shade up an inch, Dory was able to get a glimpse of what was happening. Mesmerized, she was unable to look away when she saw the body bag zipped open. Seconds later, amid muffled grunts, the body was placed in the bag, but her view was suddenly obstructed by the officer. Still shocked, straining to get a glimpse of the lively Robbie Robinson's face in repose, Dory felt saddened by the older woman's untimely death. She was sure that whatever had happened, it had to have been an accident. Robbie had appeared to love life and live it fully. Dory wondered if she had family expecting her in Chicago. What horrible news awaited them.

More blue uniforms filled the corridor, and when Dory recognized the conductor's voice she listened carefully. "Is this the woman, Kevin?" After a short pause, Kevin answered, "Yes, sir, that's Ms. Lawrence. I haven't seen her since early yesterday."

Dory's blood froze. *Ms. Lawrence. Room number eight!* She hastily pushed the shade all the way up, and could not stop the cry that escaped her lips. Lying inside the bag was the young woman from the lounge car, the same woman Dory had seen with the angry man—the man she'd seen alone ever since! She sagged against the door. Then where was Robbie Robinson? Her heart seemed to beat faster than the train when it was traveling at normal speed. Kevin answered her question with the next beat.

"No, I didn't see Ms. Robinson get off. There were no changes in the sleepers during the graveyard stops, so there was no need to let down the steps. If she did get off, she had to do it up front in coach." He paused, then answered the conductor. "Yeah, looks like she took her stuff with her."

Dory heard the bag being zipped, and it sounded like fingernails scraping a chalkboard. A shiver went down to her toes, and she couldn't help but rub her arms to get her blood flowing again. After an eternity, Dory watched the men lift their burden and disappear from her view. She opened her door. Other stunned and curious passengers stared at one another in horror. The uniformed officers told everyone to stay put. Dory sat back down and stared out the window. Several minutes later, she looked up at the sound of footsteps.

"I heard. They wouldn't allow me to pass before." Reid saw that Dory had been so shaken that she'd turned ashen.

He turned and walked away. At the beverage station that was next to the attendant's compartment, Reid prepared two containers of coffee with cream and sugar and returned to Dory's room. "Here. Drink." When she began to sip the hot brew, he sat opposite her.

They were silent as they watched the movement on the platform. Reid noticed Dory looking across the aisle to room number eight. "You were right," he said in a low voice.

Dory nodded. "I wish I hadn't been," she answered, softly. "I wonder how long she's been dead." Almost as if she knew, her body shook again. *Those noises I heard around midnight!*

"What is it?" He didn't like the trembling that had suddenly seized her.

"Reid," Dory whispered, looking at him with wide eyes. "I may have heard her dying."

"What?"

Dory explained her role-playing, ending with the intruder in the shower room. When she finished she said, "It had to be her." A soft gurgle caught in her throat. "Ms. Gilmore. She heard it, too. She called Kevin about it." Dory clapped her hand over her mouth to stifle another gasp. When she spoke her voice trembled. "Even then, she was still alive."

"We haven't even heard half the story, yet, so we can't begin to know what happened in that room," Reid said sharply. *She's really shaken,* he thought. Suddenly, he reached over and caught her hands in his. "Stop beating yourself up with guesses." In a softer voice, he said, "What was Larry's rule?"

Dory smiled. Larry Greenwood was their former editor at *The Black Press*. "If it's speculation, don't shove it under my nose."

Reid let go of her hands and sat back. "You never did

break Larry's rule." He began to relax when he saw that she'd gotten it together.

The relief started at her temples, and when it reached her shoulders she felt them drop nearly two inches. Dory threw Reid a grateful look. "I was losing it, wasn't I?" she said quietly.

"Yes," he said, not bothering to sugarcoat his answer. Coddling wasn't what she needed, at least not now. Her early-morning kiss and his reaction were fresh in his mind.

She looked at her watch. "We should have been in Chicago an hour ago," she said. "I can't believe I'll be checking into my hotel at noon instead of eight-thirty in the morning!" Dory saw the look on Reid's face, and she remembered that this was his first rail journey. "What an introduction you've had to train travel. Please don't use this trip as the norm. It really is a good way to avoid the hustle at airports."

Reid heard the real concern, and he smiled. "We'll see. I still have a few miles to go, so I'll reserve my judgment." He checked his own watch. "I think they forgot about escorting us to breakfast." He stood up. "Let's just do it."

"Good idea," Dory said, but a sudden commotion on the platform caught her eye. "Reid, look," she said calmly. She was beyond shock now, and almost expected what was coming.

Reid followed her look out the window and saw a wall of blue uniforms and what he knew to be plainclothes cops walking briskly toward the train. The next instant, train personnel hurried along the corridor, ordering passengers out of the car. Reid took Dory's hand as they were ushered into the next car. He turned in time to see the detectives, guns drawn, planted firmly outside compartment number eight. He was not surprised. Grimly, knowing what was about to happen, he made a path through the curious onlookers, who were straining to get a look at the drama, and guided Dory to the dining car. Reid grimaced. He'd never doubted her journalistic instincts. It was as he told her: she had a real bloodhound nose.

Dory stuffed her hands in the pockets of her ski jacket and shifted on the hard bench as she sat in Chicago's Union Station, wondering whether to feel glad or sad that her less than satisfying train trip was over. After all, she argued with herself for the umpteenth time, weren't the dramas that had played out on the train good fodder for her mysteries?

Another shiver swept through her, and she anticipated warmth and comfort when she arrived at her hotel. Many of the familiar faces from her train had already disappeared from the Chicago station.

Dory and Reid had waited together on the platform for their bags. His had arrived on the first luggage trolley, and after an unreasonably long wait for hers he'd gone inside to check his reservations. Confirming his accommodations would prevent another chaotic mix-up. By the time Dory had entered the crowded station, she looked for him, but gave up after failing to spot him. Deciding to wait for a few minutes in case he'd had an emergency, she found a seat in the reservations area, just in case he returned looking for her. She knew that he'd be staying at The Palmer, but she was darned if she would contact him there. If he'd had enough of her company for the last twenty-four hours, he should have had the nerve to say so. Deep down, Dory didn't want to believe he had.

Cold, tired, disillusioned, and upset, Dory gathered her shoulder bag and laptop after waiting fifteen minutes, and pulled her wheeled luggage toward the taxi stand with ease. A lump of hurt formed in her throat, and she wondered if this was the third time that the mysterious Reid Robinson would disappear from her life. The thought of never seeing him again caused her shoulders to droop, but she hailed a taxi, head held high.

Reid watched Dory from a discreet distance. For the last twenty minutes while never losing sight of her, he'd been aware of everything that moved in the station. The crowd had thinned, and he was able to watch her every move. When he saw her look around for him, a perplexed look on her face, and then settle down to wait for him, he had felt strange. As fatigued as she was, and anxious to kick back in her hotel, she was willing to put her comfort on hold, wondering where he was. But he had to make sure that she was safe.

Before, when he'd finished with the reservations clerk and Dory had still not come inside, he had spotted his name on a placard. The hotel had sent a car for its guests, and apparently he was holding up the works. Determined not to abandon Dory without a word of good bye, he had sent his bags on, choosing to wait for her. He'd be crazy to lose track of her again. When he'd started back to the gate, he had stopped in his tracks. The old man from the train was a few feet ahead of him, intently watching the doors. Was he waiting for Dory? Reid started to walk up to the man and confront him, then stopped. What proof did he have that the man was stalking Dory? He could be innocently waiting for someone else. "Yeah, just like I am," he'd muttered.

Instead, he'd positioned himself inconspicuously inside a restaurant close to the door, where he could reach Dory's side in an instant if he had to. He had grimly watched the man move from view as people started inside with their luggage. *The old fool doesn't want Dory to spot him,* he thought. His eyes narrowed, and just as Reid was about to leave his hiding place, the man, who had spotted Dory the same time as Reid had, hesitated. He looked at her, took a step in her direction. Then, to Reid's surprise, he suddenly turned and hurried from the station, shielded from view by the crowd of disgruntled passengers.

Puzzled by the man's odd behavior, Reid waited until he was certain the man would not return. Just when he'd assured himself that the stranger had gone, Reid saw Dory stand. He didn't miss the look of dejection on her face, and his heart did a cartwheel. *She missed him!* He went to her.

The taxi pulled up and the driver came around to put Dory's luggage in the trunk. She opened the back door to get in.

"Dory?"

Dory wheeled around. "Reid?" Speechless for only a second, she found her voice. "I-I thought that you'd . . ." Her voice trailed away.

"Disappeared again?" Reid said, his voice husky.

"Ye-yes," Dory replied, her heart hammering away. "Is . . . everything okay?"

He studied her. He was damned if this would be goodbye.

"Still wanna go to Embassy, Miss?" the taxi driver said in an annoyed tone.

"Yes," Dory answered. She looked at Reid.

"Dory, I want to see you again," he said quietly. He checked his watch. It was nearly twelve-thirty. "Do you think you'll feel up to having dinner with me tonight?"

Dory swallowed, a lump of happiness this time. "Yes," she answered softly.

Reid nodded. "Get some sleep. God knows we both need it. I'll pick you up at seven." He paused. "Is there more than one Embassy Suites?"

"Probably not downtown. Anyway, it's the one on North State Street." She looked at him and said softly, "See you."

As cold and windy as it was, Reid stepped back and eyed the people waiting for rides for several minutes. No familiar figure stood out. Satisfied, Reid signaled the next waiting taxi and got inside.

Settling back and closing his eyes, he was finding it hard to relax, feeling too fatigued to even think about all that had taken place on that train. He'd thought it was all behind them until he had spotted the old man. What *was* his story, and why had he looked so strangely at Dory when he'd seen her walking toward him? He looked as if he wanted to speak but something had scared him.

Reid opened his eyes. "That's it," he mumbled. *The man seemed to be afraid to speak to her!*

SEVEN

Hours after she had kicked off her shoes and flopped down on her bed at the Embassy Suites, the telephone rang, wakening Dory. Startled, she sat up. It was three-seventeen. She had slept for almost three hours!

"Hello," she said, guessing that it was her sister and prepared for a barrage of questions.

"Dory?" Willow frowned and breathed a sigh of relief at the same time. "What happened? You've had us worried to death. No matter how many times we called the railroad, we still didn't know anything. Why was the train three hours late?"

Dressed in only her underwear, Dory shifted into a more comfortable position under the covers. "Willow, stop worrying. I'm fine. I didn't call you as soon as I got here because I was wound up like a pretzel and needed some sleep."

"I thought that was why you booked a sleeper." Willow sounded puzzled.

"I thought so, too."

"Dolores Morgan, are you going to tell me what's going on or not?"

"You know my sleuth, Sara, and how I wanted her to have the train journey from hell?"

"Go on," Willow said, trying to remain patient.

"Well, I just lived it. Everything that I'd planned to have happen to Sara, happened to Reid and me. The murder, a rape—which I *hadn't* planned—and some of the weirdest characters!"

For a moment, Willow was speechless. "What did you say?" Her mouth formed a big O.

"I didn't plan a rape, but I did intend to have a murd—"

"Dolores Morgan, you know very well that I'm not talking about your murder and mayhem plot! Reid who? And if you don't tell me right now, I'm—"

"But I am telling you, and that's not the half of it—"

"Reid?"

"What?" Dory said, frowning at another interruption.

"As in the mysterious Reid Robinson from the masquerade ball?"

"Oh," Dory said, surprised. Had she mentioned his name? Realizing she had, she flushed.

"Yes, 'oh.' I'm still waiting, and don't you leave out a thing."

"Reid Robinson was on the same train. In the same sleeping car, actually," Dory began. "Willow, the whole thing was so uncanny. You wouldn't believe." Willow sucked in her breath, and Dory hurried to tell her all that had happened to her since she left Penn Station.

"Unbelievable!" exclaimed Willow after listening without interrupting the fantastic story. It really did sound like one of Dory's mysteries.

"That's what I said."

"So it really was the belligerent man in room number eight who killed her? Why? And how do you know for sure? You never did see him get arrested."

"I told you Kevin let us in on what was going on—at least, as much as he could tell us. Those two were shootin' up for the better part of the trip, apparently. So I suppose he probably didn't kill her, but just let her drug herself to death. When she allegedly overdosed, as the guy claimed, he didn't want her to be found with him because of the mess of cocaine they were delivering. So he waited until he could put her somewhere else." Dory paused. "Apparently, she was still alive late yesterday afternoon, because Kevin saw the guy fill a bag with ice at the beverage bar, and hurry back to his compartment. Said he looked desperate."

"Ice?"

"Yeah." A shadow crossed Dory's face as she remembered things she'd seen and heard when she was barely a teenager. "If she overdosed, as he claimed, she was probably in a coma. He was using the ice to try to revive her."

"Incredible," Willow murmured. "So he must have been the one who tried your door."

"I'd bet on it," Dory answered.

"Probably looking for an empty room," Willow said. She added, "Obviously with your talkative friend Robbie gone for so long, he assumed she'd gotten off, and he took the opportunity to put his friend up in the luggage rack and then hide her with the extra blankets and pillows."

"Yeah. He certainly didn't have to drag her too far in fear of being spotted. Still, he took a chance just crossing the aisle."

Willow sucked in a breath. "Uncanny is right, Dory. You practically wrote the whole scenario in your outline!" She laughed softly. "It's a good thing you're not a suspect."

Dory laughed. "You'd better believe that."

"Who would think that the story you were acting out was really happening? The noises that other woman heard, that was really the body?"

"Apparently," Dory answered. "Of course, I couldn't hear anything, but the thumps started again and Ms. Gilmore complained to Kevin. That's how they found the woman. The bedding that was used for a wedge, a shield, had come loose, and her body was rolling back and forth."

"Well, thank God you're safe in your hotel room. But I'm still not satisfied with them not being able to discover who was in that shower stall."

Dory shrugged. "With all the other mess going on, I guess they chalked it up to another deadbeat getting away without paying. After the thorough search of the train, there was no one found riding without a ticket. Not even Robbie Robinson. Kevin told us that she called Union Station, furious at the train's delay in arriving in Chicago. Claimed she'd waited for two hours in the station to retrieve her checked bags and finally left. Her message was forwarded to the chief." Dory paused. "Kevin didn't know why she'd gotten off where she did, but the chief found out later from the coach staff that she did get off at one of the whistle stops, with one of the coach passengers." When Dory had heard that, all she could do was shake her head at the woman's foolhardy actions—after she'd claimed to be so careful about letting anyone in her compartment. There was no telling about people, she thought. She stifled a yawn.

"Okay, I heard that, Dory," Willow said, "but one more thing."

"Yes?"

"You never mentioned the old man. Did you see him again?"

"No, I never did. That was the oddest thing," Dory answered thoughtfully. "I've asked myself why he scared me so much. After the first fright, I realized that he wasn't menacing, just . . . that he never smiled. He didn't have the most pleasant old face I've laid eyes on. I guess that, coupled with that serious look, made my imagination run wild."

"Well, I wouldn't be so sure about that," Willow said. "You can't be too cautious, traveling around the way you do. There's no telling how long he'd been watching you. I'd still take care."

"I will, don't worry." Dory knew what the next question would be, and her sister didn't disappoint her.

"Will you be seeing Reid again?" Willow's tone implied that she already knew the answer.

Dory checked the time. "In about two and a half hours. We're going to dinner."

Willow smiled, feeling happy for her sister, somehow sensing that with Reid around she didn't have to worry too much about Dory's safety, or her being lonely around this time of year. "After your assignment, will you be seeing him on New Year's Eve?" she asked.

"I hardly think so. That night's going to be special for a lot of people."

"Well, aren't you special, too?" Willow asked softly. "You're special to us, and we're going to miss bringing in the new year without you." She was silent for a second, then added, "It is the beginning of a new century, and who knows what the future will bring to all of us? Could be nothing but chaos, or—hope of all hopes—peace and serenity around the world. I only know that I want you to be happy, Dory."

Surprised, Dory answered, "But I am."

"I know you are, but that's not what I mean." Willow risked beating a dead horse. "I want you to experience the happiness of falling in love. I know I've teased you about finding Prince Charming, and Reid Robinson may or may not be part of your future plans, but you never can tell about falling in love. It just happens."

Dory smiled. "Yes, I've heard that, Willow, and maybe it'll happen for me one day. But I'm not certain Reid will be in the picture. He's so full of mystery."

Willow suppressed a chuckle, wondering if she should tell her sister that sometimes that was the best kind. Hadn't Jake Rivers won her heart with his soulful eyes and rare but fetching grins? Changing the subject, she put all four of her children on the line to speak to Auntie Dory.

A wave of sadness swept Dory after she hung up, but she shucked it off. One of the worst things to do was to drown in melancholia while alone at a hotel. But then, in times past, she'd always reached for the Gideon Bible that she found in most of her hotel rooms. Instead of feeling sorry for herself, she grinned at the conversation she'd had with her niece and nephews. Giselle, called Zelle from birth, was the oldest, beating her brother Troy into the world by two minutes, and was truly enjoying her role as big sister. But Troy and the other twins, David and Ronald, never let their sister's bossiness best them.

Feeling better, Dory threw off the covers and got up. She hadn't even opened a bag, and now she unpacked, hanging up clothes and studying each item as she put it away. She was eyeing her wardrobe for something appropriate to wear that night. *Festive, or not?* she wondered. *Low-key,* she decided, and selected a black wool sweater and slacks, and black boots.

Later, after leaving the bathroom, Dory noticed the blinking red light on the telephone indicating she'd had a call while she was in the shower. *Reid?* she wondered as she pushed the button for messages. Not surprised that it was the owner of the popular supper club she was doing her New Year's Eve piece about, she dialed the number.

Minutes later, Dory hung up the phone, stunned. Cancelled? The gala celebration was called off? After the surprise wore off, Dory became furious. *Two days before the event, he decides to call off everything,* she fumed. *How inconsiderate!* She sat down in the armchair and crossed her legs, swinging her foot in anger. All she thought of was her phone call with her sister, and how she could've been with them. And now here she was, stuck in a hotel room, a million miles away from her family. She wanted to hit something, but instead she stood up, hugged her arms, and let out a growl as she paced back into the bedroom. The harsh sound of a caged mountain lion startled her, and when she caught a glimpse of herself in the mirror, she stopped and suddenly let out a laugh.

"Boy, don't you look ready to eat raw meat?" she said to her fierce image. Dory grinned and plopped down on the bed, resigning herself to the fact that she was going to be alone on Friday night. *Wonder if that's a sign of what's to come on all the Fridays in the new year,* she thought. Remembering her vow not to feel sorry for herself, Dory set up the iron and ironing board and turned on the TV. Bored with all the talk of what would or would not happen at 12:01 on the first day of the new century, she listened with interest to the news report.

"Hmm. Anxiety's catching all over. Unbelievable how many establishments cancelled events," she muttered. But then, she really shouldn't have been surprised. Only days before Christmas the mayor of Seattle had cancelled his city's gala celebration. And in New York, the gigantic Javits Convention Center management had to cancel its giant gala, for lack of interest in the affair. Apparently, no one wanted to pay thousands of dollars to be entertained for one night. "Only common sense," she said, and realized that that was the very reason her own event had been cancelled. The proprietor had said just too many patrons called to cancel reservations, and one of his star performers had backed out, downed with the flu bug that was sweeping the country. Oh, well, she thought, she would just do what thousands of other people would be doing—watch TV. In New York, Forty-second Street would be ablaze as usual, and the dropping of the specially made Waterford crystal ball in Times Square would happen. She was sure that Chicago would be doing its own thing, and she'd watch a bit, drink champagne. Then she'd call it a night and ready herself for the new millennium, thinking positive thoughts.

A curious feeling swept through her. How upbeat would her thoughts be after arriving in Rockford on Monday? A shadow crossed her face when she recalled Miz Alma's strange phone call. And would she find the meaning of that disturbing dream at Miz Alma's?

"So much for thinking positive," Dory muttered.

Reid arrived at the Embassy Suites at five to seven and was told to go to Room 612. When Dory stepped aside to let him in, he inhaled sharply. She was beautiful.

"Hi," he answered her greeting. She looked ready to walk out the door, and he was feeling a little put off. He'd half expected her not to be ready, and he'd planned to spend some time with her before leaving. There was so much he wanted to ask. *Especially now,* he thought.

"Anything wrong, Reid?" Dory asked mildly. He looked so far away. Maybe he'd changed his mind about going out.

"No, nothing," Reid answered. "Ready?"

Dory nodded and reached for her coat. As Reid helped her she turned to him. "Do you really want to go out? We don't have to, you know." She held her bag and her card key in her hand.

Reid looked at her. "Yes, I do have to," he finally said. "With you." He walked quietly by her side to the elevator, and was just as silent when the doorman hailed a taxi and they got inside. He gave their destination.

"So you know Chicago?" They were going to an out-of-the-way restaurant that specialized in southern cooking.

Reid shrugged. "I don't," he said. "I visited here from time to time, saw the usual attractions, but that's about it. I asked where I could get some stick-to-the-ribs food without the fanfare and glitz. I hope you don't mind."

Dory smiled, happy that she'd selected the right outfit. "You only read my mind, that's all. I've been to Wishbone's. You won't be disappointed."

Reid nodded, but didn't speak. His thoughts were on something he'd read, besides her mind. Earlier, after checking in, unable to sleep right away, he'd toured the hotel and happened on a well-stocked wall of books and magazines. He rarely bought reading materials at airports or hotel concession stands. Most of the fare consisted of romances and mysteries, and only a handful of popular hardcovers. His occasional reading was of biographies and nonfiction. He liked keeping his feet grounded in the real world, though he realized that fiction often emulated true life. His eye had caught the name "Dolores Morgan" on two paperback mysteries. There was no accompanying photograph. With those in hand, he'd searched the wall display for her journal, and found it. The inside back flap had a picture and a short bio. It was Dory.

Back in his room, instead of catnapping, Reid leafed through the mysteries, but he soon put them aside. He read through several chapters of *A Family,* often skipping to the next, his curiosity getting the better of him. From what Dory had told him on the train, he was able to identify the characters, though she'd changed their real names. The book, fact and fiction, was a spellbinding story. No wonder it had been a best-seller and was still selling. When he closed the book, he lay back on the bed, thinking about the young woman he'd known and knew now, and the pain she'd experienced. It was no wonder that she had the saddest eyes he'd ever seen. Even Willow Rivers, nee Vaughn, and Jake Rivers had been tormented. He thanked God again for a brother like Leon, instead of the kind Jake'd had to endure. Dory's voice interrupted his thoughts.

"Reid, we're here." He was so quiet.

He looked around, then at Dory. "Sorry," he said. "I didn't realize it would be such a drive. You must be starved." They walked inside.

"Actually, I am. So it won't be a wasted trip. How about you?"

"Same," he agreed, and followed behind her as they were led to their table.

After they'd ordered and were drinking cocktails, Dory's curiosity got the better of her. She felt as if they were on a blind date that was turning sour, and the guy was having second thoughts. She drew in a breath. "What's happened to you?" she asked.

Reid didn't have to ask what she meant. He'd hardly said ten words since he'd picked her up. "Sorry," he said. "I really did mean it when I said I wanted to be with you." He gestured at the humming crowd. "Only not here."

Dory was confused. "But you said that you were hungry, and didn't mind going out. If you'd rather have stayed in . . ."

He speared her with a look. "You're not listening to me, Dory," Reid replied in an easy tone. "Yes, I'm hungry, but I wish now that I'd made other arrangements." He continued to stare at her. "You must still be tired, and after dinner you probably want to be whisked back home to get some rest." He lifted a shoulder. "I'm just annoyed that the time will pass too quickly, because I want to spend the rest of the evening talking to you."

Dory was flushed. At a loss for words, she was relieved when the waitress appeared with their food.

Remembering her shyness, Reid was amused. She hadn't lost it, in spite of all her newly acquired worldliness.

They ate and talked, their conversation bordering on the banal, each venturing far away from the personal. After exhausting mundane topics, they eventually got around to Y2K and what the doomsayers were spouting.

Dory smiled as she pushed away the last of her sweet potato pie and finished her second cup of coffee. "It's already affected me," she said, wrinkling her nose in mock disgust.

Reid didn't understand. "How's that possible?" he asked, savoring the strongly brewed coffee. He listened while she explained.

"That's it," Dory said when she finished. "But for that assignment, I'd be home with my family on Friday night."

Reid didn't miss the hint of sadness in her voice, and he wasn't surprised to find that he was having some of the same feelings. He'd told Leon that on what promised to be a bizarre raucous New Year's Eve all over the world he'd be caught up in the craziness along with everybody else. At the time, he'd been intrigued with the idea of being in a new place with new people. And it was just possible that he'd connect with someone, if only to test his virility. He found it hard to forget that recent Christmas Eve sexual debacle with an old friend. Now the idea of partying with strangers was absurd. He'd rather be alone in a room with Dory Morgan, a woman who had ceased to exist for him.

"Then are you free on Friday evening?" Reid asked casually.

"Untied," Dory said, making an unwrapping gesture with her hands. "Somehow I feel relieved . . . but I've other plans."

Plans so soon? Reid felt deflated.

"You must have big plans for the night," Dory said. She looked at him carefully. He was distant again.

Reid shook his head. "Not anymore," he answered. *In a matter of hours she'd made another date?* Outside after paying the bill, Reid signaled a waiting taxi.

"Oh," Dory said. "I'm sorry. Was your party cancelled, too?"

Oh, what the hell, Reid groused in silence. "I'd thought since your evening was cancelled we might spend the time together. But since you've already made other plans, I guess that won't be happening." He frowned at the surprised look she gave him. "What?" he muttered.

"You think I made a date?" Dory asked.

"Didn't you?" His temples pulsed when she laughed. "I fail to see what's so funny."

Dory quieted. "I don't have a date, Reid," she said softly. Was he jealous?

"You said that you have—"

"Other plans," Dory finished, wondering at his raised brow. "Yes I do. To stay in my suite, pop a cork at midnight, and then go to bed."

"That's it?" Reid stared at her disbelievingly.

"All of it," Dory answered, grinning at his incredulous expression. "Boring, huh?"

Reid unconsciously let out a breath. Holding his voice even, he said, "No, far from it. Mind if I crash?"

"What?" Dory exclaimed. "You can't be serious, Reid. It's the most special night of the year!"

"I know." He studied her face. "I'd like nothing better."

"You *are* serious."

Reid continued to stare at her.

"Yes. You won't be crashing, though. I'd love to have you join me."

Reid sat back. "I'll bring the cork to pop. Any preferences?"

"Y-you choose," Dory murmured. She stared out the window, wondering if she'd looked away in time. She'd felt like a fool when her voice cracked. Besides Miz Alma, whom she wouldn't be seeing until after the new year, Reid Robinson was the closest thing to family who'd be with her at the start of the new century.

Reid took one of Dory's gloved hands and slipped it through his crooked arm and covered it with his own gloved hand. They rode the rest of the way in silence.

At her hotel, Reid asked the driver to wait. He stood outside with Dory.

"It's still early." Dory looked at him. "You did say you wanted to talk to me."

Reid hesitated. "Are you sure?"

"I'm sure."

Reid dismissed the taxi and followed her inside the hotel.

"Ice?" Dory asked as she fixed Reid a whiskey and water. When he nodded yes, she carried his drink and her own glass of vodka and orange juice to the sofa and sat down. He was sitting across from her in the armchair. She kicked her shoes off and wriggled her toes, then sipped her drink. Her eyes caught Reid's. "What?"

"I'm seeing yet another side of you," he said. He tasted his whiskey.

"Really? What side is that?"

"Unafraid. Relaxed with me, finally." He drank some more. "Are you?"

Dory smiled. "Yes, I am. Is it all that noticeable?"

Reid nodded. After a brief pause he said, "You're an excellent writer, Dory. Congratulations, again." He saluted her with his glass.

"You've found my books?" That was what he wanted to talk about. Why was she disappointed?

"Yes." Reid noticed a slight withdrawal. "If you'd rather not talk about them, we don't have to."

"I don't mind." Dory hesitated. "Which ones did you find?" When he told her he'd read the journal, she said, "Oh."

Reading Dory's description of the attempted rape on

her when she was a child had set a blaze inside of Reid. "You're still bothered by all that happened aren't you?" he asked quietly. "Growing up without knowledge of your relatives because of your Aunt Dorcas's lies." He didn't mention the molestation.

At one time, his words would have made her uncomfortable, but Dory looked at him steadily. "My aunt did what she thought she had to do to protect Willow. It was the promise she'd made to her sister Beatrice before my Aunt Beatrice killed herself." Her eyes held a glimmer of a shadow as she remembered.

"What I didn't tell you yesterday on the train was that my mother, Vera, was a wild child. She grew up spoiled, selfish and promiscuous. She didn't care what married man she slept with, including her own sister's husband." Her voice did not waver when she added, "When my Aunt Beatrice found her husband Michael Vaughn and my mother having intercourse on her kitchen table, she went insane. After throwing my mother out of the house, she shot her husband. Then, after calling her sister Dorcas to come to Willow, she shot and killed herself."

"Don't, Dory," Reid said in a low voice. "You already told me most of what happened. I pretty much guessed who everybody was."

But Dory only shook her head. She wanted to continue. "That same night I was conceived. Later, when she knew that she was pregnant, my mother pleaded with her sister Dorcas to forgive her, but Dorcas's heart was cold. She blamed Vera for Beatrice's suicide. I don't know when it was that my mother went to Illinois, or who she knew, but that's where she stayed and where I was born, in Rockford. I believed my father was killed when I was a baby, that his name was Jones." Dory paused. "Sometimes my mother used Vera Jones, and sometimes she used Vera Morgan. I asked her about that once, and she just said offhandedly that it was convenient to use different names when it suited her. She told me that she never married my father, but she gave me his name, anyway. She refused to tell me any more."

Reid got up, refreshed both their drinks, and sat back down. "From your tone it sounds as if you never hated your Aunt Dorcas or your mother for all the lies."

Dory tasted her drink. "No," she said simply. "Aunt Dorcas redeemed herself by bringing me and Willow together. We forgave her." She gave Reid a wan smile. "She was too late to ask for Vera's forgiveness. When my mother was dying from AIDS and asked her sister to forgive her, my aunt refused. My mother died, and there's no way that my aunt can ever forget that." She sighed. "Everyone's suffered enough."

"You're right," Reid murmured. He thought about the role Jake Rivers's brother, Nat, had played in the drama; the way he taunted his brother about their mother's infidelities, also with the womanizer Michael Vaughn, and the break-up of their own parents' marriage. Yesterday, Dory had mentioned the man briefly, but he was still curious. He asked if she'd ever met him.

"Nat? No, I've never met the man," she said, then shrugged. "His daughter, Kendra, heard from him a few times, but I doubt if that's been true lately." She hesitated. "As you said yesterday, drunk or sober, it's best that he stay away. Jake's a happy man now with Willow. He needs no reminders of a painful past."

Reid looked at her. "You're not risking bringing back your own pain? Researching old haunts for your new mystery?"

Dory was thoughtful. "That's crossed my mind. I've always asked myself why I avoided coming back here. I felt a great weight lifted from my soul after writing the journal." She drew her legs up on the sofa and rested her chin in her hand as she leaned on the rolled arm. "But I'm comfortable with it."

"You're certain?"

"Uh-huh," Dory murmured. "It'll be the final closure." She smiled. "I intend for good things to happen to some of these people in this book."

Reid believed her. While he was reading her story, he'd wanted to know how she was handling returning to her past. He sensed that his question had satisfied a need in her to talk about it. She was studying him. "What?" he asked.

"Is that what you wanted to talk to me about?" Dory said.

Hesitating for a second, Reid nodded. "Yes."

"But?" Dory encouraged. He obviously wanted to say something else.

"That, and I wanted to be with you."

Dory's insides warmed. "I'm glad you wanted that. Me, too."

Later, while brushing her hair, Dory stared at herself, her image reflecting the mixed emotions. Reid had been gone for hours, yet she couldn't stop thinking about him. She'd thoroughly enjoyed their time together, at dinner and later in her suite. The only awkward moment had come after they'd admitted wanting each others' company. They'd talked of many things, and at one point Reid had joined her on the sofa. She didn't remember him ever breaking into laughter, but after something she'd said, he'd grinned broadly and grabbed her hand. She had leaned into him, her head resting on his shoulder as she shook with mirth.

When his hand brushed her cheek and her lips touched his palm, though, she had felt him stiffen. The natural moment for them to kiss had passed, and she was puzzled. Then, as abruptly as when he'd left her compartment on the train, he stood and said he'd better go, that he was sure that she was bone tired. Then he left.

Dory laid the brush down and continued to stare into her dark brown eyes. "Why didn't you kiss me this time, Reid?" she murmured.

EIGHT

On Friday Dory had awakened feeling rested for the first time in days. She'd had a spring in her step as she went from breakfast to lunch, wandering in downtown Chicago on North Michigan Avenue. Even the windy forty-degree temperature wasn't a deterrent, and when she'd gone into the Water Tower Place mall she found that watching people was still as much fun as the shopping. She quashed the impulse to buy swanky loungewear for the evening, hesitant to give Reid the wrong message. If he hadn't wanted to kiss her last night, he'd probably back out the door if she appeared in a come-hither getup. She'd left the mall without buying a thing. As she had last night, she would select something comfortable to wear and hope Reid would be dressed as casually.

After all, it was going to be a laid-back evening, and by one o'clock Reid would be back at The Palmer House and she'd be fast asleep. She'd told Willow as much when she called her a few minutes ago, and Dory could swear that Willow had smothered a laugh. They wished each other Happy New Year and hung up. Dory was glad that her sister hadn't teased her about her date with Reid.

"And that's in only two hours," Dory murmured. It was seven o'clock, and she was propped up on the bed watching TV. Already the tension was building as the whole world watched and waited for the new millennium. Depending on what station a person watched, they could celebrate New Year's several times over if they chose, as the international datelines came and went. She pressed the Mute button so she could see but not hear the action until more rockets and fireworks went boom, and then balanced her laptop on her thighs. She scanned all that she'd written since she began her trip, including what she'd typed last night.

Backtracking and mulling over the notes she'd made prior to starting her trip, she mumbled, "Something's not meshing here." She added, cut, did twenty questions, and then sat back, reading. As if a bucket of cold water had been thrown in her face, washing away mud from her eyes, she saw where she'd been wrong—the train scenarios!

"That's it!" Dory said. "The beginning, the middle, and the end happens all at once! Not prolonged from New York to Chicago and beyond," she exclaimed. "The episodes end in the whole nightmarish twenty-five hour ride!"

Feverishly, she began to type while ideas were flowing. In fiction, Sara's train murder was not solved by the time she reached Chicago. In real life, the alleged murder had turned out to be an accidental drug overdose from shooting heroin. In fiction, Sara met a talkative older woman who disappeared and was later found murdered. In real life, the older woman was a pretty flirt who lived on the edge, dallying into the unknown with strangers; and apparently turned up alive and well, waiting for the next encounter.

Dory stopped typing, let out a deep sigh, and began to read her notes. Satisfied that she was on the right track, she added a few lines and changed a thought here and there. After so much melodrama on the train, Sara should have new faces and mysteries thwart her while in Chicago. Depending on the outcome of the events, Dory would determine whether she would extend the mystery to the southwest. Encouraged, Dory began to develop another character, one who would become Sara's ally. It had to be a man, Dory thought—tall, good-looking, with a dangerous glint in his eye, and mysterious with a capital M. *A cop?* she wondered. Intrigued by the idea, Dory made more notes, giving the character a life. Movement on the TV screen caught her eye, and she guessed the new year was about to happen somewhere. She bent her head, so intent on creating her character that she missed the explosion of fireworks on the screen.

"Gotcha," Dory said triumphantly. She worried a large plastic roller in her hair, tugging at it as she read the page. "You sound like a decent guy," she said. "Just the man for Sara to even *think* about in her rare romantic moments." The more she read, the more Dory liked the guy, and she toyed with the idea of really giving her sleuth a love interest. After all, Sara was warm-blooded, pretty, thirtyish, not opposed to an occasional romp—especially if the hunk didn't get all sentimental on her and declare his love. That would hardly do for a New York City gal trying hard not to become jaded in her world, where she'd seen so much lying and treachery, and even a murder. Who would have thought that her position as secretary and sometimes courier for her wealthy industrialist employer would lead to such adventures?

Dory grinned as she had a private conversation with her fictional character. "Okay, okay," she said, "maybe, only maybe, I'll let you have a little fun. We'll see."

As she gave the page another once-over before quitting, Dory's eyes widened. She almost couldn't believe what she'd written. Frowning, she turned off the computer and pushed it off her lap. "No, I couldn't have," she murmured. But she had.

The character she'd created for Sara was a replica of Reid Robinson.

* * *

For the thousandth time, Dory checked the clock. It was only after eight, and Reid wasn't expected until nine, but she was dressed and waiting. She'd had very little to do to prepare for her date. Yesterday she'd had her hair and nails done, and after returning to the suite this afternoon, she'd showered and pressed her clothes and then done some writing. Ever since she'd realized who had inspired the new male character in her novel, she'd been as nervous as a cat. Was her subconscious trying to tell her something? Dory tried to calm down by watching the events on TV, but soon tired of it all. Where would all the excitement be when the new year came to Chicago? She found a movie channel and soon became engrossed in a mystery she'd never seen before. But she knew that she still had some questions that needed answering. Was she really ready to take up where she'd been willing to go eight years ago? Was Reid?

Reid grimaced as he got off the elevator, balancing his burden. "How do I ring the bell, now?" he muttered. When he got to the door he kicked it a few times, hoping Dory was not in the bathroom with the door closed. In a few seconds his bundles would scatter all over the hallway floor.

"Reid?" Dory asked, peering through the door peephole. All she could see was Reid's chin and bundles and—flowers?

"It's me, Dory," Reid grunted.

Opening the door, Dory stepped back as Reid hurried past her and headed straight for the table and gingerly put his bags down. The huge vase of flowers toppled, and he grabbed it before it landed on its side, swearing at the sticky mess he left on the clear glass. "Damn, the bag is leaking," he said, looking at the red smudges on his fingers.

Dory could smell hot sauce. "Hot wings," she said, smiling at his dilemma. "Here, let me help you with these while you go rinse off your hands." When he disappeared into the bathroom she carried the bag to the sink, tore it open, and then removed the dripping wings from the soaked paper and put them on a plate. While she wiped the vase, Reid returned, shrugged out of his overcoat, and looked at her.

"Hello." His eyes roamed over her appreciatively, and then he looked down at the table. "Some mess."

"Not so bad," Dory answered, setting the vase in the center of the table and trying to ignore the warmth traveling through her after his look. "These are so beautiful," she murmured. "Thank you."

"You're welcome," he answered. He began emptying the rest of the bags.

"What did you bring?" Dory exclaimed as she helped.

"Got carried away, I guess," Reid said as he checked the plastic containers for any more spillage. "In case you can't get a meal anywhere tomorrow, you won't starve. Anyway, we'll need something for the champagne to settle on."

"Potato salad. Sliced ham. String beans. And apple pie?" Dory said as she examined each container and put it in the small fridge. "I think we'll have to eat everything tonight. There's no room for it all." She eyed the two chilled bottles of Roederer's Estate and put them on the door shelf of the compact refrigerator. When all the food was put away, except for the hot wings, Dory tilted her head and raised a brow at Reid. "Don't tell me you're stockpiling just in case," she teased. "And how did you manage with all this stuff?"

"Try getting something delivered today," he said

gruffly. "I think I got laughed at after everybody finally got me off the phone. Obviously, a silly request."

Dory laughed. "The streets, Reid. They're impassable." She could imagine what he'd gone through asking restaurants to make deliveries. She placed plates, glasses, and utensils on the table. Earlier, when she was out, she'd bought a few snacks, and now she set out cheese, crackers, and fruit. She left the strawberries for later, to plop into their champagne glasses. She sat across from him, watching with amusement as he dug into the hot wings. Soon, she couldn't resist, and did the same.

"Still like this spicy stuff, huh?" she said between bites and sips of spring water.

"Can't kick the habit," Reid said, also drinking water. "Just hope it hasn't done a number on my insides after all these years."

"You probably don't have anything to worry about." Dory got up, wet some paper towels, and brought them to the table and sat back down. "Something you did kick, though," she said. "When did you stop smoking?"

Reid pushed his plate away and wiped his mouth and hands. "Years ago. About a year after I returned to Rochester. My workers weren't allowed to smoke, so I figured I shouldn't, either." He studied her. "Are you sorry you're not out celebrating with the rest of the world? It's some party out there." She looked beautiful and smelled fantastic. He'd wondered about showing up in casual slacks and turtleneck under a sweater, but he was at ease when he saw that she was also comfortably dressed. Her loose white sweater and wide-legged pants with a bold black, silver, and white geometric print were stunning. Simple sterling teardrops dangled from her ears. Her only other jewelry was the garnet ring she always wore on her right middle finger. He didn't remember it from years ago, and he wondered if it was a cherished memento from a past relationship. The thought was disturbing.

"Are you kidding?" Dory answered, aware of his admiring appraisal. "Aren't we having our own party right here?" she teased.

Instead of answering, Reid said quietly, "You're a fantastic woman, Dory."

Embarrassed, she said, "As opposed to when you knew me way back when?"

"No," Reid answered, thinking about it. "You were always something special. Now"—he searched for the right word—"you've blossomed."

"Please." Dory smiled. "You're not going to say that I was a shrinking violet, and now I've become the blooming rose." Her eyes twinkled.

Reid was serious, and didn't smile. "A violet, maybe, but never shrinking." He looked at the vase of flowers, and then at Dory. He would like to see her wear them.

She followed his look. "Oh, no, not like the beautiful orchid."

"Why not?" Reid asked. He pulled the vase toward him and turned it around until he found the one he wanted and plucked it out.

"That one is so gorgeous," Dory murmured. "It's a white cattleya, isn't it?" she asked, watching him twirl the lush green stem around in his hand.

"You know orchids?" Reid looked at her with admiration.

"No, only that one," Dory responded with a small chuckle. "I think everyone on earth knows the name. For years it was the only one we all saw on prom nights, and at award luncheons. Besides, I recognize it from the orchid calendar my sister did about three years ago. Before that I never knew there were so many different types. And so many ugly ones, too."

Reid was amused. "There are some that are unusual," he said. "Some of these, for instance."

Dory looked at the flowers. "These? You're kidding!

All of these are orchids?" She shook her head in disbelief "I thought they were fill-ins."

"Many people think that, and there are a lot of other misconceptions about the flower," Reid answered. "Most of these are cattleyas and some of their relatives."

Touching a particularly pretty drooping cluster of white flowers tipped and spotted a deep purple, Dory said, "It's so unusual to see them growing so tall, and the leaves are so large. What's this called? And where were you able to get such gorgeous flowers?"

"That's a foxtail orchid, and it's in the rhynchostylis family," Reid said. Then he added, "I know somebody." The smile on his lips was also in his eyes.

Dory laughed. "Never mind," she said, putting the orchid back in the vase. Reid didn't follow suit with his. Curious, she watched him begin to break off much of the stem and leaves. He got up and walked to her side.

Reid removed the clip from the side of Dory's hair. He pulled her hair back and fastened the flower behind her ear. He bent and kissed her cheek, then turned to the refrigerator and removed a bottle of champagne. "There's no reason we can't toast the good things about this old century, is there?"

"The good things," Dory murmured. She knew that they were both thinking about their pasts.

"Right," Reid said, and popped the cork. He poured the champagne into two wineglasses and joined Dory, who was standing by the table. He took her hand and led her into the sitting area by the sofa. He raised his glass to hers. "To the good."

Dory didn't remove her hand from his, but held it tightly as they clinked glasses. "To the good." They drank.

Reid bent his head and kissed Dory's lips, his tongue intruding into her mouth, savoring the taste of the fruity champagne on her darting tongue. It was a long, deeply satisfying kiss, and he wanted more, but he pulled back. Visions of what had happened one week ago in Rochester intruded on his thoughts, and he dreaded a repeat performance. He stared at her, and after gently kissing her lips again he sat down and pulled her down beside him. *"That* was good," he said in a husky voice. He set his glass on the table and picked up the remote. "Bet the whole world's going crazy about now," he said easily, but his heart was thumping madly.

"I don't doubt it," Dory replied, licking her lips.

Three hours later Reid and Dory watched the TV screen expectantly. They held hands and counted down the seconds. At midnight, they lifted their glasses.

"Happy New Year, Dory."

"Happy New Year, Reid." They touched glasses and drank. Dory leaned over and kissed Reid. "Well, the earth's still here," she whispered.

"Nothing went kaboom in the night," Reid remarked dryly. They listened to the commentator's comments about the world still being in business, to no one's surprise, especially since Y2K problems were nonexistent in other parts of the world.

Dory turned off the TV. "I'm glad it's all over," she said. "Now we can get on with the rest of our lives." She was very much aware of Reid holding her hand and running his finger in little swirls over the back of it.

"What are your plans, Reid?" She hesitated. "I mean after you've found . . . uh, I mean once you've—"

"Found my backstabber?" His eyes grew dark. "I may never find out now." His tone was bitter.

"What?" Dory said, surprised. "But, why?" She knew that he'd planned to look up his old friend.

"Emily's phone has been disconnected." Reid threw Dory a look of disgust. "That's it," he said.

"You've tried finding her? Another listing, perhaps? Maybe she's married and using another name?"

"Maybe."

She heard the note of finality in his voice. "Does that mean there are no other leads? No one else you can call to find out where she is?"

"I have another name, but no number. With the whole world going crazy I didn't try making any calls."

"I'm sorry, Reid," Dory said. "Maybe on Monday you'll have some luck. I know you want to put a period to the end of that story before you leave town."

Reid nodded in agreement, but dismissed talk of himself. "And what about you, Dory? What are your big plans for the beginning of this new century? Will you continue to write?"

"Uh-huh," Dory answered. "I don't want to stop now. The ideas are coming so rapidly I'm impatient to finish one project and start another. I've already picked out a big old house that's been deserted for years, and is supposed to be haunted." She laughed. "But only in my imagination. I have no idea where the house is. For all I know, it could be in the Himalayas, and I'm not about to go exploring there."

Reid raised a brow. "Want to stay closer to home?"

"Something like that." Dory noticed his curious stare. "What?"

"Is Rochester, New York, close enough?"

"You can't be serious." Dory's jaw dropped.

"I am," he answered. His eyes flickered, and he added, "I know of such a place." He was silent for a moment. "There was a murder, and it's still unsolved."

"What?" Dory perked up. "The owner deserted the house, and it's never been sold?"

"It's still boarded up."

"Incredible," Dory said, almost inaudibly. The setting for her next book was settled, without any doubt in her mind. And all with Reid's intriguing statement. Unbelievable. She poured more champagne into their glasses, and then bit into a plump strawberry.

"Problem solved?" Reid asked, amused from watching her expressions.

"A big part of it, anyway, thanks to you. Just look for me to pop up in Rochester in six months."

That long? Reid thought. "No problem," he said. "I'm looking forward to seeing you in my hometown." *Who are you kidding, man? How in God's name do you even know what kind of man you'll be six months from now?*

Dory noticed his frown and slight movement away from her as he drank. "Anything wrong, Reid?" she asked.

"No, only wondering what other plans you have. Will you still do the travel articles?"

"Yes, for a time. Of course, if I get lucky and another movie is made and it becomes a blockbuster, then I guess I'll give up the articles." She laughed and wrinkled her nose. "Besides, I'm certain that by that time, I'd rather stay home with my kids—at least until they get to some size. I can't very well put them in a knapsack and go traipsing around doing research."

"Children?"

Dory tilted her head and smiled. "Yeah, you know those little creatures that we once were?" She wondered why he looked so dazed.

"You're planning to get married?" Reid asked in a low voice. "I thought that you were unattached."

Surprised, Dory answered, "And I thought we were talking about the future. As in, years from now?" For some reason her heart dropped to her toes. *He doesn't want marriage or children?*

Reid's eyes darkened. Suddenly the thought of her realizing her dreams with another man was like a boulder dropping in the pit of his stomach. But what right had he to feel that way?

"Reid?" Dory realized he'd slipped away for a second,

but she had to know. Otherwise, why even toy with the idea of a relationship with him? When she had his attention, she said, "You don't want children?"

"What?" Reid said, startled by her question. "Of course I want children," he growled. He looked into her eyes and saw the confusion. *What the hell am I doing?* he thought. He was allowing his dark thoughts to interfere with a perfect night. Maybe it was time he left. But was this the last time that he'd ever see her? He was reluctant to leave. With an effort, he did an about-face, changing the subject.

"You've been in touch with your friend in Rockford?" Reid asked.

"Yes," Dory answered. "I spoke to Miz Alma yesterday. She's expecting me on Monday. I told her to call me at the hotel when she gets off from work and we'll get together."

"Work?" Reid said. "I thought you told me she was in her seventies."

"Seventy-six," Dory answered. "She's living on only her Social Security, which isn't that much, so she works occasionally as a home attendant when she can get the jobs. She's only a substitute."

"You won't be staying with her?"

"No. I thought it would be less bother for her not to put up with company for three or four days." Dory shrugged. "I'll pick her up, and we can do whatever she wants. It won't be a problem. She used to like taking me to the movies when I was a kid, so maybe we'll see a few. Mainly, we're visiting. I haven't seen her since my mother died." Dory hesitated. "I don't want to lose touch."

Reid didn't miss the catch in her voice, and he felt that the place held too many painful memories. He wondered if this trip was really what she needed right now. "When will you be back here?"

"Friday, though probably not in this room," Dory answered. "I'll stay another week, and then I'm off." She smiled. "At least that's the plan. You never know what can happen to alter things. What about you? Do you think you'll be going to Wisconsin, after all?"

"That depends on who I'm able to contact." Reid frowned. "If Emily's not around, I'm not all that hopeful about finding anybody from back then who can be of any help." He looked at her. "If I don't, I'll have made the trip for nothing, and might as well cut my stay short." Reid was thoughtful. "But if I'm here, can I call you on Friday? Have dinner together?"

"I'd like that, Reid." *I'm going to see him again.* She clasped her knees in a nonchalant pose.

Reid stood and retrieved his coat from the chair and slipped it on. He turned to Dory, who'd followed him to the door, and he took her hands in his. "I couldn't have asked for a better way to see in the new century, Dory." He bent and kissed her gently on the mouth, intending to make a hasty exit for his own good. But when she answered with an exploring tongue, he groaned, dropped her hands, and pulled her into his arms. *God help me.* He reclaimed her lips and crushed them hungrily.

Dory pushed his coat aside and slipped her arms around his waist. Though she had held her composure before, she kissed Reid with reckless abandon, forgetting about cautiously starting a new relationship. He was here, and she was in his arms, and that was all that mattered. "Oh, Reid," she murmured, molding her body to his. When she felt his hand cup her breast, she moaned and strained to feel more of him. She slipped her hands under his sweater, and his muscles rippled through the cloth of his shirt.

Reid shuddered when he felt the warmth of her slender hands on his back. He felt as if he were on fire, and he could feel his need for her, wanting to shout hallelujah or laugh at his getting himself into this predicament. He knew that he had to stop. *Performing inadequately with her just can't happen!* With great effort, he broke their kiss. His temples throbbed at the tiny whimper she made when he released her and stepped back. He looked down at her and had to steel himself to keep from grabbing her again.

"Dory," he said his voice husky. "I didn't mean for that to happen."

Dory looked at Reid for a long moment, trying to see whether the words on his lips were in his eves, because she didn't believe that for a second—not after what they'd just shared. She had her answer. With the realization, her heart sang. But now was not the time to find out what was bothering him.

"You didn't?" she murmured.

Surprised by her question, Reid could only shake his head.

Dory smiled and said, "Well, I did." She moved in closer to him, wrapped her arms around his waist, and held him tightly. She laid her head against his chest and smiled when she felt his arms around her. *I was right. He does care.* His chin rested on her head, and he began to smooth her hair. "You're lying to me, Reid Robinson, and I don't know why," she whispered. She lifted her head to stare into his eyes. Then she released him.

Dory kissed him gently on the mouth. "Can we talk about it when I get back?" she asked softly.

Reid stared at her. "Next Friday, Dory." He opened the door and left.

Can we talk about it? Reid was in his hotel room, staring out the window at the city that hadn't yet gone to sleep. "Sure man. Talk about how she turns you on and you want to love her madly, but you're afraid to do anything about it," he muttered in disgust. "Yeah, that's right. Afraid!" He slammed his hand flat against the wall. "Damn!"

NINE

Reid looked at his watch and frowned. Five past one, and he was still waiting for his lunch appointment, who should have arrived twenty minutes ago. It was Monday, and he was in the lobby bar at the hotel. He looked around, amused at the bustling activity. It was business as usual again, and most folks would have stared and walked away shaking their heads if asked about the Y2K bug. "Probably call me a nut case," Reid muttered. He continued to watch people walk by, hoping to spot Preston Dowdy. He doubted if he'd recognize the brother. The last time Reid had seen the man was the day he was fired from the firm. Dowdy was also a chemist, but had never worked directly with Reid. Each knew the other existed, because it wasn't too hard to notice the blacks in the firm. Theirs was a hi and bye and a quick meal in the company cafeteria from time to time relationship. Dowdy and Emily had more of a thing going.

"Man, is that you?" Reid watched the grinning man walk toward him with outstretched hand.

"Dowdy?" Reid said, and stood to grasp his hand.

"You got it," Preston Dowdy said. "You know how many times I walked past this place? I saw you, brother, but just kept passing by." He scrutinized Reid. "It was the bald head that got me. I was looking for dreadlocks down your back by now."

"Yeah, those went years ago, man." Reid checked his

watch. "Come on, we should still be able to make lunch." He led the way to the restaurant, where he'd eaten before and had enjoyed the food. They were seated, ordered cocktails, and selected their meals. Reid lifted his glass of cognac. "Happy New Year." He sipped and set his glass down. "Thanks for coming, man."

"Happy New Year to you, too, and don't mention it. I'm just glad you caught me. You must have had a devil of a time tracking me down yesterday." Preston, who was in his midthirties, was as tall as Reid but slimmer, and he looked as if he didn't have a care in the world. When he laughed it was with gusto, and his nearly black eyes twinkled like polished obsidian. Like Reid, he ordered cognac, and he savored its warmth as he sipped.

Reid nodded. "It wasn't easy. You've moved around a lot." Their food arrived and they ate, talking about their old jobs but staying away from why Reid left. When coffee arrived, Reid said, "So you haven't heard a thing about where Emily went?"

"Nah, I haven't been in contact with her for at least six years. Back then she told me that she was thinking about going into partnership with a friend. Some kind of perfume business." He shrugged. "But whether that ever came off, I don't know."

"In Milwaukee?"

"No, here in Chicago. I think the friend was already established in a shop." Preston cocked a brow. "I'm surprised she didn't mention it to you when she spoke to you last."

"You probably spoke to her after I did. She called me once after I moved back to Rochester, after my hearing. At that time she was still at the firm. She never mentioned that she was thinking of leaving." He hesitated. "I'd had enough of Milwaukee."

Preston grinned "I'm surprised she wasn't more persistent."

Reid frowned. "About what?"

"Keeping in touch with you."

"Me?"

"Yeah, you. I made a move, but she wasn't hearing it. You were the one she wanted. But everybody knew that the only thing that existed for you was that project." Preston laughed at Reid's expression. "Never knew that, huh?"

"No," Reid grumbled. Emily? He'd only thought about her as his coworker and very capable assistant.

Preston laughed. "Don't look so surprised, man. It happens. But she was so fine that we all wondered if you, well, went the other way." He held up a hand against Reid's glare. "Hey, I'm not knocking you. If that's your persuasion, hey!" He spread his hands.

"It's not." Reid thought about Dory, and his groin warmed. "It's not," he repeated. "I thought you and Emily had a thing."

"Like I said," Preston replied, "I made my move, but was rejected. We just talked. Nothing serious. That's why we didn't keep in touch all that much after I left. She left after I did, and she never called to tell me that she was leaving and going into that business. I heard the scuttlebutt from a former coworker."

"Which firm are you with now?" Reid asked.

"Chicago PD."

"You're a cop?" Not so far-fetched, Reid thought. He'd gone from chemist to newspaper reporter.

"Six years now."

"From a chemist to a cop. What made you change?"

"People. I like being around people. The lab, the quiet, the absorption." Preston grimaced. "I'd go home and have all-night conversations with my dog, and when I found myself conversatin' with the TV, I knew it was time for a change."

Reid laughed. "You like it?"

"Like anything else, you take your lumps and keep getting up. Take the good with the bad, and look on the bright side."

"Apparently that's working for you. Good luck."

"Thanks," answered Preston. "Sorry I can't be of any more help regarding Emily." His eyes twinkled. "Second thoughts about going that way, man?"

"No, it's not that," Reid answered, his forehead wrinkling. "Just thought that she could help in trying to clear up some things about that old business. Like who was the thief, and laid the blame at my feet?" He stared at Preston. "I don't suppose you heard any scuttlebutt about that?"

Preston shook his head. "Nothing," he answered. "Strange, Reid. It's like the whole thing never happened. Almost as if the subject were verboten, forbidden to speak about, in the company. It was a weird thing, man."

Both men were silent for several seconds, obviously mulling over the past.

Preston broke the silence. "Could be if you start with the perfume shops you might get a buzz. Or get a line on the suppliers to the business. If I could remember the name of the shop, that would be a start, but I'm not sure whether she ever mentioned it to me."

Reid made a gesture of futility. "The name probably changed once Emily became a partner."

"Not if the business was already established. Risky changing to something a customer doesn't recognize." Preston cocked a brow. "Unless only a name was added."

"Or unless it's not under their names, but something catchy relating to the business," Reid said, suddenly feeling deflated.

"Yeah, you're right. Well, Reid, it was good seeing you after all these years, but I'm on tonight, so I've gotta get some shut-eye. Glad you looked me up."

"Yeah. Same here, Preston." They exchanged cards,

and Reid patted his pocket. "Let's try to stay in touch," he said.

Reid paid the check and they walked through the hotel lobby to the front entrance.

Preston stopped. "Look, this may not be much help, but I just thought of something. Why don't you start with the dead phone number? Maybe you can hook up an address with that." As if he'd made a decision, he said, "I have a friend who owes me a favor. Let me see what I can find out. If there's anything, I'll give you a call. If you decide to check out, let me know."

"I appreciate that, man," Reid answered. "I'm not leaving until next Monday, so call me anytime if you get anything." They shook hands.

After Preston left, Reid went back to the lobby bar and ordered another cognac. He had no faith in Preston's ability to turn up anything. If a person wanted to disappear and stay lost, it was all too easy. And it appeared that Emily Gibbons wanted to do exactly that.

Dory arrived at her hotel in Rockford before noon. The daily shuttle bus ride from downtown Chicago was only two hours. It was uneventful, but the trip brought back memories. While she was attending college at Urbana-Champaign, her mother had forbidden her to ever come home at the drop of a hat, so Dory had stayed in Chicago, going to school and working. She remembered some of those weekends as being the loneliest of her life. She'd never been a joiner, and had few friends. Friends meant that she had to talk about family, and her mother would have had a fit if Dory brought anyone home for the weekend. Those times when she had gone home, she always left a little sadder—especially during those last two years, when her mother had gotten so sick.

When Dory graduated it almost seemed that her mother

was telling her good riddance when she encouraged her to take the job so far away in New Jersey. But Dory knew that her mother was ashamed of her own ravaged body. Even then she had forbidden Dory to come home to visit.

Dory was barely settled before the phone rang.

"It's me, Dolores. You just got there? I called a few times."

"Miz Alma," Dory said surprised. "I told you I'd be getting here about now. Anything wrong?" A feeling of apprehension swept through her, and her thoughts flew back to that strange Christmas Eve phone call.

Alma Manning hesitated. "You coming here tonight? I made dinner for us. Nothing fancy. Same as you always used to eat here."

"I'll be there, Miz Alma. I told you, anything you want to do is fine with me. It is cold out there, so I don't blame you for not wanting to venture out. Want me to bring in anything?"

"No. Got everything I need, thanks." She paused. "Dolores? What time you coming?"

"Well, I didn't think you wanted me to come too late, so we can visit awhile before dinner," Dory said. "You're not going to rush me in and out, are you?" she teased.

"Don't talk foolish, Dolores," Alma said. "I just want you to get here before dark."

Her mouth went dry. "Something happen, Miz Alma?" She tried not to let her imagination run wild.

Alma snorted. "Ain't something always happening in this building? Come before it gets dark." She hung up.

Dory hung up, too, thinking the blunt good-bye was typical. But something was wrong. Why hurry to get there in daylight? If there was a mugging or two, that wasn't unusual. Multidwelling buildings in any big city were a hazard and a fact of life. When Dory lived there she hadn't any problems coming and going to her second-floor apartment. She'd rarely used the elevator, except to visit a friend when she was younger. Sometimes she had felt she would be safer upstairs than in her home. Some of the men her mother brought home and the way they looked at her had scared her. The bad memory of her attempted rape caused a shudder, and she shook herself out of the dark mood and got busy with unpacking. She was traveling light, having stored her luggage at the Embassy Suites, since she was going back there. All she'd brought with her were two sweater and slacks changes.

When she finished putting away the clothes, Dory sat on the bed. She smiled when she looked at the flowers on the dresser. The orchids were as beautiful now as when Reid had stumbled into her suite with them three nights ago. Unwilling to toss them into the trash when she'd checked out of the hotel this morning, she'd wrapped them carefully and carried them in her lap on the bus. Now she could enjoy them for four more days. Besides, she thought, looking at them reminded her of Reid. She wished that he were there.

Dory wondered if he'd been successful in locating his friend. She was tempted to call, but quashed the idea. If he'd found her then, more than likely they would be together. With that thought, she got up and prepared to leave. She stuffed her hair under her wool hat and pulled on her ski jacket.

"Don't be jealous, Dory," she said to her frowning image in the mirror. "That man cares for you as much as you care for him." Remembering their kisses, her cheeks flamed and she grew warm inside. She left the room and walked, deep in thought, to the elevator. *Care?* Dory realized that her feelings ran deeper than that, but she was afraid to say the word aloud.

"Well, I'll be danged. If it ain't little Dolores Jones; only she ain't so little anymore."

"Hello, Mr. Johnny," Dory said, one foot on the steps, ready to enter the building. The old super's son was now the super. "Nope, haven't been little for years now. How are you and your family? Miss Loretta doing better? Miz Alma told me she had an operation around Thanksgiving." When Johnny King's father died, he and his wife Loretta took over managing the building. For as long as Dory remembered, there had been a King family in the super's apartment.

"She's doing just fine now. So, you comin' to see about Miz Alma? She'll be glad. You're about the only family she has now, 'cept for that cousin in Ohio. I know she sure misses your mama. 'Bout the only person she ever visited in this buildin'." He swept up the trash and tossed it into the garbage can, then replaced the lid. He shook his head from side to side after giving Dory a meaningful look under his bushy graying eyebrows. "No good not to have friends, though, especially when a body gets sick. Need somebody, then. She'll be glad you're visitin', Dolores," he repeated.

"Sick?" Dory said. She frowned. "Miz Alma?"

Johnny looked surprised. "I thought that's why you come," he said. "Nearly had her head busted open. Got mugged right here on these steps 'bout a week before Christmas. She never said nothin' to you?"

"No, she didn't." The words nearly stuck in her throat. *I knew it!* "Was he caught? Who did it?"

"Nah, the guy got away. Miz Alma's screams like to wake the dead. By the time I got out here he was gone and she was lyin' right here on these steps, still holdin' on to that bag she always carries. Don't know why she didn't give it up to keep from gettin' near killed over it."

"Well, I'll be seeing you again, Mr. Johnny. I'll be around for a few days. Regards to Miss Loretta." Dory ran up the steps and into the building. Rounding the curved landing, she hurried up to the second floor, her heart in her mouth. Standing outside of Miz Alma's door, she didn't knock, but turned and looked across the hall at her old apartment, the only home she'd known. The last time she'd locked the door and given the keys to Miz Alma to turn in to the super was after she'd cleared everything out—a week after her mother was cremated. It hadn't taken long to discard or give away things, and there had been nothing left in the apartment that she wanted as a memento from their life together. Dory had taken a half-filled picture album marking a birthday here and there, and some graduation pictures.

Sometimes she looked at that album and thought that her life was incomplete. Other families had scads of pictures with aunts, uncles, fathers, mothers, and cousins, all at reunions, parties, and the like. She heard voices and laughter and the TV playing, and she couldn't remember a time when all that gaiety ever happened in that apartment, except during that one week of the year—the week between Christmas and New Year's. Turning away, Dory knocked.

"Miz Alma!" Dory gasped when the door opened. Prepared to see a bandage on her forehead, Dory was shocked to see that the old woman was a bag of bones.

"Come on in, Dolores. Stop standin' out there with your mouth open. It's me." Alma turned and walked slowly back into her apartment and left Dory to close and lock the door. Her heavy chenille robe was sizes too big now.

Dory followed her old friend and baby-sitter into the living room, which was as meticulously clean as she'd always remembered it to be. She sat the gaily wrapped Christmas gift she'd brought on the table and removed her jacket and hat, draping them over the chair.

"Miz Alma, why didn't you tell me you were mugged?" Dory sat opposite her in an old green armchair that she'd sat in often in years past.

Alma Manning's intelligent deep brown eyes glittered in her equally dark-brown face, reflecting the pain that wracked her body. Dolores Jones had always been a quiet child, almost afraid to make her presence known, lest her mama got mad at her for making too much noise. But that was years ago. Staying away at college and then leaving home right after graduation had done her some good, helped her to lose some of those shy ways. Even when she'd come home after her mama died, she hadn't looked as sad as she used to. Maybe she'd been trying to find some happiness for herself working for that newspaper so far away in New Jersey.

"So old Johnny's out mindin' people's business again, is he?" Alma finally said, but her strong tone was not disparaging.

Dory smiled. "You know Mr. Johnny's good for this building, just like all the Kings were, Miz Alma. He keeps it from being a hangout." She frowned. "Except for when you got hurt. Do you know who did it? How bad was it?" she asked.

Alma's eyes were shut, and she answered, "Not bad. Guess I put up too much of a fight for him to get a good whack at me." She felt the side of her head. "Had a big knot, but it's gone now. A little sore, that's all." She shifted her thin frame on the throw-covered sofa.

Dory didn't miss the evasive look, especially from a woman who usually stared people down when speaking. Direct and to the point, and no window dressing responses. That was Alma Manning, and now Dory wondered at her shying away from answering her question. *Did Miz Alma know her attacker?* The thought was disquieting.

"You must be hungry by now, Dolores. You know where everythin' is. Why don't you help yourself? You can fix me a little somethin', too. Guess I'm feelin' a bit tired today." She eyed the package. "That for me?" When

Dory handed her the gift, Alma's bony hands smoothed the red sateen ribbon. She sniffled. "Thanks. Christmas is different after all these years, ain't it?" she said, unwrapping the package. "There's a little somethin' for you over there." She indicated a box wrapped in green-and-white Christmas paper on the end table. "Nothin' like your mama used to do for you." Holding up the robe, Alma said, "I needed another one of these. Only had one heavy one like this, and it ain't got the warmth it used to have." She nodded her head and smoothed the folds in the white cloth.

"Glad I got something you need," Dory said, unwrapping her gift. "Oh," she exclaimed when she lifted the lid. Then, almost immediately, she looked up at the woman, who was staring at her. "But, why . . . are you giving . . ." Dory swallowed.

"Not now," Alma said, sounding tired, busying herself with stuffing the robe back in the box. "That's yours, now," she said.

Dory's eyes grew misty. She removed the long gold chain from the box and held it up high, watching the gold oval locket dangle in the air. The shiny onyx facets of the stone in the center caught the light, shining as if it were a beacon in the night.

"Thank you," Dory murmured, her throat tightening up. "I've always loved this," she said. "But this should remain in your family, Miz Alma. It's a valuable antique." The eighteen-karat jewelry had belonged to Alma's mother, who'd given it to her on her sixteenth birthday. Dory had always loved to run her fingers over the scrollwork in the gold, and polish the gemstone. Miz Alma had let her wear it all day on her tenth birthday.

Alma shook her head. "There's just me, now."

"Your cousin?" Dory saw Alma nod. "Oh, I'm sorry." Suddenly, Dory felt the overwhelming desire to cry. After all these years, Alma was finally alone, just as Dory had been. And Dory knew that Miz Alma was trying to tell her something. Why else would she give away her precious heirloom? And what about her hair? The thick gray cornrows were gone. All that was left were thinning cropped tufts with more than a little scalp showing.

"Let me go wash my hands, and I'll fix us something to eat," Dory said. When she returned she headed straight for the kitchen, where the smells teased her palate, bringing memories of many nights eating dinner there when her mother was working late.

"Not a lot for me, Dolores," Alma called. She had turned on the TV, and was watching a talk show.

An ominous feeling swept over Dory as she stared at the countertop near the sink. A lazy Susan was filled with small plastic medicine bottles. She picked some up and read the labels. *Not common cold preparations, for sure,* she thought. All the words ending in *in, icine, ene,* or *mycin* sent a shudder through her, reminding her of her mother's time of illness. Alma was very sick.

"I take all of those, Dolores."

She whirled at the sound of Miz Alma's voice, dropping a bottle back on the tray. "What's wrong with you?" Dory whispered.

Alma lifted pot lids, felt the sides of the pots, then placed a clean towel over the roasted chicken. She stared at Dory. "This'll keep. Come on back inside." She returned to the living room, eased herself back onto the sofa, and turned off the TV.

Dory followed, took her same seat, and waited.

"Cancer," Alma said. "It's back."

"Back?" *Since when?*

Alma's lips moved in a wan smile. "More than twenty years ago I had a breast removed. The first year you went away to college I lost the other one. I was fine, no sign of anythin' till last year. This time, there's nothin' they can remove—unless they take all of me."

"It's spread?" Dory whispered. Her stomach was queasy, and she felt like vomiting.

"There's nothin' they can do." Alma waved a hand toward the kitchen. "Except give me that stuff in there."

"Did they say—"

"How long?" Alma's shoulders shook. "They're not God. When it's time, it's time, whether they say three months, three weeks, or three days."

"Three months? That's all?" Tears sprang to Dory's eyes and rolled down her cheeks. "Oh, no." Without warning, she broke into sobs and covered her face. Miz Alma had always been a part of her life, and now she would be gone.

Alma let Dolores cry. Her own eyes misted when she thought about all the heartache in that girl's life. But she had her half sister and the rest of her family now, so she'd never be alone again, as she once thought she was. Alma had to warn the girl of the danger she was in.

"Dolores, go wash your face and blow your nose. Then come back here. There's somethin' you have to know. It's time."

"Time?" Dory lifted her tearstained face. "For what?"

"Go. Hurry back," Alma said.

Dory left, and when she returned she sat quietly, waiting almost woodenly. *What secrets are left for me to learn? There can't possibly be more to my mother's story.*

Alma saw the dejected look. "Your mother gave me some things to keep for you. She said I wasn't to give them to you until you were grown and married, settled in your life with a house full of babies. With more important things for you to think about, other things will become smaller, and won't matter more than a ripple in an ocean."

"What things?"

"Later, before you leave," Alma said. "I have something to tell you." She closed her eyes briefly. When she opened them, they were full of anger. Her mouth was drawn in a thin line and her words were spoken stiffly, as if they grated against her teeth.

"You remember a man named Papa?"

Dory shook her head no.

"Hurley—Papa—Wilson." Alma's eyes glittered. "He's the one who whacked me."

"What? I had a feeling you knew who did it," Dory said. "But why? It wasn't for money?"

"Humph. Money ain't what he's interested in."

"Then what?"

"He's looking for you."

"Me?" Dory looked at her in disbelief. "Who is he?"

Alma's gaunt cheeks quivered. "He's the man who tried to rape you when you were nine years old."

Dory couldn't speak. She held her body taut, steeling herself against the memory. If she relaxed she would fall apart. She knew it. All the apprehension she'd had about coming back was welling up inside of her, ready to explode. The old man on the train! The one who'd stared at her, always turning up where she was. He was the one. Had he gotten off in Chicago? Was he in Rockford now? *Be calm, Dory,* she told herself. *It'll go away.* She forced herself to look at Miz Alma, and to speak.

Her voice sounded like a stranger's when she said, "Why is he looking for me?"

"The man's crazy," spat Alma. "After all these years what your mama did to him has pickled his brain, and he's obsessed with gettin' even with her by gettin' you. That's what that crazy fool told me. Been to that door more than once tryin' to get me to tell him where you were." She grimaced. "Finally tried to beat it out of me."

"He knows about me, and where I live?" Dory said.

"No. The fool's too liquored and doped up to read a newspaper, and the company he keeps is just as ignorant. He doesn't know about who you are." Alma looked hard at the young woman she'd just scared. But she had to know. "You remember anythin' of that night, Dolores?"

"As if it happened yesterday, Miz Alma."

"I thought so." Alma nodded. "Your mama always said you'd put it out of your mind, but I didn't believe that."

"I never forgot it," Dory answered quietly. "I heard them come in that night," she said in a faint voice, distancing herself from the action. "I think Mama was drunk. She would laugh too loud and too much when she overdid it. As she'd taught me, I stayed in my room with the door locked any time she brought company home. That night, I woke up thirsty. I listened and didn't hear anything, so I guessed that the man had left and Mama had fallen asleep. So I went to the kitchen. I had the water running cold, so I never heard him come up behind me. He grabbed me before I could scream. He was like an octopus, his hands everywhere—in my pajama pants, feeling inside of me. I felt his knee in my back to hold me tight against the sink while he unbuckled his pants. His other hand was over my mouth, and I bit him. He cursed, and I guess the noise finally woke Mama up." Dory looked at Miz Alma.

"You remember what happened next."

"Mama ran into the kitchen screaming, and she stabbed him with a straight razor. He screamed and let me go, but Mama had stabbed him in the shoulder and dragged the blade down his arm, and when she got to his hand she sliced it across his fingers. The man was wild, and instead of trying to attack Mama he ran from the apartment, saying that he'd kill her. Blood was everywhere."

Alma nodded. "You remember weeks later your mama was coming home from work, and was beat so bad she almost died?"

Dory nodded. "I guessed it was him. Was it?" When Alma nodded again, confirming her suspicions, she said, "I also heard that the man was a musician, and the hand that Mama cut was crippled. Months after Mama recovered he was found in the street half dead from a beating. I heard he left town and never returned."

"That's right. Stayed away for years," said Alma. "Heard he showed up here about two years ago."

"He must have heard that Mama died." She looked at Alma. "Why would he want revenge after all these years?"

"Papa Wilson played jazz piano," Alma said. "He was young, barely twenty-one, and played those black-and-whites 'till tears came to your eyes. He played like he'd been here before, dancin' around all the old-timers. That's why they called him Papa. He played like one of them. Yeah, Hurley Wilson was a name around here, and he was gonna be a big somebody. He starred on a Sonny Westbrook album, and everybody was sayin' he was on his way."

"You heard him, Miz Alma?"

"Your mama had the album, and she played it for me. The boy was good," Alma said, nodding her head. "Good."

"So after Mama maimed him, his career was gone."

"Just like that."

"And now he wants to get Mama by hurting me." Dory shook her head. "Crazy," she said. *The whole world's going mad,* she thought.

Alma's piercing eyes held Dory's. "He *is* crazy, Dolores," she said. "He's a fool with years of hate stuffed inside of him that's achin' to get out now. He wants to hurt you for what your mama took from him. Nothin' but a mad dog now, and I'm warnin' you that you're in danger."

Dory shivered at the coldness in Miz Alma's tone. There was no doubt that the old woman was scared to death of Papa Wilson. If he would hurt Miz Alma simply for information, there was no telling what he would do once he found Dory. Now she understood the strange phone call on Christmas Eve. Miz Alma hadn't wanted her to come to Rockford. Dory caught a breath. The dream! Nora in a deserted building, being chased, and no one cared. No one stopped to help her. Was she Nora?

"Dolores, you can't come back here," Alma said. "If that crazy man gets wind that you were here, he'll be back watchin' for you."

Dory's gaze landed on Miz Alma, who spoke in a weakened voice. *She's really tired.* Dory never suspected that the older woman was so ill. Always, her voice was strong, and she spoke with so much force and confidence. But all along she'd been wasting away. *She's going to die, and she wants me safe.*

"So what are you going to do if he does come back? Take another beating? Why didn't you tell the police that you knew who attacked you? They could have picked him up by now."

Alma rolled her eyes. "Humph. They have to catch him first. All they can do is keep lookin', but you know findin' him ain't their number one concern."

"Then they are on the lookout for him?" Dory was relieved. "If he knows that, then he won't be back."

"Don't go foolin' yourself, Dolores. You were never dumb," Alma said. "The man won't stop until he satisfies that rage inside of him."

A cold feeling sent a shiver down Dory's spine. She knew Miz Alma spoke the truth. But Dory also knew that she wasn't going to be scared away and leave that man to beat up on an old woman.

"I planned to spend five days with you, Miz Alma, and that's exactly what I'm going to do," Dory said. "Now that's enough talk about that crazy fool. I hope you're ready to eat, because I'm starving." She got up. "I saw all that delicious stuff you prepared, but"—she tilted her head to one side—"I didn't see my candied yams."

Alma grunted, but she looked pleased. "They're still in the oven."

"Mmm, can't wait," Dory said. "You sit here, and I'll get everything ready."

In the kitchen, out of view of her friend, Dory sagged against a cabinet. Her heart was thumping wildly, and, as if she could stop it with a magical touch, she clutched her chest.

"Dolores, anythin' the matter? I don't hear those pots. Need somethin'?"

Dory sighed deeply, and began to make some noise. "No, Miz Alma, I'm finding everything okay. I'm just going to zap our food in the microwave. Be ready in a few minutes. Want something hot to drink?"

Dory put the kettle on for some hot tea. As she took the plates out of the cupboard she nearly dropped them, but she quickly steadied her shaking hands when she felt another dull thud in her chest. She thought that she had guessed the identity of the angry musician, but she was dead wrong.

Papa Wilson was not the old man on the train. That old man had two perfectly good hands!

Then who was the man who'd watched her for a day?

TEN

Reid sat at the bar for thirty minutes after Preston left him. Disgusted at his lack of progress, he went to his room, wondering what the hell he was doing hanging around the city. He'd dreaded even thinking about traveling to Milwaukee if he'd been successful in contacting Emily, but he'd steeled himself for that possibility. Any light she could have shed on the past would have been worth the side trip. But she'd disappeared.

He had to laugh at himself. For somebody who had wanted to bury the sour incident, he'd sure carried around a lot of mementoes in his wallet for all those years. He had the names and addresses of his research team, and Preston Dowdy's name and address, but no number. He'd wondered why he had taken that man's name. They'd never socialized after work. But, maybe because he was a brother, they'd exchanged cards.

"Lucky for me," Reid muttered. As luck would have it, Dowdy was the only one he'd been able to track down after many calls. The man had changed addresses at least two times before relocating to Chicago. All the rest of Reid's team, including Emily, had moved, leaving no forwarding numbers.

Restless, Reid changed into his fleece-lined boots and slipped on a heavy turtleneck sweater. After pulling on his ski jacket and wool cap he left the room. He needed some air, and a brisk walk downtown in the cold would probably shake him into some constructive activity.

Two hours later, Reid was back at the hotel, his wanderings having ended with him freezing his butt off. *So much for arctic exploring,* he mused. The already gray skies had darkened, and furious snow flurries, while pretty to look at, obscured his view from the observatory of the Hancock Center on North Michigan Avenue. Years ago he had visited the Sears Tower, which was taller than the Hancock building, and he had been duly impressed with the miles of sights like everyone else. But sightseeing wasn't on his mind. Finding Emily Gibbons was.

When he got back to his room he found a message from Preston Dowdy. Reid wasted no time in shucking off his jacket and cap and dialing his number. Preston was at work.

"Hey, man," Dowdy said. "Glad I caught you. Got good news for you. Didn't take but twenty minutes for my man to get the scoop. Ready for this?"

Something about people prolonging whatever they had to say always irritated Reid. Get to the point, and be done with it! He took a deep breath. "What did you find, Preston?"

"The name of Emily and her partner's business was Hibiscus Perfumery. Her partner's name is Janet Steward."

"Was?" Reid frowned.

"Yeah, the business is defunct. Lost to taxes after it was seized by the Feds."

"What?"

Preston gave a dry laugh. "This is a story you wouldn't believe, man. I got Janet's number and called her. After I identified myself she was all too willing to tell me the whole story." He paused. "She wants to meet you."

"Me?" Reid was surprised.

"I think you'll appreciate hearing what she has to say

from her, rather than me. It'll clear up a lot of answers for you." Preston hesitated again. "I figured you wouldn't mind, so I took her number and said you'd give her a shout. She's leaving in two days on a business trip, and tonight's her only free time before she leaves."

Nearly speechless, Reid wrote down the number, thanked Preston, and hung up. He continued to sit on the edge of the bed, almost dreading calling the number he'd written down. Preston had sounded pretty mysterious. *And so does the eager Ms. Janet Steward,* he observed. Shaking his head, he could only laugh inwardly at the course of events. What else could possibly surprise him on this almost comedic vacation? He picked up the phone and dialed.

"Ms. Steward? Reid Robinson," Reid said in answer to her throaty, "Hello." He was taken aback by her equally throaty chuckle.

"Mr. Robinson," Janet Steward answered. "I was hoping you'd catch me. Is tonight convenient for you to meet?"

"Yes, it is," answered Reid. "Where are you?"

"Not far, down here in The Loop," Janet said, and then she laughed. "But if you don't mind, can we hook up at your place? It's been a mighty long time since I've had a business meeting in one of my favorite haunts. It sure will be good for my soul." She chuckled softly, as if at some private joke.

Amused, Reid said, "If you haven't eaten yet, would you like to join me?"

"Even if I had, I'd say yes," she teased. "What time, and which one of those many restaurants? Any one will do."

When they had decided where to meet, Reid hung up, intrigued by the frank woman. He pulled off his sweater and headed for the bathroom, thinking that Preston Dowdy must have been floored himself by whatever the woman had to say. Reid impatiently washed and dressed, and at seven-thirty he was down in the lobby. Janet Steward had hung up, laughingly telling him to look for ebony and ivory.

He ceased to wonder what she'd meant when he saw the woman. She was a vision.

Janet Steward's skin was ebony. Although she wore makeup, one could see the vibrant, healthy, polished glow of her flawless face. Creamy russet-tinted lips could only be deemed luscious in her full round face. Her hair, worn natural and shaped in a short stylish cut, was partially covered with a wide, white fur headband. The rest of her attire was all off-white, from her turtleneck sweater and pants to the low-heeled leather boots and long ermine coat. Gold glittered from her ears, fingers, and wrists.

What a gorgeous woman! Reid walked toward her, and she stood as he approached, holding out her hand.

"Ms. Steward?" Reid said, catching a breath. That the woman exuded sexuality with every move was quite evident in the appreciative stares of passing males, and some women, as well. He clasped her hand, and almost instantly withdrew it because of a sudden sexual attraction. Confused, he dropped it and stared into her smoky-black laughing eyes.

"Janet. And you're Reid?" She smiled and shifted out of her coat, draping it over her arm. Boldly, her gaze traveled over his long form. With an appreciative glint in her eyes, she said, "Of course you are. Preston's description was accurate." Her eyes lingering on Reid's bald head, she smiled at his apparent uneasiness at her frank appraisal. "Nice to meet you."

"My pleasure," Reid answered. Without another word he led her to the restaurant, where they were immediately seated. Walking beside her, he'd inhaled her exotic scent, and was surprised at his inability to recognize the base. Even though years had passed, he'd been familiar with perfume extracts and usually could identify them.

After the waiter left, Reid said, "This is a surprise. I thought I'd drawn a blank when I lost track of Emily. I appreciate this."

Janet eyed him but refrained from speaking until after their wine was poured and the server left. "Not as much as I do," she said, looking over the rim of her glass as she tasted the wine.

Reid sat back, studying the attractive woman, who made no attempt to hide her desire to seduce him. All he wanted from her was information, and then he'd thank her and leave. But Reid couldn't deny the warm feeling that was spiraling in his gut. He was getting turned on. The realization brought mixed emotions. He had not put himself in that position again since the disastrous display of his lack of sexual prowess on Christmas Eve—not even with Dory. He hadn't known this woman for fifteen minutes, and his body was ready to take all she was offering.

Janet interrupted his thoughts. "How's your steak?"

Reid had moved his food around on the plate, wondering about the disturbance this woman had caused. And he knew she was well aware of it.

"The way I like it," Reid said easily. He was determined to take control of the situation. "Preston said that you lost your business. Sorry about that. What happened?"

Janet eyed Reid for a moment. Then, as if resigned, she halted her attempted seduction. Between bites of tender asparagus, she said with a malicious smile. "Emily happened."

When Reid saw the look on her face, he laid down his knife and fork and pushed his plate away. Just as his body had warmed up to Janet Steward, it was now sending danger signals. He prepared himself to hear the news.

"I'm listening," Reid said quietly.

"Do you like the scent I'm wearing?" Janet asked. Her lips curled upward in another unattractive smile.

Anger leaped into Reid's eyes. "Stop playing games with me. Either you have something to say, or you don't. Which is it?" His hard-edged tone left no doubt that he was ready to walk.

Janet took another bite, sipped some water, and eyed Reid. "I guess you wouldn't recognize it, especially since it wasn't really fully developed before you left the firm."

"What are you saying?" Reid wasn't sure he wanted to know. He stared into her eyes.

"Emily stole the formula and laid the blame at your feet. It was all perfectly orchestrated."

Words stuck in Reid's throat the first time he tried to speak. He drank some wine that went down too fast, and he sputtered, "How do you know?"

Janet shrugged. "She told me," she said simply.

Stunned, Reid could only look at the woman, who'd just let him have one in the gut. He knew that she was telling the truth.

Janet waved away the dessert menu and accepted coffee for them both. She knew that she'd handed the man a blow, but what else could she do? There was no easy way to describe betrayal by a so-called friend. She sipped the hot beverage and waited until Reid had downed some of his. When he seemed a bit recovered, she said, "Can we talk elsewhere?"

Reid nodded, paid the bill, and led her outside of the restaurant into a quiet corner in the bar. They ordered two whiskeys and soda.

"Why don't I just talk, and you listen?" Janet said in a softer voice. Gone were all the flirtatious ways and mockery. She knew that Reid was still reeling. When he nodded, she said, "Good."

"Emily approached me years ago about buying into my business," Janet began. "Said she wanted a change from research. With her knowledge the business could develop into more than it was. I was in pretty good shape at the time, and wasn't entertaining the idea of a partner or expanding the business. I had started it from scratch with little know-how of the manufacturing end, but a lot of skills in marketing. My MBA was an asset. I turned her down . . . then." Her eyes flickered, and she laughed at herself. "Should have left it that way."

Reid fingered his facial hair, remaining silent. Janet had spoken bitterly, but when she continued her voice was even once more.

"About two years after she approached me, my business needed a jolt. I called her, and we agreed to be partners. Emily was delighted, said she would bring in gigantic new business. We changed the name of the company, brought in new fragrances, and the business took off like a rocket. She was right." Janet paused. "Little did I know that the formula she'd brought with her was stolen. That was a smart woman. She didn't leave the company right after all the mess that went down with you. Or even after your old boss died. She waited until a decent time passed, and then she left." Janet smirked. "Emily asked me not to spread the word about taking her in as a partner. Claimed people would begin to put the bite on her if they thought she was rolling in dough. The funny thing about it is, she was. She'd gotten paid big bucks for that formula. She even ripped them off."

Reid's eyes glittered. "How?"

"Emily took the original formula and added her own spin on it. That's what she brought to my business. The fragrance is a big hit. The other competitors never suspected."

Reid nodded. No wonder he hadn't been able to detect anything familiar. "Go on."

"The business was going great, and soon Emily became restless and began to travel. Appeared she was losing interest in the novelty of owning her own business. But anytime money was needed, she had no qualms about writing a check. Whatever I said I needed, I got. She moved from Chicago, claiming she needed a change. Went to live in Fort Lauderdale, Florida."

"You were still partners?"

"Yes," Janet answered. "We communicated frequently. She knew what was going on, and where we stood. She even agreed to the expansion. I wanted to open a second store in Chicago North." She laughed. "That never happened."

"What did?"

Janet raised a brow. "She fell in love."

"What?"

"Didn't expect to hear that, did you?" Janet snorted. "Love makes the world go 'round, they say. Well, it sure rocked mine, and I wasn't even the one who got bit."

"How were you affected?"

"The man Emily fell in love with was a minister." Janet laughed. "He worshipped her, made her feel like a queen. Of course, she attended his church, and of course there was no living in sin. She wanted marriage. For months she went along, believing that all was well with her soul when she knew it really wasn't. Her man was a man of God, and she couldn't deceive the love of her life by letting him marry an evil woman. It would destroy him."

Reid guessed what was coming. "She confessed to him."

Janet nodded. "And hand in hand they went to the police."

"How were you involved?"

"My store manager called me and told me the Feds had cleaned all the cash from the register, told the employees to leave, and then padlocked the place. I wasn't allowed to set foot in the place—not until months passed, and I was cleared of any embezzlement charges."

"They thought you were in on the theft?"

"Yes. If I hadn't had an attorney who could dance and

chew gum at the same time, I'd be sitting with your friend right now in Wisconsin." Janet shook her head. "A hotel like that I don't need."

"Emily told you all of this?"

Janet nodded. "I went to visit her, and she told me everything." She stared at Reid. "She was very apologetic, and remorseful about what she did to you."

Reid's temples pulsed, and he found his hand balled into a fist. He found it hard to swallow, and he couldn't drink enough water to quench his thirst. All his senses were going haywire as each one reminded him of the past: Janet's words sinking into his brain, the scent that was part of his experiments, the images of Emily's smiling face and then her look of disbelief when she had visited him in jail, the touch of her hand when she tried to console him, the sour taste in his mouth when he was in that jail. It seemed he couldn't breathe. With a giant effort he finally got control of himself, and was able to look into Janet's eyes. He could tell there was more, and he held his body rigid. "What else?"

"Emily was cleansing herself by talking to me," Janet said, obviously thinking it amusing. "It's a wonder she didn't try to track you down to confess to you, to feel completely forgiven."

Reid said nothing to that, but his look encouraged her to go on.

"The night your old boss landed on the pavement below his apartment? Well, she had been there that night. No," she said at Reid's look. "She didn't help him over the side. Drunk as he was, he did that all by himself."

Reid nodded. He'd already known that the man had been drinking. His own crackerjack attorneys had uncovered that information.

"They had argued," Janet continued. "Emily wanted to leave the company right away, and he told her that it would be too obvious if she left. The thief had never been found, and unless they got a suspect she was to stay put, and he said that she wasn't going to bring him down by doing something foolish." Janet sipped her fresh glass of whiskey, and a smile touched her lips, as if to say what happened next was no surprise. "Then he put the moves on, pawing her, and she pushed him away." Janet raised a brow. "Emily admitted that they'd both been drinking pretty heavily. But when he'd had one Scotch too many, she wanted out of there—especially when he perched up on his terrace railing. Said he loved propping one hip up there and swinging his foot like he was king of the hill. When he did that she begged him to get down, and he laughed at her. She walked to the door, and he followed her to let her out. The next day at work she got the news that he was dead."

"Obviously he went back to playing king of the hill," Reid said dryly. The image of that man's face when Reid had gone to him with his suspicions rankled him. His next thought set his teeth on edge. "That's when Emily decided to implicate me in the theft and the death, capitalizing on my argument with the man," he said.

Janet nodded. "Actually, she started planting little seeds almost immediately after you left. So when your boss died they tried to connect you to both."

Reid grimaced. "Emily called me in New Jersey to tell me that he'd died, and of the suspicion that it was murder."

Janet lifted a plump shoulder. "I told you she was a smart woman. Crafty, intelligent, she could see the scenario. She was never a suspect, and smelled like a rose."

Reid's laugh was laced with sarcasm. "Roses don't stink like that," he said. His eyes were a black flame as they bored into Janet's.

"She was the one person from that job who even bothered to visit me in that jail." Reid looked amazed. "She didn't have to do that."

"Emily was thinking about Emily. Everything she did was for her benefit. Everybody knew that you and she were friends, and if she dropped you then, wouldn't they wonder and start looking her way? She wanted things to look as normal as possible during the investigation." Janet held Reid's intense gaze. "She told me that after your attorneys got all the charges against you dismissed, she was happy for you. Since you never spent any real time in jail, and weren't convicted, she could put her own plan into action and get on with her life."

"Get on with her life," Reid mused. "She did do that, didn't she?" His voice was bitter.

Janet's look softened. "Not a good feeling, being betrayed, is it?"

Reid looked at her. She'd had her feet pulled from beneath her, too.

"How have you recovered?" Reid asked.

"Guess I'm a survivor," Janet said philosophically. "I had money. Made some wise investments early on. So when I was pinched, I had the means to pay for good advice and representation. It took a couple of years for them to sort out what was mine before Emily, and after Emily. My assets are unfrozen, and I'm free to go about my business. I'm a worker, and I like my independence."

Reid could see that. "You didn't start up the business again?"

"Nah. That left a sour taste in my mouth," Janet said. "I had to work for somebody else for a year or two, but I'm on my own again."

"What do you do now?"

Janet winked. "Keep my eye out for a rich husband." She tilted her head and said, "Orchids? Hmm."

Reid laughed. She'd gone into her seductive mode. He only shook his head, suddenly feeling at ease.

"No go, huh?" she said, winking again. "Can't blame a girl for trying." She shrugged. "Anyway, I'm a troubleshooter for floundering businesses. I come in and take a look at whatever ails the place. When I find it, I stay a couple of months, or for however long it takes, and then I move on. So far, it's been working." She chuckled. "No partners need apply."

"I hear that," Reid answered. They were silent for a moment, and then Reid asked, "The minister. Did he stick by her?"

"Until after the trial," Janet answered. "Emily told me that once she was led away, she never saw him again. Not one visit or one letter . . . oh, except the one he sent asking for the ring back. Said he'd given it in good faith, and hoped she would return it as part of her redemption in God's eyes." Janet made a face. "If that's love, honey, I want no part of it."

Anger flared up in Reid's eyes for an instant, and then disappeared. If Emily had never fallen for a preacher and sought forgiveness from God, he would probably have spent the rest of his life feeling uptight and hating whoever had wanted to ruin his life. Now he knew. He felt Janet's stare.

"You've carried that for a long time." She understood how he felt.

Grateful that he could talk about it to someone after all those years, and to somebody who'd been there, Reid relaxed, and he let out a deep sigh. "Yeah."

"I could tell," Janet said.

Reid said, "You never did let it eat you up inside, did you?" He spoke with admiration.

"Nope," Janet answered with a small chuckle. "Life's too short for all that. As long as I was able to feed and clothe myself and keep a roof over my head, I was grateful for my blessings. I had short pockets for a while, but I prevailed and thanked God my address wasn't the same as Emily's."

Reid smiled at her. "I'm glad it worked out for you,

too." His tone was thoughtful. "Janet, I don't know what I can do to thank you. Taking the time to meet me, well"—he gestured—"it means a lot." He noticed her glancing at her watch, and realized that she probably had to prepare for travel. He signaled the waiter and paid the tab.

Janet stood and allowed Reid to help her into her coat. When they were in the lobby she turned and looked up at him. "Glad to do it. I'm sure you knew nothing of what happened." She smiled, and her beautiful face glowed. "You left and never looked back, huh?" When she saw the tiny smile on his lips, she said, "That was the best thing for you. Otherwise you would never have gotten on with your life the way you did." She shrugged. "So take whatever I told you and erase it from your memory. It's ancient history now." She took a card from her leather bag and handed it to him. "If you ever need my services, call. I travel," she said with a glint in her eyes. She was barely five foot three, but she stretched her curvaceous frame to reach his mouth and kissed him, then stepped back. "I know you won't, but just in case . . ." She left the thought to Reid's imagination.

Reid stared down at her, bent his head, and kissed her again. Choosing to sidestep her unspoken invitation, he murmured, "Thank you again, Janet." He watched her until she was helped into a taxi. When the car disappeared, Reid turned away and stared around him as if he'd forgotten where he was. The feeling in his body was indescribable. Now he knew what it meant to feel weightless—he felt that he could float up to his room instead of using the elevator.

Once in his room, he still couldn't settle down. He wanted to yell and hit something, just as he'd wanted to do years ago when he was in a rage. Only this time, instead of rage he felt relief, and he wanted to scream his released emotions to anyone who would listen. He paced the room and slammed his fist into his hand. "Damn!" he yelled. Knowing he probably didn't need it, he poured another shot glass of whiskey and then sank down on the bed. After savoring the liquid, he said "Damn," again, and picked up the phone.

"Hello?" Leon frowned. It was nearly eleven o'clock.

"It's me," Reid said. He shook his head, trying to clear it, certain now that that drink should have stayed in the bottle.

"Reid? Are you drunk?" Leon frowned again. "Where are you?"

Reid grinned foolishly. "In my hotel room talking to you." He'd never felt so silly in his life.

Leon sat up in bed and put on his eyeglasses. *Something's happened,* he thought. If Reid was still in Chicago, he must have found out something. His brother was always in control, and never drank enough to get sloppy drunk. Leon was worried.

"Reid? What's going on?"

"I'm feeling good," Reid mumbled.

God, he is drunk! "Reid, are you alone?" Could feeling good mean that he'd licked his problem?

"Alone?" Reid's tongue was thick, and he wondered what his brother was talking about. Of course he was alone. "Sure am," he answered, and he chuckled when he thought about Janet. "By my own choice, too," he said. "I must need my head examined, brother." His words ran together, and he laughed again.

Leon waited until the laugh subsided. "What happened tonight?" Leon asked, trying to keep his voice calm.

"Emily fell in love," Reid said, a wide grin cracking his face.

"Emily? Who is she?" Leon tried to remain patient, but speaking to a drunk person was just like speaking to a difficult child.

"My friend, my enemy. Emily hated me, and did me

in." Reid frowned and wondered why his glass was already empty. "Hold on, Leon." He made it to the bar and poured another shot, then picked up the phone. "Was Emily who framed me. My friend Emily."

"Framed?" *So that's it,* Leon thought with relief. *He's happy drunk, not morose drunk.* "Reid?"

"Hmm?"

"Look, man, I'm happy that you're feeling good, but I think you celebrated enough by yourself. What do you say about putting the bottle away and calling it a night?" Leon had a thought. "Since you're feeling so good, I might fly down tomorrow and we can celebrate together. What do you say?"

Reid frowned. "Fly here? Leave the greenhouses . . ." He shook his head. What kind of nonsense was his brother talking?

Leon held his chuckle. Drunk or not, always the businessman. "Okay, okay," Leon said. "Just a thought."

Reid grunted.

"Suppose you get some shut-eye now, and I'll call you tomorrow. You can tell me everything then." Leon held his breath, then exhaled when his brother agreed.

"Tomorrow," Reid answered. He hung up and set his glass on the nightstand. Then he fell back on the bed and closed his eyes. *Why in the world would Leon want to come to Chicago?* he wondered.

On Wednesday, Reid awoke feeling that he was back in the world. He had a vague idea that Tuesday had come and gone, but didn't know where most of it went. He knew that he'd spoken to his brother, and wondered why Leon had called him twice. The third time Leon called, Reid had hung up on his brother and gone back to sleep. He ordered room service, and after breakfast and a shower he was back to normal. The fat head was gone, and so was the queasy feeling in his stomach, and he still mused about his drinking.

It was nearly noon, and before his brother could call again Reid picked up the phone and dialed the nursery, then waited while Leon was paged.

"Hey, man," Leon said, a little out of breath.

"Hey. Take it easy, brother," he said quietly. "I'm fine."

Leon breathed easy. "I can hear," he answered smoothly. "I'm back in the office, so take your time and tell me what happened. Don't skim, because I can't wait until you finish traveling to get the whole story. Shoot."

Reid smiled. Leon was always direct. "Put your feet up, because it's quite a tale. You already know that it was Emily. You may not remember seeing her at my hearing, but she was my friend and coworker. I didn't get the story from Emily. She's doing time for corporate embezzlement." Reid was in the chair, and he stretched his long legs to rest them on the bed. "Here it is," he said.

Leon whistled when his brother finished his story. He'd only asked one question, and had listened without further interruption. He'd gone through many emotions, but anger was uppermost in his mind. That lying, conniving woman was where she deserved to be.

"Forgiveness," Leon spat. "I'll forgive her, all right."

Reid spoke evenly. "Calm down, brother. I have. You accept it after a while."

"I don't have to accept jack!" Leon sputtered. "What she did ruined your life!"

"Did it?" Reid asked smoothly.

Leon thought about what he'd said. Finally he answered, "No."

Reid nodded. "That's what I say. If not for her there'd be no Robinson Nursery, would there? As a matter of fact, why don't we bend an elbow to Emily?" Reid said.

"Much as I'd like to, I can't," Leon answered with a

chuckle, "and *you* shouldn't. I think you lost Tuesday somewhere, don't you?"

"Something like that." Reid winced.

The brothers were silent for several seconds.

"Sounds like that Janet is something else," Leon finally said. "Damn shame she had to get burned, too."

"Yeah, it is. That reminds me. I need a favor. Hold on a second." Reid got up and fumbled through his pants pocket and pulled out her card. "Take down her name and address. I want you to personally fix up a basket and send it to her. Don't skimp."

Leon got a glimmer in his eyes. "How big?"

"Big."

"You got it. Any particular color?"

"All whites." Reid thought. "A lot of cascading Phalaenopsis. Any of the hybrids will do. Use the Amabilis and some of the Southern Snowflakes." He paused. "You get the picture. Send it to arrive on Saturday. She'll be back home by then."

"Sounds like a special lady," Leon said.

"She is."

Leon coughed. "Uh, you'll be seeing her again?"

"Don't you have to get back to work?"

"Well, you know. I thought that since—"

Reid smiled. "Mind your business, Leon."

"Okay, okay," Leon grumbled. "Guess I'll have to wait to hear news on that side of the coin."

"Uh-huh. Leon." He paused. "Thanks for lookin' out."

"Forget it, man." He took his feet off the desk and stood. "Look, I gotta get back to work. Keep in touch." He hung up before his brother responded.

"I will, Leon. I will."

ELEVEN

Dory was watching TV in the living room. Miz Alma, who'd gotten tired, had been sleeping for an hour and a half when Dory heard her stirring. She went into the bedroom to find Miz Alma getting up. The pained look on her face caused Dory to hurry to the older woman.

"How do you feel? Can I get your medication for you?"

Alma grunted. "You wouldn't know where to start. Just give me your arm. Swear I get stiff as a board when I lay down."

Dory felt a knot in her chest as she watched the woman down her pills and then walk slowly to the living room. She wondered if Miz Alma had told the truth. Were there three months left? Or less?

"Don't stare, it's rude," Alma said. A pain-wracked smile parted her lips.

A smile touched Dory's own lips. That was the closest thing to a joke that she'd ever heard from Alma Manning.

"You're sicker than you told me, aren't you?" Dory said in a direct, low voice. "And you've been sick for a long time," she added. Her forehead was wrinkled. "You haven't been going to work as a home attendant. You can barely make it through the day from the weakness and the pain. Why didn't you tell me?"

Alma turned away from the girl's moist eyes and she shifted, trying to find a soft spot on the lumpy pillow to rest her bony elbow. When she looked into those sad eyes she felt just as sad. Once she was dead, this chapter in the young woman's life would be closed. Then Dolores would no longer have to feel that something was always drawing her back to her painful childhood.

"Not many good days," Alma said. "Days I don't get out of bed, 'cause it hurts to move. Ambulette service carries me back and forth to appointments. A nurse is here three days a week." She looked around the apartment. "I'm goin' to die here. Lived here so long can't think of bein' anyplace else when my time comes."

"When?" Dory asked.

"Soon."

"Why didn't you want me to know? I could've come. You were there for Mama when nobody else wanted any part of her. You took care of her, did everything, because she didn't want me around. I could have been here for you."

Alma shook her head. "No. Just like your mama, I didn't want you here. You have a new life and family, and you're happy. No need for you to come here and watch an old lady die. Your mama protected you from that, and now I'm doin' the same." Her eyes never wavered. "That was her wish, and now it's mine."

Dory heard the finality, but she persisted. "Why did you tell me you were still working?"

"I didn't want you to still send me money. I didn't need it, 'specially since my cousin died. Like me, she never married, no kids, was all alone. Left me what she did have." Alma gave a short laugh. "Sure didn't have much time to spend it," she said. "Anyway, it'll be yours. Already took care of everythin'."

"Miz Alma," Dory said. "You don't have to do—"

Alma waved a hand. "Already know what I can and can't do, Dolores." She sniffed. "Already done, anyway." She pointed to a large, square, gray, metal box on the bottom shelf of an étagère. "Bring me that. Might as well do this now."

Dory knew there was no stopping Miz Alma once she decided on something. She got the box and set it on the sofa beside her.

"No, no, sit here near me so you can see everythin'. Can't be passin' stuff back and forth."

Dory sat next to her on the sofa and watched her open the lid.

"This is my will, and the name of the law firm that's handlin' things," Alma said. "Nothing fancy. Just that Dolores Morgan, who was once Dolores Jones, is entitled to everythin' I own." She put it aside. "You can read that later." Opening a folder, she said, "In here are bankbooks, money market accounts, all that stuff that don't make much sense to me. It's all in there. The same money person my cousin used continued to do the same thing for me." Alma looked at some papers and shook her head, as if disbelieving what she read. "This money sure grew since I got it." She gave the papers to Dory.

Dory nearly gasped at the figures she was looking at. One account had assets valued at more than five hundred thousand dollars! She looked at another. Ninety-three thousand dollars! "You're rich!" Dory could only guess at the figures in the bankbooks.

Alma's eyes clouded. "Only in money," she said.

Dory felt helpless. *She's dying, and no amount of assets can save her,* she thought. She put the papers back in the box. "I never knew you had a wealthy relative."

Alma's shoulders shook with laughter. "Neither did I, but should've suspected it," she said. "Always thought Connie was a parsimonious old maid. But she lived well."

"What did she do?" Dory was still amazed.

"Big shot in a hospital. Worked for years in that place as a nurse. She was always goin' to school gettin' one diploma after another. Tryin' to get ahead, she always said."

"Guess she did that," Dory murmured.

"Didn't retire 'til she was seventy. Guess she didn't have nothin' else to do." Alma waved a hand at the closed box. "A lot of that money came from the sale of her house. I sure wasn't going to uproot myself to Ohio to live in it." A thin shoulder moved under her lightweight cardigan. "It's yours to do what you want with. Move anywhere you want, in some big old house."

Move? Dory was happy right where she was, with her family. Cold mortar and brick didn't bring happiness.

Alma thought Dolores was going to break down crying, so she said, "Get me that other box," and pointed to a shoebox on the same shelf. When Dory handed it to her, she put it on her lap and rested her hands on top of it. A minute passed before she spoke. "These are the things your mama left for you."

Dory watched in silence as she was handed the box.

"Go on, open it," Alma said. She watched Dolores put the lid aside, as if that was the last thing she wanted to do. *The girl had so many people keepin' secrets from her. No wonder she's afraid of what could be in the box,* she thought.

"Pictures?" Dory fingered the stack of old snapshots. She recognized her mother when she was a young girl, and when she got older. There were pictures of three young girls. She knew they were the Morgan sisters: Dorcas, Beatrice, and Vera. Several other pictures showed a few relatives that Dory knew had been dead for years. Her maternal grandparents posed with their three daughters. She recognized them from pictures Willow had shown her.

"My mother had these all along?" Dory asked. "I never laid eyes on them!"

"I had them," Alma said. "You and your mother were

supposed to be all alone in the world, remember? When you got to some age, snoopin' through her things like kids do, she brought everythin' over here that she didn't want you to find."

Dory squinted at a smudged photo that looked as if it might have gotten wet. She recognized her mother, but the man's face was barely discernible. On the back her mother had written Vera and Buster.

"Who's Buster?" Dory asked, looking for more pictures of the man. She found one and stared at it. "My mother never kept pictures of her men friends." She frowned. "Was this someone she was in love with, and he threw her over for someone else?"

Alma shook her head. "More like the other way around."

Surprised, Dory said, "He was in love with her, and she didn't want him?" *Incredible,* thought Dory. *The loose woman didn't want a man who was in love with her?* Dory could never bring herself to call her mother a prostitute. When she became old enough to realize that her mother was bringing "company" home for money, it was very hard to accept. But she learned early on, even before the attempted rape, that her mother loved her and would do anything for her. And she loved her mother, who had always tried to shield her from her lifestyle.

Dory continued to look through the pictures. "Why didn't she want him?" She spoke more to herself than to her mother's old friend.

Alma got a faraway look in her eyes. "No tellin' about love."

The poignant tone made Dory look up at the woman. *Did Miz Alma love this man?*

"What was Buster's real name?" Dory asked.

"Is," said Alma. "His name is Clarence Jones."

Jones? Dory stared into the old woman's eyes. She

didn't have to voice her question, because the answer was spoken softly in the next second.

"He gave Vera permission to use his name when you were born."

Dory sat back. So there was a real man named Jones! "I never met him," Dory said, staring at the face again.

"Vera put him out after you were born. Said she wanted to be on her own, make new friends. Didn't want her daughter growin' up thinkin' that he was her father. She wanted somebody better."

"Better? With the life she led, she'd wanted somebody better?" Dory couldn't believe her ears. "What was he? A mass murderer?"

Alma was silent, almost as if she were lost in the past.

Dory looked incredulous. "Miz Alma?"

"Buster was the small time, neighborhood pimp, bad guy, whatever you want to call him. When his little nickelin'-and-dimin' started paying off, he got mighty powerful. Nobody wanted to mess with him. If they did, a body or two was left behind. Whatever corruption, drugs, was going on you could be sure most of it had Buster's name on it." Alma pulled at the pillow fringe. "He wanted Vera to move out of here, put her in a house of her own, but she wanted to stay here. She felt safe here, and we were friends."

"You were friends even then?" Dory had never known that.

Alma nodded. "I got her the job in the bar, and I got her that apartment." She inclined her head across the hall. "Sure was a beautiful buildin' back then," she said with a lift of her chin. "Buster got me mine. I was the first black who moved in here."

"You were a barmaid, too?" Dory thought she'd always worked as a home attendant.

"Yeah. It was just in another one of Buster's bars. The best one. The money was good, and I made a good livin'.

Buster wasn't stingy, and I had good customers. But I left when Buster got so full of himself, he started doin' his gangster deals right under everybody's nose. Didn't care who was listenin'." She slanted her eyes at Dory. "He fell hard for Vera. I begged her to leave when I did, but she liked the excitement of the fast life." She paused. "They started livin' together . . . right across the hall."

"Did you love him, Miz Alma?"

A long silence passed before Alma spoke. "Was a time, I did," she answered. "Before he got started good in that gangsterin'. I asked him to leave it alone, get a decent job like other folks, but the money was too good to a poor boy like him. But I took the job in his bar 'cause I needed the money. Vera, too. In her condition she needed every penny."

"So you and Buster were with Mama when I was born?"

Alma didn't answer, but reached into the box, took out an envelope, and opened it. She pulled out a picture, stared at it, then passed it to Dory. "There were more like that, the four of us, 'till you were about eleven months old. Then he left." Her eyes clouded. "Vera wanted to see other men."

"Buster didn't object?" Dory couldn't see the man simply walking away from the woman he loved.

"He loved your mama, and then you. He would never hurt either of you."

Dory looked at the picture. Buster, Vera, Alma, all smiling, surrounding a laughing baby.

"This man looks familiar," Dory said. "You sure he never came back to live with us?"

"No." Alma rolled her eyes. "He stayed in touch with Vera and his businesses, but he never moved back."

"Then, whatever happened to him?"

"Moved away, doin' his stuff in other big cities. He got rich."

"Rich?" Dory said. "I'll bet." She thought about all the drug deaths, even the most recent victim, on the train.

"Buster became Clarence Jones, legitimate businessman."

"Legitimate? As in no more gangster stuff?"

"Didn't need to," Alma said. "Much stuff as he did, he never did time. Never could make anythin' stick on him. Buster wasn't much to look at, but he was a charmer, smooth and quick. That man could live off his wits and do better than your best hardworkin' executive."

Dory stiffened. *Wasn't much to look at!* She looked at the picture and tried to see the man at fifty years older, with not much gray hair. Then she knew.

"Do you know where he is now, Miz Alma?"

"Lives in Chicago, but he told me he travels."

"You've seen him?" Dory's eyes widened.

"He was with me when Vera died. He took care of everythin'." Alma nodded. "I know you think I did everythin', but it was him. After all those years he still loved your mama."

"This man was following me, Miz Alma." Dory's voice was wooden. "On the train, he was watching me."

"I know. Told him not to do that, frighten you to death. But he wanted to see you."

"See me? You told him where I live, that I was coming here? But why?"

Alma nodded. "I told him. H-he's proud of you."

"Proud?" Dory felt that she was floating around in a wind tunnel and couldn't get her footing.

Alma reached into the box and removed a rubber band from some papers. "These are what your mama wanted you to have. Said it's not important now."

Surprised at first, Dory was silent as she looked over each sheet of paper carefully. When she finished, she put them all back in the box.

"Clarence Buster Jones paid for my college education." Dory felt numb.

"And everythin' else that came with it," Alma said. "Semester break vacations, braces when you were younger, Christmas. Somethin' happened to that man when he saw you being born. Thought you were his kid." Alma smiled at a memory. "Those months he lived with you, he was crazy about you. When Vera put him out it took him a long time to get used to not seein' you."

Dory looked bewildered. "Then why did Mama live like she did? In that kind of life she chose, when he was willing to pay for better?"

"Better? Livin' in fear of getting murdered in your bed because of the kind of people he knew?" Alma scoffed. "Your mama was her own person. She didn't love the man. But she did take what he offered her child because she wasn't stupid." Her eyes grew angry. "Remember after your mama got beat up, and then Papa Wilson got beat half to death? It's a wonder that Buster didn't kill that man that night."

"Buster?" Dory said.

Alma's laugh sounded more like a snicker. "That's why that boy is a fool for comin' back here. If Buster gets wind that the crazy man is looking for you, Papa is a dead man."

"He only wanted to talk to me," Dory whispered, almost to herself. She turned to Alma. "On the train, he looked as if he wanted to talk. I was afraid because he looked so menacing—unsmiling, staring so hard at me."

"Buster knows all about your new family, the books, and everythin' else. He's happy that he played a part in helpin' you get an education. That's all."

Dory heard the fatigue. She said, "Time for more medication?"

Alma nodded. She got up slowly and walked to the

kitchen. "Told you not to stay here after dark," she muttered.

Dory had mixed emotions. She felt she needed to get away from there, to sort out her thoughts, but she didn't want to leave her friend alone. She shouldn't be by herself. Dory yawned and brushed a hand across her eyes. When she heard Alma return she said, "Get me a nightgown. I'm staying with you tonight. Can hardly keep my eyes open."

"Don't need no baby-sitter," Alma said in a gruff voice.

Dory laughed. "Good, because I'll be dead to the world. Got an extra toothbrush?"

At three in the morning, Alma was standing over the bed in the spare bedroom. "Wake, up, Dolores," she said in a firm voice. She was shaking the thrashing young woman gently. She called her name again.

Dory tried to get away from the hand that was holding her down. "No," she mumbled. "St-stop. Leave me alone." She heard her name, and her eyes flew open.

Alma let go of her shoulder and sat down on the bed. "You were havin' a nightmare."

Dory sat up, slowly getting her bearings. She was in her old building, not the hotel. The dream she had was real, with real people. She could see Buster's face. And her mother's. And Miz Alma's. But she couldn't see the face of the man who was chasing her. Papa Wilson? She shivered and rubbed her arms.

"You all right now?"

Dory nodded and got up. "I'm okay. Just a silly dream," she said. "Sorry I woke you. Go back to bed, and I promise I'll let you sleep for the rest of the night," she teased. After she returned from the bathroom she huddled under the covers. Try as she might, she couldn't let go of the nagging thought that she wasn't herself in the dream, but Nora from her Christmas Eve dream—Nora, who was running around a building, frightened to death.

Wednesday morning, Dory was back at the hotel after spending another night with Miz Alma, who'd gone to her doctor's office. Alma had insisted that Dory leave the apartment, because she didn't want her staying there alone. She didn't want Dory coming back, she said, because she'd be exhausted and would probably sleep all day and night.

Dory had breakfast in the hotel dining room, then went back to her room and lay down to take a nap. When she awoke it was after one o'clock, and she was hungry again. She got up, rinsed her face, and brushed her hair. Why was she still tired? "Because you were sleeping like a cat, that's why," she muttered. All of a sudden she felt lonely. She should have been out, trying to get some data for her story, but she was sitting in her room, afraid of walking on the street. What if that crazy fool had found out she was in town?

"Stop it!" Dory said, jumping out of the chair, catching a glimpse of herself in the mirror. She stared at the dark circles under her eyes and swore. "I've got to get some air!" The second she reached for her jacket, the phone rang.

After Reid hung up from talking to his brother, he felt so wired that he walked from the window to the bed to the chair and back to the window. For the first time in years he felt loose. *No,* he thought, *not loose.* Trying to find the right word, he flexed his shoulders. He felt as if he were just waking up. Alive! Vibrant! That was it. Yeah, coming out of a long sleep. A chuckle escaped when he visualized what he was thinking: A dead man brought back to life.

Leon's probing about the woman thing brought a smile

to Reid's lips, and he thought about the sexy Janet and what she had offered him, and would still offer if he called her. He hadn't been ready to take it then, but he was certainly having second thoughts now, and he wondered what he'd do if she were still in town. He couldn't remember whether she had left already or was leaving today.

"Damn," Reid said, cursing his macho, selfish thoughts. He knew that making it with her would be the test of how he would do when he made love to Dory. There was no doubt in his mind that he was going to try to make love to Dolores Morgan. But would he be able to perform? Reid swore again. What guarantee was there that he'd be fine with Dory if he was successful with Janet?

As he remembered the last time that they were together, Reid's body reacted. His body had been on fire then, and now it was warm, as though Dory had entered the room. He could imagine her arms around his waist, her whispering against his chest that they had to talk when she got back. Talk? He suppressed a laugh. He wanted to love her madly. Somehow he knew that it was going to be all right. With what he was feeling now, he knew there was no way that he could fail to make love to her. No way! Reid walked back to the bed and sat, then picked up the phone, praying that she was not out with her friend. The sound of her voice would keep him from going crazy until Friday.

Dory stared at the phone. Her first thought was of Miz Alma. Bad news from her doctor? Trying to keep the worry from her voice, she picked up the receiver. "H-hello?"

Something's wrong. Reid frowned at the tremor he heard. "Dory?"

"Reid," Dory answered, letting out a breath and simultaneously smiling at her rapid pulse. Hearing his voice brought the realization that she'd been missing him since their last passionate embrace. Without pretense, she spoke her feelings. "I miss you."

Taken aback by her admission, Reid was unable to control his reaction to her soft voice, and a groan that he couldn't stifle escaped with a whoosh. At that moment he knew he'd be a fool if he ever let her out of his sight after Friday.

"I miss you more," he said with ease, but he didn't forget the caution he'd first heard in her voice. "How's your visit with your friend going?"

Unwilling to spoil his vacation or burden him with her problems when he had his own to deal with, Dory hesitated.

Reid drew in a breath. *Something is wrong,* he thought. "Dory?" he prompted.

"Good, everything's going well. It's just cold as the devil, as I'm sure you already know. Did the wind stop kickin' over your way?"

"Not at all, but we're not going to talk about the weather instead of what's bothering you, are we?" Reid asked. He heard the soft intake of her breath.

"Miz Alma has cancer, and she's dying." Dory was so overwhelmed with relief that she started to shake. Speaking the words to someone else helped to ease her own hurt at the shocking discovery.

"You never knew," Reid said.

"She kept it from me all these years," Dory said, feeling more in control. She was thankful for Reid's matter-of-fact tone, knowing it was keeping her from falling to pieces. She loved him for it. An involuntary "oh" escaped her lips. She did love him, she thought. Really loved him!

"What happened?" Reid frowned at the exclamation and her silence.

My life just happened, love, Dory thought.

Ignoring his concern, she answered, "Miz Alma's in so much pain. She sits there pretending she can handle it." Dory hesitated. "I guess she's been doing just that, anyway," she said. "All I was doing was sending her money when I thought she needed it."

"Why do you want to berate yourself for doing that?" Reid asked. He intended to keep her talking. The bitterness in her voice was out of character.

"Because I was being so happy in my own new world that I couldn't fly out here to look in on an old friend."

There was a short silence.

"That's not the real reason you never came back," Reid said. He already knew the pain she felt when she remembered her mother and the attack made on her when she was nine.

She gripped the receiver.

"Is it, Dory?" He softened his voice.

"No. It's not."

"Then stop what you're doing," Reid said. He lowered his voice. "At least until I see you."

Dory shivered at his tone. "Stop doing what?" she asked.

"Beating your head against that wall." Reid paused. "I'd rather it was done against my chest." His voice was a little ragged.

"Oh, Reid." Dory's voice dropped to a murmur. "I wish I could see you now."

"Not more than I do." Reid's voice was even lower. Did he really have to wait until she came back here on Friday?

Suddenly, Dory didn't know how she could wait two more days. She wanted to grab him and hold on tight.

"Are you going to take Alma to dinner tonight?" Reid asked, curious that the two hadn't spent the day together.

Dory explained about the doctor's visit and Alma's plans to sleep the rest of the night. "She's probably just getting back home now. I'll call her to see if she needs anything." Dory thought about the mugging. "A nurse accompanies her in the ambulette and then sees her back home and makes her comfortable, but she'll be alone after that." *Maybe I should insist on staying the night again,* Dory thought. *Who knows when that crazy fool might show up and start beating on her again?*

"Dory?"

"I'm here. I was just wondering if I should spend the night again."

"Again? You did last night?"

"And the night before."

"Is she that bad?" Reid asked. He hadn't realized that Alma's time was so near.

"Not only that," Dory said, "it's that she . . . well, we talked a long time and then it got dark. She was worried about me leaving then."

Dark, as opposed to leaving at a late hour? Reid frowned.

"The neighborhood is that unsafe?"

"Not as bad as some," Dory said. "But I guess bad enough for her to get hit in the head in the daytime without a soul seeing a thing." Too late, she realized she'd said more than she wanted to. The man that she realized she was in love with was far from being dense.

Reid tensed. "She was mugged in the daytime?"

"Yes," Dory said, wanting to kick herself.

Reid had been sitting in the chair with his feet propped up on the bed, and now he got up and stood looking out the window. It had stopped snowing. He sat back down.

"Dory?"

"Hmm?"

"Why won't you tell me what's going on?"

Dory sighed again. "Because you have your own problems to deal with, Reid," she answered. "Have you been able to contact your friend yet?"

"In a manner of speaking," Reid replied. "My problems have been resolved, Dory."

"They have?" Dory was surprised, yet happy for him. "So quickly? How?"

"Strange, but true," Reid answered. "I'll tell you about it when you get back. First I want you to tell me what's going on."

"It's really not important," Dory said. "When we meet on Friday, you'll tell me your story and I'll tell you mine." The laugh she emitted was false and weak. She groaned inwardly at the inept way she'd handled her slip.

Reid's voice turned as hard as the look on his face. "You're upset, and I know it. What I don't know, and can't guess, is why you won't trust me enough to tell me who or what has bothered you since you got there on Monday." A sudden thought made him grimace. "Is it the old man?" he asked, in his tone razor-sharp. "You've seen him?"

"Old man?" Dory said. "From the train?" A sudden hysterical laugh bubbled in her throat, and when she opened her mouth it gushed out like an explosion of seltzer. She sputtered. "Yes . . . yes. I've seen him." Another peal of laughter burst out.

"What?" Reid was on his feet. "Where?"

"At Miz Alma's," Dory said, wiping the tears from her eyes. She really was trying to control herself, because she could only imagine what Reid was thinking.

"Dory," Reid snapped sharply. *What the hell is going on?* When he heard her suck in her breath, he called her name again. This time he got a coherent response, and he began to breathe easily.

"I'm sorry," Dory said, completely composed. "I just found the whole thing so funny. But you haven't the slightest idea why. I'm okay."

Reid sat down. "Can you tell me now?"

"His name is Clarence Buster Jones."

"Jones?"

Dory was proud of her astute man. "As in Dolores Jones," she said. "Surrogate father Jones?" she added.

Stunned for only a moment, Reid grew angry. *And she's there, facing this alone? What other secrets did Alma reveal?*

"What do you mean, you saw him at Alma's?"

"Pictures." Suddenly, Dory was tired, yet she wanted to be active. If she stayed in through the night she'd be a basket case by morning. She didn't even have the urge to write, or do research. She had to get out of the room.

"Reid," Dory said, "I'm going to go for a walk. I'm feeling claustrophobic. Would you mind if I called you later, if you're not going out?"

"Are you going to Alma's tonight?" Reid asked.

Dory hesitated. "No," she finally said. "Miz Alma was pretty sure that she would sleep the rest of the night. If I showed up there she'd only be scared that that cra . . ." *Oh hell,* Dory fumed. *Miss Foot-in-the-mouth!*

"Scared that what?" Reid asked, trying to remain calm. He knew she hadn't told him everything. Was it herself she didn't trust, or was there some other reason she wouldn't talk to him? He rubbed his temples, not even wanting to go there.

Dory heard the pregnant silence, and wanted to kick herself for real this time. She sat on the bed and took her shoes off. She was not going to hang up with a cloud of mistrust hanging over his head. That time was past.

"Reid?"

"I'm here."

"Are you comfortable? This will take a while, love," Dory said softly.

Reid knew he'd heard right, and knew that she didn't speak lightly. That was no slip of the tongue. He did as she suggested. Kicking off his own shoes, he positioned himself on the bed, propped up against the pillows.

"Shoot, sweetheart," Reid said. He grinned when he could feel her smile.

Quite a while after she began her story about Papa Wilson and Buster Jones and Miz Alma's new wealth, Dory stopped talking, her throat feeling parched. She excused herself to get some water and then returned to the phone. When she spoke, there was no answer. She wrinkled her forehead. Had he fallen asleep on her?

The second time she called his name, Reid answered. "I'm still here."

"That's the whole story," Dory said. "Everything."

"Did you mean what you said about not going over there tonight?"

"Uh-huh. I'm sure." She felt relieved after clearing her mind of the gray shadows. "Guess the most I'll do is take a brisk walk around the block for some air, get a bite to eat, and head back in for the night."

"Are you sure?"

"Yep. What about you? Don't suppose you want to share your story now." Although she wanted to go out, she wanted to stay and listen to his voice. She had the feeling that disconnecting the call would make her feel isolated and lonely.

"It'll keep until I see you," Reid answered. "Go on and take that walk, and I'll talk to you later."

After Dory hung up, Reid dialed her hotel number. When the operator answered, he said, "Reservations, please."

TWELVE

At eight-twenty in the evening Dory picked up the phone, thinking that Miz Alma was calling her back. A few minutes ago they'd spoken, and Dory had heard the exhaustion in her friend's voice. The nurse had gone for the day, and Miz Alma was worried that Dory would try to come and visit, anyway. After assuring the tired woman that she was in for the night, Dory had said good-night and hung up.

"Hello?" she said.

"Have you eaten?" It was Reid.

Dory smiled, suddenly feeling wide awake. "I had a bite when I was out earlier. What about you?" she asked, settling down for a long conversation. She was already undressed, lounging on the bed watching TV. Her ears tingled from hearing his voice, and she was pleased that he wasn't out doing the town celebrating his good news, that he wanted to talk with her.

"Only a bite?" Reid asked.

"Uh-huh, I wasn't too hungry. I'll probably regret it later on."

"No, you won't, because you can help me eat mine. I was starving, but I think I bought too much."

"What?" Dory's jaw dropped. "Where—"

"Open the door, sweetheart," Reid said. "I'm on my way up."

When Dory stepped back from the door, Reid could

see tears misting in her eyes. He swallowed the lump in his throat, walked past her, and dropped his bags on the table. He slipped off his coat and cap and turned to her. His twinkling black eyes roamed over her, and he broke into a grin.

Dory had not taken the time to toss on her robe. She was dressed in a long-sleeved flannel gown that covered her from neck to ankle. She stood staring at Reid as if he'd appeared from another planet.

"What's so funny?" she whispered, watching him walk toward her.

"You," Reid murmured. "Too many clothes."

She walked into his outstretched arms. "Reid," she whispered. "Oh, Reid."

"Shh, love," he answered. "Kiss me."

Dory did as he commanded. She stood on her toes and kissed him. Her arms were wrapped around his neck, and without shyness she smothered his lips. She was as starved for the taste of him as he'd said he was for food. Hungrily, she sought his tongue, and the firm, warm moistness sent shivers down her spine.

"Ooh." She swooned against his mouth. "Mmm, you taste so good."

If Reid had been uncertain about what her reception of him might be, all doubt was erased when he held her tightly in his embrace, relishing the aggressive onslaught of her tongue.

"How good?" Reid murmured, teasing her by removing his tongue. The tiny noise she made, sounding deprived, warmed him down to his toes. Aware of his body's reaction, he refrained from yelling his joy. "Tell me," he said in a low whisper, but she couldn't speak because he'd covered her mouth again with his. She sagged against his body and pressed against his erection, and he nearly hit the roof.

Dory's arms slid down the taut muscles in his back

until her hands were on his buttocks. She pulled him into her, slowly moved her fingers toward his groin, and touched his bulging front. She broke the kiss to stare into his eyes. "Indescribably delicious," she whispered.

Reid jumped as if burned by her touch. Her smoky dark eyes smiled at him, promising delightful things. He groaned when he bunched up her gown to touch her bare skin. She was naked. His fingers felt scorched, and he removed them instantly and stepped back. Reid lifted her arms, and in seconds the gown was on the floor and he stood looking at her, taking in her smooth skin, brown as a butternut tree.

Dory saw the need in his eyes and wondered if hers mirrored it, because her body was straining for his as much as his was for hers. There was no doubt about that. The moistness between her thighs felt as if a dam had burst, and she wondered if he could tell. He was staring at her as if she were a mirage.

"Reid," she murmured, tugging at his belt buckle, "I want to love you."

The sound in his throat was meant to be her name, but was unintelligible as Reid tried to kick off his heavy boots, cursing them.

Dory saw his dilemma, and giggled as she led him to the bed. In seconds, with her help, he had unlaced his boots and kicked them aside.

"I suppose you think that's funny," Reid grumbled as he undid his belt buckle and slid off his pants, dropping them by the side of the bed.

Reid looked down at Dory as she lay watching him expectantly. Vaguely he wondered why he was still erect, but dismissed all negative thoughts. This woman that he desired wanted him, and there was no way that his body was going to disappoint her.

"Reid?" Dory murmured.

"I know," Reid said, feeling that he had all the time in

the world to savor this moment. "I want to look at you. Touch you. Feel you." With one finger he touched the dark maroon circles of her breasts and watched in awe as they responded by peaking into taut mounds. He cupped her breast, then bent and sucked at the hardened nodule, moaning at the tender sweet taste. Her skin had the essence of sweet jasmine. Slowly he took the other nipple in his mouth and circled it with his hot tongue. His hand was roaming sensuously up and down her body, and he felt pleasure at feeling her writhe under his touch. When he touched her inner thigh and felt the moistness, he drew in a breath at her readiness for him.

"I always imagined how you would look when I undressed you with my eyes," Reid said in a ragged voice. "Now that I see you, I know I didn't do you justice. You're more than I imagined. You're so beautiful." He closed his eyes, anticipating loving her. When he opened them, he stared at her. "I'm going to love you now, Dory Morgan," he whispered.

Dory's body burned from the heat emanating from his, parts of her that he had touched seared to sweet agony. She could only nod her head as she touched his nipples, kneading them, and watched Reid draw raspy breaths. When he moved from her for an instant and fumbled around on the floor, she heard him prepare himself. Then, when she felt his hot body settle atop hers, she opened her eyes.

"Love me, Reid," she said.

Without another word, Reid kissed her lips, her eyes, her neck, and recaptured her lips in a crushing kiss. Her hands on his erection guiding him into her secret place jolted his body like a giant wave of electricity that had a life of its own.

"Dory-y-y!" he yelled. He plunged into her, losing himself when her legs entwined his and she rode with him to wherever lovers went when the rest of the world ceased to exist.

Not surprised that her urgency matched Reid's, Dory unleashed her pent-up emotions and unfulfilled love for Reid with savage intensity. She gave her body and her love unstintingly. Each caress of his hand on her body, every touch of his hot tongue tasting her contours, wrenched a moan from her throat. When the heady sensation had her feeling that she was going to faint, she felt the slow ebbing of their desire.

Reid's body shuddered one last time. "Ah, sweet love." The words were meshed with a last agonized groan as he lay panting on top of her. Unwilling to move, he made himself slide to her side. All of a sudden, he hesitated to look at her, wondering if he'd met her expectations. He'd had no idea of how passionate she would be. She had not held back. He felt her stirring, and then her hand caressing his belly. His body stiffened. Suppose she wanted him again, and he couldn't become erect? Reid's chest started to heave, and almost instantly he cursed himself, forcing himself to relax.

Dory propped herself up on one elbow. She looked down at Reid, curious at his sudden heavy breathing. She kissed his closed eyelids.

"Hey," she said. "You're not going to have a heart attack on me, are you?"

Reid opened his eyes and stared into her laughing ones. He smiled and pulled her down beside him and kissed the tip of her nose. "Only that would keep me from enjoying an encore," he said. He felt her stiffen. "What's wrong?"

"That was a stupid thing for me to say," Dory answered. She looked at him. "I-I wouldn't know what to do if you . . ." She couldn't finish.

Reid met her stare. "Yes, you would."

Startled, Dory said, "What? You're not . . . sick?"

His eyes flickered, but he said, "No, there's nothing wrong with my heart, Dory. I only meant that you're a survivor, and you'd be able to go on no matter who left you. You've already proven that." *Was he warning her to stay away from him?*

Uncomfortable with the morbid conversation, Dory shook herself and snuggled under the covers, pulling Reid with her. "Let's change the subject, love," she whispered, and kissed his bald head. She liked the sensuous feel of the smooth skin on her lips.

Love. Reid liked the sound of that. "Am I?" he asked. *Do I want to be?*

Dory fidgeted, suddenly feeling shy about speaking her feelings to him. But there was no denying the emotional high she was on.

"It's only a figure of speech."

Reid turned to look at her. "Is it?"

Dory didn't meet his stare. "You know. It's always being said, and it means nothing most of the time."

"Most of the time," Reid echoed. "Not this time." If anything, his tone oozed confidence.

"You're so sure?"

Reid touched her chin, forcing her to face him. He nodded. "As sure now as when you said it earlier."

Dory remembered. Then, she'd had no such inhibitions and she wondered why she did now. Then she knew: wanting him to want her was making her uptight. "You're right," she murmured.

"I know I am." Reid bent to kiss her. "I feel the same way about you, love." He nibbled her lips, then probed with his tongue until he found hers and drew it into his mouth. He kissed her long and hard. When he felt her relax against him, he pulled away and saw her eyelids flutter. He kissed them and then cradled her in his arms.

Dory smiled at the light touch of his lips and struggled

to open her eyes, but the effort was too great. The smile was still on her lips when she fell asleep.

Reid had listened to her even breathing for a long time before easing her out of his arms. Now, after turning out the bathroom light, he was sitting in the chair by the window. Occasionally he turned to look at Dory, who slept without moving. Once in the past hour she had turned over, but she remained asleep.

If he had felt euphoric on Tuesday, losing a day in his life, what was he feeling now? Reid had never before in his life told a woman that he loved her. He'd never met such a creature. He still hadn't said the words to her, though he implied them. All he'd answered was that he felt the same, and he'd called her love. What was that supposed to mean? Far from the commitment that she deserved, because he suspected that she had fallen in love with him. No, he knew as sure as his erection that she had fallen in love with him. Now what?

The churning in his stomach was signaling Reid that he was making himself tight, so he flexed his shoulders, pulling and stretching until he felt himself loosening up. He tried to remember some of the pointers in the mountain of literature the doctor had given him that would help keep him loose. Losing negative thoughts was one of them. Staying away from stressful situations was another.

Reid nearly laughed at that one. If this wasn't a stressful situation, he didn't know what was. He'd had a damned incredible sexual experience with the woman he was falling in love with, and he was toying with the idea of not putting himself in that situation again. This time he did emit a slight chuckle. What if she'd wanted him again, and he had to get the hell out of there? He tried to envision the look on her face, and he scowled and swore under his breath. He was breathing normally, and he probed his conscience. Starkly.

A passionate woman like Dory needed a man who could satisfy her sexually all the time, he thought. Was their one time a fluke, or would he be able to perform at will? Risking failure again and seeing the puzzled look in her eyes would drive him over the top.

"What are you doing talking to yourself?" Dory mumbled. "Want some company?" She peered at the clock. "Ten-forty?"

Reid swore. He'd never heard her stir.

"Sleep well?" He did not trust his body to react the way it was supposed to, so he stayed put. The sheet had fallen away, and the inviting contours of her breasts beckoned him.

"Mmm," Dory answered. "You?" She wondered why he stayed so far away.

"What do you think?" Reid answered in a low voice. He watched her closely, but he saw no signs of regret about what they'd shared.

Dory blushed. His sexy voice made her shiver.

Reid smiled at her sudden discomfort. Taking her robe off the chair, he handed it to her. She put it on and belted it, and when she threw him a curious look he indicated the untouched bags on the table. "We never did eat anything, but that's garbage now. I'm going to see what I can scrounge up at this hour. Afraid we'll have to take potluck."

Dory stood on her toes and kissed his mouth. "Whatever you bring will be devoured," she said. "Hurry back." She stopped on the way to the bathroom. "You are sleeping here tonight, aren't you?" Reid hadn't brought an overnighter with him.

Reid shuttered his eyes. "That depends on someone being able to hang." He winked at her and left the room.

"Oh, is that so?" Dory said with a smile on her face.

"We'll see about that, Mr. Robinson." Her body tingled from her sudden lascivious thoughts.

An hour later, Dory was on the bed in gown and robe, feet tucked beneath her, while Reid sat in the chair still dressed. He'd never removed his boots, and Dory was curious about his distance. They'd stuffed themselves on giant sausage heroes, greasy potato chips and red wine. She was feeling sleepy again, but fought it, anticipating falling asleep in his arms.

"Is that for me?" Reid asked, wondering at her smile. He'd been watching her while watching the TV.

"What?" Dory asked.

"That smile."

"Yes," she answered. "I was thinking how you were able to get a car service on short notice to drive you here. And you managed to get a room on this floor, only two doors away. You're very resourceful."

"People are very accommodating when you line their palm with green." Reid inclined his head. "You've forgotten?"

Dory remembered her reporting days. "How could I?"

Reid studied her. "What else do you want to ask me, Dory?"

Another smile touched her lips. His reading her mind could become unsettling, she thought. Serious, she said in a soft voice, "You can talk to me about anything, Reid. You know that."

"I do." *Except for one thing.*

"Then if you regret what we shared tonight, I wish you'd tell me now."

Briefly, Reid closed his eyes. Chancing being so near, he went to her and sat on the bed. "Regret?" He caught her shoulders with his hands and kissed her eyes and then her lips. The kiss was deliberate, yet gentle. "Regretting what you gave to me would make me the biggest fool who ever lived in the twenty-first century!" He kissed her again. Then, holding her gaze, he said, "Don't ever let that thought enter your head again. Understand?" He frowned at her sudden smile. "What?"

"But the century isn't even a week old!"

"Then you get my point," Reid said. He whispered in her ear. "In a thousand years you'll never meet a bigger fool, sweetheart."

Dory's arms went around his neck, and when he held her close she rested her head against his chest and closed her eyes. She had doubted his feelings for her, and she vowed she'd never put herself through that uncertainty again. He loved her. If he never said the words, she would always know it. Her sister's words echoed in her head. *That man touched your heart.*

And my soul, Dory thought.

The next morning, Reid and Dory were finishing breakfast in the hotel restaurant. It was a few minutes past nine o'clock, and they were dawdling over second cups of coffee. Dory mapped out her list of old haunts she would visit to make sure they were still standing before she included them in her story.

"So will you be checking out today? Going back to Chicago?"

"I don't plan to." Reid shrugged. "I've never been to Rockford. Thought I'd take a look around your hometown. Besides, I don't have to be back there until tomorrow evening, when I have a date."

"Tomorrow night?" Dory asked. "But that's when—"

Reid's eyes twinkled. "Exactly," he said.

"I never knew you to be such a tease, Reid Robinson." His date was with her.

"Way back then, I wasn't," Reid answered as a shadow came and went in his eyes.

Dory caught his hand and squeezed. He'd told her the horror story that the woman Janet Steward had told him, and she'd listened in disbelief. *So much for old friends,* shc thought. A person never knew.

"Thank God it's all over now," Dory said. Reid appeared to drift for a second, and she called his name. When she had his attention, she said, "I know you can't keep from being bitter, but don't let Emily's greed continue to mess with your head." She hesitated. "Do you think if you met her face-to-face, it would help?"

It wasn't my head I allowed her to mess up, Reid thought, but he laughed at Dory's question.

"God, no!" he said. "There was a time that I wanted to kill the guy who framed me. I was young, full of hate and anger. Who knows? If I could have gotten my hands on her years ago, maybe I wouldn't be sitting here with you now." He shook his head, still amused. "Emily's a loscr. She lived in style for a while on her stolen money. Thought she'd gotten everything she desired in life. Sitting on top of the world. Then, she fell in love. But"—he lifted a broad shoulder—"if I saw her now I'd only pity her. She has nothing. And me?" Reid covered Dory's hands with his. "I'm the winner."

His meaning was very clear, and Dory let him know she understood by leaning over and kissing him lightly on his mouth. "I'm glad," she murmured.

Reid signaled for the check, and once in the lobby he said, "What time did you tell Alma you were coming?" He didn't want Dory out of his sight, but didn't want her to know it. Whenever he thought about the crazed Papa Wilson, a chill settled in the small of his back. The man had obviously turned psychotic after all these years. Reid cringed. Didn't he know about revenge?

"When I spoke to her this morning, she sounded a little

groggy. Said she had to get up during the night a few times."

"The pain?"

Dory nodded. They were in her room, and Dory tossed her bag on the bed and sat down. Reid sat across from her in the chair. "I think she's getting worse, and doesn't want me to know. I really think that she's putting off seeing me again, knowing that I'm leaving tomorrow."

"You think she lied about having three months?"

"I believe she did."

"What do you plan to do?"

Spreading her hands in a helpless gesture, Dory said, "There's nothing much to do. She's left all her affairs in order. I know where to find everything, including the funeral arrangements." She turned her head away for a second. "The super has my address and phone number, so he can contact me immediately. Nobody's to do anything until I get there."

"You're going to be away for another month," Reid said.

"I've thought of that."

"She doesn't have another month, does she?"

Dory shook her head. "I don't think she does," she murmured.

"What about your research? Will you continue?" Reid asked.

"I'm so far behind now. I really have to," Dory said, and gestured toward her purse. "That list I made just now? Well, I had planned to take Miz Alma around town, wherever she wanted to go, and then visit some of those places she used to take me. You know, get a feel for the place again. I thought she'd get a kick out of that." She paused, lifting a shoulder. "I never realized she was so sick. She's suffering."

Reid could hear her uncertainty, and he refrained from advising her. The decision she made to stay in Illinois was one she had to make on her own. But he already knew that he'd be around when she did decide. His intended stress-free vacation trip southwest would have to wait. He went to her and pulled her up off the bed.

"Remember that wall you were beating your head against the other day?" Reid asked.

Dory looked up at him, curious, then she did remember. "Yes."

He wrapped his arms around her and pressed her head against his chest. "Use me."

After a long while, Dory lifted her head and looked into his eyes. "Are you sure you don't have a psych degree, too?"

Reid kissed her nose. "Sat through a few of those courses. Guess something stuck."

Dory felt warm and safe in his arms, and she didn't want to leave the comfortable haven, but she stepped away and reached for her jacket and hat. "I'd better get started," she said. "What will you do today?"

Reid stared at her and shrugged.

"Well, since you're not sure, why don't you come along with me? Then later you can meet Alma Manning." Her eyes brightened. "Maybe she'll feel well enough for us to take her to dinner. She hardly eats anything, but maybe being out will perk her up."

"I thought you'd never ask."

"You *wanted* to do this boring stuff?" Dory accused. "Why didn't you say so, instead of letting me miss you before we even parted?" She tugged on his goatee, then kissed him.

Reid helped her shrug into her jacket. "Guess I remember more of that psych than I thought. Ouch," he said, as she pulled his chin hair again.

After stopping by his room, where Reid got his outerwear, they left the hotel. It was a gray day, and snow was predicted for later in the evening. When not thinking of

Alma, Dory couldn't help but feel happy. What better way to spend the night than wrapped in Reid's arms? She could hardly wait for day's end.

"Now tell me that you weren't bored," Dory said, snuggling against Reid's shoulder in the taxi. She was pleasantly tired after accomplishing all she'd set out to do for the day, and now they were headed for Alma's apartment.

Reid gave an exaggerated yawn and grunted when she poked him in the ribs. "Uh-uh," he said, his teasing tone absent. "I liked watching you operate." He raised a brow. "You've developed some sneaky little interviewing techniques."

"Sneaky?"

"Yeah. I thought we were stopping for a quick lunch at one of your old hangouts, then taking off"

Dory sat up, but still linked arms with his. "All I did was ask Soupy how his restaurant celebrated New Year's." Her eyes twinkled. "How did I know that he planned a gala celebration for two hundred people? It was easy to ask permission to make him the subject of my article. He ate it up."

"He sure did," Reid said, and he turned to look out the window.

"What's that supposed to mean?" Dory suppressed a smile at the tinge of jealousy she heard.

"Sounded like you two went way back."

"We're the same age, and went to school together. Old friends."

"Friends?"

Dory grew quiet, remembering the past. She, too, looked out the window for a while, then turned to Reid. "One of a few I had back then. Dickie Porter lived on the top floor in the building. He was an only child, like me. We had another friend who lived on another floor.

Her name was Margaret. We were all pals. Margaret's family moved to Texas, though, and when we were in high school Dickie's family bought a house. I didn't see him too much after that, only in school."

Reid sensed her change of mood, and he knew his question had brought it on. Whatever memories he'd stirred, they were painful. He listened to her without interrupting.

"Everybody in the building and some kids in school knew about my mother and her men. I tried hard not to pay attention to their teasing." Dory's forehead wrinkled with the memory. "News traveled fast about the attack on me, and my mother's beating, and then later that man almost getting killed." She grimaced. "Happenings like that are hard to keep secret in the black community."

Though Reid remained silent, Dory felt him stir, and she appreciated the slight pressure on her arm.

"Boys started to bother me." She shrugged. "You know. Like mother, like daughter."

Reid made a sound, but didn't speak.

"Dickie took care of all of them. He became my shadow from that time on, until our senior year. Then, people just went about their business and left me to myself." Dory smiled. "Of course all his girlfriends had to be very understanding about where Dolores Jones fit in the scheme of things. But they were all very friendly."

"Sounds like there were quite a few," Reid said.

"You'd better believe it!" Dory chuckled. "He's a handsome guy, and has a personality to match."

Reid grunted at that. "How did Dickie turn into Soupy?"

"Most of the soups in the restaurant are his concoctions. When they opened the place years ago, he experimented at home, and it wasn't long before his folks realized he had a knack."

Imagining the humiliation she must have experienced, Reid could feel the tension in his temples, but he soon relaxed. She didn't sound bitter, and he knew that he was right on the money when he'd called her a survivor.

"I'm glad he was a friend," Reid said.

Dory didn't answer, but continued to hold on to his arm. The taxi slowed and turned the corner onto her old street. She peered outside at the darkening skies. It was almost five o'clock, and she hoped that Alma felt well enough to want to go out to dinner. Now that Dory had a potentially fantastic New Year's Eve article, and had gathered enough material on the historic sites for the last of her two articles, she was free to spend the rest of her time researching her mystery story. In between her stops she'd called, but had not received an answer. Afraid of keeping the woman from her needed rest, she didn't bother calling again. The driver's voice startled her.

"What's wrong?" Dory asked, looking out.

"Nothing," Reid answered. "I think we're here." He could feel her tense up.

"Yes. This is it."

The taxi left, but they were still outside, and Reid wondered if she was afraid of even entering the building. He looked around. There were a few people walking hurriedly, huddled against the stiff wind. No one stopped or spoke. The entrance was deserted, but well-lit. Old and showing evidence of a grandeur long gone, with its marble floors and iron railings, the building appeared to be in good condition. Reid estimated that there were about seven floors.

"She's probably just asleep. Come on. Let's go up," Reid said, catching her elbow.

Dory nodded. "So quiet."

A door opened, and Dory saw the super come from his apartment. "Hello, Mr. Johnny," she said.

"Saw you get out of the taxi, Dolores," the old man said, peering up at Reid. "I know you didn't hear, else you wouldn't be here," he said, still staring at Reid.

"Reid this is Johnny King. Mr. Johnny, this is my friend Reid Robinson." She turned worried eyes on the old man. "Hear what?"

After acknowledging Reid with a handshake, Johnny King, satisfied, squinted at Dory. "Alma's in the hospital," he said, shaking his head as if the idea were preposterous. "Ambulance came almost one o'clock. Her nurse was with her when they went."

"What?" Dory couldn't believe it. "What happened? Did she—"

"Don't know. Just that the nurse gave mc the keys before climbin' inside the ambulance. Said Alma told her to give them to you when you got here." He pulled a ring with three keys from his pocket and gave it to Dory.

"That's all? She didn't say what happened?" Dory took the keys, squeezing them in her gloved hand.

Johnny shook his head. "I saw when the ambulance came and I went outside, wonderin' who they come for. I saw them bring Alma down in the elevator, holdin' her up 'tween them. She was fussin' about wantin' to walk by herself, but they half-carried her outside and put her on the stretcher and lifted her inside." He stopped as if trying to remember more. "That's all I know." He paused. "Except for where they took her."

Dory could only nod. "Thanks," she managed after he told her the name of the hospital, and then returned to his apartment.

Reid swore under his breath. What a homecoming!

"What do you want to do?" he asked quietly.

"She may need things," Dory said as if Alma's comfort was the uppermost thing on her mind, but she made no move toward the elevator or the stairs.

Reid could see the indecision. He steered her toward the stairs. "Suppose we go on up. You'll get an idea of what to bring." She caught his hand, and they walked up the stairs. She led him to the door. Reid took the keys from her hand, and after successfully opening two locks he pushed the door open.

The apartment was eerily quiet, and Dory shivered when Reid locked the door. She sighed and shrugged out of her jacket. "This is such a shock," she said, looking at Reid in disbelief. "I thought she was just a little tired, so I hated to disturb her."

"How could you know?" Reid asked, studying her. "She made the decision to keep her illness from you until . . . well, until now."

"You mean until she went into the hospital to die."

Reid nodded. "Apparently." He noticed her little shiver, and he shrugged out of his jacket. "You could use something hot. Why don't you start packing whatever you think she needs? I'll zap the water for tea and it'll be ready when you finish." He gave her a little nudge. "I'll find things."

Dory found it strange pawing over her old friend's things. She looked in drawers, absently thinking that the woman had always had a neatness fetish. Everything had a place, including the hosiery that nestled in Styrofoam egg cartons. She turned to see Reid at the bedroom door.

"Tea's ready," he said.

"Okay. I'll only be a minute." When Reid left, she packed a gown, robe, slippers, and some socks in a small canvas shopping bag. After finding toiletries in the bathroom she joined Reid at the kitchen table.

The hot beverage warmed Dory's insides, and she could almost feel the tension dissipate. "That went down pretty well." She smiled at Reid. "Thanks."

"Feel up to going?" Reid asked, accepting her thanks with a nod.

Dory sighed. She surveyed the space around them. "I only saw her for two days and nights, you know? When she opened that door and I looked into her eyes, I knew before she told me a thing that she didn't have much time." She waved a hand. "You know what I mean?" Without waiting for an answer, she said, "It was like trying to push away water. I didn't want it to touch me, but it covered me, anyway. When she was telling me, I didn't want to hear it, because it was like I already knew what she was going to say. You know?"

"I know." Reid looked grim. There was nothing he could do to help her sort through her misery but be there for her.

"Maybe we should go now," Dory said, getting up. She rinsed their cups. Alma never went to bed with anything in the sink.

Dory had called for a car service, and while they waited downstairs, shivering in the doorway, Reid hugged her close and kissed her forehead. He could almost read her thoughts.

"We may be thinking the worst," Reid said. "Alma could be raising hell for being taken there in the first place. You might be bringing her home tonight."

Dory could envision the scene, and she smiled and held Reid tightly around the waist. But she believed her own gut feeling. Alma wasn't coming back home. Dory closed her eyes briefly, resting her head against the firm wall of Reid's chest, and breathed her thanks that he was there.

THIRTEEN

Reid waited for Dory on a bench outside Alma's hospital room. He'd refused to accompany Dory inside. He'd never met her, and he was certain that the strong-willed woman would not appreciate his looking on while she was dying. When they'd arrived, Dory had spoken briefly to the doctor. Explaining that she was from out of town, she had insisted on being told the truth. As they had suspected, Alma had lied. It was only God's will that her ravaged body had survived so long after her terminal diagnosis, over a year ago. Reid looked up as Dory came and sat beside him.

"How is she?" Reid asked.

"She wants to meet you." Dory glanced at Reid. "Said, besides Soupy, who doesn't count, I never in my life brought a boy home. Now she wants to see the man I brought here with me." Dory smiled. "Think she wants to approve of who I'm hangin' with."

Reid took her hand. "What do you think she'll say?"

"She always told me to set my sights high—one day I'd find a boy to bring home." Dory stared at Reid. "I brought you home," she said softly. She swallowed the lump in her throat. "Want to meet her?"

"Wouldn't miss the opportunity." Standing with Dory, Reid kissed her lips. "I'm glad I'm the first boy you wanted to bring home, Dory." They entered the room.

Alma was heavily sedated, but she fought drifting off

until Dolores returned with her man. *Nothing wrong with my mind,* she thought, *it's only my body that's had enough.* She was satisfied that she'd done all she could, done right by Vera's kid. She'd promised all those years ago. Alma wanted to laugh, but the effort was too painful. If Vera only knew that her little girl was going to be a rich woman. One thing was still scaring her—Papa Wilson was waiting to hurt that girl.

"Miz Alma," Dory said, touching the woman's shoulder. She seemed to be sleeping.

Alma opened her eyes. She could see a big man with broad shoulders, but had to lift her head to see his face. It hurt to move. "Sit down," she said.

"Alma Manning, this is Reid Robinson, my friend," Dory said. She and Reid were sitting close to the bed.

Reid hadn't known what to expect, and he wasn't prepared for the shrunken body he saw. The most vibrant part of her was her sharp eyes hawking him. He said hello, and waited until she finished appraising him.

Alma looked from Dolores to the big man, who didn't flinch under her gaze. She studied the couple for a long time. The man didn't say a word, but Alma watched the way he was sitting close to Dolores. They weren't touching, not even holding hands, yet Alma sensed the cloak of protectiveness surrounding Dolores. She closed her eyes. This stranger was going to help her child.

Dory saw Alma's eyelids flutter. "Miz Alma?" she said softly.

Alma opened her eyes, but looked into Reid's. "Be careful," she said.

Reid knew exactly what she meant. He nodded his head. "I will."

"Dolores." Alma struggled to keep her eyes open. "Buster's comin' here. Told them to call him. Want you two to meet." She moved her hand toward Dory, who caught and held it. "Remember, he loved you and your mama. Always meant well."

"Shh, I know," Dory said, patting Alma's hand. She could see that the effort to stay awake and talk was a strain. Alma's eyes closed, but she held on to Dory's hand.

Reid touched Dory's shoulder and stood up. "I'll wait outside." He wanted the two women to have privacy. Deep down, he knew that Alma did not have long. He stopped when Alma's eyes flew open and she called his name. He listened, but her first words were lost. Reid understood the last three: ". . . care of her."

Reid touched the back of Alma's hand and shook his head. "Yes," he answered, and he knew he'd understood what she was trying to say, because she smiled. He left the room.

The old man sat on the bench outside the room. Reid noticed that he was dressed in the same manner; extremely conservative in a tailored overcoat, hat, and pinstripe suit. He stood up and met Reid's stare.

"You know who I am?" Buster Jones said, eyeing Reid.

"I do."

Neither man extended a hand.

Reid moved closer to the bench. "You scared the hell out of her, you know." His dark eyes were accusing.

Buster's sharp eye assessed the man, who was twice his size and was staring at him with a cold look. "I know." He removed his hat and coat and sat down, gesturing for Reid to join him.

Reid sat. "Why?"

Ignoring the question, Buster studied the younger man with shrewd dark eyes "I saw you with her." He blinked and his thin eyelashes skimmed the tightened skin of his face. "You've got feelings for her like I had for her mama."

Reid looked at the man. His gruff voice probably used to command attention when he spoke. Now it sounded tired and old. Reid wanted an answer to his question. "Why?" he repeated.

"Hah. Who would have thought that Buster Jones would let a little slip of a woman stop his tongue?" A soft laugh escaped, and he played with his hat, twirling it around in his hands. "Scared like some damned rabbit when I got up close to her on that train. Sat next to her, and couldn't open my mouth." He appeared surprised at his behavior. "She's her mama all over again."

Reid's mouth twisted in a grim line. "I don't think so."

Buster's hard look swept Reid. "Vera was what she was," he said, a nasty glint entering his eyes. "What she wasn't, was a bad mother." He glared at Reid.

Reid held the man's look. "I agree," Reid said easily. "She knew who she didn't want raising her kid." He ignored the old man's evil look. "That makes me wonder, why are you bothering her daughter now?" Reid didn't flinch an eyelash, but he could see the sting of his words. The former gangster looked beaten. "How many fathers does that girl have to mentally bury? Real, or otherwise?"

"Hello, Mr. Jones." Dory watched the old man snap his head around at the sound of her voice. "Miz Alma wants to see you," she said, moving away from the door.

Buster stood and walked toward Dory. He stopped, looked at her, and was about to speak, then clamped his mouth shut and went into the room.

Dory sat down next to Reid. She slipped her hand in his.

"You heard?" Reid asked after a few minutes passed in silence.

Dory nodded. "Did you see his eyes?" she said in a low voice. "He's probably losing the last person who knew him when he was a young man. It's like he's trying to hold onto something of the past." She rested her head on Reid's shoulder. "Me."

Reid was thoughtful. "Do you want his friendship now?"

Low murmurs drifted from the room. Dory listened to the gravelly voice, and after a second she said, "Miz Alma told me he wants to talk to me just once. All these years he's been afraid of rejection. Said he wants to hear my voice." She rose up and looked at Reid. "I'll talk to him," she said. "The next time I see him will probably be at Miz Alma's funeral."

Buster Jones appeared. "She's sleeping." He looked from Reid to Dory, unsure of what to do. He started to walk by them, then was stopped by Dory's voice.

"Mr. Jones, if you haven't eaten, would you join us for dinner?" She looked at Reid, who nodded his approval.

Buster hesitated. He coughed and sniffed. Then, in his gruff voice he said, "Yes."

The next morning, Reid was in Dory's room watching her pack. He had spent the last half hour trying to talk some sense into her, but she'd refused to listen. He tried again.

"Dory," he said. "Look at me." When she zipped her bag closed she sat down on the bed and turned to him.

"Alma is dying." Reid saw the pain in her eyes, but he continued. "You heard the doctor. She may go at any time in the next few hours, or she may hang on for days. You can't put your life on hold, waiting for the inevitable." He indicated the room with a wave. "Checking out of here and staying in her apartment until she dies is asking for trouble with a deranged man who's walking the streets."

"I don't want to come back here, Reid." Dory's voice was adamant.

"What?"

"When she dies. I don't want to come back here."

Reid heard the anguish. "I know," he said, "but you have to. Alma expects you to take care of her business."

Dory threw him a half smile. "Remember when I told you that I was coming back here to give happy endings to my characters' lives?"

"Yes."

"So far that's not happening." She spread her hands in a hopeless gesture. "That's why I'd rather stay. I can't go off tripping merrily along knowing she's going to die with no one there. I want to stay and face things."

"Including coming face-to-face with someone who wants to attack you?" Reid was annoyed. And the thought of someone trying to hurt her made his stomach churn.

"That may never happen. Papa Wilson, with his muddled thinking, probably realized what he'd done to Alma, and scared himself to death. He's probably miles away from here."

"I wonder why I don't believe that you believe that."

"Reid, I have to wait around, see what happens. If Alma looks like she's improving, then I'll continue my trip. But, to leave when she's like that, is hard. She was there for my mother, and I want to be here for her. There's no one else."

"How long do you plan to stay?" Reid asked. He understood her feelings, but she was taking the threat of Wilson too lightly.

"Only a few days. I won't take foolish chances coming and going at odd hours. The super is around, and can walk me up when I get home from the hospital." Her throat tightened. When they walked out of this hotel would they be walking out of each other's lives again? They'd only had a few days together. But that was all she'd needed to fall in love with him. With his own mystery resolved, there was really nothing to keep him there. He was free to leave on Sunday to continue his vacation, and the thought of him not being with her brought a lump to her throat.

"What time will your luggage arrive?" Reid asked. Earlier she had called the Embassy, to have them forward her luggage to Alma's apartment.

"This afternoon. I want to be there to receive it." Dory looked at him. "Well I guess I'll go down and check out now." She reached for her jacket. Reid had not mentioned when he was leaving. He was standing there in a black bulky sweater and black slacks, watching her. She flushed under his intense gaze, and suddenly wished that he would go before she broke down. How many times would she lose someone she loved?

Dory picked up her jacket. "What time will you be leaving for Chicago?" she asked Reid, who was by her side.

"Now. There's no reason to stay here."

Dory's heart sank. *No reason?*

Reid took the jacket from her hands and tossed it back on the bed. He pulled her into his arms and kissed her forehead. "I have to leave now so I can check out of there. I don't want to be late tonight."

"Tonight?" Dory frowned.

Reid leaned back and cocked a brow at her. "Didn't you promise to have dinner with me?" His voice dropped to a huskier tone. "Or maybe you find your old friend who concocts soups more intriguing?"

"What?" Warmth flowed through her. "You're coming back!" she whispered as she hugged him tight.

He held her close, burying his face in her hair. God, he'd fallen in love with her. But had he the right to claim her love? Her arms went around his neck, and she lifted her eyes to his. The love he saw turned him inside out. He bent his head and captured her lips, brushing them tenderly and slowly, as if savoring their sweetness, as if the kiss had to last him for a long time. The hours that he would be away from her would be pure agony as he thought of the potential danger she was in. The thought caused him to increase his hold, crushing her body as well as her lips. She squirmed from the pressure, and he loosened his hold.

"Sorry, love," he murmured, reluctant to release her mouth. Her tongue was sweet and searching, and when her hands slid down his back and she pressed her hips into his, he was jolted to his senses. He couldn't chance not knowing whether the warmth in his loins would result in an erection or not. Preferring to remain in ignorance, he stepped back and dropped his arms.

Dory, bereft at the swift disentanglement, opened her eyes and looked into his. She was surprised at the confusion she saw, but then it disappeared so instantly she wondered if she'd been mistaken.

"I think the sooner we leave, the quicker I'll get back here," Reid said, speaking in an airy voice. He avoided the puzzled look on Dory's face, picked up her jacket, and helped her into it. She zipped it and reached for her hat and bag.

Reid lifted her small overnight bag and said, "Have everything?"

"Yes," Dory answered. The room key was in her jacket pocket. She threw him another curious look and walked to the door. "I'm ready," she said. They left the room.

Hours later, Dory was in Alma's apartment. Her luggage had arrived, and she was relieved to have fresh clothes. She showered and changed into a pair of dark brown wool slacks and a beige-and-black turtleneck chenille sweater. She'd called the hospital, but Alma had been sleeping and the nurse refused to wake her. There was no change in her condition. Dory planned to visit her for about an hour and then come back to change for her date with Reid. She busied herself by dusting and vacuuming and changing the bed linen. She'd washed and dried the few clothes in the hamper, and was now folding some lingerie and towels. After putting them away, Dory looked around for something else to do, and she couldn't help wondering why she hadn't heard from Reid. She thought he would call her once he got back to his hotel. It was after three o'clock.

She stood. If she were to be back on time to meet Reid at seven, she should leave then. Dory left the apartment and walked down the stairs. She knocked on the super's door.

"Hi," Dory said. "I'm on my way to the hospital. I hope to get back in time, but if you see the gentleman I was with the other day would you ask him to please wait for me?" She hesitated. "If I'm too long, would you let him into the apartment?"

Johnny looked a little skeptical. "Well, I don't know if Alma would appreciate strangers sittin' around her place," he said.

"They've met, Mr. Johnny. I'm sure she wouldn't mind," Dory answered.

"Well, okay, if you say so. Give Alma my regards, and tell her that Loretta sends her prayers. She went to visit my wife in the hospital, and now Loretta's sorry she can't do the same for her. Still can't do much after her operation." He shook his head. "Sure is a shame. Nobody knew Alma was that sick, always wantin' to go and do for herself. Didn't ask a soul for a thing." He shook his head again. "Shame."

Dory said, "Thanks. I should be back in a couple of hours. I'd better wait outside so I won't miss my ride." She walked toward the door, but was stopped when he called her name.

"I forgot to tell you when you got here this mornin' that some fool was upstairs bangin' on Alma's door yesterday. Neighbors had to call me to get him out of the buildin'."

Dory stiffened. "What? Who was it?" Her gaze darted to the stairwell, and she turned to search the long hallway.

Johnny noticed, and sniffed. "Ain't nowhere around here now, I saw to that," he said, proud of his actions. "Don't know who he was, but I told him to get out and stay the hell away from here. He won't be back."

"W-what did he say?" Dory asked.

"Nothin' that made any sense," Johnny said, tilting his head as if trying to recall. "He mumbled somethin' about 'that girl', gave me the evil eye, and shuffled out of here with my help. Didn't smell no liquor on him, but his head must be all messed up with that crack cocaine garbage. Wasn't talkin' a bit of sense."

"What did he look like?" Dory was afraid to know. The next words stilled her blood.

"Just another bum, Dolores. Could use a bath and a shave and some clean clothes," Johnny said. "Kept swingin' one arm back and forth and waved it in my face before he walked out of here. That's when I saw his fingers. Looked like two of 'em was stitched together. Looked like one big finger."

Dory shivered. *Papa Wilson has been here.* "Did you tell him where Miz Alma was?"

He made a face. "I didn't, but the neighbor in your old apartment did. Thought that'd make him go away." He tugged on the jangling bunch of keys that hung from his thick leather belt and gave her a reassuring look. "You don't have to be scared of nothin', Dolores. That fool won't be comin' back in here." He peered outside. "Better go now. Looks like your car just pulled up." He started to walk away and called back, "I'll look out for your friend for you."

"Thanks," Dory whispered. She walked down the front steps and looked up and down the street before getting into the car. The thought came to her that it would be dark when she got back—the very thing that Miz Alma had warned her against. She sank back against the cold plastic vinyl cushion and—using an old trick her mother had taught her when she was scared—tried to think of things that made her feel good. She thought of Reid.

In Alma Manning's apartment, the phone rang. It stopped, and after a few seconds, the ringing started again. Finally it stopped.

At twelve-thirty Reid was listening to Ms. Wind at the Rochester Travel Service office. She was explaining that it would be a few hours before she got back to him with his changed train and hotel reservations.

"Thanks, Ms. Wind. No rush," Reid said. "I'll get back to you on Monday. Enjoy your weekend." He hung up and lay back on the bed, wondering how Dory was going to accept his plan. Although he would keep the room at the Rockford Hotel, he intended to stay with her at Alma's apartment, at least for as long as Alma remained in the hospital and Dory insisted on staying in that building. His gut feeling told him that she was in more danger than she believed. He would stay with her as long as she needed him. A soft chuckle rumbled in his throat. Leon wouldn't believe the events of this so-called stress-free vacation in a million years. "What's next?" he mumbled.

Reid got up and started to undress, wondering how things were going in Rochester. Thinking that he should call, he immediately tossed that idea. His brother was perfectly capable of running things, and if there was a major problem Leon and Gilbert Lane knew where to contact him. Reid's brow cleared, and he stepped into the shower. With the relaxing stream of water pelting his head and shoulders, he was unaware of the ringing telephone.

Dressed only in a knee-length, white, terry cloth robe

provided by the hotel, Reid lathered on some cologne and then left the bathroom. He was going to Rockford dressed for his date. There was no sense in leaving Dory alone longer than he had to. He'd drop his bags at the hotel and then go immediately to Alma's. He eyed the navy blue suit and light blue tab collar shirt he'd hung up. Selecting an abstract print maroon-and-gray tie from his bag, he tossed it on the bed. The doorbell rang, and he looked up in surprise. He hadn't called room service.

Reid stepped back from the peephole. "Damn!" He opened the door.

Janet Steward studied Reid's reaction to her unexpected presence with amusement. She twirled a cascading orchid in her hands. "I called, but didn't get an answer," she said. "I figured I'd try, anyway." Her eyes roamed over his body, and she was certain he was buck naked under that robe. "Can I come in?" Her tongue darted out of her mouth as she smiled up at him.

Stunned, Reid moved back into the room. "Janet," he said. In that second, he had a sense of how a woman must feel when boldly undressed by a man's roving eyes.

"I had to thank you personally for the beautiful orchids," Janet said in a deep voice. "I've never seen such a display." Her eyes traveled from his hairy chest and down the belted robe to his muscled legs, then traveled back up just as slowly. "Never," she said.

"I thought you were still out of town," Reid said, moving back as she moved closer. *Damn, Leon. I told you to deliver them on Saturday!*

"My business was finished, and I decided to return early." She smelled the flower. "I'm glad I did. Otherwise I might have missed the opportunity to thank you."

"Janet," Reid said in a finn voice, "there was no need for you to come here for that." *She's more gorgeous than the first time,* he thought, watching her walk slowly toward him. She was dressed in the same white ermine coat and matching headband, but the coat was flung open and her ivory V-neck dress did not leave her contours to the imagination. He could feel his body react the same way it had before. What in God's name had he done to deserve this? Temptation was this woman! He was trying to stay away from Dory, the woman he loved, because he wasn't sure of his ability to always satisfy her. Here was the perfect opportunity to test his sexual performance for a second time, proving that there wasn't a damn thing in the world wrong with him.

Janet reached out, touched the loose knot in his belt, and tugged. "Mmm. Why don't you let me be the judge of that?" She slid her hand up, and the tip of her long fingernails scraped his chest. She slipped her hand inside his robe and tilted her head to look into his eyes.

"Jesus!" Reid flinched when her fingers touched his nipple and it jumped to attention. He felt fire in his loins and a wild thumping in his chest. He was swelling. She stood on her toes and waited for his kiss. "Jesus, help me!" Reid said. He bent his head.

Dory reached Alma's hospital floor, and had started toward the room when the nurse at the desk stopped her.

"Ms. Morgan. I tried to call you before you got here, but you'd probably just left."

"What's wrong?" Dory stared at the woman, her expression anxious.

"Ms. Manning slipped into a coma a little more than an hour ago."

"What?" Dory wanted to sit down. Maybe then her knees would stop shaking, she thought.

"The doctor is with another patient," the nurse said, "but he'll pass by this way in a little while if you want to speak to him."

"Can I see her?" When the nurse nodded, Dory went to Alma's room.

An hour later, she was still sitting by Alma's bedside. She continued to stare at the sleeping woman, who was breathing without artificial support. The doctor had come in and spoken to her briefly about Alma's condition. They had to wait and see. There was no telling how long the coma would last. Hours, days, sometimes weeks, could pass before something happened he'd told her. But even then there was no hope of reversing her terminal condition.

As if she were reliving the events of Alma's life for her, Dory thought of her own childhood, which had included Alma Manning for as far back as she could remember. Why was it that Alma had never married? Dory couldn't for the life of her ever remember seeing a man in the older woman's apartment. She'd never seen her getting dressed for a date. She was always there, doing her home attendant's job during the day and staying at home at night. It seemed she'd always been there when Vera needed a baby-sitter. Many times Dory had ended up spending the whole night in the spare bedroom and run across the hall in the early morning to get ready for school.

Yet Alma had admitted that there was a time that she'd been in love with Buster Jones. Had the man ruined her chance of ever falling in love again? Dory stirred as she patted the hand of the still woman.

Last night, at dinner, which hadn't lasted long, Buster Jones had talked about his life as it was now, not years ago when he'd terrorized the neighborhood on his way up the crime ladder. He was the owner of a chain of barbershops and beauty salons in black communities all over Illinois. He'd made his home in Chicago, so that he could watch Dolores Jones grow. He'd never been very far away from Vera and her daughter. As she and Reid listened to the man, who appeared tired, and older than his seventy-nine years, he said that many times he'd wanted to contact Dolores after her mother died, but when he saw that she'd found her family, he didn't interfere. He'd followed her successes, and he was proud that he'd played a part in helping a young life instead of taking one. That was the only reference he'd made to what he'd once been.

Dropping Alma's hand, Dory sat back in the chair. She had to think about what she was going to do now. She couldn't, as she'd told Reid, wait around until something happened. Alma could be comatose for weeks. She had to decide whether to go now and continue her research, or to hang around for another day or two. Maybe she could stop back here once she was finished in Albuquerque. She'd leave her itinerary with Johnny King so that she could be contacted about any change—or if Miz Alma died.

Loud voices outside the room made Dory turn. The nurse was arguing with someone. Dory's eyes widened when she saw a disheveled man at the door trying to enter the room. When he flailed his arm, knocking away the nurse's hand, Dory gasped. His mangled fingers were just as grimy as the rest of him. She stood and faced him.

Hurley—Papa—Wilson looked at the girl who stared at him. His jaw dropped as if he were looking at a ghost. "Vera," he muttered. Then his mouth twisted in a sneer. Without another word he backed away from the door, turned, and disappeared. Dory ran to the door, only to see the elevator doors closing. The man was gone.

Dory looked at the nurse. "Has he been here before?" she asked.

The nurse sniffed. "Got in here last night with his dirty self," she said. "When Ms. Manning saw him she tried to say something, and was looking upset. That's when I chased him out of here."

"Thanks," Dory said. She went and sat back down by Alma's bed. Was he the reason that sent Miz Alma into a coma? Dory wondered. She shuddered. He'd found her!

Dory was awakened by a hand on her shoulder.

"Ms. Morgan," the nurse said. "There's nothing more you can do. She doesn't even know you're here." She saw the young woman hesitate. "You can come back anytime, but why don't you go and get some coffee? There's a waiting room at the end of the hall that's quite comfortable. You'll find vending machines. I can always come for you if there's any change."

"Okay," Dory said, glancing at Alma. She left the room. She was about to put change in the machine when she realized she was hungry. Maybe she'd feel better once she had some real food in her stomach. The cafeteria was on the second floor, two flights down. She'd get a sandwich and some real hot coffee, then return. It was after six, but she didn't worry about missing Reid. Johnny would let him into the apartment.

Dory walked slowly down the stairs, deep in thought. When she reached the bottom landing, she made a face. Her jacket was in the room, and the little change purse she carried with her money was in the pocket. She went back up the stairs, only to see a no reentry sign on the door. Annoyed, she went back down to the third floor. The same sign sent her down to the second floor. The door was locked. The sign read that that door was closed when the cafeteria closed at six o'clock.

"Damn," Dory muttered as she started down to the lobby. She heard a door close above. *Good,* she thought, *at least I'll have company trying to get out of this maze.* The stairwell was clean and well-lit, but that didn't make her feel better about being caught in the place. She welcomed the company.

"Hello," she called. "We're locked in here, and we'll have to make it down to the first-floor lobby."

There was no answer, and Dory frowned because she heard the thud of footsteps on the metal steps. "Hello," she called again. Suddenly her heart started thumping, and she realized the worst—Papa Wilson had followed her! As she ran down the stairs she heard the quickening steps of the stranger. She reached the first floor, but the sign there read EMPLOYEES ONLY. The door was unlocked, and Dory was startled. This wasn't the lobby! It was a long gray corridor with many doors marked Staff. *Where's the lobby?* she cried to herself. "Oh, God," she whispered. "Somebody, anybody, help me!" Dory ran from door to door, and at the end of a corridor she saw a guard walking toward her. She ran wildly toward him, but just as she reached him he opened a door and she yelled.

"No, wait! Help me!" She heard footsteps behind her and she ran faster, before the guard could disappear.

"What are you doing down here?" he yelled at her. "You don't belong on this floor."

"The lobby," she gasped. "I'm looking for the lobby. Someone's after me."

The guard pointed to the door at the end of the corridor and said, "You don't belong here." He disappeared through the door.

"No, wait!" Dory screamed. She turned to see a figure coming toward her, and she ran as fast as she could toward the door. She reached it and pushed it open. Her eyes hurt from the light. The lobby. There were people, and more guards. Dory sagged against the wall and tried to keep her body from shaking, staying where she was, expecting the door to open to an enraged man. But nothing happened. People began to look at her strangely.

Dory walked to a row of brown leather chairs and sat down. The shaking did not subside. She realized that she'd just experienced her Christmas Eve dream. *She'd been Nora!*

"Miss, are you all right?" The guard looked down at her curiously.

Dory looked up into the eyes of the concerned man. She knew he'd never believe her story, so she stood and said, "Yes, I'm okay. I had some bad news, that's all." She looked around. "Where's the elevator to the fourth floor?" He gestured that it was around the corner. Dory hesitated. "Would you mind walking me there?" she asked.

"Sure, I'll show you," he said.

In a few minutes, Dory shrugged into her jacket and she smiled down at her friend. "The danger was here in this building, Miz Alma," she whispered. "Not yours." She bent and kissed the woman's cheek. "Good-bye," she said. "I'll come again tomorrow."

FOURTEEN

Dory caught a taxi as soon as she left the hospital. Instead of calling ahead to see if Reid had arrived, she decided she'd just get to Alma's as quickly as she could. She hoped that Johnny was home and had let Reid into the apartment. Feeling drained after the fright she'd had, she relaxed against the cushion, throwing her head back and closing her eyes. Now she realized how silly she'd been. There was no proof in the world that the person on the stairs was Papa Wilson. It was possible it had been some staff member going to his locker room, anxious to clock out, who didn't bother to answer a foolish person who'd lost her way.

Dory never noticed the black Mercedes Benz that followed at a discreet distance behind her taxi. When the taxi left and she entered the building, she was unaware of the Benz pulling into a shadowed space a few doors away.

As she'd done years ago, Dory went straight to the stairs without a thought of danger. She put Papa Wilson out of her mind. He couldn't possibly be fool enough to come to Alma's after meeting up with Johnny King. The cops would be there so fast it would make his head spin. She made a face. "Probably why he went to the hospital looking for me," she muttered.

Surprised not to hear a radio or the TV, Dory frowned. It was past seven. Thinking that Reid should be there, she unlocked the door and went inside. Could the super have gone out? Missed seeing him waiting? Annoyed, she shrugged out of her jacket, guessing that Reid must have gone back to the hotel. Picking up the phone, she placed the receiver back when the doorbell rang, thinking that it had to be Reid.

"Mr. Johnny." She looked past him. "You haven't seen Mr. Robinson?"

"No, Dolores. Just came up here to tell you to keep this door locked. Your neighbor"—he inclined his head across the hall—"said that that fool had the nerve to come in here again. Found him waitin' at the other end of the hall. She yelled that she was callin' the cops, and he ran down the stairs. After she called me I went over the buildin', but he musta took off."

"When was this?"

"Not long before you came in. Thought of callin' the cops, but since nothin' happened they wouldn't have come." He shook his head. "Fella's got a lot of nerve comin' back here," he said.

"Thanks for coming up to tell me. I appreciate it, and I certainly will be careful."

"Okay, and if I see your friend I'll let him know you're here." Before he left Johnny said, "Alma about the same?"

"No. She's lapsed into a coma. They'll keep in touch with me."

"Damn shame," Johnny muttered.

After Dory closed the door she felt better, knowing that Johnny had searched the building. She put the kettle on to prepare a hot cup of tea, and wondered what was keeping Reid.

Besides the driver, there were three other men in the black Benz that was parked outside Alma's apartment building. They were silent and watchful. Every person who entered the block, walking on either side of the street, was under surveillance, but only those stopping in front of, or entering, number eleven hundred had their undivided attention.

The phone rang just as Dory finished her tea and was rinsing her cup. Worried that something might have detained Reid, she grabbed the phone, dreading the thought of not seeing him.

"Hello?"

"Ms. Morgan, please."

"Speaking." Dory recognized the nurse's voice. "Ms. Pratt?" she said. "What's wrong?"

"Ms. Manning is awake. She's asking for you." Her voice faltered. "Can you come now?" she said softly.

"I'll be right there." Dory put down the receiver and sank slowly onto the kitchen chair. "She's dying," she murmured, looking around the silent apartment. "Miz Alma's not coming back here." Dory shook as if a cold hand were massaging her chest. Absently, she tried to rub some warmth back into her body, and then she stood mechanically and put on her jacket and hat. When she locked the door she stood for a moment looking at her old apartment door and the one that had always been Alma Manning's. A kaleidoscope of events and snatches of conversation invaded her senses, and she could almost hear her mother's deep mellow laugh, her own childish one, and Miz Alma's gruff one, then laughter at something silly she had said or done that amused the women. Tears formed in the corner of her eyes, and she walked away.

Once outside, Dory realized she'd forgotten to call for a car service. There were never any passing taxis cruising down that block. She'd have to walk two blocks to hail one, and hoped one would stop. Head down, bracing against the wind, she walked down the few steps and onto the sidewalk.

Before Dory reached the next building, a figure jumped out from the shadows and grabbed her from behind, trying to drag her into the alley, and she screamed. He had his arms around her waist, and he tried to cover her mouth. She kicked and was able to scream again, but suddenly the man let go and yelled in agony. She looked into the angry face of Papa Wilson. Dory fell to the ground in her haste to get away from him. She watched, stunned, as two men grabbed him on either side, lifted him off his feet as if he were a rag doll, and tossed him into a black car. The car pulled away from the curb slowly enough for Dory to hear Papa give one loud yell. Then he was silent.

Dory was still on the ground trying to pick herself up, when Johnny King came running from the building, along with two neighbors who lived across the street.

"Dolores," Johnny said, helping her to her feet. "Are you okay? Who was that? Was it that fool?"

Dory shivered. "Y-yes," she whispered.

The neighbors all began talking at once, each telling what they'd seen and heard. None of them recognized the car or the men who got out and took the mugger away. They'd never seen any of them before. After making sure Dory was okay, they all left, except the super, who helped Dory back to the building. She explained where she was going, and he offered to call the car service for her while she waited in his apartment.

While walking beside him, she felt a violent shudder coursing through her body, and she wondered if she'd ever be warm again. The still figure in the back of the car, the man who'd never gotten out, was Clarence Buster Jones. While Dory was down on the ground, she'd stared straight into his eyes. He touched the brim of his hat and then turned, stone-faced, to stare straight ahead. He never said a word as the car door slammed shut.

A car pulled up, and Johnny and Dory turned to look. Reid got out, looking surprised to see them standing there. Dory was brushing herself off, and the super looked angry.

"Dory. What's wrong?" Reid asked quietly. He sent a swift look to the older man, who was muttering under his breath.

"Nothing, Reid," Dory said. All she wanted to do was to get to the hospital.

"Nothin'! Humph," Johnny said. "That fool was here, knocked her down and tried to hurt her." He grunted. "Didn't get the chance. He was carted out of here, thrown into a car like a sack of old clothes. I saw from the window, but couldn't get out here fast enough. That car sure moved quick." He turned a puzzled eye on Dory. "Was almost like they were waitin' for somethin' to happen," he said. "You sure you never saw them before, Dolores?"

Dory shook her head. "I never saw those two men before," she said. *And that's the truth.*

The car Reid had stepped out of was still standing, and Dory said, "I have to go to the hospital. Can we use this car?"

Reid asked the driver to wait. Turning to the super, he said "Thanks." He got inside the car and it pulled off.

Johnny King stood looking after the car for a few minutes, and then walked into the building, a puzzled look still on his face.

Dory's cold hands were in Reid's, and he was rubbing some warmth back into them. Her cheek was cold against his lips when he kissed her, and he frowned at her lack of response. She hadn't spoken a word.

"Want to tell me about it?" Reid asked. His lowered voice was meant to calm her, because he could feel her fear. Something was bothering her besides being attacked.

I have to get to the hospital, she'd said. "Is it Alma?" he asked.

Dory nodded. She told him about the coma and Alma waking up. "The nurse called me. She's dying."

Reid suspected the inevitable. "Did she tell you that?"

"No. I just know it."

Reid nodded. They both knew Alma was dying. The doctor had said it was imminent. Something else was weighing on her mind. "What else?"

"Nothing," Dory answered. She pulled her hands from Reid's and tucked them under her arms and hugged herself. She thought that she would never be warm again. The coldness she'd seen in Buster's eyes was something she'd never forget. The yell that reached her ears as the car rolled away was Papa Wilson's. Dory was sure that was the last sound that man would ever make. She couldn't tell Reid. Not now. She would scream if she opened her mouth to talk about it. Her arms tightened around her body.

Reid felt her withdrawal. She seemed to be in shock. Instead of forcing her to talk, he put his arm around her shoulder and pressed her head against his chest. She shivered, and he held her close.

Dory never spoke to Alma again. When she and Reid got off the elevator, the kindly nurse, Ms. Pratt, was there and Dory guessed. "She died."

"About ten minutes ago," the nurse said.

Reid waited outside on the bench while Dory paid her last respects to Alma. He stared darkly at nothing, silently cursing himself. The old woman had counted on him to protect Dory, and he hadn't been there when Dory needed him. Whatever she'd seen and heard tonight had turned her numb. Papa Wilson had attacked her, she knew. But the men in the car, men Dory had never seen before, who were they? Reid recalled the super's words: "Almost like they were waitin' . . ." he'd muttered. Waiting? The furrows in Reid's brow disappeared. It all became clear. Dory's refusal to speak about what she'd seen. Those men who'd abducted Papa Wilson. "Buster Jones." The name came easily to his lips. There could be no other explanation. Alma had spoken to that old man, and Reid could only guess the request she'd made. His mouth twisted wryly. Buster Jones had kept his promise.

"Reid," Dory said. He was unaware that she'd been standing in the doorway and wondering what was wrong. She went to sit beside him.

Reid looked up. "Are you okay?" he asked.

Dory nodded and sighed. "There's nothing more to do here," she said. "We can go." They stood, and as they passed the desk Dory stopped and said a few words to the friendly nurse. Then she joined Reid by the elevator.

Outside, Reid signaled a waiting taxi, and they got inside. When he gave directions, Dory stopped him with a hand on his arm. He looked at her.

"I was worried about you before. Is everything okay?"

"Yes. Everything's fine."

"I'm glad," Dory said. She linked her arm in his, settled against his strong shoulder, and closed her eyes.

When they exited the car, Dory stood outside for a moment, surveying the street and the building. At last it was over, she thought. Miz Alma had no more worries about her health, when she was going to die, or whether Papa Wilson would get his revenge. She'd known that Buster would take care of everything. Dory said a silent prayer for the old woman and for Buster, and then held on to Reid's arm as they walked inside.

Almost as soon as they entered the apartment, it was as if a dam burst inside her. She shrugged out of her jacket and kicked off her shoes. Complaining that she was starving, she made huge cheese omelets, bacon, toast, and coffee. She felt the urge to talk, and she did.

Reid sat with his arm around Dory as she talked. Long after they'd eaten and left the kitchen, she was still talking. He hardly interrupted except to laugh at funny stories about her mother, Alma, and her friends Soupy and Margaret. She showed him the box of pictures, the will Alma had made, and finally the money accounts. Finally, she told him about Papa Wilson forcing his way into Alma's hospital room, the fright she'd had in the stairwell, and—at last—about seeing Buster Joncs in the car. And then she stopped.

"That's it," Dory said. "Who could have dreamed up such a story?" she asked. "Not even me." Dory grimaced and gave a little laugh as she thought about racking her brain when trying to think of adventures for her fictitious sleuth, Sara.

"You know what?"

"What?" Reid asked.

"He's a broken old man."

He knew she meant Buster Jones.

"He's lost. After all these years of being legit, he reverted to type."

"You don't know what happened in that car," Reid said. "Years ago the man was beaten and run out of town. Tonight he's probably still running, scared out of his witless mind."

Dory hoped that was true, but she'd heard Papa Wilson's yell. Reid could be right. She hadn't seen what was happening in that car, and maybe the man *was* now running for his life. Suddenly she didn't care. There was a sense of peace surging through her that she wasn't going to deny or question.

"I'm glad you're here, love," Dory murmured. She snuggled against him.

Reid stiffened. Had he the right to respond in kind? He

closed his eyes briefly and then kissed her forehead. "I'm glad I came," he finally answered.

Came? How odd, Dory thought through her sleepy haze. *Why wouldn't he have?*

Hours later, Reid awoke and eased himself out of Dory's arms. They were in the queen-size bed in the spare bedroom. She had been half asleep when he insisted that she undress and climb into bed. She refused to close her eyes until she felt him beside her. Once in his arms, she'd fallen into a deep sleep. He lay awake listening to her fitful breathing. Finally, when her breathing was deep and rhythmic he'd found himself relaxing and dozing off.

Now, dressed only in briefs and a T-shirt, Reid slipped his pants on and left the bedroom, closing the door softly behind him. He heated the leftover coffee and carried his cup to the living room, where he sat on the sofa, thinking about the woman in the next room. The stale brew was acrid in his mouth, and he grimaced as he drank. But it was hot, and that was what he needed. He had to make some decisions, soon. Otherwise, he would break the heart of the woman he loved, and she would never know the reason why. He'd messed up earlier today, allowing himself to be put in a position that had confused the hell out of him—to the point where he'd wanted to pack his bags and get out of town. Afterward, he'd made excuses for himself, all in the name of his "condition"—whatever that was. Either he was impotent, or he wasn't! What the hell was this trying to take it easy crap, trying to avoid stressful situations because it would precipitate the "condition?"

Reid grimaced. For the thousandth time that day he asked himself a simple question. Was he going to go through life letting the wrong head do his thinking for him? Putting himself in situations that would justify his reassuring himself that he still had it going on? "Damn," he muttered.

He remembered the look in Janet's eyes, and he knew she wanted him. His body had been responding, and he couldn't stop what he'd allowed her to put in motion. He'd bent his head to take what she was offering.

When his lips touched hers, he'd managed to mumble, "I love someone . . ." But she'd pressed into him, and he crushed her lips in a bruising kiss.

"Sure you do, sugar," Janet had responded. "But I'm here now. Just let go." She unbelted his robe and slid her hands around his waist and down his thighs. "Now you got it," she'd whispered against his mouth as he tightened his arms around her. She caressed his buttocks and pulled herself into his erection.

Reid had yelled when she touched him. "Damn!" He'd opened his eyes and appeared dazed. *Lord, what am I doing?* He stepped back from Janet, who looked surprised. Reid had kept moving back, pulling his robe closed.

Janet, who'd shrugged out of her coat, let it fall to her feet, bent to pick it up and sling it over her arm. She stared at Reid, unbelieving.

Reid had padded barefoot to the bar and poured himself a shot of whiskey. He looked at Janet, who was sitting on the bed, and without asking he poured another and walked back to her. She accepted the glass.

Reid sat in the chair and downed the liquid that burned his throat. They'd stared at each other for a few moments before either spoke. Both had finished their drinks.

"I'm sorry," Reid said. "I was wrong to put you through that." He'd seen the look in her eyes, and couldn't tell whether she was hurt or disappointed. Either way, she didn't deserve what he'd done.

Janet eyed him thoughtfully. She tilted her head and spoke in a serious voice, all coquettishness and acerbic wit absent. "You're really in love," she said. She touched her ermine headband in a smart salute. "I tip my hat to her. She must be something special."

Though Reid had never spoken the truth before, he did then. "I do love her, and she is very special."

The familiar sexy look had returned to Janet's eyes. "I'm envious," she said. "I don't blame you for not being a fool and risking her love." She stood up and slipped into her coat. "You're my kind of man, Reid Robinson," she said, and walked to the door.

Reid stopped her from leaving when he stood and went to her. His look had been direct, and his voice intense. "You're a desirable woman, Janet. But I wanted you for the wrong reasons. I couldn't put you through that."

Janet smiled. She reached up and touched his rugged cheek. "Good-bye, Reid."

After she left, Reid lay on the bed for a long time thinking about himself. The idea of leaving immediately to be with Dory after what he'd almost done left a bad taste in his mouth. He had to think about what he needed to do from there on. Could he have a future with such a passionate woman? For several hours he rode and walked around town, stopping in the nearly deserted Grant Park. Tired and nearly frozen, he'd made up his mind. He would return to Rockford, stay with Dory through her nightmare, and then he would try to love her as he did before. Life itself was all chance, he thought. And not taking a chance on keeping her in his life would make him the biggest fool of the twenty-first century.

The sound of the bedroom door opening made Reid turn and see Dory walking toward him. He had to smile. She was covered from head to toe in her granny gown, and he wondered if she even owned any slinky nightgowns.

"Mmm, what are you doing in here at three in the morning?" Dory said, stifling a yawn. She noticed his smile. "Hope you were thinking about me," she said, plopping down beside him. She kissed his lips.

Reid kissed her back. "How did you guess?"

"I'm psychic, too, sometimes." She touched her nose to his.

Reid grinned at her seductive look. "I confess. You have the power."

"I knew it." Her laugh was deep and mellow.

He kissed her brow. "Sorry I wasn't here for you earlier," he murmured against her hair.

"I missed you," Dory said. "I was afraid something had happened to you and you couldn't come back."

Reid was glad she had her head on his chest. "Something did," he said, "but I . . . took care of it." The cadence of her breathing changed, and Reid sensed she was holding back. When she caught her breath, he was sure. "What is it, sweetheart?"

With difficulty, Dory fought to control her emotions. She wanted to admit that she would have been a lost soul if he hadn't come back to be with her. How could she blurt out that she was in love with him, and never wanted him to leave? And how could she cope with the knowledge that all he was offering was his strong chest and shoulders to lean on, that he would soon be on his way? This wasn't a destiny thing for him. A hiccup escaped.

Reid frowned at the sound. "You're upset," he said. He shifted so that he could see her face. Surprised at the confusion he saw, he caressed her forehead, trying to smooth away the creases. "Tell me," he murmured.

The concern in his voice was too much, and nearly tore up her insides. Her stomach in knots, she forced herself to look him in the eye. "I've fallen in love with you," Dory whispered. He started to speak, but she touched his lips with her finger. "No. I have to say this."

He remained silent.

"A few times I had the impression that you felt the

same. Then, the other day, after we made love, I was certain that I was right." Apprehension entered her eyes. "But you never said the words, and once or twice I thought you wanted to be far away from me."

Reid tightened his hold around her shoulders.

She felt overjoyed at the movement. It wasn't one of rejection. "Once this is over"—she gestured around the apartment—"you'll be leaving." A lump caught in her throat, and she forced a smile. "I can't stand the thought of another eight years slipping by without seeing you again."

Believe me they won't, if all goes well, Reid thought.

"You were right. I am in love with you." Reid stroked wispy strands of hair that swirled in stubborn tendrils around her face. He expelled a deep breath. "I've never been there before, sweetheart." He buried his chin in her hair and inhaled deeply. Her warm scented skin heightened his senses. He recognized the essence, and he breathed in the violet-based scent.

Dory raised her eyes to his, and she flushed at the smoldering fire she saw in them. She kissed his lips. "It's a heady sensation, isn't it?" she murmured.

Reid smiled. "In more ways than one love," he whispered in her ear. "Come here."

His silken whisper sent chills down her spine—the kind of chills caused by love, not fear—and her body reacted with delicious tremors. "I am here," she said in a sultry voice. His hand was under her gown, caressing her thigh. She squirmed when she felt his hand cup her breast.

"Uh-uh," Reid said. "Closer." He lifted the flannel gown over her head and tossed it to the floor. As before she was naked. He was rigid at the sight of her. He dipped his head, and took one of the berry-colored nodules in his mouth. "Ah, Dory, love," he murmured as he tasted each brown berry. He had no fear of needing to rush through loving her. An impatient frown wrinkled his brow. His protection was in the other room. Reid stood, reached for Dory's hand and when she took it he guided her to the bedroom where she lay down on the bed. Reid stripped. Naked as she, he lay down beside her, deftly flipping her over until they were belly to belly, her breasts once again the object of his fiery tongue. Her toes tickled his ankles, and the sensuous feel of her soft skin against his sent spirals of heat to his loins.

Dory pressed into his erection and rotated her hips in a circular motion, savoring the excruciating pleasure-pain she was receiving and giving. Reid squirmed under her, and called her name. She murmured, "Yes, love, I feel you." She kissed his eyelids, his cheeks, and his lips. Her tongue darted in his ear and he called out her name again. At last she kissed his nipples. With her manipulation the stiff buds became warm plump cherries under her fingers and when her moist lips closed over them Reid bucked his hips.

"Dory, you're killing me softly," he rasped.

"Then love me," Dory whispered as she reached for him.

Reid groaned at her touch and moved swiftly until she was on her back. He stared into her eyes, and, condom in place when he entered her, he smothered her lips, stifling the yell in his own throat.

Dory arched into *him* and instantly they were as one, their heated bodies moving in perfect syncopation. Her instant cry of delight was breathtaking as she gasped at his mastery over her body. His passion was turbulent, sweet and uncontrollable, and as hers matched his, she was swept away.

Reid felt drained as his throbbing body sank, satiated, against her warm damp flesh. To keep from crushing her, he slid to her side. He positioned her on top of him and held her close. His eyes were closed, but he opened them at the touch of her lips on his eyelids. "What?" he said, wondering at her smile.

As if they were not alone in the room, Dory scooted up to his ear and whispered, "You love good."

Reid felt a grin go from ear to ear. Her words were like music, and he felt like dancing. He kissed her, and his body reacted. His grin grew wider.

Dory tilted her head, infected by his joy. She laughed. "Now what's so funny?"

Reid grew serious, but his eyes twinkled as he caressed her back. "Me," he said. "Just laughing at myself, sweetheart. Haven't you ever wanted to jump for joy when you got something you'd always wanted, but never expected to have?"

Dory thought. Solemn, she said, "Yes. When I found Willow."

Reid traced her cheek with his finger. "Then you know how I'm feeling right now," he said. "I'm glad I found you again." He brought her head down to his and kissed her lips gently. "I love you." He closed his eyes when she moved against him.

Dory buried her cheek in Reid's crinkly chest hairs. She couldn't help but think she'd been wrong. Happiness *was* waiting for her here in Rockford, after all. It wasn't all doom, though she was sad. Her old friend was gone, but she was free from pain, and at peace. Dory liked to think that the two old friends, Vera and Alma, had already hooked up and were watching her right now. *Heaven forbid!* She squirmed at the idea.

"Dory?" Reid said. He thought he'd heard a cry. "What's wrong?"

"Everything is good. I love you, Reid," Dory murmured.

FIFTEEN

A week later, Dory looked around the stripped apartment with satisfaction. Everything that was good and useful was gone. The super had agreed to discard the rest, a few cardboard cartons of unwanted items.

The day after Alma's cremation and the flight of her ashes to her cousin's grave in Ohio, Dory had been overwhelmed by what to do with the furniture and clothing. Dory had always believed that the quiet woman had stayed to herself, and didn't speak to a soul except Johnny King and his wife. But Alma had befriended many of the people in the building. That was evident in those who came to Dory to offer their condolences. They spoke of her generosity when a few dollars were needed to meet the rent, and how she had often been called to visit a shut-in until a home attendant arrived. But she'd never wanted or accepted help from anyone else. The building residents had attended the memorial service. People from the home services agency were there. Dory had been pleased, though she knew that Alma would just grunt and scoff at the attention.

Meeting all the well-wishers had given her the idea. She just opened the door to them, inviting all to come and take what they wished. In two days the clothing, furniture, and kitchen appliances had disappeared. Dory had boxed all the personal items and papers and mailed them to Willow.

She swept the floor and emptied the trash. It was finished.

Dory locked the door and took the elevator down with her luggage. She knocked on the super's door.

Johnny King looked at Dolores. "Sure is going to be strange addressing any mail that Alma gets to a Dory Morgan," he said.

She smiled. "That's my name now, Mr. Johnny." She reached out and took his hand. "Thanks for everything you and your wife did for Miz Alma," she said.

"She had her ways, but she was a good woman," Johnny said.

Dory handed him the keys. "I know. Well, I see my car outside. Thanks again for forwarding the mail. Hardly anything of importance will slip by, because I already took care of the change of address with the post office. There're some reliable folks over there." She smiled at him and walked outside.

While the driver put her luggage in the trunk, Dory looked over at the building. *I'll probably never come this way again,* she thought. As the building disappeared from view, she chose to remember the good and happy times. All the bad things couldn't overshadow her happiness. Who could have known that this would be the place that the man she loved would confess his own deep love for her in his warm and passionate way?

Yes, she was truly happy. And it would only be a few days before she and Reid met in Albuquerque. She was sad that she couldn't fly to him, but she'd made commitments along her train route.

Dory watched the familiar streets turn into unfamiliar ones as the car took her to meet her train. Her heart felt light as she began to plot new scenes for Sara. Just as she'd wished, she was going to give her sleuth a lover—the man of her dreams, who was so like Reid Robinson.

* * *

Seated comfortably in the wide, superliner coach seat, Dory had her laptop on the foldaway tray table and was finishing up her article. She was on the upper level of the train with its huge panoramic windows, and it was hard to concentrate because of the sweeping view of the countryside.

She'd just left Topeka, Kansas, after a daylong stopover, where she'd interviewed the owners of one of the city's fastest growing, unique, African-American businesses. Glassblowing by mouth, an art thought to be dying, had been given new life by two brothers who resurrected the skills they'd learned from their grandfather. Gabriel and Lincoln Hayward, each in his late thirties and trained in another field, had started the business only five years ago. Neither had expected it to garner such interest and skyrocket.

Dory had found their stories interesting, and she promised her readers an update on the progress of the fascinating brothers in a holiday article. She would visit the brothers again after they'd completed their surprising designs for next Christmas. Dory was looking forward to going back.

After the interview, Dory had been so excited that she'd called her editor, telling her that the article was practically in the mail, and of her plans for a follow-up. She asked about payment for the last two articles she'd done, with a reminder that payment was long overdue. She'd been told that one check had been mailed and the other was coming soon. Dory had to laugh. She'd heard that many times before.

Dory closed her laptop. Waiting for those freelance checks had been a constant in her life, but now that money seemed insignificant. She was rich. The idea was slowly sinking in. She didn't feel any different, and a sudden smile touched her lips. Was she supposed to? She no longer needed to supplement her writing career with the travel articles. No more combining side trips and novel research. Dory refrained from giggling, for fear of waking her seat companion. She put the laptop under her seat and sat back, marveling at the flat expansive fields of Kansas, and knew that she'd miss these trips.

But, she thought, instead of diligently ferreting out interviews for income, now she could just do those that interested her—like coming back for the Hayward brothers's article, and possibly for the next interview, if she was impressed. She was scheduled for a three-day stopover in Dodge City, in Southwest Kansas along the Santa Fe Trail, to interview the proprietors of a bed-and-breakfast inn. It was a family business that had been in operation since the early sixties, before the Civil Rights Act was passed. Back then it hadn't been called a bed-and-breakfast. It was just a big old house that had gained a reputation for putting up black travelers who weren't welcome in white establishments. The word about good food and large clean rooms had spread throughout black organizations, whose members needed additional sleeping quarters during conferences.

The popularity of Monroe's Bed and Breakfast Inn was brought to Dory's attention by Willow, who had stayed there during one of her exhibition tours for her calenders. Since then Dory had planned to do an article, and had been pleased by the friendly reaction she'd received during her initial phone call.

Dory sat back in her seat and closed her eyes. She was happy that she hadn't booked a sleeper for this part of her rail journey. The coach seats were as comfortable as beds, especially when reclined in the sleeping position. Like many passengers, she'd brought her own lightweight blanket, and the pillows were complimentary. She liked the give-and-take with the other passengers, and most important were the spectacular views.

Thoughts of Reid, who was never really out of her mind, replaced all else. By the time she left Dodge City, three weeks would have passed since she'd last seen him. He had left Rockford almost immediately after the memorial service, and she'd begun missing him the instant his taxi disappeared from view. She'd heard from him once when he got settled in Albuquerque, and again just before he boarded a flight to Los Angeles. He was spending a week there, attending an Orchid Society convention.

She drew the blanket close around her, reveling in the delicious tremors that moved through her body. Anticipating his crushing yet gentle and passionate hugs and kisses, she couldn't wait to be enveloped in his embrace. From the sound of his voice, and the words he'd spoken, she knew that he missed her as much as she was missing him.

Dory didn't give too much thought to what must happen after their three weeks together in Albuquerque. The inevitable separation was going to be painful, with Reid flying back to Rochester and her taking a different flight to Irvington. It was a scene she didn't want to envision. Although they would only be about an hour's drive apart, she wondered if career demands would interfere with their relationship. She closed her eyes, hoping that there would come a time when they would never be separated again.

In Albuquerque, Dory checked into a rustic two-room cottage with delight. The accommodations were exactly what she wanted. For once the brochure pictures and the description of a place didn't lie to potential visitors. Dory had chosen such a setting for the final chapters of her novel, in which Sara would solve her mystery.

The Dancing Waters Bed and Breakfast Inn and Cottages was composed of one big house and several small cottages on a few wooded acres. The sprawling main house, which consisted of ten guest rooms with private baths, a dining room, sitting room, and other amenities including a pool and spa, was also built in the rustic manner, simulating a log ranch home. It had two levels and a spacious deck on the main floor. Although the cottages were only several feet away from the main house, they were unobtrusive and did not intrude on the view of the main house occupants. The atmosphere was that of a secluded retreat, although the inn was not in a remote area. It was situated in the downtown woods of Albuquerque, within walking distance of historic Old Town.

Dory dropped her bags on the long beige-tweed sofa, which she knew was an extra bed, and went into the bedroom. She sank down on the queen-size bed and stretched her limbs. "What a place," she said, her discerning eyes roaming over the eclectic mix of artifacts and antiques. The color scheme—earth tones interspersed with the bright hues of turquoise, coral, and pink—connected the two rooms. The effect was serene and relaxing. She kicked off her shoes and began to unpack. The smile on her face told her she was going to get a lot of work done in the next three weeks—if she wasn't deliciously distracted.

It was past five o'clock, and Dory was anxious for the next hour to pass quickly. Reid was due to arrive at six, and they planned to go to dinner. She grinned. Not that that was really the first thing she wanted to do. *But all good things come to those who wait,* she thought. And she'd waited.

Weeks ago, when they'd decided they would be together in Albuquerque, Reid had changed his accommodations from a huge hotel chain to the inn. He was unable to get a cottage, so had settled for the only room available in the main house. Dory was glad that he would at least be nearby. However, both kept their car rental reservations. Dory knew that they would both need space—she to write, and Reid to do whatever came to mind when he awoke in the morning.

There was a knock at the door, and Dory stopped midway to the bathroom, a frown creasing her brow. Had Reid's plane landed early? She stayed where she was. This couldn't be happening. In her story, immediately after checking in, her sleuth Sara opened her door to a knock and had come face-to-face with the very man she had been following. The knock sounded again, and Dory mentally kicked herself. "Don't be silly," she murmured.

"Ms. Morgan?"

Dory moved woodenly to the door and looked through the peephole. "Yes?"

"Staff, Ms. Morgan. Delivery."

The chain in place, Dory opened the door and then let out a deep sigh. She unlatched the chain and opened the door wide.

"For you. Just came." A coatless young man with a mop of wavy black hair looked curiously at the startled guest, then handed her the big bouquet of orchids. "Good night," he said, and left to walk back to the main house.

"Thank you," Dory called when she found her tongue. "How beautiful," she murmured. Her heart back in its place, she placed the bouquet on the small dinette table and plucked the white card from the envelope. It read simply, I love you. Reid. She placed it back in the envelope and gently ran her fingers over the beautiful blooms. She recognized the old-fashioned, pinkish, purple cattleya, and a Phalaenopsis that was greenish white and had a purple center. The display of orchids he'd given her before had contained only one of the white flower. Reid had called it a violacea. It was very fragrant, and Dory bent and inhaled the sweet perfume. With a smile on her lips, Dory fairly skipped to the bathroom, undressing on the way.

Reid drove his rented bright red Toyota at a leisurely pace along the famed highway, Route 66, now Central Avenue. He was already familiar with the area, and drove with confidence. The forty-eight-degree temperature was a change from the balmy eighty-two degrees he'd left in Los Angeles. Before his trip to LA, he had taken in quite a few of the tourist attractions, but most of the time he'd stayed on the grounds of the inn. The peacefulness that was in the air put his mind and body at ease. The first few days he'd started his mornings wondering why in the world he wasn't home in Rochester, working. He almost felt guilty vacationing, when he felt that there wasn't a thing wrong with him.

Reid had taken the time to study the literature his doctor had given him about erectile dysfunction, and decided that he didn't fit into any of the serious categories. There was nothing physically wrong with him, and he didn't do drugs or abuse alcohol. He'd cooperated by removing himself from job stress for a period, and he'd never felt better. As far as he was concerned, stress was only a word in the dictionary. He'd wanted to call his medical man and tell him exactly that.

When he'd left Dory standing in front of that building watching him leave with love shining in her eyes, he'd wanted to jump out of that taxi and grab her and never let go. But once he was on the train, his mind and body had settled down. He realized she'd needed time to be alone with her grief, and to take care of necessary business. He would never let her get too far away from him again. That was paramount in his mind.

He flexed his shoulder muscles, not from fatigue, but because he was feeling good. For a whole week, he'd spent time with fellow orchid growers. Some he'd met in the past, many he'd spoken to over the phone, and others were customers, who had been surprised to meet him there. He'd enjoyed the warm moist smell of earth in the greenhouses, and found himself sticking his hands in the soil. Except for the fact that he was going to spend days with the woman he loved, he would have been on a flight to Rochester.

A half hour after arriving at the inn, Reid was knocking on the door of Dory's cottage. It was six forty-five. When he heard her footsteps he had to stuff his hands in his jacket pockets, fearful of crushing her ribs on sight.

"Hi," Dory breathed. She drank in the sight of him and then caught his hands and pulled him inside.

The touch was electric. Reid's hands tightened over hers, and his approving gaze roamed over her face, searching her eyes for any hint of sadness or regret for her decision to meet there. All he saw was the same look of love.

"Hi, sweetheart." Reid bent his head and kissed her lips gently.

Dory pushed aside his unzipped nylon jacket and slid her arms around his waist, holding him tightly. She pressed her head against his chest and closed her eyes.

They embraced for several seconds, lost in the heavy emotion of the moment.

Reid stepped back and kissed her forehead. "I missed you," he said, searching her eyes. He kissed her nose. "You look beautiful." He kissed her lips. "Good enough to eat." Recapturing her lips in an aggressive searching kiss, tasting her sweet tongue, he inhaled sharply. He was aware of the tantalizing scent she wore, and he recognized it as the exotic sweet smell of gardenias. "Yes," he murmured, "definitely delicious."

Dory approved of his hands caressing her body, moving sensuously over the curve of her breasts and over her buttocks, pulling her closer to him. He wasn't wearing his black cap, and she put her arms around his neck and reached up, running her fingers over his head. She shuddered. She'd always loved the tactile sensation that she felt through her fingertips. The warm smooth hardness was erotic and, sent the juices in her flowing. She stood on her toes and brought his head down to hers. Her tongue found his, and she sucked it softly, refusing to let him capture hers, selfishly reveling in the velvet warmth.

"Mmm," Reid murmured against the onslaught. "Greedy." He took control, reversing the attack. He devoured the softness of her mouth with deep exploratory kisses, and her response sent shock waves down his spine.

Dory moaned with pleasure as his mouth left hers burning with fire. "You're dangerous," she whispered, but she didn't want him to douse the flame. She gave in to his ravishment of her mouth.

After a long while, Reid and Dory parted, both breathing heavily from their passionate greeting.

Reid slipped out of his jacket as they walked into the spacious room. He looked around with an approving eye at the tiny kitchenette and the combined eating and living room. His glance went toward the bedroom.

"Comfortable," he said. "Satisfied?"

Dory nodded, still holding him around the waist as they looked around. "I like it," she said. "I'll get a lot accomplished here."

Reid's dark eyes twinkled. "You will?"

Dory blushed. "That's my goal," she said.

"There's something to say about the best laid plans, huh?" he teased.

"That they get stymied at times?"

"At times."

Reid steered her toward the table and stared at the orchid display. He pulled out the violacea. "Especially for you," he said.

"They're all so beautiful," Dory said, taking it and inhaling the perfume. "I think this is my favorite." She looked at him. "How did you guess?"

"Your face when you saw it among all the others."

Dory kissed him. "Thank you."

"Hungry?"

She just wanted to lie on the bed, stretched out beside him, but she realized he probably hadn't eaten on the plane.

Her hesitation made Reid give her a quick look. "Is that a no?" he asked, not realizing there was a tinge of hopefulness in his voice.

"Yes."

"Yes, you're hungry, or yes it's a no?"

"Yes, I'm hungry. Not for food."

Reid laughed. "I think I understand." He tilted his head. "Do you think maybe your writing goal is about to be stymied a little?" he asked in a lowered voice.

Dory glowed inside. "I believe so." They walked to the bedroom. "Just for a little while," she whispered as he took her into his arms.

"Only for a little while?" He was rising against her. "We'll see," he said, his voice husky.

Dory couldn't believe that two weeks had passed. A wry grin twisted her mouth. She thought that it must be true that time ceased to exist when a person was happy and in love. One week from today, she and Reid would part. She shook her head at the thought, and brushed her forehead as if to wipe away the inevitable. She slapped her hands and rubbed them together, seeking warmth against the nippy cold as she stood with Reid in the chairlift line. They were at the Sandia Peak course, where Reid and other downhill skiing enthusiasts spent the day. This was their third trip during the past two weeks.

"Sure you won't change your mind?" Reid asked, his ski poles in one hand and his other arm around her shoulders. "Probably be the last time we come here." He, too, was thinking about the coming days. Time had passed too quickly.

"No, thank you, sir," Dory said emphatically. "I'll just watch you as usual."

He laughed and squeezed her shoulders. "Once we get back home we'll have to see about snapping some skis on your feet. This is the one pastime I do indulge in, and I can't be going off leaving you at home on weekends," he said. He kissed her cheek and inched up as the queue moved.

Dory looked at his handsome profile. *He hasn't even realized what he just said,* she thought. In the last few days he'd made a few similar remarks about their future, almost as if they would always be together, as if that was the most natural thing in the world to say. She didn't answer, but kissed his cheek and said, "This is where we part, Mister. I'm going to go get warm." She waved and hurried back to the big restaurant, where other nonskiers and skiers alike huddled together in the big toasty room.

Finding a seat in a corner with a mug of hot black tea, Dory removed her mittens and jacket and hat. She waved to a few people she'd seen before, and looked around at the scene with interest. The second time she had been there, she had smelled an article. There had been a group of about thirty black skiers who were part of an international African-American skiing organization. She'd met the president, who agreed to do the interview. It wasn't common to run across so large a group of black skiers. She smiled wryly at that thought. It wasn't common at all to see African-Americans walking the streets of Albuquerque.

Dory had been intrigued to learn that the group traveled to several different ski areas around the world during the season. She was impressed that they also held fund-raising functions for several charities. They gave scholarships sponsoring youngsters who were avid skiers. It was the group's goal to sponsor an African-American Olympic hopeful one day.

After writing the article that night, Dory had chuckled to herself. She hadn't needed to do the article for the income, but because she couldn't ignore her nosy instinct. She wondered if she would always have that instinct, and realized that she'd never want to lose it, money in the bank or not.

Watching the skiers come down the peak, Dory had no trouble spotting the man she loved. The tall, imposing figure clad in royal blue neon, was grace in motion as he sailed down the steep slope. Her proprietary air was evident as she raised both brows at the three snow bunnies practically edging each other onto the snow to get next to him as he unsnapped his skis. He was looking down at them, and from the set of his head Dory could only imagine his grin, the flash of his even white teeth, and the twinkle in his dark eyes. When he turned she did see the big grin.

"What's so funny?" she mumbled under her breath. She could remember when his smiles had been rare, and big grins even rarer. Now it was no longer startling when he gave a loud guffaw at something on the TV, or at something she'd said. The sound was pleasant and amusing. She often wondered if Reid would find it so easy to laugh now if he had not met that woman Janet Steward, who'd told him everything about the vicious Emily Gibbons.

She stayed put, knowing that Reid would soon join her inside to warm up before they left for the day. Her frown was gone. Dory knew that she played a big role in Reid's life now, and was happy that she was part of the reason for his easy laughter.

Reid spotted Dory and made his way to her, a mug of

hot tea warming his big hands. Like others around him, he sat on the edge of a huge, square, oak table and drank the beverage.

"Hi," he said, enjoying the warmth sliding down his throat and heating his insides. "Told you. One day," he said, "you'll love it!" He winked at her.

Dory's dark hair was limp from the steamy room, and when she shook her head from side to side it swung lazily across her cheeks. "Uh-uh," she said. "I'm not that adventurous." She cocked her head. "But one day Zelle and Troy will give you a run for your money. At six, they already want to race their father and mother." She'd accompanied the family to a ski resort last winter, and had been amazed at the prowess of the then five-year-old twins. They'd called their Aunt Dory a big chicken when she wouldn't even rent a pair of skis.

"They sound like a handful," Reid said. "Can't wait to meet 'em."

"You will," Dory said. She chuckled at the vision of her nephews and niece clambering over Reid's long legs. When she realized the implication of her words, she became quiet.

Reid became somber as he watched her look change. "Guess we're both wondering when that will be," he said.

Dory stared into his probing eyes, but she didn't speak.

Reid was careful to place his emptied mug in the middle of the big table. He took Dory's hands in his. "Aren't you?" he asked, watching her intently.

"Yes," she murmured.

Reid held her hands for an instant longer, then released them. "But this isn't the place to talk about that, is it?"

"Not really," Dory said, shaking her head.

"Ready to go, then? I'd like to talk about it."

"Me, too."

Although the New Mexico sun kept the wind at bay, it

was still cold at the peak, and they hurried to take the tram down to the car.

Reid and Dory relaxed on the plump sofa, in the cozy comfort of her cottage. They had brought in a meal, and after warming spicy barbecued ribs, baked potatoes, and mixing up a salad, they were now savoring glasses of red wine. No impostor, it was a true red burgundy, from Burgundy, France: the one hundred percent Pinot Noir.

Reid pressed the OFF button on the TV remote and turned to Dory, his expression serious. "I don't want to lose you," he said. "On Sunday, when we go our separate ways, my gut tells me that is exactly what will happen. Sometimes I believe you're thinking the same." He searched her face. "Tell me if I'm wrong."

"You're not." Dory's hand rested on the back of his as it lay on the cushion beside her, and she moved her finger in a circular motion on the hard ridges.

Reid's lips were drawn in a grim line. "My psychic talent tells me that neither of us wants that. Am I right?" He caught her fingers. The gentle caress was taking him to a place he did not want to go. Not yet.

"I'd say that your talent was right on," Dory answered with a smile.

"Any suggestions on what we should do?"

"Not a clue."

"Not one?" Reid gave her a skeptical look.

Dory lifted a shoulder. "I don't know what you want me to say, Reid."

"Only what you feel."

When she looked away in confusion, Reid touched her chin and gently turned her face back to him. "Then I'll tell you what I feel. I don't want to have an electronic relationship. I know it's the twenty-first century, but I don't want that to define how I spend time with you. E-mail, voice mail, an occasional snail mail." He shrugged. "That's not what I want." He ran a finger down her soft cheek. "Dory, I can't bring all my greenhouses to Irvington and plop them in your backyard."

Dory drew in a breath. *He couldn't possibly be making such a request!* "Reid, you're asking me to move in with you?"

Reid didn't drop his gaze. "If not that, come to me. Spend days, weeks, with me."

"But my work," she said.

He inclined his head toward the bedroom, where he knew she worked on her laptop at night. "Can't you bring it with you?"

Dory laughed. "Reid, you can't be serious," she said. "Typing into the computer isn't all there is to writing."

"No?" His eyes were teasing.

"No. I have my library, research materials . . . there's tons of stuff. I'd need a room all my own."

"It's a big house," Reid said solemnly.

"You *are* serious."

"We're at an impasse." Reid sat back, feeling defeat.

"I have my life in Irvington. You're asking me to leave my family."

Reid heard the catch in her voice. *Her family.* He remembered her poignant account of finding the family she'd never known she'd had. How could he compete with that?

The silence in the room was broken by the laughter of the family occupying an adjacent cottage.

Finally, Reid leaned over and kissed her forehead. "Forget I suggested that, sweetheart," he said.

Dory felt miserable—not only because of the disappointment in Reid's voice, but because she couldn't deal with the possibility of leaving her family. The thought had never entered her mind.

"Reid," she said, folding his hand in hers. "I never

considered that I might . . . well, I never . . ." Her voice trailed away.

After a moment, Reid said, "I know. You thought you'd fall in love with the guy around the corner."

Dory smiled ruefully. "Now, wouldn't that be convenient."

Making light of the situation wasn't working, and they were both quiet with their thoughts.

Finally, Reid stood and pulled Dory up with him. He hugged her and kissed her lightly on the mouth. "We're not going to solve our problem just like that, are we?" he said, looking steadily into her eyes.

"I don't think so," she answered, dropping her gaze. The uncertainty she saw in his eyes frightened her.

"You're writing tonight?" Reid asked.

"Yes," Dory said. "I'm pretty close to fitting all the pieces together."

Reid smoothed a wayward strand of hair from her cheek. "Maybe we should engage Sara to solve our own mystery," he said softly.

Dory didn't like the sound of hopelessness she heard, and she shuddered when his lips brushed hers. His kiss seemed so final.

"What's wrong?" Reid felt the slight tremor.

"Are we saying good-bye?"

"Good-bye?" Reid frowned. "Why do you ask that?"

"Only a feeling."

"Then lose it," Reid said, embracing her again. "We agreed, remember?"

Dory nodded. They had agreed that there would be no more long separations, but neither had given thought to the reality of their situation. She walked with him as he got his jacket and shrugged into it.

"I'll leave you and Sara to tie up loose ends," Reid said. "We still have a few days to work on ours." He caught her and held her close. "Right?"

Dory kissed his cool lips. "Right," she murmured.

Reid opened the door. "Breakfast at my place?"

"I'll be there at eight."

"Good-night, love."

Dory watched him walk up the slight grassy incline to the main house. His step wasn't as light as it normally was. She closed the door.

Hours later, just after midnight, Dory closed her laptop. She was already dressed in nightgown and robe, but instead of heading for bed she went to the kitchen and poured a glass of the burgundy. As she lounged against the pillows on the bed, her thoughts went to her conversation with Reid. Why had she asked him if they were saying good-bye? Deep down, she knew that wasn't what she wanted. There was no doubt in her mind that she wanted Reid in her life. But had she expected the man to just pick up and move away from his livelihood?

Dory finished the wine and set the glass on the table. He wanted her to disrupt her life to live with him—without the offer of marriage. More than a month ago she'd known that she wanted to spend the rest of her life with Reid Robinson—but as his wife, not as his live-in lover. Yet, he hadn't proposed marriage to her. *Why?* she wondered. Even if he had, she thought, there would still be the fact that her family would no longer be near. Confused, Dory went to brush her teeth.

Once back in bed, she turned out the bedside lamp. She lay in the dark, thinking, sleep elusive, as she tried to make sense of her contradictory feelings. If he did propose, it was normal that a wife should live with her husband. Dory, naively, had never given thought to moving away from her family, even if she did fall in love and marry. She had supposed that any stumbling blocks to her dreams would just fall in place, like a fairy tale's happy ending.

But the fact remained that he hadn't proposed, and if

she agreed to spend time with him, as he put it, she would only be living with him. Could she do that? Traveling back and forth for weekends, or even a few weeks at a time? That wasn't the sort of life she had planned for herself. She wanted a family like her sister had, children who would light up her life, like Zelle and Troy and Ronald and David. She wanted to fall asleep in the arms of her husband every night, and kiss him awake in the morning.

Dory closed her eyes. Her last thought was of Reid and the pain she would feel if she couldn't be with him, and she almost knew what her decision would be. But why hadn't he asked her to be his wife?

SIXTEEN

"Why didn't you ask her to marry you?" This time Reid asked himself the question aloud as he drank another glass of wine. Unable to go to sleep, he had spent the better part of the night probing his subconscious trying to find an answer to his question. But he already knew, and was in denial. In spite of all his self-examination of a few weeks ago and his making the conscious decision that there wasn't a thing wrong with him, there was a dark and shady doubt rolling around in his mind. What if he did have a problem and married her, only to have it surface days into the marriage? In all fairness to her, he would have to walk away, give her the opportunity to have a decent, fulfilling sex-life with another man.

"God," Reid blurted out. "That can't happen!" *Then what are you going to do about it?* he asked himself. *Marry her, you fool!* Reid closed his eyes. God help him. He was going to propose.

The next morning, Reid awoke with mixed emotions. Today was going to be one hell of a day. There was a lot he had to do. The decision he'd made just before falling asleep sent a tidal wave of new feelings sloshing through him. He felt as if he were riding the high surf in Hawaii. He grinned widely. That thought brought to mind honeymoons, and wild loving on the beaches of the lush island.

He'd been there years ago for an orchid convention, but at that time romance was the furthest thing from his mind as he networked for his fledgling business. As he dressed, he hoped Dory had never been there. He wanted to be the one to bring the wonder to her eyes as he took her around to exotic places. By seven forty-five he was in the dining room, waiting for her to appear.

Dory saw Reid get up and wave to her. When she reached him, she could feel the energy that enveloped him. His eyes twinkled, and he gave her a lazy grin. They kissed and sat down, and she wondered at the vibrancy of his movements. Last night there had been no pep in his step when he left her.

"Sleep well?" she asked, picking up the menu.

"Like a log," Reid said, casually setting the menu aside. He already knew what he wanted.

Wish I could say the same, Dory thought, a little jealous of his exuberant mood.

Dory listened in amazement while Reid ordered sliced pears, flapjacks with side orders of sausage and bacon, and three fried eggs. He was already drinking hot coffee. He ordered scrambled eggs and bacon for her.

"You're not hungry?" Reid asked when the waitress left. "Did you work too long last night?" he asked solicitously.

"No," Dory said crossly. *What's happened to this man?* she wondered.

Reid's eyebrows shot up. "Hmm, I think you did," he said, eyeing her critically. He drank some more coffee. "Maybe instead of going to Old Town like we've planned, you should rest for a few hours. You really have been going at it pretty steadily the last few days."

She stared at him. "A few hours?"

"Sure," Reid answered. "After lunch you'll be refreshed and ready to go. But," he said, "dinnertime and the rest of the night belong to me."

"But," Dory protested, "I thought we were going to shop for souvenirs together. You said you wanted my opinion on that necklace for your sister-in-law."

Reid shrugged. "We can do that tomorrow," he said. "You look tired, and getting some rest is more important."

"Humph. You certainly know how to take away a girl's appetite," Dory said.

Reid grinned as he sat back in his chair. He helped the waitress make room on the table for all their dishes. When she left, he winked at the scowl on Dory's face.

"Don't let your eggs get cold, love."

At five o'clock, Dory was dressed and waiting for Reid. He'd called about two and asked her to be ready for dinner. Their six-thirty reservations would be cancelled if they were late. He'd hung up so quickly she didn't have a chance to tell him that he'd been right. After breakfast she'd slept for a couple of hours. Her sullen mood of the morning had disappeared. She awoke refreshed, and ready to put in a couple of hours of writing. Dory smiled because Reid had read her so well, although he would never guess why she hadn't slept well last night. Whatever the reason for his buoyant spirits, she was glad. Maybe he had found a solution to their dilemma, and was planning to share it with her at dinner tonight.

Dory knew which restaurant they were going to, and had dressed simply but elegantly. People rarely dressed up anymore, a practice that she and Willow had remarked on several times. But sometimes a person had to dress in a manner that matched the mood. It did something for the event and the psyche, she thought.

Although the sun was burning hot with temperatures reaching the sixties on some days, the cool evenings required warm clothing. Dory had chosen a white, long-sleeved, hip-skimming top with a V-neck. The matching sheath skirt skimmed her ankles, the side slits showing her shapely legs as she walked. She wore red strap sandals, and a heavy red wool serape draped her shoulders. For jewelry she wore only her gold watch. Dory had taken off the gold dangle earrings that she loved, preferring to let her dark curls cover her ears. She wore very little makeup, because the sun had tanned her skin to a deep golden brown.

Reid rushed to get dressed. Earlier, he had spent more time than he wanted to, shopping for what he had in mind. Picking up just anything was out of the question, because he hoped this was going to be a perfect evening. Reid picked up his packages and left the room, satisfied that he was making the right decision.

Dory opened the door to Reid's knock. Curious about the packages he carried, she stepped back. The clean-smelling sandalwood scent that he wore tantalized her as he walked by. He wore a mysterious smile as he took a bottle of champagne out of a bag and held it up to her before putting it in the refrigerator.

"For later," Reid said, still smiling at her. From another bag he pulled out a large violacea encased in cellophane. "For now," he said, and walked to where she was standing by the sofa. He removed the wrapping and placed the beautiful flower in her hands.

"Oh," Dory managed as she caressed the velvety blossom. She looked up at Reid, who was staring at her, and thought how serious he'd become in an instant.

"You're so beautiful." Reid stood away from her so that he could take in everything—from the sun-kissed skin at her neck to the red toenails that matched her sandals. The bare leg that peeked through the slits in her skirt brought visions of the rest of her that he'd come to know so well, and he wished the evening was nearing an end instead of just beginning.

There was no distance between them now as Reid took her in his arms. He held her for only a moment, then released her. With a gentle kiss on her lips, he took the flower from her hands. After placing it on the table, he guided her to a seat on the sofa and sat beside her.

From inside his light gray suit jacket he pulled out a long flat box. "For you," Reid said, and handed it to her. "I love you, Dory, and I want you to be my wife. Will you marry me?"

"What?" Dory whispered. Although her ears might deceive her, she knew her eyes could not. He was looking at her with all the love in his heart. And he wanted her to be his wife. Tears misted her eyes.

"Yes, Reid," she murmured. She caressed the rugged lines in his cheek. "I will marry you."

Reid let out a breath. When her arms snaked around his neck, he captured her lips hungrily. Neither had words for several minutes as they shared the intimacy of the moment. Reid opened his eyes to find hers closed. He kissed her eyelids, and she raised them. "I'll always love you," he said. He brushed the damp lashes with his finger.

"And I, you." Dory was choked up, and when she moved the black box on her lap slid to the floor. "Oh, I'd forgotten about this."

Reid picked it up and handed it to her. "A token of my love." He stared at her while she opened it.

Dory gasped. "It's beautiful," she said. Nestling on black velvet was a long, traditional, squash blossom necklace. The symbol of the desert flower was made of hundreds of matched turquoise gemstones and sterling silver. She lifted it from the box and Reid helped clasp it around her neck. There were dangling pierced earrings to match, and she put them on.

"Reid," she said, "they're gorgeous!" Today was the day that she'd been going to buy the necklace for herself. She'd always loved the turquoise, and since she'd been in

Albuquerque she'd seen many necklaces. One was more beautiful than the next, and she could never decide. None had been as different as the one she now wore.

"I hoped you'd be pleased," Reid said in a solemn voice. He reached in his pocket for another item. The turquoise and silver circlet looked tiny in his large hands, and when he slipped it on her finger it fit perfectly. "Would you wear my ring for now? Later, when we get back to New York we can search for the kind of perfect diamond that you ladies prefer." He made a mock grimace. "Too much confusion for me."

Dory lifted her hand to stare at the slim band. It looked as if it had always been there. Her heart was full, and she found it hard to speak.

Reid smiled at her, and he knew she was overcome.

"I'm proud to wear your ring, love." Dory kissed him gently.

The soft touch stirred Reid down to his toes. "Let's go eat, sweetheart."

Reid shrugged out of his suit jacket and tossed it onto the kitchen chair while Dory unstrapped her heels and padded to the bedroom. Reid watched her go with a wicked grin plastered on his face. It widened when she reached behind her to unfasten her skirt before closing the bedroom door.

The champagne was on the table, and before sitting down to wait for Dory he loosened his tie and draped it on top of his jacket. Tonight couldn't have been more perfect if he'd taken a year to plan it. He had to laugh at himself when he thought of all the mess they'd gone through last night trying to decide about their future together. The solution had been simple. All that was needed was for him to screw his head on tight and stop thinking in negatives.

Reid frowned at the knock on the door. He opened it to find a young man who worked in the main house.

"Sorry to bother you, Mr. Robinson," he said, "but you left word to contact you here in any emergency."

"Yes, that's right," said Reid, his frown deepening. "What is it?"

"This fax came for you. It requires an answer. The office is still open if you want to send a return fax tonight." He said good night and returned to the lodge.

Reid read the short message. "Christ!" He sank down on the kitchen chair, shock blinding him. He read the message again, then let the paper drop from his hands as his mind went blank.

Before Dory opened the bedroom door, she checked herself out once again in the dresser mirror, pleased with what she saw. She'd put on an ankle-length, red satin nightgown that skimmed over her curves. The three spaghetti-thin straps on each side went over her shoulders and crisscrossed down to the deep V at the small of her back. Over it was a calf-length matching jacket with kimono sleeves. She had treated herself to the confection after Reid had left for Los Angeles. He was always amused at her flannels, and never wasted any time in tossing her gowns aside. Maybe he'd want to look at her a little longer tonight, she thought. But not too long! She smiled. She opened the door.

"Reid!" Dory knew instantly that something was wrong. She went to him, but he stared at her bleakly. "Oh, God, what's happened?" she said. She saw the paper on the table and picked it up and read it. It was from his brother. There had been a fire. Without a word she went to him. He opened his arms and she sat on his lap, cradling his head against her breast.

Dory could feel the rise and fall of his chest as he struggled to gain his composure. She knew he was still in shock from the news. When his breathing quieted, she said, "Gilbert Lane is the manager you mentioned?"

"Yes." Reid closed his eyes. He could only imagine the scene at the nursery. He held Dory for a moment longer, then eased her off his lap and stood.

"I have to call Leon, love," he said. He shrugged into his jacket. "I'll use the phone up in my room."

"Okay," Dory said.

Reid sank back down in the chair in disbelief and looked up at Dory. "A fire!"

Dory saw that he wanted to talk. She took the chair beside him. "Were any visitors hurt?" she asked softly.

Reid shook his head. "I won't know more until I speak to Leon," he said. "The tours through select greenhouses are well supervised. Nothing has ever happened to make us even think they could be unsafe." He paused. "Gil is proud of the place, and he's always been willing to conduct at least one of the tours on weekends. Now he may lose his life! Sometimes my nephew Matthew follows behind Gil. He wants to conduct the tours himself when he's older." Suddenly the thought hit him that Matt might have been there. He stood. "Wait up for me?"

Dory nodded. She didn't close the door until he'd disappeared into the building. She rubbed her arms to keep from shaking. She missed her flannels.

"Leon," Reid said, trying to keep the fear out of his voice. "What the hell happened?"

"An explosion," Leon said. "The fire chief thinks it could have started from fumes from the propane tanks or maybe from a cigarette. They're investigating."

"A cigarette!" Reid exploded. "Gil would never allow that. *Nobody* would allow that! Who the hell was it?"

"I said *maybe.* A visitor sneaking a smoke during the

tour could have tossed it without putting it out. For now, it's still a mystery."

Reid swore. "W-who was with Gil?" he asked.

Leon heard the anguish. "Matthew was in another greenhouse with his mother. He wasn't hurt," Leon said.

"Thank God." Reid expelled his breath. He paused. "Why was Gil so badly burned? He didn't try to put it out, did he?"

"You know Gil," Leon finally said. "It's like every one of these buds are his children. He wanted to save as many as he could. It was windy, and fireballs were flying all over the place. One latched on to the tail of his jacket. Before he knew what was happening, he was engulfed." Leon swallowed. "He's pretty bad."

"Will he live?" Reid didn't want to hear the answer. He and Gil had been friends since Reid had hired him six years ago.

"It doesn't look good."

Reid shook his head. "God."

"One house was lost."

"Which one?"

"All the laelia and cattleya hybrids."

Neither man spoke as the loss penetrated. A year's work, gone.

"I'm coming home, Leon. I'll be on whatever can get me out of here tomorrow." He paused. "Tell Gil to hang in there, and I'll see him in a few."

"I hear you," Leon said. He replaced the receiver and pushed his glasses up. Stress, he thought. Exactly what his brother was trying to get away from. "Damn!"

Dory opened the door to Reid, and her heart went out to him. His expression reminded her of when she'd first met him again on the train—bitter. The softer side of him that he'd let her see in the last month was gone. She knew it was still there, but shock had buried it. She led him to the sofa, and they sat.

"Tell me about it," Dory encouraged. Holding in his hurt and anger was the last thing he needed.

"My nephew's okay."

"Thank God," Dory murmured. "And Gil?"

Reid shook his head. "Leon said that he . . . might not make it." He closed his eyes and rubbed his forehead. The possibility of losing his friend was hard to swallow.

Dory wanted him to talk. "And the greenhouses?"

Reid talked, telling her all that he knew. In the end, he felt the first wave of shock and anger dissipate, but he felt drained.

"Carelessness! Stupid carelessness," he said. "A great guy might die because somebody wanted a smoke." Reid slapped the palm of his hand with a rock-hard fist.

Dory felt the tightness in his shoulders, and his pulsing temples alarmed her. He needed to relax. She stood up and took his hand. "Sit here," she said, forcing him to sit up straight on the strong pinewood coffee table. Slowly she began to massage the muscles in his neck and shoulders. The tension eased, but she continued until he went limp. Satisfied, she made him sit back on the sofa and went to put on the kettle.

"Here, drink," Dory said, handing him a mug of strong black tea. When he took it she sat beside him and sipped from her own mug.

Minutes passed before either spoke.

Reid put his mug on the table. He took Dory in his arms and pressed her head against his shoulder. "Thank you," he said, resting his chin on her soft curls. His fingers caressed her arm under the wide sleeve of her satin robe. She smelled delicious, and her skin felt like his finest orchid petals. "I always knew you had undiscovered talents," he said. "That's what I'm going to like about being married to you. More mystery." He kissed the top of her head.

Dory squirmed in his arms until she faced him. She raised her lips to his and kissed them. They tasted of the sweetened tea. "Mmm," she said. Sticking her tongue in his mouth, she savored the warmth. "You're the mystery," she murmured against his mouth.

Reid responded with a deep kiss of his own. He wanted to love her right on the spot, but he eased her up and stood, pulling her with him. His eyes roved over her sexy lingerie. He smiled at her. "Bet you thought I didn't notice," he said.

"You were preoccupied," Dory said, but she was pleased.

"Beautiful." He started tugging the robe off as they walked to the bedroom. "Still too many clothes," he whispered. The robe fell to the floor.

Reid pushed the wispy straps off her shoulders, slowly caressing her satiny skin. When her breasts were uncovered, he bent and tasted each tender bud, and his pulses quickened. Slowly he eased the gown over her curvy hips, pausing to smooth his hands over her rounded buttocks. He could feel the throbbing in her thighs as he touched her inner softness.

"Mmm," Dory murmured, "you make me feel so good."

"Look who's talking," Reid whispered against the softness of her cheek. Then he frowned. As much as he wanted her, he should have been swollen by then. It had never taken his body this long to react to her. Just one of her deep sexy kisses was enough for him to get an erection. Once her hands were on his body, that was the end for him.

Reid's chest started to heave, and his temples broke out in beads of perspiration. Dory's hands were all over him, and there was no reaction from his body. He was not getting erect! Visions of the last time that had happened, which had seemed a vague memory, ancient history, were now vivid images in his mind.

God, no! Don't let this happen to me. Not with the woman I want to marry!

Dory frowned and her hands stopped their explorations when she felt Reid stiffen. His breathing was labored, and he had broken into a cold sweat. The warmth of his body was gone, and he stood with his eyes closed. The look of anguish on his face scared her.

"Reid, love, what is it?" she said. Her arms were around his waist, and he opened his eyes. Their icy blackness made her step back, and she dropped her arms. "Reid?"

Reid looked at Dory as if she'd just materialized and he wondered what she was doing there. Then he realized. He'd frozen. He couldn't get to the point where he could make love to her. "God," he rasped.

That onc word torc a holc in Dory's hcart as shc watched the pain in his eyes turn his face into a cold hard mask.

Reid backed up, and after one long look at her he left the bedroom. He picked up his jacket and tie, draped them over his arm, and walked to the door. He turned to Dory, who was standing by the bedroom door watching him. The look on her face brought anger to his eyes. *Why have I done this to her?* he thought.

"Reid?" Dory's heart was pounding in her chest. He couldn't be leaving her!

About to go to her, Reid stopped. No. What could he say that would make any sense? "I'll call you in the morning, Dory." He opened the door, and the need to put distance between him and the look in her eyes caused him to hurry out—as if those haunted eyes were following him.

* * *

Dory was huddled in the bed. Even her flannel gown could not make her warm as she rubbed her arms vigorously. She stared at the red satin gown and robe where they still lay on the floor. Just looking at them brought fear to her heart and sent cold shivers up and down her spine. Trying to make sense of what had happened, she was still mystified by Reid's behavior. A smile tugged at her lips. She *did* tell him that he was the one that was full of mystery.

After mulling over his behavior and abrupt departure, the answer that Dory came up with was the fire. The reality of what had happened was just sinking in. Reid was not so much concerned with monetary loss, but the fact that his friend was not expected to live was eating him up. And it was all so needless!

Reid was angry. He wanted to blame somebody. But who? There was no one to beat up on but himself. He'd warned himself, played games with his head, tricking himself into believing that he was going to be fine. He'd scoffed at the doctor's warning that stress would lead him right down that path to candidacy for hypertension and, possibly, impotence. Well those two dreaded visitors were knocking on his door right now, he thought bitterly.

A thought hit him, and he laughed. Apparently, he should have put himself through the test with Janet Steward. Maybe he wouldn't be sitting there now kicking his butt for messing up with the woman he loved—the woman who'd fallen in love with him! What was he going to tell Dory now? "Sorry, but go find another life—I'm out of yours."

Reid, sprawled in a big tweed-covered armchair, rested his head against the hard back and closed his eyes. A long while later, cramped and stiff from sitting in one position, he looked at the time. It was late, but maybe he would be able to find somebody at the airline who could help him get out of there. He walked stiffly to the telephone and dialed the operator.

The next morning Dory awoke to an urgent knock at her door. It was six-thirty. She hurried to the door and opened it to Reid, who stood there dressed in his ski jacket and heavy boots. Stepping back to let him inside, she knew that he was leaving.

"I was able to get a flight out," Reid said, studying her closely. She was hurt. He rushed on. "It's not straight through, so I'm looking at hours of stopovers. Eventually I'll get home."

Dory nodded. "I hope you get there in time. Your friend is in my prayers," she said softly.

"Thanks." The distance between them was more emotional than spatial. There was no way that he could wrap her in his arms. The thought of touching her lips was scaring him to death.

Dory didn't miss his hesitation. After seconds of watching his discomfort, she intuitively didn't embrace him, but stepped to him. Raising her head, she kissed his lips. She moved away before he could react.

"I'll miss you," Reid said. "Will you stay until the end of the week?"

"Yes." Dory gestured, taking in the grounds of the inn. "I want to be in this space when I end things for Sara."

End. The finality of the word gnawed at Reid. He reached out and ran one finger down the side of her cheek. "Then I'll call you here," he said. "Good-bye, Dory." At the door he said, "I love you." He opened and closed the door before she could respond.

Dory didn't watch him from the window, but got back into bed, then glanced at the time. It was just after eight-thirty in New York. The nanny was certain to have taken

Zelle and Troy to school, Jake was long gone, and Willow was getting the twins ready for a busy day.

Last night Dory had wanted to call home. Telling Willow about falling in love with Reid had been one long phone call. But calling now to tell her that Reid had proposed was another, and Willow would have insisted that she bring Reid home to the family. Dory held up her hand and stared at the turquoise ring. She couldn't help wondering if the whole thing had indeed been a dream. The thin circle was proof that she'd agreed to marry the man that she loved, yet she had the feeling that she might never become Mrs. Reid Robinson.

At about two in the afternoon, Dory closed her laptop. She'd written nonstop since early morning, skipping lunch. Satisfied with what she'd accomplished by missing a meal, she dressed to go to lunch. The knock on her door was unexpected.

"Hi," Dory said. One of the young women who cleaned the rooms was staring at her quizzically with bright brown eyes, set deeply under thick black eyebrows.

"Ms. Morgan, I thought you might want this." The young olive-complexioned woman, who looked to be in her twenties, held the book out to Dory. "That's you, isn't it?" She pointed to the inside back cover flap, with the headshot of Dory.

Dory took the hardcover copy of her published journal. "Yes."

"I found it in Mr. Robinson's room. I thought you might want to give it to him." Her Hispanic accent made it sound like a question.

"Of course," Dory answered. "I'll be certain that he gets it."

As Dory put the book on the table, a brochure fell out. Reid had probably used it as a bookmark. She picked it up and frowned at the broad white type in large script:

Erectile Dysfunction. An Overview. Another smaller pamphlet inside had a bold headline: Are You Impotent?

Stunned, Dory pulled out a kitchen chair and sat down. *Erectile dysfunction? My Reid?* She burst out laughing as scenes of their lovemaking flashed before her. Thinking about him made her squirm on the hard seat. Sobered, Dory scanned the literature. The content was not unfamiliar, so she was not surprised at what she read. As a matter-of-fact she was quite knowledgeable on the subject.

When she'd first moved in with her Aunt Dorcas, they had run Wildflowers Cove, a Writer's Retreat, together. Her aunt was a single woman, but while living in Connecticut for a while, Dorcas had fallen in love. Dr. William Hammond, once he retired, moved to Irvington and married her aunt. The three of them had operated the retreat until Dory began to write full-time and moved into her own place.

Her new uncle was a surgeon who'd performed penile implant surgery during his career. Dory, who was curious, had often had conversations with her frank uncle. Bill loved his work, but after years of performing surgeries on men who required implants, he gave it up because of his worsening arthritis. He joked that there wasn't enough malpractice insurance in the world that could pay for a slip of a knife.

Dorcas had also joined in those discussions, and she'd mentioned that there had been many times during her nursing career that she'd seen male patients of all ages leave the hospital, swearing that they'd made a mistake in opting for the uncomfortable procedure. But in the months to follow, on their return visits, there wasn't a complaint to be heard, and the smiles were pretty broad.

Dory left the pamphlets on the table, put on her jacket, and left the cottage. Sunshine and fresh air were what she needed to clear her muddled thoughts. Of course, there could be any number of reasons why those pamphlets had been in Reid's book. Coincidence was not one of them, she decided.

In Old Town, Dory shed her jacket under the blaze of the hot sun. The temperature had gone up to sixty-two degrees, and while she was driving around looking for parking she'd used the air-conditioner. After eating a spicy sausage and pepper hero, she left the restaurant feeling melancholy. That was the kind of sandwich that she and Reid had eaten in her compartment on the train. It seemed almost eons ago. As she walked from store to store picking up souvenirs for her family, her melancholia worsened. The shops, the galleries, and other amusements increased the emptiness she'd felt since Reid left. Her necklace hung proudly from her neck, and she constantly ran her fingers over the smooth blue-green gemstones. Did she really need something tangible by which to remember him? *Hardly,* she thought.

The sun was still hot, and back at the cottage Dory stripped down to her underwear. The sheets were cool, and she plumped up the pillows on the bed and closed her tired eyes. About that time she and Reid would be having dinner together, here or at a place downtown. Since she hadn't brought anything back with her to eat, and she was too lazy to cook, dinner would be another skipped meal.

Dory switched on the TV and channel surfed aimlessly. When she found a movie, she watched for a bit, but soon switched stations. As solemn as she felt, the tearjerker *An Affair to Remember,* with Deborah Kerr and Cary Grant, certainly was not entertaining fare. Looking around, she failed to see a Gideon Bible anywhere in the place.

Restless, unwilling to try to write, Dory suddenly made the decision she'd been wrestling with all day. She was going home. The cottage and its memories were closing in on her. She picked up the phone. After several calls, she found out the earliest arrangements were for Thursday afternoon. Dory booked the flight.

By Thursday, Reid still hadn't called. Dory waited until the last possible moment before checking out, realizing that his friend, Gilbert Lane, might have died. A funeral could very well be taking place that day.

On the plane, a sense of peace enveloped Dory. All her plans for articles, for her novel, had worked out to her satisfaction. There was more material packed away in her luggage than was needed, but that was good. Sara had resolved her problems, found a new love, and was going back to her job in New York as a secretary and sometime courier, to await the next adventure. In a few days, Dory would begin writing the first chapter, just as she'd planned.

Dory sighed and closed her eyes. As so often in the last few days, she fingered the turquoise on her finger and wondered about Reid. A question was never far from her mind: Was she still engaged?

Reid returned home from the hospital at eight-thirty in the evening. He and Leon had visited Gil, and for the first time in days were given some uplifting news. Gil had improved, though he was still listed as critical. There was a long painful battle to recover facing the man. Reid was brought to tears when he'd first looked at his friend, who was doped up with pain medication. Gil hadn't recognized him.

It had been nonstop since he got off the plane. Though Dory was on his mind, he couldn't think straight, and had no idea what he was going to say to her. Whatever she was thinking about him, she had a right, and he wouldn't think a bad thought about her if she kicked him out of her life. But he knew he had to call. After the good news about Gil, he felt that he could talk without sounding like an idiot.

Several minutes after he called, Reid hung up, his brows knitted into a frown.

"That party has checked out, sir. The room is unoccupied."

The words still stung his ears. Checked out? Had she found another location to research? Come home? Where had she gone?

Reid walked through his big empty house without turning on the lights and went straight upstairs to his bedroom. For the first time in years he felt lonely.

SEVENTEEN

On Friday morning, the loud ringing of the doorbell awakened Dory. It was just past nine, and she knew that it had to be Willow. She got out of bed and hurried to the door.

"I know you're in there, sleepyhead. Let me in." Willow leaned on the bell again.

The door opened, and the two sisters hurried into one another's arms.

Willow kicked the door shut. Still hugging her sister around the waist, she walked hip to hip with her back to the bedroom, shedding her jacket on the way.

"Now, you're going to tell me everything right now," Willow said, making herself comfortable in a big chair.

Dory laughed. "Oh, no, you don't," she said, jumping up. "My mouth is full of cotton and you know I can't function without caffeine. You're just gonna have to wait a few more minutes, sweetie. Suppose you make the coffee. I'll be right there." She headed for the bathroom in the hall, and Willow followed.

"Wait, what is this?" Willow said, catching her sister's hand as she walked by. "It's lovely." She stared with accusing eyes. "This looks like a wedding band."

Thoughtfully, Dory looked at the ring. "Hmm. It does, doesn't it?" she said, and left her sister standing in the hallway.

Willow had done more than just make coffee. When

Dory exited the bathroom, she smelled bacon, and knew her freezer had been raided. Besides the honey-cured slices, Dory saw English muffins and shredded hash browns.

"Mmm, I'm starving," Dory said, sitting down.

"Your fridge is bare. No eggs or juice. But I'm not taking any chances on you hopping up in the middle of your story," Willow said, biting into a muffin. Her eyes were still on the ring.

Dory sipped some hot coffee and sat back. "Delicious," she said. "Hits the spot." Finally, she smiled at her curious sister. Ending the suspense, she said, "Not a wedding band, but it is my engagement ring." Dory's voice was soft. Remembering the night it was given to her brought a faraway look to her eyes.

All thought of teasing and badgering Dory for information left Willow. There was no denying or ignoring the sadness in her sister's eyes, and in her voice. All was not right. Willow remembered a time when she'd confessed her love to a man, and had then given him up for reasons she thought were real. But that was a long time ago, and she would spend the rest of her life giving thanks for that loving sensible man—Jake—for not letting her throw their love away. She shuddered to think that the same thing was happening to her sister.

"I'm sorry about Alma," Willow said. She had a fleeting memory of the woman. She'd seen her for barely ten minutes, years ago. The face was a blur, but Willow remembered those accusing eyes that had bored into her Aunt Dorcas's with such hatred. Now, everyone from Dory's past was dead.

"Thanks," answered Dory. She paused. "It was a shock to find her like that."

"She did what she thought was best for you." When Dory had called her from Rockford, Willow had heard her pain and confusion, and had done her best to console her.

"I know. Everything she did in the end was for me." The part about Buster and Papa Wilson was left unsaid.

"Do you want to talk about Reid?"

Dory looked at her sister for a long moment before speaking. They always shared everything, and why should now be any different?

"Yes. I already told you that I love him," she began. "I still do. But whether a wedding will ever happen . . . I'm uncertain about that."

"What happened?"

"The night he proposed to me and I accepted, he heard from his brother. There was a fire, and Reid's good friend was not expected to live."

"Oh, I'm sorry."

Dory explained all that had happened that night and the next morning when her lover had left so abruptly, all except the book and the literature that she found inside it. Whatever it meant, that was Reid's personal business, and not meant to be shared with anyone else.

The kitchen was quiet as each reflected on Dory's story.

"You haven't heard from him?"

"No." Dory stared at Willow. "I felt awkward calling, and wouldn't have known what to say if he was grieving over Gil's death."

Willow responded in a sympathetic voice. "But he's your fiancé."

Dory felt a wave of something unknown flow through her. *Is he really?* she wondered, but she said, "Yes."

"Maybe he did try to contact you, but you'd already left. Can't you call him now? You'll find the right words."

"Possibly."

"I know you will."

"You're probably right. I'll try to reach him later."

Willow sensed that her sister had left some things unsaid, but didn't push for any further explanations. The fact that Dory was willing to call would probably set things right, whatever might have gone wrong. "I'm going to miss you," she said.

Startled, Dory said, "Miss me?"

"When you're married." Willow raised her brow. "I hardly expect Reid to move his greenhouses to Irvington," she said.

Dory looked at her in amazement. "That's what Reid said."

Willow stared at her. "Well you didn't expect him to relocate here, did you?" Her sister's look made her stare with suspicion. "You discussed it?"

Dory nodded. "We talked about it."

"I don't believe you!" Willow sucked in her breath. "Are you thinking of breaking your engagement because he's there, and you're here?"

Dory didn't answer. How could her sister have hit the nail on the head, just like that? They'd become so close that their thoughts were simpatico. At times, it was unsettling. Like now.

When Dory remained silent, Willow pursed her lips. "Is it because you don't want to leave us? Your family?" she asked in her mellow voice. "It is, isn't it?"

"How can I do that?" Dory answered, anguish filling her voice.

"Dory, six years is such a short period in a lifetime. That's all we've had together so far." Willow's eyes grew misty. "But that was only the beginning of our lives as a family. We have the rest of it ahead of us. Years. No matter where we are we'll still have and love each other."

"I know, but it won't be the same," Dory said, her voice faltering. She gestured. "Would you be sitting talking to me like you are now? Dropping the kids with Marcy and running over here any old time? To the kids I would be just a voice on the phone."

Willow didn't answer. Her sister was intelligent, and she knew that Dory was upset with the thought of wrenching herself away from all that she'd only come to know in the last few years. Once she realized what she would be giving up if she let Reid go, she'd come to her senses. Willow knew that. But she was worried that Dory might wait too long. She would do her best not to interfere. A long time ago, her best friend, Mellie, had talked until she was hoarse, trying to get Willow to go back to the man she loved. But Willow'd had to make up her own mind. Before she was too late, she had gone back. And Jake had been waiting.

Willow went to Dory and gave her a hug. "Do you think a few miles will break us up as a family?" A smile brightened her eyes. "Can you imagine the fun the twins will have traveling back and forth to Aunt Dory's house? And all the second honeymoons Jake and I will have without going away?" Her eyes glittered. "Mmm, I think I like the idea better and better. How far away is Rochester?"

Dory grunted. "Yeah, right. You two will never let those kids come stay with me for more than a night. Both of you will be on that phone every hour on the hour, and I'll be forced to put them on the first plane out of there." Both her eyebrows were raised. "Besides, I'd have to contend with Kendra, Aunt Dorcas, and Uncle Bill, too, 'just popping in' as they'd put it." She gave a mock grimace. "On second thought," she said, "maybe the greenhouses *can* be moved. To California!"

Willow laughed. "You wouldn't!" she said. An amused look settled over her features. "It's a wonder with all the love and attention they get, they're not the world's worst menaces."

"Never happen," Dory answered fondly.

They both cleared the table, and when the kitchen was

clean they went to the living room, each carrying a second mug of coffee.

"How's Kendra doing now?" Dory asked. Willow had told her about the young woman's distress after she'd heard from her father, Nat Rivers.

"She's back in school now, so I haven't talked to her in a few weeks." Willow frowned. "She almost didn't go back, her mother told me. Just wanted to see if she could find her father and get him some help."

Dory felt sad for Kendra, and angry with a man she'd never met. *Nat Rivers is still messing up people's lives,* she thought. "Obviously, he loves the bottle more than he does his daughter," she remarked dryly.

"Apparently," Willow said. "Jake's done what he could. If the man insists on messing up, dropping in and out of rehabs like they were hotels, there's nothing anyone else can do. I wish Kendra could understand that before she lets it affect her studies."

"I hope she will," Dory answered. After a moment they changed the subject. Somehow having a Nat Rivers conversation didn't go with morning coffee.

It was almost two hours later that Dory hugged her sister, promising not to be late for dinner. Aunt Dorcas and Uncle Bill were coming to welcome her back home.

At six-thirty, Dory was driving to her sister's house. The day had gotten away from her. Before she knew it, the time had come to shower and dress for dinner. After dusting and vacuuming, she'd gone shopping to put some food in the house. Upon returning, she'd unpacked and sorted her clothes, washing, drying, and putting them away. A quick trip to the dry cleaners eliminated having a pile of clothes taking up space on the chair in her bedroom. While locking her door, Dory knew that she'd deliberately kept herself busy so she wouldn't find the time to call Reid. After all, she reasoned, she couldn't very well rush him off the phone, what with all the things she had to do, could she?

Dory pulled into the driveway of the Rivers home, parking behind her aunt and uncle's black Infiniti. Smoothing her leather gloves over her hands, she was acutely aware of the bare third finger on her left hand. She'd removed he turquoise ring before she left the house. There was no need for the older couple to know anything about Reid Robinson. Not yet. Willow knew enough to keep quiet about the romance, and would not go against Dory's wish to keep the engagement a secret.

Engagement? Once again, Dory had to think about that. All the consoling in the world from her sister could not erase Dory's doubt. When Reid had said good-bye, was it meant to be good-bye, as in, I'm sorry, but we made a mistake?

Dory rang the bell. Before the door was opened, she shrugged off her gloomy mood, put a smile on her face, and hoped it showed in her eyes.

Reid called Dory's number for the second time since he'd arrived home. And for the second time he swore in the empty house. It was almost nine o'clock. *She never went home,* he thought. If she checked out yesterday and was headed for Irvington, she had to be there by now. He was sitting at the big square table in the kitchen, warming a cold bottle of Corona beer between his hands. After taking a long swallow he nearly choked at the thought that had flashed into his mind. Had she left on her own, after telling him that she was staying until the end of the week? Or was she forced to leave? He slammed the bottle down on the table with a bang.

"Cut the crap, man!" Reid said, running a hand across his shaved head, thinking that listening to her plotting her mysteries must be messing up his mind. It sure wouldn't be dull living with a mystery novelist! His thoughts turning serious, Reid knew that there was no one stalking Dory. She must have gotten another idea and decided to follow up on it. But where?

Reid refused to give up. Short of calling Jake and Willow Rivers and risking scaring them to death if Dory hadn't gone home, he decided to try her number again. It was past eleven, and if she didn't answer, the Rivers would be getting a late-night call.

When the phone was answered on the second ring, Reid breathed again. She was home!

"Hello," Dory mumbled, partly sitting up in bed. She was half asleep.

"Dory, it's Reid."

"Reid?" Dory's eyes snapped open, and she turned on the bedside lamp. "Reid," she whispered, afraid of hearing bad news. "What's happened? Are you okay?"

"No," Reid answered, both angry and relieved at hearing her voice.

"No?" Her mind went numb. What more could have happened to him? Wide awake now, she said, "I'm so sorry. I know how you must be feeling. When did he die?"

Immediately, Reid realized his mistake. She thought Gil was dead, and she was trying to console him. *Idiot,* he swore at himself.

"Dory, you don't understand. Gil is alive, but still critical."

"Then what happened?" Dory asked, puzzled. "You said you weren't okay."

Reid took a deep breath. "I meant that I wasn't okay when I couldn't reach you," he said. "When I called the inn last night you'd already gone. I didn't know where."

"You called me yesterday?" Dory felt relieved and happy.

"Last night. And several times today, and this evening." He paused. "I didn't know what to think."

She heard the relief in his voice, and her heart sang. He had called!

"The cottage was too lonely without you. I decided to come home."

"Why didn't you let me know?" Reid asked.

"I thought your friend had died, and you were probably busy."

Reid was silent. Hearing her voice sent a surge of relief through him. The need to have her close and to hold her was driving him nuts, but he couldn't ask her to come to him. There was something he had to take care of first—once and for all.

"I was doing a lot of running," Reid said. "You would have had difficulty in reaching me." A note of bitterness crept into his voice. "There was a lot of damage, and things are in a mess. It'll take a while to sort things out."

"Nothing could be salvaged?" Dory heard the controlled anger.

"Not in the one house that was destroyed," Reid answered. A laugh escaped. "So much for spending time taking a stress-free vacation," he said. "Guess I'll have to do it again."

"Reid, that was out of anyone's control. You and your brother are taking care of business, and you're certain to have things running smoothly before too long."

"You're that confident, huh?" Reid had to smile at her brave attempt to console him.

"I've never met Leon, but I know his brother," Dory answered. "Yes, I am."

Reid laughed. He could imagine the fiery sparks in her dark eyes, and the fullness of her lips pursed in a thin line. God, how he missed her!

"I'll be sure to tell Leon you said so."

Dory heard the light note in his voice and relaxed. She didn't realize how tense she'd become.

Then, abruptly, Reid said in a low voice, "I love you, Dory."

Surprised at the sudden change, Dory shifted in the bed, moved by the sensuousness of his voice. Vivid memories made her squirm. "I miss you," she murmured.

"I miss you too, love."

Dory hesitated. "Would you like me to come there for a while?" What had made her say that? She frowned, wishing to retract her words. When he hesitated, she said, "Forget I asked. I know what must be going on, and I'd only be in the way," she said, hoping that he would agree.

Reid grimaced. "You'd never be in the way, sweetheart. Don't say that." He hesitated. "But, now isn't a good time. Things are hectic, and we wouldn't have that much time together."

Dory was relieved. She knew deep down that he had other things on his mind. There was no way that she could broach what she was thinking. Instead she answered, "You're right. I should have never asked." She paused. "I just want to see you," she whispered.

Reid held back the groan in his throat. "Me, too."

After a moment Reid cleared his throat. "We never got a chance to talk about our wedding plans. Have you given any thought to the date?"

"No," Dory answered. Was that really what he wanted?

"No?" Reid didn't believe her.

"So much has happened, Reid. Besides, it wouldn't really make sense to begin picking dates alone. I have no idea what's on your calendar."

"Why does that sound like an excuse to me?" he asked softly.

Dory didn't respond. What could she say to the truth?

"Have you had second thoughts, Dory?"

Only because you have, Dory thought. Deep down she

knew that the last night and the next morning that they were together, Reid had wished himself far away from her. She'd yet to discover the reason why. Maybe what he needed was time to sort things out in his own mind.

"Dory?"

She sighed heavily and closed her eyes. Breathing deeply, she said, "Yes."

Reid's heart dropped down to his toes. He'd heard exactly what he'd pushed her to say, and he felt lousy. He'd given her the opportunity to break their engagement, and she had. But he had to make sure.

"Second thoughts about us, or about setting a wedding date?" Reid asked.

Dory hesitated. Finally she said, "Never about us, Reid. I'll always love you, and I know you love me. What we shared could never have happened otherwise." She paused, trying to form her next words. "I think our timing is all wrong. The fire and other . . . things that you have to sort out, and me having to write this story to meet my deadline . . . we both have full plates right now."

"You're right, sweetheart. I'll always love you."

"Then you agree that we should break the engagement for now, and postpone our wedding plans?"

"Is that what you want?" Even though he'd prayed for it, Reid didn't like the finality.

"I think it's the best thing to do for right now."

Thoughtfully, Reid asked, "Have you removed your ring?"

"How could you know that?" Dory was startled.

Reid shrugged. "A hunch. Sounds like you've given this a lot of thought. Is that a yes?"

"Yes."

After a pause, Reid said, "That's probably the best thing. No need to put yourself through an interrogation by your family."

"True."

For seconds both were lost in the unreality of what had just happened.

"Reid," Dory finally said, "I'll keep your friend in my prayers. I hope that the next time we talk that you'll have good news. About Gil and . . . the business."

The next time. *As if there will ever be one,* he thought.

"Thanks. I hope so, too," Reid said. "I'll let you know how things are going. Good luck with your writing." His voice lowered. "Good-bye, Dory."

"Good night."

Dory forced herself to maintain control over her emotions. Her temples throbbed, and she rubbed them methodically, trying to ease the dizzying sensation as Reid's words steamrolled over her numbed brain. She'd gotten her wish: to postpone their engagement and eventual wedding. She hadn't expected the finality in his tone until she realized that he'd said it as easily as he had in Albuquerque. He'd said *good-bye.*

EIGHTEEN

Two months after the fire, Leon finished making his rounds of the greenhouses. Satisfied that all was as it should be, he'd spent extra time admiring the newly built house, inhaling the fresh new smell. The fiberglass and aluminum alloy structure had been completed a week ago, and was ready for occupancy by thousands of germinating seedlings. It had taken giant effort and many work hours by everyone to make up for what had been lost. A week was needed just to bulldoze and clear out the rubble from the old building and prepare the ground for the latest in greenhouse technology. An updated computer system, which monitored the changes in temperature, ventilation, and everything else that went on in the nursery, had been installed.

It was eight-thirty in the evening and the staff had been gone for hours. Exhausted, Leon was calling it a night, but knew his brother was still around after spying the black Lexus in the parking lot next to his SUV. Leon wasn't surprised. Reid often didn't leave the place until midnight.

He found Reid in the spacious laboratory, hunched over a flask. Reid looked up, then bent to his task of growing orchids from seed. "Hey, man. You still here?"

Leon grunted and sat on a stool opposite his brother. "I could ask you the same thing." Reid shrugged, but didn't look up. "Look, man, why don't you come home with me and get a good meal? Cerise's orders."

Reid carefully filled a glass flask with seedlings. Satisfied with the amount of seeds, he secured it tightly with a stopper and set it aside. He reached for another bottle. "Not tonight, man. Tell Cerise thanks. How about the weekend?" he said, carefully dropping seeds in the bottle.

"You know that's okay. You need a meal tonight, don't you?" Leon said impatiently.

"Uh-uh, I'm okay. Had something before." Reid labeled the bottles with the species and the date. He carried the two flasks to a large table that held hundreds of other similar flasks, and fit them into the last two spaces. "Wanna give me a hand with this?"

Leon slid off the stool and went to help his brother. Together they draped a large spread of wire mesh netting over the table, covering the flasks.

"Okay, the babies are sleeping," Leon said. "Now, how about us?"

Reid pulled off his rubber gloves and lab coat, looking around the room.

"Stop looking for something else to do," Leon said, waving his hand in the air. "There's still plenty of work here, but you can't do it all at once—especially not all by yourself! You have dedicated people who'll be here at eight in the morning to help. That's what you're paying them for."

Reid gave his brother a curious look. "What are you getting so bent out of shape about?" He was washing up at the sink. He splashed water on his face and dried off, tossing the towel in a canvas bin. He walked to the door "Coming?"

Leon followed Reid into his office. He sat down, watching him sift through some papers that his secretary had left for him. "Now what? You're not calling it quits?"

"In a minute," Reid said absently. "Just want to get a jump on this stuff."

Angry, Leon reached over, took the papers from Reid's hands, and laid them on the desk.

Surprised, Reid stared at Leon. Pushing away from the desk, he put one ankle on his knee and folded his arms across his chest. "You got it," he said.

"What?" Leon growled.

"It's obvious you want my attention."

Leon let out the steam. "And damned time, too," he mumbled.

Reid waited, amused at Leon's rare display of grumpiness. "Okay, shoot. Something going on I should know about?"

"Yeah."

Reid's face lost the humorous smile. "What is it?" He steeled himself. What else could go wrong?

"You."

There was a second of silence.

"I'm not laughing," Reid said, glaring at Leon.

"Well, I'm not surprised. You probably forgot how!"

Reid rocked back in his chair. "Anything else?" He relaxed his body.

Leon noticed the dropped shoulders. "We're doing okay, Reid. Why don't you back off some? Gil's replacement is doing a bang-up job. You can afford to keep godly hours again."

"Temporary."

"What?"

"Temporary replacement," Reid answered.

"We all know that. John, the temporary replacement, knows that. So what does that have to do with you acting like you're a robot?"

Reid didn't answer. He was thinking about Gil. He knew as well as anyone else in the place that it would be a long time before his friend came back.

Leon's voice lost its bark. "We all miss him around here. Place ain't the same. But we all have to keep doing what we have to do."

Reid looked up. "I know," he said.

A cough broke the silence, and Leon shifted in the chair. *No time like the present,* he thought, since he had Reid's attention. "You feel like talking about it, man?"

"What's that, Leon?"

"You never talked about your vacation. Nada. Nothing. Like it never happened. You flew back here and got caught up with Gil and the fire, and haven't taken a minute to sit down and breathe." He spread his hands out. "When you think I'm about to ask you something, you change the subject, or make some excuse to get away. What went on with you?"

Reid stopped rocking, stood, and walked to the window. He rubbed his smooth head, then jammed both hands in his pockets. After a long while he sat back down.

"What do you want to know?"

Leon didn't miss the note of resignation, but he decided he might as well finish what he'd started. "You never told me whether the doctor had the right prescription. If it's none of my business, just say so. I'm worried about you, man."

"The prescription worked."

Leon refrained from grinning. There was more.

"I met a woman on the train. We were together for nearly two months. I proposed." Reid's eyes flickered.

Leon's jaw dropped. "You're engaged?"

"Was. She ended it." Reid looked at Leon, disgusted. "I goaded her into it."

Leon didn't know what to say. Reid had carried that burden all this time without letting on what was eating him up inside.

"You dropped a bomb on me, man. I expected to hear that you'd gotten it on and had a ball." He pushed his eyeglasses up on his nose and shook his head, as if to clear away cobwebs so he could see his brother better. Reid's expression was grim. "Look, you don't have to tell me any more," Leon said. "I know something heavy must have gone down." He started to stand, but Reid stopped him.

"Let me finish." Reid pulled on his goatee moodily. "I don't know whether I can talk about this again."

Leon sat and crossed his knees. "She must be a special woman," he said.

"She is." Reid raised a brow. "Would you want anything less for a sister-in-law?"

"What's her name?" He was glad that Reid had settled down.

"Dolores Morgan. She's called Dory." Reid saw Leon frown. "What's the matter?"

"Dolores Morgan? Name sounds familiar, that's all." Leon couldn't put a face to the name, so he said, "Go on. What does she do?"

"Dory's a writer."

Leon knew his brother had fallen hard from the way he spoke about her. "So what happened?"

"I proposed to her the night you faxed me." Reid saw the understanding in Leon's eyes, and nodded. "Whatever you're thinking is correct. After I phoned you, I went back to her." His look was direct, and his voice even. "I couldn't get it on, and I got the hell out of there. The next morning I said good-bye, and that was the last time I saw her."

"You never spoke again?"

"I called her. That's when we decided to forget about everything."

"At your suggestion?"

"More or less."

Both men were silent.

Reid started stacking the papers in the same neat pile

that his secretary had left for him. He turned off the desk lamp and stood up.

Following Reid's lead, Leon stood and shrugged into his jacket. Once outside, Leon secured the lock on the front entrance and both men walked to the parking lot in silence.

"So that's the end of it?" Leon asked. "You're going to let her go?"

"No. I'm going to get her back." Reid deactivated the car alarm and opened the door. "I'm working on it."

"What do you mean?"

"I'm taking care of business," Reid said, getting into the car. "When I'm successful, you'll be the first to kiss the bride. After me, naturally." He grinned at his brother. "See you tomorrow."

Leon drove carefully on the snow-slick roads. His thoughts were on his brother, and what Reid might have meant. Working on what?

After work the next day, Reid drove slowly to keep his appointment. It had started snowing again at noon, and hadn't let up. There were already four inches of new snow, and he hoped the doctor hadn't canceled his evening patients. For the last month Reid had made this trip once a week. Tonight, especially after talking to his brother the night before, he felt that he'd bared yet another layer of himself. Talking about Dory so openly to someone other than his psychologist had felt like the most natural thing in the world.

Reid thought about how he had gotten to that point in his life. When he first returned home from Albuquerque, his world had stood on end for a while. It wasn't until a week after speaking to Dory that his head had cleared, and he'd realized what he'd done. He had condemned himself to a life of uncertainty and endless stressful situations, especially in sexual encounters. Losing the only woman that he'd ever loved was a hard pill to swallow. It wasn't long before he'd visited his doctor, and—after a thorough physical exam and some tests—he'd taken the previously scoffed at advice and sought the services of a psychologist. For possible E.D. psychological reasons, that was sometimes the only way to get at the root of the problem. In such cases, there was nothing physically to operate on, and there were no drugs to take. If talk and reasoning didn't do it, then there would be a major problem.

Later that night, Reid found himself tapping his foot to the groovin' sounds coming from his CD's while he prepared his dinner. He'd had the urge for a rare home-cooked meal, and if it hadn't been so late after leaving the doctor's office he would have barged in on Leon and Cerise. But he dove right into thawing chopped meat in the microwave, chopping and sautéing onions and green peppers in olive oil, and rolling the meat into plump balls. The bottled sauce was simmering, and the water for the spaghetti was boiling.

Reid ate his meal in the kitchen while watching a basketball game on the small TV on the counter. The wine he had selected was the same burgundy he had bought in Albuquerque. As he drank, his mind drifted to that time, but he quickly brought himself back from the past. What was done was done, and he was through kicking himself.

When the kitchen was cleaned Reid turned out the light and went into the living room, where he kicked off his shoes and resumed watching the game. Lying on his roomy, black leather sofa, he set the remote on the table, placing it next to the book that had lain there since he'd received it.

Reid picked up the book and ran his fingers over the raised lettering, as he'd done when he first bought it in

Chicago. Dory had mailed the book to him about two weeks after they'd spoken. The literature that he'd left inside it was still there, and it had slipped out when he opened the book. There was a little yellow square of paper stuck to the larger pamphlet. She'd written a simple note: I love you. Dory.

Reid had been stunned when he'd read that understated message. She knew!

That night, after the first wave of panic swept him, he'd recovered enough to think about what receiving the book and the note meant. There was no way that Dory could be sure what his having that literature meant. She could only suspect. But, whether she thought he had a sexual problem or not didn't matter. She was still in love with him. Without asking him outright whether he was impotent or not, she'd let him know that her love was unconditional. Reid was even more pleased about the professional advice he had sought even before receiving her message. He would do all in his power to get to the root of his problem.

The back jacket flap slipped open, and Reid stared at the glamour photo of Dory. He ran his finger over the contours of her face, wishing he could feel the real thing. The image was not the real Dory. He'd never seen her wear so much makeup. The vision of her in her flannel granny gowns came to mind, and he grinned. If only her fans knew!

Reid found thinking about her too difficult. He wanted to hear her voice, and feel her touch. Weeks of preparation had made him ready for that. The only thing standing in the way of going to her was her schedule. But he could wait. In another few months she would be finished with her book, and there would be no stopping them from being together.

* * *

Dory stretched and turned off her computer. A big grin was plastered on her face as she went to the bedroom. In minutes, she was dressed for bed. Only a small smile remained, but she was overjoyed and amazed at the progress she'd made in only two months. She calculated that Sara's mystery would be solved in another month.

In the last few days Dory had been able to loosen up a bit, and she'd cut her work hours. No more writing past eleven at night. The strain on her eyes and back was getting to her. The TV was on, and she was watching the eleven o'clock news when the phone rang. Unperturbed, Dory smiled. At that hour it could only be her sister.

"Hi, what's up?" Dory said.

"It's Reid, Dory. How are you?"

The phone slipped when Dory scrunched up in the bed, absently smoothing her hair as if he could see her.

"Reid. I'm fine." From his voice she couldn't tell what was on his mind.

"You sound like it. The mystery is coming together?"

"Fabulously," Dory answered.

Reid heard the smile in her voice, and he couldn't help but respond in kind. "That good, huh?" he said. Did he dare hope that he'd see her soon?

"Yes," Dory breathed, suddenly flushed. He sounded so near, and she wished he were. "You wouldn't believe how it's flowing. The train scenes fit like the perfect glove. I can't wait for you to read it." She chuckled. "There's no way you won't recognize Robbie." Then she frowned. "I hope she doesn't read mysteries."

Reid laughed at her enthusiasm.

Dory sobered. "But that's not why you called. Is Gil recovering okay?" she asked.

"That's not the reason, either," Reid answered mildly. "But, yes, he's doing better. He's still in a rehab center, taking constant physical therapy. He'll be there for another few months before he can live on his own again. Thanks for asking."

"I'm glad." Dory hesitated, wondering why he had called. When she returned his book there had been no response, and she'd wondered if he'd tossed her note aside. There was no way that he couldn't guess that she was willing to share whatever he was going through. He'd never called.

Reid's throat was dry, and he sipped some more of the burgundy. "I was wondering how far along you were in your book and . . . if you would consider taking a break." He sucked in his breath. "A long weekend?"

She frowned. He was serious.

"Dory?"

"Reid, we have to talk."

"I know."

Her thoughts raced. She was due for a needed respite, to get her second wind for the last third of her story.

"What are you thinking, Dory?"

"That I'd like to see you."

"Are you sure?"

"Yes."

"In Irvington?"

Dory felt comfortable with that. "Yes."

"When?"

"Next weekend?"

"I'll be there," Reid answered. Then he frowned. "Will I be staying with you?"

Where else, love? Dory thought. "Yes," she murmured. "Unless you prefer a hotel. I'm some distance away from the closest one."

"Prefer? I don't think so, love."

Dory smiled. "Then I'll see you next Friday. Early?"

"Very early."

"I'll be waiting. Good night, Reid."

"Good night."

* * *

Wednesday morning of the next week, Dory was stacking her cupboards and fridge with all the foods she needed for her recipes. Going out for several meals was not how she wanted to spend time with Reid. There was so much they needed to discuss, and she was certain that public restaurants were not the right places. A cleaning service had given the place a thorough scrubbing, as vacuuming and dusting always fell into the "to do" category on her list of tasks.

Willow had been excited at the news of Reid coming, but Dory had discouraged her sister from inviting them for dinner.

If they were going to have the conversations she thought they would have, Dory didn't want to put Reid through her family's scrutiny the first time they got together again. There would be other weekends for that.

Dory pulled the lid off a carton of lemon yogurt and sat down at the kitchen table, eating and checking her menus again. The phone rang, and she reached for it, making a face when she realized she'd left sharp cheddar cheese off her shopping list.

"Hello?"

"Dory, it's me," Willow said.

Something had happened. Her sister's voice was never teary. "Tell me," she said, trying not to think the worst. Her thoughts were on the kids.

"Nat's dead."

Dory's mind went blank for a while. Nat? She'd expected to hear Zelle, Troy, Ronald, or David's name. Nat Rivers had never entered her mind. She was almost shaking with relief. "What happened?"

"He was stabbed to death in a fight. They found him in a rooming house in Philadelphia." Willow paused. "It happened two days ago, but they had trouble locating his family."

"Oh, my God," Dory murmured. "How's Jake?" Strong kindhearted Jake watched over his family with all the intensity of a lion.

Willow sighed. "He's shaken up. When Nat's ex-wife called him this morning, it was hard for him to talk about it."

"I'm so sorry," Dory said. "What do you need me to do?"

"Kendra is on her way from school, Annette said. You know how close the two of you are. Would you mind spending some time with her until after the funeral?"

"Not a problem. I'll be here. Annette made the arrangements already?"

"She asked Jake to take care of everything," Willow answered. "The body will be here tonight, and the cremation will be on Friday after a small service. Jake wanted to have something, for Kendra's sake."

"I'll go over to Annette's in a couple of hours," Dory said. "Kendra can decide what she wants to do. She's perfectly welcome to stay with me for a few days, if that's what she wants."

Willow remembered Dory's plans for the weekend. "Will Reid still come?"

"No, I don't think so. It'll be a little awkward with Kendra here. I'll call him."

"I'm sorry, Dory."

"That's okay. It's a family thing. He'll understand."

Willow thought about that. "One day he'll be our family, Dory. Don't exclude him totally."

After her sister hung up, Dory sat in the kitchen for a long time, thinking about past and present events. Nat Rivers had brought a lot of pain to a lot of people, had disrupted lives all his life. Now, even in death, he was still messing up people's lives. But he was Jake and Kendra's family, and had to be treated as such.

Although he had been a stranger to her, his death was affecting her life, too. She hoped Reid would understand. Friday was to have been the day that whatever was between them would dissipate, and they would be free to plan the rest of their lives. Reid was looking forward to that as much as she was. She knew that in her heart.

Dory couldn't help wondering if postponing their coming together at such a crucial point in their relationship was a bad omen for their future.

"Hello, sweetheart," Reid said after his secretary had forwarded Dory's call to the lab.

"Hi. I hope I didn't catch you with your hands full."

"Actually, you did," Reid answered, pulling off his skintight rubber gloves. A big grin split his face at his lascivious thought. His voice was low and husky when he said, "I could think of other things I'd rather be holding right now."

Dory warmed at his seductive tone, a flush enveloping her like a soft cocoon. She missed him so much.

Reid sensed her somber mood. "What is it, love?" he asked, his voice back to normal.

"Jake's brother's dead. The funeral's on Friday," Dory said in a rush.

His exuberant feelings plummeted. Reid sat down on the edge of a cluttered table. "My sympathies," he managed.

"Thank you."

"Are you okay?"

"Yes, it's Jake and Kendra, Nat's daughter, who are shaken up."

"Do you want me to cancel our plans for this weekend?" Reid knew that was her reason for calling.

"That would be best, I think. I'll be tied up with the family," Dory answered.

The family. Dark thoughts sent a chill through Reid. "You don't want me with you?"

Taken by surprise at his response, Dory said, "No, that's not necessary. I'll be fine."

Reid held his temper. "I didn't say that out of necessity, Dory. I'd think my presence would be wanted, not needed," he said evenly.

Dory groaned inwardly, realizing she'd hurt him. "Reid, I didn't mean it that way."

Now was not the time to discuss what she meant. Reid said, "Forget it, Dory. Is there something I can do?"

"No." What else could she say?

"Will you call me if you want to plan another weekend?"

"If?" Dory said. "I want to spend time with you Reid." She thought. "What about the following weekend?"

"No, that's no good for me," Reid answered. Finally he said, "Let's not do this now. Call me after everything settles down and you can think better." He paused. "Give my condolences to Jake."

"I will," Dory answered.

Reid left the lab and went to his office and poured himself a cup of coffee. He sat down behind his desk and sipped the brew, his thoughts spinning. The very thing he'd feared was happening. Separating Dory from her family when they married would be wrenching her from the security and happiness she'd come to know. Could she be happy and content living any distance away from them?

Leon caught his brother frowning into a mug of coffee. "Hey, what's that look for, man? Friday can't get here soon enough for you?" All week Reid had been tripping on air. Leon was happy for the man, who was finally getting it together with his woman.

Reid looked up at the interruption. He knew Leon was in his corner one hundred percent, and he wasn't going to take his disappointment out on him.

"It's off, man. Until further notice," he said in a matter-of-fact tone.

Leon sat down, surprise covering his face. "What happened?"

Reid explained, and when he finished he said, "I told you if anything would keep us from getting together, it would be her family."

"Not her family, man. Her. She's the one who has to come to understand that you'll be her family." Leon grinned broadly. "And me and Matthew and Cerise," he said. "When I told my wife who you were seeing, she couldn't believe it. Almost called me a liar. I went home and looked on her bookshelves, and there was every book of Dolores Morgan's. Thought I recognized that name," he said, proud of himself.

Reid smiled. "They should hit it off pretty well," he said.

"That's what I'm talking about, man! We're just her extended family."

"She's obviously not thinking that way, man."

Leon shook his head. "Then, it's up to you to show her where she'll be living, and with whom. She probably never set foot in Rochester." He laughed. "Like a lot of folks, she's thinking it's the end of the world."

Reid laughed. "Maybe. But you've got a point there."

Leon rose and walked to the door. "I know I have. Think about it."

An idea hit Reid. "Wait," he called, stopping his brother from leaving. Leon was watching him curiously. "Next weekend, that Saturday meeting we have planned with the building inspectors. Do you think John could handle it with you?"

"John? No problem. He's a good man." Leon looked

at Reid thoughtfully, knowing his brother was thinking about Gil and was missing him especially at times like these. "John can handle it."

Reid nodded, agreeing with his brother. "I know," he said. "I wanted your opinion."

Leon pushed up his glasses and walked back to the door. "Go on to Irvington, man." He grinned. "When you get back here, I want to know the wedding date *and* when I'm going to meet my future sister-in-law!" He left, tickled that he'd given his brother the nudge he needed.

Reid rocked back in his chair. His mind was spinning again, this time with thoughts of Dory and what he needed to do to convince her that he loved and wanted her. Abandoning her family for him was the last thing he wanted her to do.

On Friday morning, a week after the funeral, Dory woke up puffy eyed and sleepy. The mattress hadn't sunk under the weight of her tired bones until one in the morning. Her body was crying out for more sleep. Since the Wednesday when Willow had called her with the news, she hadn't been able to write as much as she wanted to. Visiting with Jake and the family, doing whatever she could, and spending time with Kendra, who wanted to talk her heart out, had exhausted her. Kendra had finally felt up to going back to school two days ago, and Dory had written practically nonstop to make up for the time she'd lost. Only last night she had finally gotten the rhythm of the story back, and she'd been hard put to stop, but her eyes had seemed to yell, "Enough!"

Dory pulled a woolen robe over her flannel gown and returned to the kitchen, where the coffee was finished brewing, and poured herself a mug. Sipping gingerly as she walked to the living room, she decided that she wouldn't change her clothes. This was how she was going to stay all day and night. If tonight was going to be another writing marathon, she'd just flop into bed at the end. As always, her thoughts turned to Reid. But for his commitment, she'd be snug in his arms right now. Waiting one more week was going to be torture.

A few days ago, Dory had called Reid to thank him for the beautiful spray of orchids he'd sent to Jake and Willow. She had asked him then if next weekend would be convenient for him to come to Irvington. Without the slightest hesitation he had said yes.

Thoughts of him and their times in Chicago and Albuquerque crowded her mind. Absently, she reached for the ringing phone.

"Hello. How are you?"

"Reid?" Dory's glum mood brightened. "I was just thinking about you!"

"Hmm. And not writing? Why does that make me feel good?"

"Don't tease," Dory said with a smile. She heard the amusement in his voice. "You know I think about you all the time. I just tuck you away in a corner of my mind while I'm typing."

"Not too deep, I hope," Reid said. He had to grin at the image.

"Never." Dory sighed. "As a matter of fact I was just about to tuck you away while I go boot up," she said.

"Not before coffee, I know."

"Uh-uh. I'm having my first cup now," she answered. "You're probably on your second, I'll bet."

"Actually, no," Reid said, doing a good job of sounding a little sad. "I was hoping to have that one with you."

"With me?" *He can't be!* Dory breathed a prayer. "Reid Robinson, where are you?" She didn't wait for an answer, but rose from the chair and hurried to the window and pushed aside the curtain. She saw him leaning against a black Lexus, cell phone in hand.

Reid saw the curtain move, and he smiled up at the window. "Right here, love." He pushed himself off the car and walked to the town house.

Dory hung up the phone in shock. "I'm a mess," she said, exasperated. Helplessly, she looked down at herself and finally drew a deep breath. There was nothing in the world she could do about the way she looked. *If he doesn't run away now, it must be true love,* she thought, but her heart was singing. By the time he rang the bell she was at the door, all thoughts of her imperfect appearance disappearing as she stared at him.

"Reid," she whispered. When he was inside she locked the door and led him to the kitchen, where he dropped several bundles and removed his jacket. A feeling of déjà vu swept over her as she remembered Rockford.

Reid looked at her hungrily. "You're . . ." He choked up. "God, how I've missed you, sweetheart." Slowly he took her in his arms, savoring the moment he'd waited an eternity for. Her arms clinging around his waist caused him to crush her against his body. He laid his cheek against her tangle of curls and gently rocked her from side to side.

Dory clung to him. As if he might suddenly be transported to another world, she held on, all her pent-up emotions surging together, causing violent shudders.

Reid held her tightly, his own body pierced with sharp quivers. He closed his eyes and breathed thanks that he'd been given the chance to make her his.

Dory didn't want to leave Reid's warm embrace, and his hot breath when he whispered in her ears sent more delicious tingles down to her toes. She raised her head to look into his eyes. "I've missed you too, love," she whispered.

Reid stepped back, but didn't let go of her waist. His roving look scanned every inch of her, and his eyes twinkled when he stared into hers. With one hand he fingered the top button of her gown and tugged on the tiny ruffled edging. "Still too many clothes," he murmured.

"We can do something about that right now," Dory whispered. She began to unbutton the gown while leaning in to him and kissing his lips. Her tongue darted into his mouth, and she moaned at the sweet taste of his lips as they crushed hers. Dory wondered if she would ever be able to let him know just how much she loved him.

Reid wasn't ready for her quick moves on him, and he groaned as his body reacted involuntarily. He caught her hand, which moved slowly from his waist down to his thigh, steeling himself, unable to resist her seductive movements against his hips. Reid was already rigid. He swore inwardly.

"Dory, wait," he gasped. "We have to talk first. I have to tell you—" He groaned when she touched his erection.

Dory shushed him with a gentle finger to his lips. "Love me, Reid." She took his hand and placed it under her gown, pressing it against her breast. "Just make love to me."

"God, yes," Reid groaned as she took his hand and led him to the bedroom. An eternity seemed to pass before they stood naked and Reid enfolded her in his arms shaking with the sensation of flesh against flesh. He smothered her face with kisses and then eased her down on the bed, drinking in the sight of her. He closed his eyes, vowing he'd never let her go again.

Reid opened his eyes at the touch of her finger on his eyelids. "Wait," Dory whispered, and he watched her slip from his arms. Her curvy hips swayed, and he ached to love her. When she returned to him she sat on the edge of the bed and opened her hand. He stared at the turquoise circle.

Dory held out the ring to him "Reid" she said softly, "as husband and wife there's nothing we can't share and handle together."

Reid understood, and his throat burned with the deep feelings of love that were searing his insides. She had no idea that he didn't have a sexual problem now, yet she was willing to take a chance with him. He took the ring from her. "Will you marry me, love?"

Dory held out her hand, and Reid slipped the ring on her finger. "Yes," she said.

Reid pulled her down beside him and kissed her nose. "Then let me love you, sweetheart." He reached for the condom packet that he'd removed from his pocket and had placed on the nightstand.

Dory sank under Reid's deft ministrations to her body. When she touched him as he prepared himself, he shuddered, and then, whispering his love, entered her. She closed her eyes. Whatever he had been thinking about himself, he could not have been more wrong, because her body hummed under his touch. Her lover was just fine!

When Dory murmured, "I love you, Reid," she was secretly overjoyed at his body's spontaneous response.

EPILOGUE

Two years later
Rochester, New York

Dory left her study, which was next to her son's room, and stood in the doorway. Eric was still sleeping, and Dory smiled as she glanced at her watch. It was twelve-thirty, and any minute now she would hear the front door open and close and footsteps on the stairs. Reid was going to be disappointed again to find his son taking an afternoon nap.

Sure enough, minutes later Reid was standing by her side. He stopped when Dory put a finger to her lips. "Don't tell me I missed him again?" Reid whispered, disappointment in his voice as he hugged and kissed his wife. It was the second time that week he'd stopped by and found his son asleep.

"It's the medication for the ear infection," Dory whispered. "It makes him a little drowsy and cranky, so his schedule is off."

Reid went to the crib and stared down at his son, who was his spitting image—except for the bald head. He grinned. For the first twelve months of his life, the baby'd had a mop of hair like his mother's. But last month, on his first birthday, he'd had his first haircut. Reid bent, kissed the baby's cheek, and followed his wife from the room.

Downstairs in the kitchen, Dory helped Reid raid the refrigerator of last night's leftovers. While they were eating, she teased, "I wonder what Leon and Gil say to each other when you disappear every so often at such an odd hour."

Reid grunted. "It's none of their business," he growled. "Leon's been there, and Gil soon will be," he said.

Dory laughed. "I know. Cerise said Leon was the same way with Matthew." Her tone sobered when she thought of her husband's best friends, Leon and Gilbert. Both had been best men at their June wedding two years ago, and were Eric's godfathers. Gil, who'd had a slow recovery after many skin graft operations and was back at work, had fallen in love with his nurse. They were getting married in June, and Dory heard him tell Reid that they wanted to get pregnant on their honeymoon.

Reid noticed Dory's silence. "What's up, love? Thinking up another best-seller?"

Dory smiled. "That, too, but I was thinking about Gil and Marian going to Hawaii for their honeymoon. They're going to love it," she said dreamily.

Reid smiled. He had taken Dory to the big island, just as he'd promised. He had never seen her so beautiful and happy. It was no wonder that little Eric had been conceived, with all the love they had shared in those two weeks.

He rose and cleared the table. "Got to get back." Reid raised a brow and said, "So what's this about a new story? Another Sara mystery?"

"No, not this one," Dory said, helping to clear. "Sara's taking a rest. I had no idea that that story would come pouring out of me like that when I saw your house of mystery."

Reid bent and kissed her lips. "Would I lie?" he asked. "Told you." Months after they settled into his house, she'd started her new Sara mystery. Released only two months ago, it was a runaway best-seller.

Dory walked Reid to the front door, where she hugged him around the waist and kissed his mouth.

"Happy, love?" Reid asked, kissing her back. His family had taken to Dory, and they were all inseparable.

"What kind of question is that?" Dory asked, looking into his eyes. "Don't I look happy?"

Reid gazed into her eyes. They were still full of love for him. "Yes," he said. A lazy grin parted his lips. "You remember what you promised would happen when Eric turned a year old?"

Dory knew what was coming. "I do," she said, snuggling against him.

"Then what's wrong with tonight?" he suggested. He nuzzled her ear, then whispered, "We don't really need Hawaii to get pregnant again, do we?"

Dory gave him a seductive look. "I'll have the leis ready for you, love."

Reid laughed and opened the door. "You're a funny lady," he said, and sprinted down the steps. He was still laughing when he drove away.

Dory watched her husband go. She was the happiest she'd ever been in her life. After the second time Reid had proposed and they'd loved, they had talked for a long time. He had expressed his fears about having erectile dysfunction, and about chaining her to his problems. When he had come to her he was fine. Whatever had caused his inability to perform sexually was gone. The doctors had found nothing wrong with him, and they had been right. Reid thought his sessions with the psychologist had helped a lot.

Dory had her own family now, as well as her growing extended family—Gil was soon taking a bride, and Cerise was pregnant again after thirteen years, and Leon was beside himself.

Willow and Jake visited often, and Zelle, Troy, David, and Ronald were crazy about their baby cousin. Dory was happiest for Kendra, who had bounced back from her father's death and was a proud senior. She was a drama student, and hoped to become famous one day.

Dory went back upstairs to her son. He was still sleeping, and she sat down in the rocking chair and closed her eyes. Just before she dozed off, she smiled. This time next year, Eric would have a sister. There was no doubt in her mind that she and Reid would make a baby girl that night.

Dear Reader,

Thank you all for the wonderful letters and e-mails you've sent to me about *Precious Heart.* Diamond and Steven's story is still in my thoughts. It is purely coincidental that *Just One Kiss* touches on a medical condition. I don't intend to consciously zero in on health issues although during the time that I was writing this story, erectile dysfunction was a frequent topic in the media.

I've received many of your requests to give certain characters their own stories. I elected to do the story of Dolores Jones from *White Lies,* since so many of you told me that she was too sad and needed some happiness in her life. It was also an opportunity to get a glimpse of Jake and Willow Rivers, and how their two sets of twins have enriched their lives.

I hope you weren't disappointed to find I gave Dolores the name Dory Morgan. But it was her wish to adopt her mother's family name, especially since she'd never known the man named Jones. Dory and Reid were meant for each other, although they didn't realize it when they first met. Fate being what it is, their reunion and falling in love were simply destiny.

Reid, like so many men of all ages, had an inkling that he had a sexual problem, but was in denial at the beginning. Unlike so many, his erectile dysfunction never materialized. He chose the option that was offered for his particular problem, and that was psychological counseling. Of course those who are affected have a world of opportunity to take advantage of the help that is available, and to have a satisfying intimate lifestyle.

Please continue to write. For a reply, include a self-addressed stamped envelope.

Thanks for sharing,
Doris Johnson
P.O. Box 130370
Springfield Gardens, NY 11413

E-mail: Bessdj@aol.com

ABOUT THE AUTHOR

Doris Johnson lives in Queens, New York, with her husband. She is a multipublished author. She enjoys lazing on beaches, poking around in flea markets, and collecting gemstones. Frequently the lore of gemstones is incorporated into her stories.